## Praise for *The Adults*

"This cri de coeur carries a freshness and charm—honorable, too, for its cutting accuracy."

—*San Francisco Chronicle*

"[An] outstanding coming-of-age novel . . . one of the funniest books I've read in a long time. Ms. Espach's coup is to chart Emily's growth through her maturing sense of humor."

—*The Wall Street Journal*

"It's hard to be a teenager, but it's even harder for a writer to capture a teen's voice in fiction. . . . [Alison Espach] masters her teen's voice exceptionally well."

—*The Washington Post*

"Wry rather than out-loud funny, laced with melancholy and angst, this book is an enviable first effort."

—*Kirkus Reviews*

"[A] smart first novel."

—*People* magazine

"[A] razor-sharp debut novel . . . a wry, devastatingly funny coming-of-age tale."

—*Marie Claire*

"Teeming with clever insights, witty acerbic dialogue, and a helplessly loving acknowledgment of family quirkiness."

—*School Library Journal*

"Espach is a gifted writer, making Emily brave, bold, and timid all at once."

—*St. Louis Post-Dispatch*

"Sharp and witty."

"With shining prose and razor-sharp wit, Alison Espach writes about the murky landscape between childhood and adulthood, the mistakes and misunderstandings, the betrayals and the beauty. *The Adults* is a piercing and authentic journey through adolescence, filled with squeamish missteps and laugh-out-loud insights, wrenching heartache, and characters so rich and tenderly drawn that one can't help but love them through all their flaws and failures. I absolutely adored this book."

—Aryn Kyle, author of *The God of Animals* and *Boys and Girls Like You and Me*

"Alison Espach has written her debut novel in one of the most authentic and memorable voices I have ever read. Finding myself on every page of this heartbreaking and hysterically funny book, I began to have the same strange suspicion I had the first time I read Salinger's *The Catcher in the Rye,* Yates's *Revolutionary Road,* and Eugenides's *The Virgin Suicides*: the impossible belief that the author might have written this book specifically for me. Like those classics, *The Adults* is wholly original, astonishingly true, and absolutely vital."

—Stefan Merrill Block, author of *The Story of Forgetting* and *The Storm at the Door*

"In her impossible-to-put-down debut novel, Alison Espach manages to marry youthful exuberance with deep adult sorrow, quicksilver wit with trenchant observation. The world of *The Adults* is a familiar one, but the voice and the brain at work here are anything but, sparkling and unexpectable and irresistibly wise."

—Kathryn Davis, author of *The Thin Place*

# The Adults

*A NOVEL*

## Alison Espach

Scribner

*New York London Toronto Sydney New Delhi*

SCRIBNER
A Division of Simon & Schuster, Inc.
1230 Avenue of the Americas
New York, NY 10020

First Scribner trade paperback edition September 2011

SCRIBNER and design are registered trademarks of The Gale Group, Inc., used under license by Simon & Schuster, Inc., the publisher of this work.

For information about special discounts for bulk purchases, please contact Simon & Schuster Special Sales at 1-866-506-1949 or business@simonandschuster.com.

The Simon & Schuster Speakers Bureau can bring authors to your live event. For more information or to book an event contact the Simon & Schuster Speakers Bureau at 1-866-248-3049 or visit our website at www.simonspeakers.com.

Manufactured in the United States of America

10  9  8  7  6  5  4  3  2  1

Library of Congress Control Number: 2010029697

ISBN 978-1-4391-9185-9
ISBN 978-1-4391-9186-6 (pbk)
ISBN 978-1-4391-9187-3 (ebook)

*For my mother, my father,*
*and my brothers Gregg and Michael*

Everything Was Like My Mother Said

# 1

They arrived in bulk, in Black Tie Preferred, in one large clump behind our wooden fence, peering over each other's shoulders and into our backyard like people at the zoo who wanted a better view of the animals.

My father's fiftieth birthday party had just begun.

It's true that I was expecting something. I was fourteen, my hair still sticky with lemon from the beach, my lips maroon and pulpy and full like a woman's, red and smothered like "a giant wound," my mother said earlier that day. She disapproved of the getup, of my yellow fit-and-flare dress that cradled my hips and pointed my breasts due north, but I didn't care; I disapproved of this party, this whole at-home affair that would mark the last of its kind.

The women walked through the gate in black and blue and gray and brown pumps, the party already proving unsuccessful at the grass level. The men wore sharp dark ties like swords and said predictable things like, "Hello."

"Welcome to our lawn," I said back, with a goofy grin, and none of them looked me in the eye because it was rude or something. I was too yellow, too embarrassing for everyone involved, and I inched closer to Mark Resnick, my neighbor, my maybe-one-day-boyfriend.

I stood up straighter and overemphasized my consonants. There were certain ways you had to position and prepare your body for high school, and I was slowly catching on, but not fast enough. Every day, it seemed, I had to say good-bye to some part of myself; like last week at the beach, my best friend, Janice, in her new shoestring bikini, had looked down at my Adidas one-piece and said, "Emily, you don't need a one-piece anymore. This isn't a sporting event." But it sort of was. You could win or lose at anything when you were fourteen, and Janice was keeping track of this. First person to say "cunt" in two different languages (Richard Trenton, girls' bathroom, *cunnus, kunta*), an achievement that Ernest Bingley decried as invalid since "Old Norse doesn't count as a language!" (Ernest Bingley, first person ever to cry while reading a poem aloud in English class, "Dulce et Decorum Est"). There were other competitions as well, competitions that had only losers, like who's got the fattest ass (Annie Lars), the most cartoonish face (Kenneth Bentley), the most pubes (Janice Nicks).

"As a child, I shaved the hair off my Barbies to feel prettier," Janice had confessed earlier that morning at the beach.

She sighed and wiped her brow as though it was the August heat that made her too honest, but Connecticut heat was disappointingly civil. So were our confessions.

"That's nothing," I said. "As a child, I thought my breasts were tumors." I whispered, afraid the adults could hear us.

Janice wasn't impressed.

"Okay, as a child, I sat out in the sun and waited for my blood to evaporate," I said. I admitted that, sometimes, I still believed blood could vanish like boiling water or a puddle in the middle of summer. But Janice was already halfway into her next confession, admitting that last night, she touched herself and thought of our middle school teacher Mr. Heller despite everything, even his mustache. "Which we can't blame him for," Janice said. "I thought of Mr. Heller's hands and then waited, and then nothing. No orgasm."

"What'd you expect?" I said, shoving a peanut in my mouth. "He's so old."

At the beach, the adults always sat ten feet behind our towels. We carefully measured the distance in footsteps. My mother and her friends wore floppy straw hats and reclined in chairs patterned with Rod Stewart's face and neon ice cream cones and shouted, "Don't stick your head under!" as Janice and I ran to the water's edge to cool our feet. My mother said sticking your head in the Long Island Sound was like dipping your head in a bowl of cancer, to which I said, "You shouldn't say 'cancer' so casually like that." A woman who volunteered with my mother at Stamford Hospital, the only woman there who had not gotten a nose job from my neighbor Dr. Trenton, held her nose whenever she said "Long Island Sound" or "sewage," as if there was no difference between the two things. But the more everybody talked about the contamination, the less I could see it; the farther I buried my body in the water, the more the adults seemed to be wrong about everything. It was water, more and more like water every time I tested it with my tongue.


Our backyard was so full of tiger lilies, nearly every guest at the party got their own patch to stand near. Mark ran his hands over the orange flower heads, while my mother opened her arms to greet his mother, Mrs. Resnick.

My mother and Mrs. Resnick had not spoken in months for no other reason than they were neighbors who did not realize they had not spoken in months.

"Italians hug," my mother said.

"We're Russian Jewish," Mrs. Resnick said.

"Oh, that's dear," my mother said, and looked at me. "Say hello, Emily."

"Hello," I said.

It was unknown how long it had been since they borrowed an egg from each other, but it didn't even matter because my mother noticed how tall Mark had become. "Very tall," my mother said.

"Yes, isn't he tall?" Mrs. Resnick asked.

"How tall are you, Mark?" my mother asked.

Everybody suspected he was taller than he used to be, but shorter than our town councilwoman, Mrs. Trenton, who was so tall she looked like King Kong in a belted pink party dress observing a mushroom garlic cream tart for the first time. She was so tall it only made sense she was granted a position of authority in our town, my mother said once. And Mark was a little bit shorter than that, in a very small, unnoticeable way.

Most of the adults stood at the bar. Some reported flying in from Prague, Geneva, Moscow, and couldn't believe the absurdity of international travel—it took so long to get from here to there, especially when all you were doing over the Atlantic was worrying about blood clots, feeling everything clumping and slowing and coming to an end. Some needed to use the bathroom. Some couldn't believe how the roads were so wide here in Connecticut and, honestly, what did we need all that space for?

"It's presumptuous," said Mrs. Resnick. She took a sip of her martini while a horsefly flew out of her armpit. "So much space and nothing to do but take care of it."

I looked around at the vastness of my yard. It was the size of two pools, and yet, we didn't even have one. My mother had joked all summer long that if my father wanted to turn fifty, he would have to do the damn thing outside on the grass. We had all laughed around the dinner table, and with a knife in my fist, I shouted out, "Like the dog!"

"If we had one . . . ," my father said, correcting me.

"It's the nineties," my mother added. "Backyards in Connecticut are just starting to come back in style."

But soon, it turned out it wasn't a joke at all, and at any given moment my mother could be caught with a straight face saying things like, "We'll need to get your father a tent in case of rain," and after I hung up on Timmy's Tent Rental, she started saying things like, "We'll need three hundred and fifty forks," and my father and I started exchanging secret glances, and when my mother saw him scribble THAT'S A LOT OF FORKS to me on a Post-it, she started looking at us blankly, like my father was the fridge and I was the microwave, saying, "We'll need a theme."

"Man, aging dramatically!" I shouted at them across the marble kitchen counter.

"And a cake designed to look like an investment banker." She wrote it down on a list, her quick cursive more legible than my print.

"No! A map of Europe!" I said. "And everybody has to eat their own country!"

"No, Emily," my mother said. "That's not right either."

Everybody was invited. Was Alfred available? Alfred was our neighbor who always gave the comical speech about my father's deep-seated character flaws at every social event that was primarily devoted to my father, which was every event my mother attended.

"Like how he questions my choice of hat at seven thirty in the morning," my mother said, as though my father wasn't there pouring himself some cereal. "It's just that the brim is so notably wide, he says. Well, that's the point, *Victor!*"

Or how he called the Prague office with a mouthful of Cocoa Puffs every morning and my mother said, Victor, you're a millionaire, that's gross, and my father chomped louder, said, *it's puffed rice*. He just doesn't get it, my mother said. He walks out to the car every morning and comes back in asking me how is it that a car can get so dirty!

At some point, they always turned to me, the third party. "Emily, would you explain to your father?" my mother asked.

"Well, Jesus, Victor! We drive it!" I shouted. I never considered the possibility that we weren't joking.


"Isn't Emily so beautiful?" my mother asked Mrs. Resnick, twisting her gold tennis bracelet around her wrist.

My mother asked this question everywhere we went. The grocery store. The mall. The dentist. Nobody had yet disagreed, though the opinion of the dentist was still pending.

"Don't you think that if the dentist really thinks I am beautiful he can notice it on his own?" I had asked my mother once, fed up with the prompt. "Don't you think pointing it out to the dentist just points out how *not* beautiful I must be?"

"It's just a point of emphasis," my mother had said. "It has nothing to do with you, Emily. Just a way into conversation."

"Adults need things like that," my father sometimes added.

But Mrs. Resnick hesitated, while Mark scratched a freckle on his arm like a scratch-n-sniff.

"*Mother,*" I said, and rolled my eyes so Mrs. Resnick and Mark understood that I too thought this question was unacceptable.

Mrs. Resnick had a bad habit of never looking at me, so she tried to size up my entire existence using only her peripheral vision. Medium height. Dirty blondish brownish hair. Scraggly, mousy, darling little thing that apparently had no access to an iron or a bathtub.

Hours before the party, my mother tugged at her panty hose, wiped her fingers across my cheeks, and said, "Go take a bath. You'll come out smelling like the beach." This was strange, since I just got home from the beach. And I never knew why smelling like the beach was always considered a good thing, especially when the closest beach was the Long Island Sound, and I wasn't even allowed to stick my head under.

"I don't want to take a bath," I said. "I don't like baths."

"Everybody likes baths," my mother said.

I did not like baths. I understood the warm water felt nice against my skin, but after five minutes of sitting in the tub, it became painfully apparent that there wasn't much to do in there. I would pass the time by shaving every inch of my skin, including my elbows, and reciting jingles I heard on the television—"Stanleyyy Steemmmmer," and "Coca-Cola Classic, you're the one!" When I would be older, one of my boyfriends would work as a flavor scientist for 7Up and would be addicted to bathing with me, his body on mine nearly every night, spilling water and secrets about the beverage industry, explaining that New Coke was an elaborate marketing scheme, designed to taste bad, predicted to fail, so they could reintroduce Coke as Coca-Cola Classic and make everyone want it more. "It worked," he would say, filling my belly button with water as I sang. "Look at you, giving them free advertising in the tub."

"I've thought about it," I had told my mother in the kitchen, "and I don't want to smell like the beach. I'd much rather smell like something else, like a wildflower or a nest of honeybees."

"Emily," my mother had said. "I don't even know what that is supposed to mean."

I had explained that Mark, who was a junior lifeguard at Fairfield Beach, had found a box of dead kittens floating at the edge of the shore when he combed the sand before his shift was over. Mark said they were the saddest things he had ever seen, floating by a broken buoy, curled up like they were sleeping. "But they weren't sleeping," he had whispered in my ear. "I mean, they were *dead*." I explained to my mother that smelling like the beach meant smelling like a place where tiny animals could not survive, where cardboard boxes contained not presents but sad corpses of beautiful things that were now impossible to love. My mother sighed and blended the garlic.

* * *

"Yes, very beautiful," Mrs. Resnick finally said, and this settled all of us into a strange sort of ease. Mrs. Resnick straightened out the hem of her lime green dress, and my mother pointed out that my father had recently planted tiger lilies in our backyard. Did they go with the neighborhood décor?

"This neighborhood has a very specific floral nature," my mother said.

Mark and his mother nodded. They already knew this.

"Well, you kids be good," my mother said, and stuck her fingers to my lips in a not very covert attempt to remove the Revlon. "And take some pictures, please."

That morning my mother had shoved a Polaroid camera in my face and said, "We need a party photographer! It could be you!" like it was a career move she might make me interview for. I snapped a picture of the two women walking away from us, our mothers, mine tall and alive in a coral party dress that was cut low enough to suggest breasts, and Mrs. Resnick walking next to her, rounder at the hips, in a lime green fabric with pearl embroidery so high on her chest it suggested that once upon a time, in a faraway land, there were these breasts. The skirt was cut at the calf, making her ankles look fatter than they should have. "Cankles," Mark said in my ear. "Calves and ankles that are the same width."

My mother picked up two empty beer bottles and a dish of shrimp tails off the ground before making a full waltz back into the center of the party, Mrs. Resnick wiped her glasses clean with a napkin, and I thought, Those poor adults. Doomed to a life of filth, finding it everywhere they went. At the beach, the only thing my mother could see was the empty Fanta bottles, sandwich wrappers, Popsicle sticks littering the sea, and when the sun set over the water, Janice's mother said it looked just like when she sorted through the garbage can with a flashlight after Janice threw out her retainer. My mother and Janice's mother shared a big laugh and quickly grew hot in their chairs, dried out from Saltines and peanut butter and talking. They walked to the water but never went in, moving away from the waves like the mess was nothing but an accidental oil spill that would turn their toes black. Janice and I sat on the wet sand and rubbed the water up and down our newly shaved shins, while our mothers looked on, nervous about the way we were already abusing our bodies. They held up sunscreen bottles, rubbed cream on our noses. We fussed, squirmed, accused them of horrible crimes, threatened to wipe it all off in the water, stare straight into the sun until our corneas burned and our flesh flaked off, until we had taken in the worst of the Sound with our mouths. They sighed, tugged at our faces, threatened to bring us home, to end our lives right there! But I was never scared. I knew our lives were just beginning and that their lives were ending, and how strange it seems to me now that this was a form of leverage.

# 2

"I like the feeling of Belgian endive against my upper lip," I said to Mark an hour later at the vegetable table, running a piece of it against my mouth. My mother thought it was best we served vegetables with names nobody felt comfortable pronouncing. Stuffed Belgian endive for the Americans! she had shouted, and witloof chicory salad for the Europeans! And if anybody is to say, *Where's the pâté de foie gras?* tell them the God's honest truth, Emily: 'tis not the season for ridiculous meat spreads.

"I like foods based on their textures," I continued.

"You're weird," Mark said.

"Shut up," I said. When Mark insulted me, it felt like praise.

I looked around for my father but instead saw his two brothers, Uncle Vince and Uncle Vito. Our last name was Vidal, so their names always seemed like a joke to me—Vince and Victor and Vito Vidal—but my grandmother believed names that invoked alliteration produced successful people. Galileo Galilei. Harry Houdini. Graham Greene. And my grandmother would have continued the list if she were still alive.

My uncles were talking to Dr. Trenton. Dr. Trenton's son Richard was in my class at school and had told everybody that his father gave Mrs. Trenton a brand-new nose (and removed our senator's jowls). "Mr. Trenton was literally redesigning his wife the way he wanted to!" I had told my parents at dinner, my rage calculated and ultimately irrelevant.

"Where's your father?" I asked. Mark's father hadn't attended a neighborhood function in over two years now, and I wondered how he got away with that. I could barely remember what he looked like, even though he was one of the few adults who had always made it a point to talk to me at these patio things, probably because the other adults wouldn't talk to him. He wasn't a crowd favorite, my mother had said once, as though people should be ranked like sports teams. She said Mr. Resnick asked too many questions. "He was always like, 'Quick, what's the only river that goes north and south on the equator!' Honestly? This isn't school. It's a party!"

"The Congo," I had said.

"Don't be absurd, Emily."

It had been years since anybody had seen him. I missed Mr. Resnick, how he would walk by me, put a hand on my shoulder, point to his forehead, and say, "Quick! A widow's peak, or a man's peak?"

"He's at home," Mark said. "Where's your father?"

"Whereabouts unknown."

We laughed. Mark and I liked the adults most when they were gathered together at parties. Alone they were boring—boring and powerful—saying any boring thing and getting away with it. At dinner, all my mother wanted to know was, "Have we estimated our summer expenditures?" even though there were a million other good things to be discussed, and my father looked at the pot on the stove and all my father wanted to know was, "Is this actual seaweed?" And when I stabbed my fork into the kale before my father properly sat down (his arms had to be fully rested on the table so we knew he was almost relaxed), they both said, "Emily, have you no manners?" Or rather, where did I last leave them? And I said, "In my locker at school," because sincerity was a form of weakness at the dinner table. My father looked down at his plate of kale and said, "And thus the carnivores went extinct."

My mother narrowed her eyes and said, "Well, who needs them anyway?"

But when they were all together at my father's fiftieth birthday party, when I lifted the aluminum foil covering the food trays to sneak a shrimp in front of all the adults, my mother smiled and said, "Oh, children." Just like that, the differences between us were darling.

The birthday party was so much like a corporate networking event, some of the adults introduced themselves with name, title, business;

Henry Lipson, vice president, Stratton and Stratton. My father was one of the more successful investment bankers with Lehman Brothers. Everybody knew this. That was why he was leaving the New York branch soon, to bring his talents overseas. Everybody knew this too. Alfred announced it by the vegetable table.

"He's leaving," Alfred said. "Even though nobody will talk about it. But it's final. He's moving to Prague."

"I know," Mrs. Resnick said. "I heard."

My mother approached gravely with a tray of dead shellfish. "Alfred," was all my mother had to say to end the conversation and make Alfred eat some shrimp. Mrs. Resnick walked away, claiming shellfish allergy. "Everybody is so allergic these days," said my mother. "Don't you think it's getting a bit pretentious?"

Whatever their title, the adults all had the same question. Where in the hell are the napkins, Emily, if not right on the table?

"I don't know," I said to Alfred. "Don't worry. I'll take care of this."

I took a picture of the empty spot on the table where the napkins should have been. I was a fourteen-year-old girl documenting the invisible failures of our party and Alfred thought that was the funniest thing he had seen so far that night. He puffed on a cigar and the white smoke curled out his nostrils and some seemed to get caught in his nose hairs. Sometimes, when he smiled, he looked as though he couldn't even breathe and that this was hardly relevant.

"Mom," I said. "We have a problem."

"Photograph the guests," she said, without even turning around.

My mother pointed to the napkins and sent me to light the candles that had gone out. I meandered through the white chairs with white lace tied around the backs and watched Mark by himself at the vegetable table appraising the squash. I wanted to return to him, but as soon as the party started, I had acquired all these chores from my mother, whose lipstick was starting to crack at the corners of her mouth, something that happened to her when she was talking and drinking too much, which was something that happened to her when she was nervous, wiping her mouth with a napkin after every sip. I lit the candles and listened to the adults around me, the way their words sounded coming out of their mouths.

"Get this," said Mr. Bulwark. "My wife counted up all the deaths in the Old Testament. Took her two years."

"Good fucking God," Mr. Lipson said.

"Fish babies," Mr. Lipson said. I lit the candle on their table and held up the camera. Mr. Lipson opened his mouth to put in the caviar and stopped midbite as though I had caught him red-handed, eating my peers. I took the picture.

"Anyway," Mr. Bulwark said. "It's a stupid project. But a project nonetheless."

Mr. Lipson agreed; wives should always have their projects.

I wiped crumbs off their table like a waiter and walked over to the Trentons.

"The mother and child aren't going with him," Mr. Trenton said as I approached from behind.

The mother and child. I didn't like the sound of that. In the entire canon of Western literature, nothing good ever happened to the mother and child, and Mrs. Trenton could see I understood that.

"Edward," Mrs. Trenton said. "Have a carrot."

Mr. Trenton looked up and saw me. "Such a wonderful party," he said to me. I nodded because I knew that was something everybody at this party was forced to agree with.

I lit their candle. "Thank you, sweetheart," Mrs. Trenton said, suddenly sweet over her drink. "Richard will be coming by shortly, to say hello." Mr. Trenton turned the carrot in his mouth like a lollipop.

I returned to Mark, my stomach sour.

"Mrs. Bulwark self-published a book. Called *God: A Murderer*," I said. "Mr. Bulwark thinks it's a ridiculous idea, to count up all the deaths in the Old Testament and write a book about it. Embarrassing, frankly."

"Alfred thinks Bob should get a shingles vaccine," Mark said, leaning closer. "But Bob already had chicken pox. Alfred doesn't understand why that matters."

"Mrs. Hanley is going to spend the night testing the predictability of vodka," I said. "It's an experiment."

"Just this morning, Mr. Smith said he was considering his mortality," Mark said, and we couldn't bear it. We fell into giggles. "He said it just like this. 'Ladies! This morning! When I was considering my mortality!'"

It was the first time I laughed all day.

"Your father and I are getting a divorce," my mother had shouted at my back that morning as I went upstairs to bathe for the party. My mother believed there were certain ways of delivering bad news that were better than others, that bad news felt better when it came at you fast, from behind, like a bullet. That way, there was a chance it could exit before you even felt it inside you. I turned around to see her in yellow control-top underwear that was pushing her love handles farther up her torso. It got so hot there in Fairfield, Connecticut, during the summer my mother said there was nothing more suitable to wear besides your underwear. Plus, she had added, being pantless was only a phase.

"Gloria, can't you put on some pants?" my father had asked walking through the kitchen. "You're running around like a goddamned Viking."

Turning fifty had put my father in a mood.

"Vikings wore pants, Victor," my mother said.

"Vikings did not wear pants. That was the whole point of being a Viking, Gloria."

"This is how I relax," she said.

"By taking off your clothes?"

That was my father's way of calling her a whore.

I picked off the top of a blueberry muffin sitting on the counter. I waited for my mother to yell at me, to say Emily, are you that narcissistic to think you are the only one in the house who enjoys the tops of muffins, for Christ's sake, nobody likes the bottom, we only eat it out of obligation to the rest of the muffin! But she didn't.

"Anyway, you can see why your father and I are getting a divorce," she said again.

"You told her?" my father asked. The vein in his forehead had emerged.

My history teacher Mrs. Farbes had told us in class last year that in the early Arab world when a man wanted to divorce his wife, all he had to do was stand up straight and say, "I divorce you, I divorce you, I divorce you!"

"That's stupid," Richard Trenton said at the time, and I agreed. "That solves nothing."

"It was enough to make it real," Mrs. Farbes said. She said it was important for the man to hear out loud what he was doing to the woman.

"Your mother and I are no longer going to live together," my father said. "We're no longer going to be married."

When I was younger, my father told me you had to hear something seven times before you internalized it. "What do you mean, internalize?" I had asked.

"Bring it inward," he said, pointing to his stomach.

"Like all the way to your liver?"

"Doesn't have to be the liver. Could be the spleen. Maybe even the kidney," he said, and I had mistaken the point of this conversation to be that the kidney was a lesser kind of organ.

But when my father came home a few weeks ago and told my mother that he was being offered a position in the Prague office, that he would move after the New Year, that it was a great opportunity, I said, "Can you feel it in your liver?" and he looked at me and said, "Huh?"

"The thing is, Emily, we're getting a divorce," my mother said.

I mashed a piece of the muffin between my fingers, rolled it into a ball. My mother leaned against the counter, wrote *SWISS CHARD* on the list and said, "Anyway, Emily. Your father and I have been thinking," and then stopped. I waited. I rolled the ball of muffin and I waited and after my mother said, "That you should really take a multivitamin," my father threw up his hands in disgust, and I was positive I had no family at all, certain it was not my mother but the solar wind that carried me into this universe.


It was ten when Dr. Trenton cornered me and Mark in the side lawn and blamed everything on the vodka. Dr. Trenton blamed most things on the vodka. His son was rude (his wife got drunk off Belvedere in her sixth month), and his wife was rude (drinking a martini right now), and he even ate caviar earlier (he only did that when he was drunk).

Dr. Trenton sneezed. It was wildly messy. He excused himself to get a tissue. Mark and I stood side by side and watched adults smoke cigarettes and lean against my house. Mark drew a correlation between someone's age and the messiness of their sneeze. I laughed. I wondered how Mark always said exactly what I wanted to say.

"At an exponential rate," he said.

"That's something to look forward to," I said.

"I'm going to be a smoker soon," he said. "I love the smell. Don't you?"

"Oh, yes," I said, trying to show him how many cigarette smokers I knew: my mother, my grandmother, my great-grandmother. Generations of women in my family had regularly been inhaling smoke like it was better than air.

"Mr. Jackson ate fifteen wontons," I said. "I saw the whole tragedy myself."

"Mrs. Miller has a herniated back," Mark said.

"What a weird word."

"'Herniated.'"

"Can you imagine what it'd sound like if people used the word 'herniated' instead of 'beautiful'?" I asked.

"The herniated princess," Mark said.

"Hello, this is my herniated wife."

"You're so herniated."

"Oh, why, thank you, I get it from my mother."

I heard my mother call for me, asking me to pass out pieces of the cake, which ended up looking more like Bill Clinton than my father. I saw Richard Trenton coming out of his house across the street, headed toward the party. I wanted nothing to do with either of them. "Let's get out of here," I said, before Mark could get stolen away by Richard. Mark and I ran into the woods behind my house. The trees were tall and thin and webbed. The twigs cracked under our feet with an unsteady beat.

Before I knew it, Mark was ahead of me.

"Alfred thinks I'm cuter than a bug's ear," I said behind him.

"Have you ever even seen a bug's ear?"

"No."

"I have. They aren't very cute."

And everything truly was like my mother said: of course men think they know everything, but you know, Victor doesn't even realize how much of his happiness is based off the fact that he has such a lovely living environment, one I created for him. With Italian vases and miniature ivory elephants sitting on his desk. It's like he thinks they're just for pretend or something, like they came with the house and so did we, like a man is always entitled to be around beautiful things! It's like he doesn't realize an elephant was murdered for him, the tusks ripped from the mouth, carved into a string of tinier elephants, it's like he doesn't realize I bought them at a store where they were shipped in a box from somewhere very far away, like Italy! It's like men don't even realize how far away that is!

I wondered what Mark realized. Did he realize what I had done to prepare for this moment? I practiced articulating my *t*'s, a letter my mother said I didn't emphasize enough in conversation. I put lemon juice in my hair, which according to my mother was the equivalent of rubbing my head against the frying pan after breakfast. "I'll do that too," I had warned her. I stood in front of the mirror, dripping with lemon, reciting, "Button, mutton, glutton."

I wondered if Mark could see me like I saw him, a body in the dark, a distinct member of the opposite sex.

"The penis," my health teacher Mr. Heller had said last year, "is an organ of the mammals and the reptiles." With no shame, he drew a human penis on the board. It looked like a long carrot wearing shoes. "I have kidney stones," Mr. Heller said, "and I can't pass them. So when that happens," he said as he moved his finger across the diagram of the urethra toward the stomach, "they put a rod up your urethra to break them up."

"That's the problem with these things," he said, "these *penes,* plural."

The boys groaned. Ernest Bingley grabbed his crotch. Janice was intrigued. "Wouldn't you dic from that?" she asked, determined to love him forever.

"No," he said. And he was right. He didn't die. He limped for a week, while everyone made fun of him behind his back. "Mr. Heller is gay," Richard said in the lunchroom. "So gay he put a rod up his own dick."

I had watched Mark squirm in his seat. I watched Mark every day really, whether he realized it or not. He was always next door, pulling weeds in his yard and stuffing them into black plastic garbage cans. His father had a bad back. That was what my mother said at least.

"It explains a lot," she said, and opened her mouth wider for rigatoni.

It was why we hadn't seen Mr. Resnick in years, or why sweat soaked Mark's neck instead of his father's while Mark trimmed the hedges. Mr. Resnick had been outside only once this year. It was last winter, and the yard was full of snow. I saw him standing on the sidewalk with a shovel. He was wobbling like he was going to fall over. He couldn't quite grip the shovel, and it hung lazily in his hands like a spoon, and then just as the shovel fell to the ground so did Mr. Resnick. Mark ran out the front door, saying, "Dad! What are you doing outside!" Mark helped his father stand up and led him back into the house as though nothing had happened, as though his father had dropped the mail.

My mother said his bad back was why Mrs. Resnick was always around town toting shopping bags by herself. It was why Mr. Resnick never took out the recycling bin and why there was never the sound of four feet and a basketball in their driveway. It was why they were all so unhappy. My mother said the constant silence around their house made everybody in the Resnick family seem older than they were.

I agreed. Mark was fourteen going on twenty. I knew this better than anyone. I tracked his growth daily. His arms were thicker by the month. His legs became logs instead of sticks. He had cut the sleeves off most of his shirts, started to read books by Tom Wolfe, books his father read, *Lonesome Dove, Ulysses*. Mark was entering the world in a way I was not, strong and informed, armed with a vocabulary and questions—did I know that James Joyce wrote the word "cunt" in his novel? Did I know that in Japan poisonous fish was a delicacy? Did I know that if I rubbed chili peppers on his balls the pain could actually kill him?

"Did you know I have BO?" Mark asked one hot day, sniffing his armpit.

There were so many amazing new developments.

His hands were opening jars for me weekly. I watched with fascination, or maybe it was frustration, not sure my weakness was good or bad. Either way, I was slowly devoting myself to him, adopting his speech patterns, dropping the g's off all my gerunds, devising ways in which Mark might have to touch me even though every time he brushed against me, I felt my whole body empty, all of the heat leaving my body for his. By August, I was nearly empty inside, and I began to understand what my father meant when he whispered quietly and harshly to my mother in the stairwell when they both thought I was out, "Gloria, I have lost myself in this marriage."

Mark took my hand. "Let's sit here," he said with some enthusiasm, like he was picking out a home for us.

I took a stick and drew lines in the dirt. Around Mark, I acted aimless. There was no reason why I looked up at the trees, or scratched my knee, or cleared my throat, or stood up and put my hair behind my ears when I offered to comb his leg hair for five dollars a minute.

"*Joke,*" I added.

"Do you know what I realized today?" Mark asked.

"No."

"None of the statues in our house have pubic hair. But they are all naked."

Mark was staring at me, looking at the way my bottom lip was too large for my top lip.

"Maybe your mother had them shaved."

He rolled a cigarette in his hand and put it to his mouth. He pretended to eat it. I smiled.

"Don't eat that," I said.

Something incredible was about to happen and yet, neither of us could stomach the idea of it. We couldn't even look at each other. I stared back at the party, which was either dying out or at its peak. It was hard to be sure. Adults always had a different idea of what a good time was. When my parents and I went to Disney World, we rode the teacups, spun around in a thousand circles until we couldn't remember our names. I was exhilarated. I laughed until I peed a little. My father's sunglasses flew off his head, Ray-Bans lost forever. "Let's never do that again, huh?" my father said, and straightened out his shirt. My mother fussed over her bangs. My father squinted the rest of the day. At night, we went to Epcot and sampled breads, and both of them got a perverted satisfaction out of agreeing with each other—the Irish soda bread had the perfect ratio of raisin to dough, why go to France when their bread is here, and isn't Emily being rude? I laid my body on a stone wall nearby, so bored I threatened to harden into rock, swim to Cuba, sell my body to Donald Duck, if he would even have me. They ignored this, continued nodding at the vendor.

Adults, I was learning, were not a people of dramatic gestures. When they approved of something, they gently nodded, and when they wanted something, they gently nodded, and when they were upset by something, they gently nodded and then shifted their body weight to indicate a significant change of attitude. Everything they wanted was within reach, or at least one nod away, so mostly, the adults stood upright, their arms stuck to their sides, like manikins unaware of the night dimming around them. They were getting blinder, more immobile every day, and I felt it was my duty to warn them, to shout through the trees with a megaphone: *Do you adults see how old you are getting?* My father was getting so old. Every day, I noticed new ways his body was failing us. Last night, he'd gotten a piece of chicken stuck in his esophagus at dinner. He put one finger in the air, which signified to my mother and me to wait, and then put one hand around the bottom of his throat. Then, he swallowed slowly. When the food passed, he said, "This happens from time to time." When it wouldn't pass, he went to the bathroom, where he forced himself to throw up. Either way, he continued eating, and I was heartbroken by the simplicity of it, my father's body broken.

"You're very herniated," Mark said.

I forgot what I had planned to say. Mark reached out and touched my hair. I couldn't believe it. The thought of reaching out to touch him felt as criminal as reaching out to trace the lines of a Picasso painting at the MoMa. But Mark seemed confident in his action, as though touching each other was becoming the right thing to do.

"You have knots," he said, his fingers stuck at the end of my ponytail. The dried lemon juice was coarse in my hair.

"So?" I said. "All girls have knots."

"So?"

"I'm just saying," I said.

He leaned closer, took me in.

"You look a lot like Michael Bolton with that greasy ponytail."

My stomach sank. Nobody ever knew how to talk about anything.

It was all so disappointing. After my mother told me about the divorce that morning, I stormed upstairs, stood in the bathtub, and refused to bathe. Why bathe? I shaved my legs without soap or water and cut my knee. I stuck my nose to the coconut shampoo and tried to imagine my mother's reaction if I stormed down to the kitchen and said, "Mother, are you sure you know what beach smells like? I don't think you understand what kind of beach I go to." But I didn't because she would have said, "Since when do you call me 'Mother'? That makes me feel so old." I just did not understand her sometimes, though I had always tried, a project bigger than I realized at the time. I studied her face over her cereal bowl, her skin tight against her cheekbones, while my father's sagged toward the milk like a man who was so so tired of everything, especially cereal made 100 percent out of fiber, a breakfast that made him "shit all the goddamned time," he told my mother. "I'm a working man," he said, holding up the box. "And I can't be shitting between calls."

My mother had laughed in his face. My mother was thirty-seven, thirteen years younger than my father, and she often used her youth as leverage to win arguments, something I didn't realize was even possible since it was youth that was always my handicap. But my mother was always successful in her attack, walking around the house in her underwear to show my father how smooth her legs were; she was only thirty-seven and still happy in her skin. She had only about three visible varicose veins and they were on the backs of her knees. My father refused to look at her when they fought. He would sit down, stroke his chin, and look out a window like he couldn't believe the world was ending in this particular way. My mother would stare at him across the room in disgust, squint her eyes as though she was counting his wrinkles. Every day she denied my father the peace he had hoped would come with age and in response my father always shouted some variation of, "You knew that when I married you, Gloria!"

You knew my pants would shrink! You knew I would move less, hum more, analyze important American revolutionaries at dinner!

"A pretty Michael Bolton," Mark said.

"That's still mean."

Mark moved his head toward mine. As I leaned in, and felt only the air against my lips, I realized that I was accepting a kiss that was not being proposed. I opened my eyes. Mark was looking at something behind me.

"Who's over there?" he asked.

I turned around to see two figures in the dark, holding each other.

"Let's go find out," I said.

We crept over to get a better view of the adults. We leaned against the tree and watched them kiss deeply.

"I bet it's Mr. Bulwark and Mrs. Trenton," I said. "She was leaning into his large ear earlier."

"Nah, Mrs. Trenton's a wolf."

"Like, good wolf or bad wolf?"

"Bad wolf."

"Is that like, a wolf you wouldn't sleep with?"

"Shh. Get your camera."

I got my camera, steadied it against my eye. I focused on the two adults, centering them. I pressed down on the button.

The flash illuminated my father's face. But my father didn't even notice, didn't even budge. His arms were steady around Mrs. Resnick's waist. He was burying his face in her neck. His mouth was on her throat, and the rest of her neck looked raw under the moonlight. Mark and I stood by our tree, watching my father's mouth pull away from Mrs. Resnick's neck while her skin remained so covered in him.

I was going to be sick.

A caterpillar crawled away from my hand like he was fleeing the scene. For one moment, I thought about picking it up, holding the caterpillar in my hand like a friend who needed to see the animals too but wasn't tall enough. I thought about putting my hand on Mark's back, pretending that was all I needed to keep me from falling over from the sight of our parents. But balance was what the tree was for and Mark probably would have looked at me and said, "Emily, then what is the tree for?" and I would have had to respond, "Oh," or "Yeah," or something equivalent as though I had never stopped to consider that things had another function separate from being all around us.

Mrs. Resnick laughed. Apparently, my father was being incredibly funny.

"Baby, shhh," my father said. "You're going to wake up the party."

Mark turned away from the sight, but I kept staring. We stood quietly and then suddenly I remembered everything I wanted to say earlier. Uncle Vito hated carrots, especially the baby ones, and Mrs. Trenton didn't think it was right for someone to hate *baby* anything. Alfred groped his wife's butt by the rutabaga dip and Mr. Hemley thought this was absolutely an inappropriate thing to do.

"I guess my father thinks your mother is very herniated," I whispered.

"Shut up," he said, quietly and in my ear. "Don't make stupid jokes. Don't make your voice all high-pitched like that, all curious and interested and stupid and shit."

"Don't tell me to shut up," I said.

"Your father's a shithead."

"Your mother's so old!"

Mrs. Resnick was thirty-nine, two years older than my mother.

"Your father's a *fuck face*."

"Shut up."

He came closer. For a second, I still thought he might kiss me.

"A giant bloody cunt," he whispered in my ear.

The word felt wrong coming out of his mouth, uncomfortable, like a new pair of jeans still stiff around your body. He was staring at me like he could kill me, while I felt certain that I loved him, that I would have sat back down on the log and pretended nothing had happened if he would; even in that moment when his cruelty was desperate and barbaric, clinging to my face, I would have asked him to reach out for me. But I stood there, so deeply openmouthed, a bird could have flown in.

"Do you know what he does for a living?" Mark asked.

"Of course I know what he does for a living," I said. "He's my *father*."

Though I didn't actually know what my father did for a living because every time I asked, he said, "I'm an investment banker," and I'd say, "What's that?" and he'd sit me down all serious, as though I was on the brink of learning something incomprehensible. With a hand on his knee, he'd say, "Well . . ."

I'd beg him to stop. "No more! No more! I can't take any more!" I'd shout, and we'd laugh.

"He fucking steals money from companies," Mark said. It felt typical for some reason that Mark would know my father better than I did. Sometimes I got the distinct feeling that everybody knew my father better than I did, even our mailman, whom he chatted with at the end of our driveway. "And everybody hates him. My father hates him. He said that nobody at the golf course liked to play with him because he tried to make bets with money that nobody had."

"My father is a good golfer," was all I thought to say.

"Your father is a bastard. I should kill him."

"You can't kill him," I said. "He's my *father*."

"Fathers get killed all the time," he said.

I could almost feel my mother looking around on the deck with an empty drink, sucking on the green olive, grimacing with bitterness but only because she had nothing else to do. My father was not dancing with her, not dipping her until the bobby pins fell from her bun and between the cracks of the Brazilian wood.

"I'm out of here," Mark said.

"Oh my God," Richard said, pointing at my father. Richard had followed us in the woods and stood between two oaks gaping at us. My father and Mrs. Resnick were still oblivious, huddled together, two bodies sharing a mouth. Mark pushed by Richard and left.

"Your dad's in serious trouble," Richard said to me, seeming somewhat pleased about this.

"Fuck you, Trenton," I said, and ran after Mark. "I'm going to vomit," I said to Mark when I caught up, the Polaroid developing in my hand.

"Don't be such a child," he said. "Vomiting would change nothing."

When we got to my side yard, my lawn became his. I stopped and watched him go. He opened his front door and walked inside. He did not even say good night. He did not even turn around. I stood like this, in between our lawns, until I had to sit, until I started running my hands up and down my legs. Everything was moving too fast. The hair on my legs had grown back into stubble. The cut on my knee had crusted into a scab. It was already brown. I was already picking at it with a nail and the blood was already at my shoe. Dr. Trenton was already sober.

Mrs. Bulwark's eyes were already clumped in mascara like it was the next morning. Mrs. Hanley was asleep on the deck. The Polaroid in my hand was already fully formed, a picture of people who were already unidentifiable, my father and Mrs. Resnick, dark blurry figures among the trees as though they were a people before my time, their customs outdated, already myths.

My mother was at my back with her hand on my shoulder, telling me the bad news: some of the adults were tired; they were getting their purses and hats and into their cars, and even though their departure was penciled into the invitation from the start, I felt their absence in my gut like abandonment, a wide and expansive bullet through my stomach, carving a path for the wind.

"What do you have there?" my mother said, looking at the picture.

"See for yourself." I handed it to her.

"Emily," my mother said. "You were supposed to take pictures of the guests. Not the trees. We already know what our backyard looks like."

"Then maybe you should have hired a professional," I said. "For Christ's sake, Mother, I am only a child!"

She flinched as though this was a terrible secret I had been keeping from her.

And everything was always intolerably like my mother said: your father's birthday was such a fiscal success. Mr. Lipson got your father to invest in an expanding branch of Bubble, International. Which, you know, means good things for your father. I don't want you thinking that just because we're getting divorced we won't benefit from his wealth. We will. And that still makes us a family, right? You don't just stop being a family because of a stupid piece of paper. It's not like today we are a family, and tomorrow, there is a piece of paper, and we're not a family. That's not how it works.

My mother sat down on the white chairs and sipped the last of her martini and sighed.

"Really," she said. "I don't know why Mrs. Resnick just doesn't hire a gardener. That poor boy Mark. Did you see that look she gave me when I mentioned your father planted lilies, like I was rubbing it in, like I was trying to brag about how I have a husband who is concerned about the vegetative state of our yard? And her dress, I mean, *right*?"

Right. I understood. "It was a terrible dress," I said. "Too wide on the shoulders. She looked like a really excited cardboard box. And can a cardboard box even be excited? She defies all logic. And her hair. It's like she went to the hairdresser and said, 'Francois! Make me look more like a gerbil than a gerbil!'"

My mother looked at me. "You're funny," she said. "I'm not very funny. How did you get so funny?"

"I used to watch a lot of television," I said.

My mother did not laugh like people normally do when they discover someone who makes them laugh. Instead, she reached out and touched my arm and said gravely like it was the last time she would ever recognize the comedy of the situation, "Thank you for making me laugh."

My mother picked up her drink. I watched her move through the crowd, her crowd, the crowd she built on a pad with a pen three months ago in our living room when she said, "Victor, how about a giant party?" And my father had said, "What's the occasion?"

"Your turning fifty!" she said.

My father pointed to his bald head and explained what it meant to be fifty.

"Being fifty means you finally have enough money to throw a decent party for a change," my mother said. "We'll invite everybody and it's perfect timing, we have the new deck. We'll invite the neighbors and your coworkers and good cheer."

"And what do we do if the cheer does not RSVP?" my father said. "What shall we do then, Gloria?" They laughed. I know I heard them laugh. I know this because I laughed too, and thought, This is exactly how I will talk to the people that I love when I get older.

I sat back on my chair and watched my mother keep her head up and smile, her hair tightly wound in a bun. She was so thin and restrained in her movement. She was sticking out her hand, saying thank you so much for attending our party, we'll see you soon. It was like she always said: there are better ways of saying good-bye than others. Don't just stand there, with your mouth all agape, Emily, it's unbecoming. Be an adult. There's nothing more impressive than a child who is really an adult and vice versa. Stick out your hand, keep a firm grasp, no, no, not a limp noodle, Emily, not like that, do you want people to think you are just a noodle? Do you want them to say, "You throw a good party," for a noodle? No. Stand tall, look people in the eye, and say, "Good-bye and thank you so much for attending our party."

The Other Girls

# 3

At first, it was intuitive. You could spot an Unfuckable the same way you could identify a bird sitting outside a window. This was what the Other Girls told me as soon as we sat at our desks in the back of biology. One of them pointed a finger and proclaimed, "Unfuckable." Debate followed. Consensus reached. Annie Lars, an Unfuckable indeed. It was an archaic system of justice; we passed judgment with only suspicions of Unfuckability, and all the while, our teacher Ms. Nailer stood in the front of the room trying to teach us how to be grateful for things we never knew we had to be grateful for.

"Eskimo women chewed on their husband's shoes when they got back from hunting," Ms. Nailer said between sips of her coffee. "Their teeth would wear down over time. I want you all to rub your teeth and feel grateful."

We did as such.

These were the things we learned freshman year: Even Eskimo women (who did not like to be called Eskimo women) needed to get married in order to survive (one person couldn't tend to the igloo and also hunt all day for the seals); it took fifteen days for a peeled banana enclosed in a jar to be fully infested by tiny maggots, and it took another fifteen days after that for all the maggots to consume the banana, and this whole affair was called decomposition (something that would happen to us one day, said Ms. Nailer). We learned that most records were not necessarily achievements: Janice's ancestors were responsible for executing hundreds of "witches" in seventeenth-century Germany; Brittany Stone's parents had been divorced and remarried three times; soda cans have nine teaspoons of sugar (which makes you fat); William Taft, heaviest president of all time, was so fat he couldn't get out of his tub, which wasn't supposed to be funny, Ms. Nailer said. It was wrong to make fun of fat people (Taft couldn't help it), or the mentally challenged (extra chromosome), or the Unfuck-ables (they'll never get fucked), or girls wearing their mothers' gold jewelry (their mothers were usually dead), and we knew all of this, even though none of us could recognize the difference between "dis-creet" and "discrete," Missouri or Mississippi, good people or bad people (but I was pretty positive reptile eggs had tough outer cover-ings and amphibian eggs lacked outer coverings, which was why they were laid in water, water that contained over nineteen species of box jellyfish, the most venomous animal in the world, a bite that nearly no one ever survived, unless you were smart and had on your panty hose).

Ms. Nailer pushed up her yellow Dior glasses. The Other Girls were cross-legged behind their desks, whispering hurtful things about every-one sitting in front of them.

"Annie's nose is so large, she descended from a rare line of prehis-toric bird."

"Annie the Bird's ears stick out so bad, from the back, she actually looks more like a bear than a bird."

"Annie the Bird or Bear hasn't shaved since the Cambrian Period."

"Annie the Bird or Bear is so tall, she can fuck all the teachers stand-ing up," Richard Trenton said, chiming in from across the room.

At Webb High you were either Fuckable or Unfuckable. Anything else you might have been was secondary. There were so many students, nearly two thousand, it was very possible, if not guaranteed, you would know only 50 percent of your graduating class. The only way to survive was to organize everybody into categories, so every five people could be treated as one, four hundred as two. That way, you felt like you knew everybody without actually having to.

Ms. Nailer made us put unpeeled bananas in jars so we could draw pictures of decay in our notebooks for a whole semester. We had to observe the banana turning to mush, and then draw every new mag-got that hatched. We had to open the jar every week and describe the scent. *Nasty*, I wrote on my lab sheet. *Even nastier*, I wrote a week later.

Annie the Bird or Bear was Richard's lab partner and she was standing tall and proud, holding their banana jar level with her massive breasts, confident that Richard was not someone who could ever hurt her, even though I figured he was the only person who would. She took pride in her new high school identity the way a superhero uses their defining mutation as a source of power. She made boys bleed in the parking lot. She scared away lunch tables just by sitting down at them, the students scattering like sparrows. She embraced her solitude and used it as a form of freedom. She spread her lunch out on the whole table like she was happy about all the room, made animal sounds down the hallway, bird calls, bear cries, lion roars. Mostly everybody thought this was hilarious; they fell against their lockers, crippled by laughter that spread like a disease as Annie the Bird or Bear walked by, neighing like a dying, vengeful creature.

I could hardly watch. But, of course, I did.

It was September of freshman year, when the earth began to tilt away from the sun, the flowers still upright, the shrubs on their last breath, the bees slowing in flight, making dizzy, drunken loops in the air like parade planes. *EVERYTHING IS CHANGING,* Ms. Nailer wrote on the board in all caps and drew an arrow pointing to the outside. Her observations, while not mind-blowing, were at least correct. Caterpillars were lined up on my driveway like remains of a drive-by shooting, and when I added their souls to our dinnertime prayer, my mother said, "Emily, enough about the caterpillars." My mother and father started to maximize the efficiency of our dinnertime appeals to God as though prayer was a science of exclusion. We no longer prayed for a successful town apple festival like we normally did at the start of fall; or for Ms. O'Malley, my thirty-year-old algebra teacher who needed a new heart pump, because she got one; or for my father's gums to quit receding, because it stopped being funny.

My father was still living with us until he moved to Prague after New Year's Eve, but if you weren't listening hard, you wouldn't even notice. Every night, my father kicked his shoes off and they hit hard against the wall, the bed squeaked as he slid under the sheets across the hall from my mother, and if I was tired enough, I mistook the creaks of his bed for the cracks of his bones. I had nightmares of his skeleton breaking at the joints, and I woke to his spoon clacking against his six A.M. cereal bowl. From my bed, I could hear him put the coffee grinds in the trash can, the bowl in the sink like any good father, and for a moment that was what he sounded like—any good father who cleared his throat and walked out the door to go to work.

But he couldn't just leave like that, like any good father. One morning before school I jumped out of bed to say, "I saw you, *Dad*," to stand wounded and victimized in front of the door until we both remembered everything: my father and Mrs. Resnick with their mouths pressed together; my father and my mother both teary-eyed and pink-faced on the porch in August, blowing their noses and then laughing deep sorrowful laughs, and me listening from my bedroom wanting to shout, *It's not funny!*; my father and mother ten years ago at the kitchen counter, my mother spreading stone-ground mustard on wheat bread, my father singing with the bread knife to his lips, me in baggy green jeans shouting, "Make me a turkey sandwich, please!" and my father tapping me on the head, saying, "Poof! You're a turkey sandwich!"

I ran down the stairs, but by the time I walked into the kitchen, my father was out the door. I looked at the clean table and the orange bowl in the sink and my throat went dry. He was gone. Not even a crumb left on the floor. And when my father was gone, sometimes he didn't come back for days. Sometimes he went on business trips to California. Sometimes he went to Europe. Sometimes he just went places and I didn't know where, and I wouldn't even know he was away on a trip until I woke up at eight in the morning fully rested.

My father's blazer was hanging on the back of one of the chairs. I grabbed the jacket and ran out the front door as fast as I could. "Dad!" I shouted, but his black car was already at the end of the street. I ran after the car, waved my hands, screaming his name, but he didn't hear me, and I wondered afterward if I even shouted it at all.

My mother stood in the frame of the wide-open door with a glass of orange juice waiting for me to return.

*"What?"* I said, mortified.

"Emily," my mother said, frowning. "Why don't you stop worrying about your father, okay?"

I threw the jacket back on the kitchen chair, but it slid and fell to the tile. I had no idea what she meant, but she put her hand on my head and said, "Good girl."

"If Annie the Bird or Bear was an amoeba," Richard said to a bunch of the Other Girls, "I bet she wouldn't even reproduce with herself asexually, she's that ugly."

*"Richard!"* Ms. Nailer yelled, finally hearing us, or finally recognizing us, turning away from the chalkboard to look at Richard, and then Annie, and then Richard again. Her white bra was visible through her shirt. She spilled her coffee on the desk, stepped backward, got chalk on her ass, and then laughed like it was an accomplishment that something finally touched her ass. She wasn't a disciplinarian by nature. Ms. Nailer's presence in the room offered no more protection than a fruit fly; she just buzzed from one shoulder to the next. Her interests were elsewhere, and she always reminded us that she was only a high school biology teacher as a last resort. She had been in the seventh year of her Ph.D. in body history when her funding ran out.

"This is high school, kids," Ms. Nailer said, wiping the coffee off her desk with her hand.

I stood hopeful with my banana, waiting for Ms. Nailer to slap us across the faces if that was what it took to put an end to all this misery, to save us from the horrors of each other, from Richard. Richard was constantly taunting Annie the Bird or Bear, created a comic strip of her nose doing absurd things every day, like "ABOB's Nose Goes to the Grocery Store" or "ABOB's Nose Goes to the Doctor," and passed them around the room. Everybody unfolded the paper, smiled, said nothing when he did this.

Ms. Nailer put her hands on her hips and smiled too, as though our cruelty was playful, a game we used to get closer to her.

"You can't go around making statements like that until you properly understand what you are saying," Ms. Nailer said. She was a skinny but doughy woman, like someone had ripped the muscles out of her body. "Richard, your comment implies that beauty is some objective thing, when really beauty is an evolving process of natural selection."

The class was silent.

"What does 'ugly' even mean? Can anyone define ugliness? Or beauty, for that matter?" she asked.

Ernest Bingley tried his hardest. "Beauty is the unconscious pleasure of looking at something artistic," he said.

"Let me teach you all a lesson," she said. "And this is going to be the most important lesson of your lives."

We groaned. It was too early in the morning to understand such things.

"Just like everything in science," she said, writing SCIENCE on the board, "beauty has evolved over time. Beauty is real, but it is also crucial to keep in mind that it is equally an ideal established by the culture in which you exist. Beauty in the eighteen hundreds was much different than what we think beauty is now."

The Other Girls were fascinated, the first time all year they had visibly reacted to something Ms. Nailer had said. One of them raised her hand and wanted to know what was considered beautiful back in the day. One of them couldn't imagine a world where Brittany Stone wasn't the most beautiful girl in school. Brittany Stone said she couldn't imagine a world where Ms. Nailer was the authority on all matters of beauty. Neither could I really. Every day, I tried to be surprising in my footwear, and Ms. Nailer did not, standing in front of the classroom, fully formed in her ugly suede flats and her two-piece suits that she probably got from Talbots, where we sat on benches outside the fitting rooms in snug tubular dresses that made me feel like a hollow tube of toothpaste, picking our scabs, watching Janice's mother try on mustard suits that were too broad in the shoulders.

"Back in the day," Ms. Nailer said, "scientists used a mathematical formula to decide who was beautiful and who was not. There was such a thing called the Facial Angle."

"Huh?" asked Ambrose, the albino boy who sat in front and answered most of Ms. Nailer's questions with, "According to Satan."

"Richard," Ms. Nailer said. "Please come up here."

Richard looked around, nervous. He rose from his seat. Ms. Nailer got out two rulers from her desk and Richard halted in front of the class rabbit.

"I'm not going to hit you," Ms. Nailer said. "Come closer."

Richard walked toward her. She put two rulers to Richard's face and measured him vertically and horizontally, the two rulers intersecting at his ear.

"The angle that the two rulers create determines if a person is more human or more primate," Ms. Nailer said. "This is obviously an imprecise measurement, but I'm getting one hundred degrees!"

"Richard's a primate?"

"Actually, no," Ms. Nailer said. "Far from it. One hundred degrees was approximately the angle you will find in the faces of classical Greek art."

Richard smiled as though he had known it all along. People booed.

"Scientists theorize that people are attracted to other people with similar facial angles. Meaning, Richard is most likely attracted to women who best represent the ideal of classical Greek beauty."

"That's racist," someone said. "Richard's a racist."

"It's not racist," Ms. Nailer said. "It's evolution."

"My dad said evolution is racist."

"People picked partners based off similar facial angles for thousands of years, but subconsciously. It wasn't until recently that people started to understand attraction through the lens of science."

"Measure my face!" Brittany Stone shouted out.

"And my face!" Martha Collins said.

I knew Martha from elementary school, but we stopped being friends in the sixth grade when she asked me if I wanted to play this game called Cats in the House, which required taking off all our clothes, including our socks. When I protested, she said, "You don't see cats walking around the house with clothes on, do you?"

"I just don't see why we have to be naked," I said. I left her house and the shame of it all kept us from speaking for three years, until we ended up in biology together. She was the only person I knew sort of well, and it seemed that when you were a freshman walking into a classroom, you saw only a string of people you couldn't sit next to for some reason or another: girls who didn't know you, girls who thought your angular features were obnoxious, or Richard, who spent his whole life battling me for Mark's full attention and publicly exposed my armpit hair in the fifth grade. He had pointed at my armpit in the lunch line and said, "Ew, look, she's got armpit hair." "That's just dog fur, you idiot," I had said. Richard laughed at me and shouted, "Emily is growing dog hair."

"Why don't you pair up and measure your lab partner's face?" Ms. Nailer said. "More efficient that way."

We took out rulers and began to measure. Martha put the ruler to my cheek. "I don't know how to tell you this," she said, "but your face is three inches on the left side, and two and a half on the other side."

"What?" I asked, getting hot. "You're doing it wrong."

"No," she said. "I double checked."

"Holy shit! ABOB's nose is almost four inches!" Richard announced from the other table. "That's almost a finger! That's almost a Twinkie! That's twice the size of Ernest Bingley's di—"

"Noses!" Ms. Nailer shouted, and wrote *NOSES* on the board. I wrote *NOSES* in my notebook. "If you could believe it, they have their place in history. The black nose, the Jewish nose, the Irish nose, the Italian nose, the syphilitic nose. So many different noses. Right now, the Irish nose is in style, but in the early 1900s? The Irish nose, the tiny stub, meant you were an immigrant, poor, most likely diseased, unable to work. Many Irish people underwent aesthetic surgery to look more 'American.'"

"I don't think this is right," someone said.

"To be honest, I think this is a little bit racist."

"Shut up," Richard said to the class. "Just because you aren't classically beautiful doesn't mean you have to cry about it."

"Hey, *hey*," Ms. Nailer said. But it was too late. A girl threw an eraser at Richard's head. Ernest Bingley's Coke exploded when he opened it. One of the Other Girls tried to free the rabbit but he just sat there in his opened cage. Ms. Nailer saw two girls whispering from desk to desk. She put her hair behind her ears and made nervous jokes about syphilis. One of the Other Girls leaned over to me and said, "Isn't the point of syphilis that it's *not* funny?"

I agreed too quickly.

This was the girl who had smooth firm calves that made the rest of us feel Unfuckable. This was the girl who said she wanted to stay Unfuckable for as long as one could remain Unfuckable. She said it was more Fuckable to look Unfuckable, "like one of those paradoxes."

"Well, you can probably stay as Unfuckable as you want for as long as you want," said the girl who ate meals only on Tuesdays, Thursdays, Saturdays, and major commercial holidays and never muttered a complimentary, "Just kidding," after she was cruel the way I did.

Ms. Nailer gave us the vocabulary to turn cruelty into a legitimate science, something we didn't have to apologize for, a formula we passed along to the school as proof that we had been on to something. Certain people truly were more Fuckable than others! People walked down the hallways and said, "Of course they're going out, their facial lines are structured the same way." "Of course they boned, they both have European noses." "Of course they want to get married, they want to have a symmetrical baby."

In biology, I watched Richard measure Annie's nose with a ruler, and Brittany leaned over to me and said, "ABOB's nose is so long, nobody will ever be able to kiss her." Boys pulled her long red hair, drew her body on pieces of paper in the backs of classes, and discussed what it would be like to have sex with her in exaggerated, excited ways, but girls were the ones who wouldn't even look at her as she passed, as we spread secrets about her, like ABOB got her period when she was five, ABOB once had sex with an alligator. She was more similar to a monument than a person, and our insults splattered on her face like pigeon shit. It was impossible, then, to understand how really alive she was.

# 4

Our new principal Dr. Killigan sat the school down in the auditorium and told us what it meant to be participants in a Hug-Free School.

"Hugs are supposed to be handshakes from the heart," he said too closely into the microphone. "But most of the time, these hugs I see taking place in the hallway are not that innocent."

Dr. Killigan said all the hugs did was cause traffic jams in the hallways when other students needed to get to class. All a hug did was allow boys to press against pairs of breasts. He said, Girls, boys are just using hugs as devices to get to you. He said that if we really gave it some thought, it wasn't all that logical to press our genitals together as a form of greeting. Asians bow, he said, and why would the Asians do something so random like that, like bow?

"There's a reason for everything," Dr. Killigan said.

The auditorium booed, someone shouted out, "Drugs not hugs!" and everybody laughed. I started to get worried. High school was not going very well. Why did Janice immediately gravitate toward the Other Girls? Girls who caked their eyes in grease. Girls who looked good even when they looked like they stuck their face under the hood of a car. Girls who sat on boys in the parking lot like they were nothing more important than a piece of leather, and I'd watch Janice steal Richard's Yankees hat every single day. She'd hold it behind her back and he'd reach around her body for it. He'd accidentally hit her breast and they'd smile. They would hug. Everyone would hug. Hugging became a new form of rebellion. "Press against me!" people would laugh in the hallways. "Press your genitals to mine!" People would make plans to meet in the stairwells. "Hello, genitals!" they would shout as they greeted each other.

Janice and the Other Girls made it a game to chase after the young male teachers, especially the ones who played soccer with the freshman boys after school, boys who made me sick, who were suddenly unworthy and uneducated and followed us around the halls like they had nothing better to do than stare at our asses and write *Cunts 'R' Us* on the girls' bathroom door while they waited for their beards and bodies and brains to grow in. We popped bubblegum in our mouths on the sidelines of the football games that nobody actually cared about, where Janice would cheer for a boy, sometimes Peter Barnes or Ben Mulligan or even Richard, always as a joke, screaming, "Woo!" That was another thing: enthusiasm had to be fake. When you were caught genuinely excited over something, it was worse than getting caught with your pants down. An older couple in matching navy blue fleeces, parents, turned to look at Janice, a girl all crazy for a guy, and whispered to each other. I could tell they thought she was dumb. That was just something you could tell by looking at Janice. You looked at her and thought, That girl is probably dumb, but in reality, she was the only person in our geography class who knew that Mississippi was a Southern state, and Missouri was a Midwestern state. She knew that women were supposed to stick mints in their vaginas so they wouldn't taste so much like vaginas, and bleaching the labia was important too. This was what she told me at two in the morning that August night I called her crying after I saw my father kissing Mrs. Resnick. Janice leaned her bike against the side of my house. "Want to try?"

I laughed. She put the hair behind my ears and said, "Now, don't you feel better?"

"No," I said. "Bleaching your vagina is sad, I think."

"That's why I brought this," she said. She held up a container of yogurt.

"What's that for?"

She grabbed my hand, and we walked toward the Resnicks' house. She opened up the yogurt and took a spoon and started flinging the yogurt at their windows. "It's all I could find," she said, apologetic. "Try."

I flung the yogurt at their window, and while this didn't necessarily make me feel any better, it was nice to know that Janice really was my best friend, and when I asked her things like, "Do boys want our vaginas to taste like mouths?" she always knew the answer. She knew things nobody else did, just as I knew things nobody else did, like if Janice had to be a lesbian she'd do it with ABOB since ABOB was the manliest girl she could think of, or that Janice was five pounds under the normal weight for a five-foot-six girl, but that she still believed herself to be twenty pounds overweight, and whenever she thought she was getting fat she fasted and cleansed, stirred lemon and cayenne pepper and molasses into a tall glass of water and drank it all—her only meal for two days—then ground her teeth at night, wearing away the enamel, not to mention building up a fluid in her jaw that hurt when it got below freezing.

I knew that her dermatologist grabbed her breasts once to "look for skin cancer underneath." I knew her father practiced witchcraft in the secrecy of their basement. I knew that she cried whenever Sneaker Pimps came on the radio because theirs was the song she masturbated to for the first time (wrapped a carrot in Saran Wrap and inserted it inside her), and while "6 Underground" was blasting in her room, her younger brother Ed fell down a flight of wooden stairs. He was knocked unconscious, and Janice had no idea, until her mother got home from the grocery store and flung open Janice's door, finding her, carrot and all. She called her a "dumb shit," a "filthy whore," and I knew this was what Janice still believed about herself (though she would never tell the story in this way).

Before I introduced Janice to the Other Girls, I had always referred to them as just that: these other girls in my biology class who liked to swear excessively in casual conversation. At lunch, it was fuck green beans, fuck milk, fuck eating for the sake of eating, fuck everyone in line—"Would you?" one of the Other Girls asked Janice. "Would you fuck everyone in line?"

Janice laughed. She took to them immediately. There was nothing that anyone could ever say that would shock Janice ("Your brother will never walk again," the doctor told them all), nothing that anyone could ever do to make her open her mouth in surprise. Janice had always been bolder and brighter than me—even her eye shadow seemed to scream as she walked down the halls—always discovering the world one second before I did, even drew me a map of my own vagina once so I could put in a tampon for the first time, and I was in the bathroom wide-eyed, saying, "*Not* the pee hole?" and she was arms crossed, on the toilet, saying, "Of course not the pee hole."

Janice admired what she called the Other Girls' "enterprising speech patterns," while I feared them, and we both felt we had to resort to mockery in order to survive the day. Janice called me after school and said, "Hello, my fucking friend."

I laughed.

"Let's go to the fucking beach so I can wear my new fucking bikini," she said. So we went to the beach nearly every day that September, and Janice wore her new fucking bikini that was purple and had white fucking flowers adorning the bottom.

"It's still so fucking hot," Janice said. We were sitting in the back of her mother's car like professional passengers, French manicures on our toes, hemp bags across our chests. We were freshmen now. This meant no more pink, no more looking good on purpose, and no more laughing too hard. Half of our new friends starved themselves for religious reasons, though they never went to church and prayed only before a history test, and if we had religious thoughts, they were only worries that we would die while wearing our retainers and then have to wear them for the rest of eternity. "Isn't it fucking fall?"

"Technically, not until the fucking autumnal equinox," I said.

"Girls," her mother scolded. We laughed, then apologized.

We didn't let our mothers stay at the beach with us anymore because my god, we were grown women with breasts, and standing around in our bikinis was like standing around in our underwear, and we couldn't act naturally at the beach, or anywhere really, with our mothers looking at our bodies.

Instead of staying, our mothers dropped us off with the same warning: "Don't stick your head under!" and a newly added, "Don't talk to any of the boys!" This was always Janice's mother though, as my mother was at home watching *The People's Court*. Her only warning before I left the house was, "Emily, don't ever lend your cheating boyfriend your brand-new Pontiac."

"Okay," I said. "Noted."

"Actually," she said, "don't ever buy a Pontiac new."

This was supposed to be a sad joke, but I was impressed. My mother *knows* things about cars, I thought as I ran out the door.

"Aha!" Janice said, pointing her finger. "There they are."

We sat down with the Other Girls. They were in striped bikinis. One of them was peeling the skin off an almond with her teeth. One of them had pubic hair coming out the side of her bottoms. One of them looked like a young Barbara Walters, which was Martha, chomping on a hot dog.

"God, Martha," said one of them, her teeth grating at the almond.

"What?"

"You're so fat in your intent sometimes."

"Huh?"

"You're like, not actually fat, but you desire all the things fat people desire, like hot dogs and ice cream," she said. "So really, you're, like, fat in intent."

The Other Girls, of which there were six including Martha, were thin with arms that looked like needles. They could prick and deflate you with one word. They were the kinds of girls I desperately wanted to like; life would be so much easier if I just liked them, I thought.

One of them licking salt off a rice cracker asked, "Uh, what's a tenor sax?"

I got up and walked to the edge of the beach. The water cooled my shins.

There were certain things I could see more clearly now. The Sound sat at the margin of the Atlantic to collect things. Nitrogen levels were on the rise. Mercury was being dumped, and the jellyfish were growing like tumors in pockets along the shore, the clear ones that slipped into our baggy bathing suits and made us scream for no reason.

I could still hear the girls from their towels.

"This is how you know a guy is a liar," one of them said. "He shrugs his shoulders a lot and creates an obstacle between you and his mouth."

"Like a fence?" another one of them said, to which I heard Janice exclaim, "Wow, that's so true actually. Mr. Basketball always puts a Coke can up to his mouth, especially after we've slept together."

The Other Girls laughed. Mr. Baskette, a teacher at our school whom Janice started calling Mr. Basketball for fun, was the most Fuckable teacher at Webb High, determined by poll. He had an Irish nose, a classically Greek jawline, and so did Janice. Janice belonged with him, everyone decided, at least facially; "Your kids would have the best faces," Brittany said. But he had eyes like mine, I thought as I submerged myself in the water. I could feel the fish mutating at my feet, the insecticides nesting between my toes. My hair spread out around me. The water flooded my ears until it felt like an invasion.

## 5

On Sundays, Richard and Mark chucked crab apples at each other across the street. From my window, I was able to see the objective of the game: they were trying to hurt each other.

Five years ago, Richard, Mark, and I would have been at the cold spring that ran through our woods, where Richard held one of my Barbies facedown in the water until I was positive it had drowned, until I said, "Richard! Stop!" and he looked at me and said, "Emily, it's just plastic." Richard was the boy who knew things like this, and I was the girl who didn't realize that the things I chose to love were never meant to be seen in any real, human way. Mark, who always just wanted to get along, was in the background and said, "Why do you guys have to fight all the time? I don't understand why you have to fight."

Inside my house, nobody was home, except everybody, but it was easy to feel like those were one and the same. My mother was watching television. My father was in the basement. My father was on the verge of leaving us. He didn't say it like this. In fact, nobody said it like this. We weren't allowed to speak of his distance. It only upset my mother. We just watched him move slowly out of the house one box at a time, as though it were becoming a tiresome project to leave this life behind, an operation that required way too much packing tape. I was at the window, or outside on the driveway, or somewhere else entirely, and if anybody bothered to ask what I was learning in school, this was the answer I was preparing: a person can feel equally alone anywhere; you can be just as lonely in biology class holding a rabbit as you can standing next to a window in the middle of September as you can watching older people on television take each other's clothes off.

My mother and I watched *Dr. Quinn, Medicine Woman* at eight. *Touched by an Angel* at nine. Every Sunday we decided something different. We decided we probably wouldn't watch *Touched by an Angel* if it didn't come on right after *Dr. Quinn,* if they didn't show a small preview before we had time to lose interest. We decided we liked eating grapefruit, but then my mother declared that the labor of eating it was too demanding for a snack. We decided the hot one on our favorite after-school soap opera was never going to find out that his brother, who was blind with a heart condition, was having sex with his lover and we decided that you could never justifiably get mad at someone who was sleeping with the blind, considering the woman who was doing so also had amnesia, and we decided we had enough energy to tolerate this tease of a story line. We decided it didn't matter who made their beds when. This meant we were finally liberated.

"From what?" I asked my mother.

"From linens," she said. I had never felt particularly oppressed by linens, so it made more sense to me when my mother added, "From rules, from intolerable mornings, and that includes linens."

At some point, my mother would ask, "What's new?"

"The right side of my face is smaller than the left," I said, munching on a pretzel.

My mother laughed. "That's ridiculous."

"It's true. We measured it in science class."

"Who measured it?"

"Martha."

"Well, Martha obviously doesn't know how to measure correctly."

"How would you know?" I asked. "You don't even know Martha."

"I'm your mother. I've stared at your face for fourteen years."

"Well, that's just sad," I said.

Janice called. Over the phone, Janice and I laughed about all the things the Other Girls had said that week, and I welcomed the relief from my mother. "Brittany told Mr. Basketball that she was worried about him because he had such an amazing body," Janice said, and when I laughed, she added, "I'd die without you." I agreed, even though I knew I wasn't the type of person who would die from grief. I was the kind of person who would sit with grief on the couch until grief died, who would watch reruns of game shows while grief guessed the price of a can of green beans. Seventy-nine cents! Grief was always right. Grief went to the supermarket a lot.

I hung up the phone.

"Shouldn't you *be* somewhere?" I asked my mother accusingly.

"Like where?" my mother asked.

"I don't know," I said, and I didn't.

"Let's just watch the show, Emily," my mother said.

When my father came up from the basement, my mother got up and made chicken fajitas. As she seasoned the chicken, she nonchalantly dropped comments about the plumber and the water that dripped from the upstairs shower into the basement, and didn't that bother him? How could that *not* bother someone? This was what my mother needed to know.

My father got out the vodka from the liquor cabinet and when he caught me staring, he dropped in two ice cubes and looked at me like, *Well, this is still my house, Emily, still my liquor,* and then to distract me from his lingering presence, he asked, "What have you been learning in school?" By this point in the night, the kitchen had overheated from the chicken on the stove, my parents held crystal glasses of iced vodka between their fingers, and my milk was warm and forgotten in front of the television.

"Women are the inversion of male body parts," I said, and when my mother stayed silent at the stove and didn't argue, I added, "Men literally *turned inside out.*"

It was my father who protested and said, "That's barbaric, Emily."

"Ms. Nailer said so," I said.

"I don't care who said what," my father said. "Don't repeat things like that inside or outside of this house." He gave me the stern look that reminded me he was my father, six feet tall, hands nearly the size of my head, and even though he was the one who slept with the neighbor, even though he needed to be punished somehow, denied his meals like a misbehaving Victorian child, the truth was, he owned this house. He had bought the vodka, the refrigerator, even the space between the doors was his, as he filled up the frame every night with his tall body, announcing, "I'm home!" His largeness always seemed so unfair to me—a man was born with all the power—so I picked up my father's glass of vodka on the table, took too big of a gulp, and said, "My fucking friends are fucking sleeping over Friday," proud and defiant. Both of my parents looked at me like I had thrown up all my carrots. It was moments like this when I couldn't stand either of them, when I blushed and excused myself from the table and said, "Well, don't you people see that I live here too?"

"Did you know that blow jobs are like when your brother used to shove ice pops really far down your throat and you wanted to gag?" one of the Other Girls said Friday night, leaving unwelcome kiss marks on my bedroom mirror.

"My brother never did that to me," Janice said. "That's really weird your brother did that to you."

Janice and I looked at each other and laughed. Even though I was distinctly aware in which ways I was losing Janice during freshman year, I was always aware of the moments she chose to stay with me.

We were eating marshmallows in my room and bad-mouthing our parents like they were nothing to us but drunk blond people.

"It's so annoying when they look at you," said Brittany, draped in her mother's mauve nightgown, the breast cups large, lacy, and unfilled. The truth about Brittany Stone was that she got ugly at night; she popped her pimples and wore thick red glasses and her retainer was too large for her mouth. This was a great relief. "My mom was just looking at me the other day. And I was like, '*What* do you *want*, Linda?'"

The packing tape ripped loud from down the hall like crows crying out in an emergency. The Other Girls were sprawled out on my rug like sickly dogs that hadn't eaten in days. The heaviest one claimed she hadn't.

"Well, a corn on the cob," Martha said. "Yesterday. My dad, like, seriously made me. He, like, shoved it down my throat, shouted out something about anorexia being an artificial disease of the rich, a product of too much time on my hands, and he wouldn't tolerate it in his house, and I was like, 'Dad! Don't you see how Freudian this is?' My dad's stupid like that."

"My dad is stupid too," Janice said. Janice was a slobbery talker, saliva sometimes flying out of her mouth when she got too excited. "The first time I got my period I was in my bed and my dad came in and saw the blood all around me and said, 'What the hell happened, Janice?' I was like, 'Dad, I've been murdered in my sleep.' He was like, 'You couldn't have been murdered, you are talking.' He's always acting like a doctor. He's like, '*I am a doctor*.'"

"I didn't know your dad was a doctor," Brittany said.

"He's not really," Janice said. "He's a natural pathologist. He thinks he can cure people with herbs and tapping on parts of their bodies and things and chanting in their faces. Like a witch. Like, he thinks he's a witch."

The refrigerator hummed downstairs. Outside, a metal trash can was knocked over. Martha pressed her ear up to the window screen and asked, "What *was* that?"

Martha was scared because someone on my street got robbed for the first time ever last week. Mrs. Bulwark stood outside her brown house and cried while waiting for the police to show up. My mother stood with her at the curb, going over which items had been taken. Television, she said. The microwave. The toaster oven.

"Or maybe not," Mrs. Bulwark said. "Maybe I didn't have a toaster oven? I can't remember."

When the police showed up, the adults were gathered on Mrs. Bulwark's lawn, wiping their long bangs off their faces and adjusting their postures as if it was the first time they had to act human all day. I was in the front of the crowd fingering the blades of grass like I was the head of the search team and my curiosity was something professional, listening to my mother win over the affection of Mrs. Bulwark with gentle affirmation. "Of course you had a toaster oven, dear," my mother said. "Everybody on the block has a toaster oven."

Mrs. Trenton whispered to Mrs. Resnick next to me, "What a terrible brown house."

The neighborhood had gotten really into pastel the last few years. It started when Alfred's wife painted their whole house a soft pink during menopause. Looks Like Linen it was called. People raved. A magazine came, made the family hold up a rotisserie chicken, and then photographed it. A few months later, Mrs. Trenton's house was Mint Leaf. Ours became Celery Powder. The Resnicks' house turned Yellow Feather. Mark and Richard painted one side of the house black last year when his parents went to St. Thomas for a week. When they returned, Mrs. Resnick screamed so loud, our salt and pepper shakers rattled together.

"Lucy," Mrs. Resnick said in a halfhearted attempt to scold.

I stared at Mrs. Resnick. My one and only skill at fourteen: yelling at people without actually yelling. From where I was standing, Mrs. Resnick looked heavier than she did at the party. The evil part of me was glad. There had to be some kind of punishment for what she had done and if it was only twenty pounds, so be it. I stared and stared and Mrs. Resnick never looked at me, not once, and I didn't understand how she could stand there and not fall to her knees asking for everybody's forgiveness.

"Maybe it's the White Lady," Janice said.

The White Lady was a ghost story that all the parents of Fairfield told their children. She was rumored to be a tall, thin, pale woman of average height who haunted the Holy Church, the oldest church in our town with a tiny graveyard in the back, for no apparent reason. Janice believed in the White Lady but only because she had nothing else to believe in. Her father was pagan and her mother was Jewish. She said it was either the White Lady or Janicism, which sounded too much like racism, so she doubted it would ever really catch on. But mostly it was because her father swore he saw the White Lady one night, and she worshipped her father. We all did really. Our fathers were the ones who were constantly leaving us, but they were also the men who would always love us, despite our broken conversation and frizzy hair and periods in our beds. Fathers were men who were just trying to understand, while mothers were women who were trying to change us, buying us pads instead of tampons, clarifying shampoos when all we wanted was moisturizing.

"Your father is a liar," Brittany said to Janice. "That's what it all boils down to."

"All fathers are liars," Janice said. "If you want to be a father, you have to be prepared to become a liar. Like, just the other day my dad told me that when I was seven he accidentally stepped on my hamster on the stairs. I wasn't mad. Because, I mean, what was the hamster doing on the stairs? That's what you've always got to ask yourself."

This diffused the tension. We laughed, and I thought, Maybe I did like my new friends. It was nice to have people to talk to like this. And Janice was probably right. Fathers are liars, and the noise was probably a raccoon or something; I'd probably find all my garbage eaten in the morning. "That's so boring though," said Brittany, shifting her retainer. "I wish it was a killer. The White Lady. I'm bored."

She took out her retainer and the saliva dripped on my rug like fishing line.

Everybody began to slowly fall asleep, but I couldn't. Life moved in opposite directions at dawn and it was too unsettling to watch the world fight with itself, the sun and the moon awkwardly present at the same time, everything so disappointingly circular, like a dog trying to eat its own tail.

I got up to get a glass of water. Janice and the Other Girls were passed out on my white shag carpet, their mouths open like drunks, chapped at the corners. I crept over their bodies, passed my mother and father asleep in separate beds, and walked downstairs to the kitchen.

The kitchen was ambient and still at dawn, the light refracting through half-filled jars of sugar and dried fruits, making everything appear a little invisible, a little godly. I walked across the tile, compelled to pray for something. I was religious at the most unexpected of times, in the morning, when the world seemed empty and unused, and I tried to feel grateful for the peace, the cleaned spatulas. Someone always restarted our life at dawn and this was supposed to be comforting.

Chrome faucets, I would tell my clients when I was older, were the best for creating light. Everything in the kitchen could be a source of light, everything down to the spatula, your whole house illuminated from every angle, if that was the kind of life anyone was looking for.

I put my lips to the glass. The breeze through the window was new against my cheek.

The weather was turning and this should have made everything feel less full of possibility, but the morning air had taken on a cryptic chill, filled me with a giddy terror, similar to the way that mischief felt around Halloween, when egging the neighbor's suddenly became the neighborly thing to do, toilet-papering streetlights was less a crime than it was a rite of passage.

I saw Mr. Resnick outside through the window, walking toward a rock between our lawns, the large one Mark and I used to pretend was a spaceship capable of transporting our brains to Venus. I hadn't seen him in so long, I nearly pressed my nose to the windowpane. What was he doing outside his house so early in the morning? He wasn't shaking in the way that he shook the last time I saw him. He was taking long smooth steps. He stood on top of the rock, paused for a moment, casually dressed in a polo shirt as though he was waiting to be convinced into a morning game of golf.

He had a long rope in his hands, which he threw over the branch on the tree beside him. Then, his knees began to wobble, and for a moment, he looked scared, like he was worried about falling off the rock and to the ground. I was about to run outside, when he grabbed the rope that was now hanging down from the branch and regained his balance.

It was a noose.

He put the rope around his neck, and that was when I saw his wrists were dripping with blood.

I want to say that I tried to scream, or wave my hands and get his attention, but all I managed to do was drop my glass. I turned to run and the pieces of broken glass etched into my heel. I flopped like an empty sack on the tile, and when I stood back up, Mr. Resnick was dead. His body was as still as a wind chime in a glass case, the earth so completely balanced that morning.

I didn't move. Life came and went so fast. I was warned about this by my mother and father, who yelled when I ran down the stairs in slippery socks, or by my teachers, who kept us off the street during recess, and here it was—the end—dangling in front of me on a rope, Mr. Resnick, dead before the morning paper arrived.

I looked around for help.

There was broken glass over the floor. I waited for someone to yell at me, for my mother to scream, "Emily, pick up this mess!"

But the kitchen was empty.

The broken glass was spread around me like a rug.

I was the only person in the world who knew Mr. Resnick was dead, and the only person who could see me was Mr. Resnick through the window, but his eyes were fixed, pointing in two different directions, making it appear as though he wasn't there at all, or like there were so many interesting things to look at before you died, he couldn't choose.

I ran for my father. The glass dug farther into my foot with each step. I was at my father's bed, shouting something none of us can remember, and my mother told me later that it made all too much sense when she woke up to an empty house, following a child's bloody footsteps over the oriental rug and out the door to find our poor neighbor hanging from a tree.

# 6

I would tell all my boyfriends that the most tragic part about the whole scene was Alfred, who ran out of his house in a red Starship Enterprise shirt that read, SHATNER FOREVER! on the front. Men would laugh and laugh at this, stroke my neck, my thighs, their beards tender like feathers between my legs. They would love me for the way nothing remained sacred in my presence, seek me out for this, kiss me down to the bone.

"I just don't understand," Mrs. Bulwark said in her workout suit, not ready to give up on the idea of a morning jog. The adults circled around her like concerned hawks. Mr. Resnick's body had already been photographed, put in a bag, and taken away in an ambulance. "I just can't believe they are putting him in a bag like that. Like he was some bad fruit at the grocery store."

The police had sectioned off the Resnicks' house with yellow tape, and all the morning joggers and dog walkers stood on my driveway to rubberneck. A beagle barked loud from the back of the crowd, pissed he couldn't see.

"And he just mowed his lawn yesterday," Mrs. Trenton said. "God, this is sad."

"That wasn't him," Mrs. Bulwark said. "That was Mark."

"Tom never mowed his lawn," Alfred said.

"That's a bad sign."

"The sign of a deeper sense of apathy. A man who doesn't care about his lawn probably doesn't care about anything around him."

Janice and the Other Girls had been picked up by their mothers, who hurried them into their vans with one arm, half-asleep. It wasn't until Janice looked back at my house like the whole place was damned, the grass, the lamppost, the American flag, the potting soil against the garage, that I realized, yes, we *were* damned—I had suspected this two days earlier when I saw my father watering the drooping tiger lilies and asked, "Dad, why are you doing that? They're nearly dead."

"Why eat?" he said. "Why anything?"

My father had run outside and then back inside to reschedule a conference call, and I stared at the basement window knowing that he wasn't returning because Mrs. Resnick was standing in front of her house now, my mother's arms wrapped around her body like a sheath, and Mark was at their side, an unreachable figure, brown hair uncombed, his eyes wild and heated like an abused animal's, ready to bare his claws and attack my father should he dare show his face again. Mrs. Resnick pulled away from the embrace, and that whole time I was talking to some policeman who stared at my mother's nipples on display through her sheer nightgown.

The cop nodded some. "Right," he said. "Looks like a suicide."

"A suicide," Mrs. Resnick said aloud to nobody, to everybody, to the mailbox.

The policeman led Mark and his mother to the cruiser. The car drove away and never turned on its sirens.

"He threw raw meat out the window once," Mrs. Bulwark said.

"What?" Mrs. Trenton asked.

"He threw a leg of lamb out the window once. I saw him."

"Why?"

"Probably to prove some kind of a point," Alfred said.

"What kind of a point would that be?"

"A man can do anything he wants," Alfred said.

"To think," Mrs. Trenton said, and hung her head like nothing was possible anymore. "I had just promised myself that I would eliminate stress in my life."

"Go put on some real clothes," my mother said to me as she went inside to yell at my father. I heard my father's office door slam open, the knob hitting against the wall. "Victor!" she yelled. *A man has died in the yard* was supposed to be her next line, but instead, she said, "It's a *Saturday*."

I sat on the stone stoop as the scene cleared, and everyone started to make their way back into their homes, dispersing in different directions like a compass made out of humans. They had lives too, which needed to start. They had to go inside, turn on their ceiling fans, call their distant relatives, and explain what happened to the poor Russian Jewish man down the street, the one who threw raw meat out the window, the one who was never happy anyway. They had to tweeze their eyebrows and wake up their children for Saturday soccer games, the girls' teams named after flowers and the boys' after cars (Richard had been on the Ferraris and Mark on the Volvos). They had to cut oranges into quadrants; turn off the cartoons; French-braid hair; brush teeth; think about socks, shin guards, and staying hydrated, Gatorade and brake fluid; and don't kick the cat, don't hang on the banister, pack the cooler with raisins and gluten-free crackers, edible ice packs, parkas in case the weather turned, and then explain to the kids in the backseat on the way to the field: the weather always turns; death finds us anyway.

There was a man still standing on my driveway. It was Mr. Basketball. He was looking around, with a beagle on the end of a leash. He was in mesh shorts and a T-shirt that said PEPSI. He walked over to me on the stoop. He looked anything but professional. Like a college student. The picture of a man I might hang on my wall, if I had done things like that as a teenager.

"Hi," he said. His body was illuminated in front of me as he blocked the rising sun. We had never met before.

"Hi," I said.

It was cold. October. I had run outside in my pajamas, white fleece pants, and my father's I CLIMBED DIAMOND MOUNTAIN AND SURVIVED! T-shirt.

And then I remembered: the bottom of my foot was bleeding.

"Jesus," Mr. Basketball said, picking up my bloody foot to see the tiny bits of glass wedged into the thick skin of my heel. In the light, the sole of my foot almost looked diamond studded. "Are you all right?" And he was the only person that morning to suggest I might not be all right.

He took my foot in his hand.

I nodded.

He pulled out a Swiss Army knife from his pocket. Without even asking, he began to carefully remove each piece of glass with the tip of the blade. When he pushed too hard, I shifted uncomfortably, and he was gentler the next time. From far away, I imagined it looked like a holy offering, like a painting of Jesus washing a woman's feet.

"I like your dog," I finally said. "What's his name?"

"Her. Her name is Penelope. And she's not mine. I'm watching her for a friend."

"Hi, Penelope," I said, and held out my hand to the dog.

"I was giving her a walk," Mr. Basketball said. "I live two blocks down, off Crab Apple. And then I ran into this whole mess."

My nipples were still cold through my shirt and on any normal occasion I would have thought of a reason to go inside and help my mother with breakfast. But I sat there, looking at him. It didn't seem necessary to get embarrassed about being a woman in front of Mr. Basketball. It was as though that was exactly what he had wanted me to be from the start.

"Breathe," he said, to signal that this wasn't going to be a good one. He removed the last visible piece of glass. It cut my foot more as he removed it, and blood spotted the cement steps, but I didn't cry. It was a relief to know that I was still a person, connected inside by a network of nerves and blood, and Mr. Basketball was here to observe that. Sometimes, I didn't even notice I was alive until somebody else did, and what was weirder, more incomprehensible than that?

I reached out and put my hand on Mr. Basketball's arm like my mother would have. "Thank you," I said.

He was an older person I hardly knew, a teacher at my school, a *man,* and I should never casually touch a man, Janice told me once, because a casual touch reminds a man of a less casual touch and so on. But everything seemed arbitrary all of a sudden. Right or wrong, things happened anyway. Suicide or no suicide, at eight A.M., Mrs. Bulwark would pull out of her driveway in her blue minivan, my mother would get in the shower, and the sky would open up. Alfred would walk to the end of his driveway and get his paper. The dogs would begin to bark, and it would sound like an act of charity, the animals filling the silence, starting the day when we failed to notice it had begun, the sun already tired above us.

# 7

W ho knows what would have helped him, you know?" I said, suddenly the expert three days later in my mother's bedroom preparing for Mr. Resnick's funeral. My mother was drawing a thin black line across her lids, and somewhere else, Mr. Resnick's eyelids were being sealed with glue, his lips tied with sutures.

I was fidgety, sleepless from the previous night when Janice and I had read from the "Embalming" section of the encyclopedia. I was overheated in long sleeves, laid out on my mother's bed in a black polyester dress and my hands crossed over my chest like today was my burial. I told my mother I'd do her makeup. She looked at me like I asked to file the taxes, shifted in her brand-new off-the-shoulder chiffon dress, picking lint from the hem, and said, "No, thanks."

Germicide-insecticide-olfactant rubbed inside his mouth with cotton swabs, Janice had read. Massage cream rubbed onto his face for softness.

"Don't you think you're a little dressed up?" I asked my mother.

"It's a funeral," she said. A burst of anger hummed between us. As though I had not been aware. As though I had not watched the man die. As though I could not feel the lanolin, carboxymethylcellulose, humectants, hydrolyzed proteins being injected into his arteries while the blood was drained from his heart.

My mother leaned closer to the mirror and swept purple eye shadow across her lids.

"That's a mistake," I said.

There was an energy that came with sudden death. My mother sprang to life, shut off the television, curled her hair for three days straight, listened to the weather report on the radio as though it suddenly mattered what the chance of rain was, while my father fell farther away from us, sequestered in the basement with a phone and a new computer that virtually connected him to any part of the world he wanted, except the upstairs of our house. I didn't know what to say to my family in the car on the way to the funeral; death made everything so awkward all of a sudden. Surely my mother thought the suicide was all Mrs. Resnick's fault, and surely my father thought the suicide was all my mother's fault, as he wouldn't have slept with another woman if he didn't *have* to, but the truth was, we all knew it was my fault: I was the one who couldn't run outside in time to stop him. I never reacted properly to any situation, something my parents told me at dinner when I spilled the milk, and instead of getting a napkin, I watched it drip off the table, to which they said, "Emily, don't just sit there like an idiot. Get a napkin."

There we were, in the quiet car, like a bunch of idiots, doing nothing. So I tried to be the adult, right there in the backseat, in my black clogs, and engage my parents in discussion about the recent events.

"I sure do feel bad for Mark," I said, folding my hands on my lap. "Don't you?"

"And poor Mrs. Resnick," my mother said, flipping down the dashboard mirror. "It's just awful."

"Nobody's pain is worse or better," my father said, making eye contact with me in the rearview mirror of the car. "Just different."

This made me so angry because I was sure I had said the perfect thing, something nobody could ever disagree with, and so I stared at all the mailboxes and said, "You know they drain the blood from your heart after you die," and my mother put her hand on my thigh and said, "Calm down, Emily."

"If you need to see a therapist, Emily, just tell us," my father said.

"We should bring the Resnicks a lasagna later this evening," my mother said, looking at her face in the mirror, and I wondered if she would still be going to the funeral if she knew my father and Mrs. Resnick were lovers, and I felt I should shout it out right there in our car, and I almost opened my mouth to do so but saw her slowly apply lipstick and became afraid that maybe she already did know, that her goodwill toward Mrs. Resnick was something else entirely, something I couldn't quite understand.

My mother seemed so invested in the idea of Mr. Resnick's suicide and all the tradition that surrounded death—flowers and lasagna platters and phone calls and jewelry so dull it wouldn't offend—yet couldn't bring herself to cry. I had never actually seen my mother cry. She didn't even shed a tear when her own mother died four years ago. I remembered when she got off the phone with my aunt Lee, my mother sat upright at the dinner table and explained to me and my father: Nana has a blood disease.

We nodded our heads and looked her in the face and thought, Ah yes, blood disease, as she picked up her dull spoon and funneled in the beef stew like the structure of consumption was all she needed.

After that, we spent most of our time at Stamford Hospital. My father and I communicated silently, sitting in the hall, kicking someone else's French fry between our feet. My mother walked back and forth from tiled places to tiled places. She didn't get very far, but I could feel her changing with every step. She looked at us. She looked at me especially and said, "I can't believe this blue room is the room in which my mother will cease to be."

This was as much a warning as it was a threat.

Then she would say, "Hey, guys"—just like that, like me and my father were a gaggle of something indistinct—"let's go get some coffee." I reminded my mother: I am only ten, my legs are barely covered in peach fuzz, I just found out there are two r's in "library," this whole time it had never been "ly-bary," and how embarrassing, I'm so so embarrassed, Mom, can I have a ginger ale instead?

"Of course," my mother said, and took my hand. My father got on a plane to Munich.

Two weeks later, Nana's heartbeat was dangerously slow. I sat and crossed my legs and counted my toes as I listened to my mother schedule Nana's funeral for the next day. Mahogany at eleven, lilies in the afternoon, buried by dusk. Ten, nine, eight, seven, six, five, four, three, two, one, and I wondered if this was what your heartbeat sounded like as soon as you started to lose it.

"Don't ask me why," my mother said to the doctor, "but she wants to have her funeral the day after she dies. This sounds awful, and I can't believe I'm going to ask, but will my mother be dead by tomorrow?"

Nana wanted to be fresh.

"That's only when you are Jewish, Mother," my mother had argued a week earlier.

"And the Jews do it for good reason," Nana said. "Who wants to smell like an old dead body? I want to be fresh!"

"You won't smell," my mother said. "Jesus, let's not talk about this like that."

"Gloria, you need to face the facts," Nana had said. "You know, that has always been your problem."

Nana was the wisest woman anyone knew. She did the crossword puzzle every day and knew about words my father didn't. She knew how to keep all of her flowers fully bloomed through October, and whenever I fought with my mother over the last grocery bag in the car, Nana would recite a Bible passage from memory. We'd be silenced by the immediacy of God standing before us in a knit sweater, burgundy heels.

When we were sitting in the hospital cafeteria and my mother dropped her seven-dollar noodles on the floor, she swore loudly and threw her fork.

"Mother," I said, looking her straight in the eyes, *"your noodles are gone."*

"Emily, for Christ's sake, don't be so weird," my mother said, picking up the noodles with an American flag–imprinted napkin.

Nana was hooked up to ten different tubes regulating ten different parts of her body and insisted the next day was the day she was going to die. She insisted it's something you can feel inside you, as though your feet have already stopped understanding their responsibility for the toes. If anything, I was comforted by how organized her death was becoming. My mother called my father, who was flying home from Munich for the funeral. He'd try to get there in time. "Damn right, it's a big ocean," my mother shouted to him on the black phone at the hospital. I stood next to her in knee socks, a sponge, absorbing her rage. When she hung up, she bit her painted thumbnail and said, "I love your father. I do."

My mother phoned everyone about the event that was to occur:

Nana was due to stop breathing any minute now. Until the nurse told us that Nana's heartbeat was strong enough to last until the next night. "You mean she's not going to die tonight?" my mother asked.

"I don't think so," the nurse said.

And I really thought this had to be it. This was the moment when my mother would put her face in her hands and cry. But she began to laugh. She was always doing this, being so painfully unpredictable. I stared at her in shock until I realized how funny it was. Nana not dying was the funniest thing that happened all day, maybe our whole lives thus far, and soon we were bent over on our seats from laughing so hard. Sometimes, I loved my mother so much.

Nana died.

I felt so guilty for laughing, I pinched my thighs while I slept. The morning of her funeral, I threw a tantrum outside the shower and shouted to my mother, "Don't make me go!" My mother plucked me off the floor like an undressed doll that she put in the wrong part of the dollhouse, like I was over in the kitchen holding a plastic egg and she needed me in the bath, like I was a child who did not understand age and location and dress code, and my mother stuck me in the tub as though she could see this about me too, and I remember knowing for certain that oh my god that was my mother holding me naked.

"I don't want to see her!" I shouted through the plastic curtain.

"Don't worry, Emily," my mother said. "You won't be able to see her."

This made me even more confused, because why would we be going somewhere just to see Nana if it wasn't to see Nana, so I sat on the tub floor and shaved the hair off my legs for the first time with my father's razor. I bled in three places.

I put on thick black stockings as a Band-Aid. The limousine was so big, I remember feeling instantly colder than I should have during March. I remember feeling like we should have had a beverage in our hands, like we should have been going to a party instead. I remember nobody saying anything at all. And this happened so early in the morning, as if the whole point of saying good-bye was to shower first, and the only thing I can distinctly remember being surprised about was that I had to set my alarm the night before like I was an older person waking up for work.

Halfway through Nana's funeral, I stared at the door hoping my father would walk in and I peed through my dress.

But my father did not show up until after the burial, after the reception, after we had eaten cold eggplant bread and shared nostalgia for her acute criticism, wishing she were there to explain how the meatballs were too damn dry and that nobody in this goddamn country knew how to make anything worth a dime, after all the pots and pans had been scrubbed and put away in the cabinets and the cheese dish grew green fuzz across the top because we forgot it on the piano for two days.

*"Dobrý den,"* my father said in Czech, which at the time I thought was German. He was cold in the doorway and reeked of dark, faraway lands. *"Mám tě rád."*

My mother did not even ask him to translate. She just scraped the cheese into the garbage can and went to bed without washing the platter. I wrote MOM TAY ROD down in my notebook and asked the German exchange student in my class that everybody called Scheisse—German for "shit"—what it meant in English. The fat life, he said.

"I peed," I whispered to my mother in the pew. My mother looked at me and her face fell. I was intolerable. I knew it. But she didn't even admit this, or say, "Now why would you pee in your pants?" or "My God!" She picked me up and put my arms around her neck and carried me to the bathroom and this is what I will remember when I am most scared about being alive, abandoned in a room years later, the heat of her cheek against mine, someone else's skin around me, mistaking it as my own.

# 8

It cost ten thousand dollars to take your life in Connecticut, which didn't surprise me considering Connecticut was the most expensive state to do anything in. Mrs. Trenton announced the total to everybody at the coat rack. She sounded like a bad advertisement. "Ten thousand dollars," she said. "What a waste . . . you could rent a flat on the Seine with that kind of money . . . go to Budapest for a month . . ."

The rest of the adults were stabbing cheese cubes with toothpicks. It seemed wrong to eat and talk about death, like something my mother would have advised against, similar to eating and running or eating and going to the bathroom or eating and being mean, but there she was by the cheese platter, offering cheddar to a curly-haired man. It was obvious the man wanted to fuck her. Even more obvious that she didn't mind. The whole performance made me sick, gave me the same feeling I got when Janice brought in tiny tuna sandwiches after she gave a forty-five-minute presentation on the Holocaust last year, complete with photos of corpses and a short slide show of the mass graves at Terezin and then held up a platter and said, "Who wants sandwiches?"

Mr. Resnick's value suddenly seemed measurable by everybody's grief, which didn't seem to be much at all. The adults hardly looked changed, their hair still the same color it was two days ago, as they picked the stems off the strawberries before they ate them. They sat down in red leather recliners, crossed their legs, but most of them never took off their fall coats, perhaps not fully convinced by the warmth of the house or the idea of a suicide in the neighborhood, *this neighborhood,* where it was officially recorded that in September of '94 there were more tulips than people. I caught my mother bragging about this to our cousin Rex at the town pool once, to which he said, "The parties you must have . . ."

My father shook hands with some white-haired ladies who flittered around the cocktail tables like overdressed children, nodding their heads, and my father nodded back as if to say, *Yes, it's hard—very hard. Very hard to never see a man you never saw.* They were like kids at the playground, trying to decide whom to play with, and was the conversation worth the fuss? Adults were constantly auditioning, but for what? For the next conversation, for the next conversation, for the next conversation? They touched each other on their sides as they passed, or sometimes pressed a hand to the small of a back to signal they were still in love, still alive, chock full of organs. Everybody wore black, except for the bright blue scarf wrapped so high around Mrs. Bulwark's neck, she looked like a character from Dr. Seuss if a character from Dr. Seuss ever went to a funeral. I was walking away from one of Mark's third or fourth cousins, who was trailing behind and informing me how strange Mr. Resnick's suicide was considering summer suicides generally preferred to go naked. "It's *October*," I said back. I ran my hands against the smooth maroon walls, seeking out a crack, searching for Mark, listening to everybody.

The girl hung at the curly-haired man's knees in a plaid jumper and exclaimed, "This is sooo boring, Dad."

"Go talk to someone," the curly-haired man said.

"Talking is boring," the girl said. "All you people do is talk."

"If you're looking for more than that in life, Melissa, you're going to be disappointed. That's what we do. We stand around and we talk."

"Hell," my mother interjected, with a drunk finger pointing in the air, "we might go to a movie sometime, but you know what we do after it? We sit around and talk about it."

"Exactly," the curly-haired man said.

They both sipped on their drinks.

"It's the permanence that makes the dead beautiful," the curly-haired man said at some point, as though my mother had asked, which I knew she didn't since the only possible question that would have preceded such an answer was, What do you think makes the dead so beautiful?

"I wrote my dissertation on it," the man said, continuing. I had always hated curly-haired men. Sometimes, they looked too much like children who didn't brush their hair in the morning.

"Well, it's certainly up for debate," my mother said, playing with his daughter's long ponytail, and I could tell even from across the room that was the hair, the daughter, she had always wanted: golden, tame, quiet at her hips. My hair was darkening from a dirty blond to an ashy brown like my father's, and my mother was so disappointed. Last year, she announced that the "sun had left it," and my father picked up a chunk as he walked by, rubbed his bald spot, and said, "Why is *my* hair growing out of *your* head?"

My father stood in the hallway with Alfred and a few other tall men I didn't know. Tall men always seemed to have such purpose, with their heads next to the cabinets and hands in their pockets, so tidy and neat and civilized these men were, even their hands had storage units when they weren't needed in the conversation. Nothing these men did could be carelessly executed; removing a fallen olive from the floor was an event they seemed to have written into their calendar weeks ago. Their laughter was impossibly loud and soft at the same time, the kind of laughter that could kill you if you weren't a part of it. Every boom and hush made my heart quake and seemed to kill Mr. Resnick even more, buried him farther into the ground. When they were done laughing, they nodded their heads, passed judgment on the high Gothic ceilings. These were the living men, leaning against walls, sipping on whiskey, being accurate.

I looked around for Mark. I hadn't seen Mark since the burial. I had stood directly opposite him at the graveyard, next to my mother and Mrs. Trenton, who whispered to us, "She got a flat headstone so he wouldn't seem so *dead* when everybody went to visit."

My mother was dipping raw broccoli in blue cheese dip. She was still talking to the curly-haired man. She was leaning against the bookshelf. She was wearing a sweetheart neckline, and she was flirting. If she had known she had blue cheese on her lip, or that the curly-haired man had a hole in his back pocket, or that my father was walking toward Mrs. Resnick at that very moment, that my father could look at Mrs. Resnick across a room and think about her legs spread on a bed for him, that he could close his eyes and feel her breasts still on his hands like a film of soap, the way they had consumed each other, deeply and consistently, with their hands and mouths—if my mother had realized any of that at all, she would have cried right then and there. But she was laughing, talking about property tax.

"Don't," my father said to Mrs. Resnick, who was about to pour herself a glass of wine. He took the merlot and set it down, and the moment took on an eerie, holy air, like a battlefield torn apart by bombs, and the only movement for miles was the smoke rising to the clouds, revealing everyone on the ground dead.

"Oh, seriously, Victor," Mrs. Resnick said, and walked away with the bottle as a brown chunk of hair fell loose from her updo.

Richard stood next to me, watching me watch them. He looked evil and sad in a suit, like a shrunken mobster.

"What?" I asked, shrugging my shoulders.

"You know what," he said.

I panicked, so I said, "Listen, my psychology teacher told me that sometimes people kill themselves just because they're overwhelmed by the largeness of everything, like this guy who was promoted at his law firm five years ago. So he slit his throat."

"That's dumb," he said.

It was, sort of. I didn't understand it either. Mrs. Resnick came back in the living room, her hair loose around her face now, drinking the red wine. My father watched her from afar.

"She must be trying to kill the baby," Richard said.

"What the hell are you talking about, Richard?"

Richard and I became worse people around each other.

"She's pregnant. You didn't know?"

I glared at him. "Just because she's fatter doesn't mean she's pregnant," I said.

"It's your dad's baby," he said.

"I don't even know what you are talking about," I shouted at him.

"My mom told me."

I had to get out. Mark had to be somewhere. I slipped on my clogs and headed to the front door, which was blocked by Mrs. Trenton and Mrs. Bulwark, holding tiny plates of food.

I stood tall and forced them to reckon with me.

"So she's pregnant?" I asked, my arms crossed.

Mrs. Trenton blushed, looked away, then muttered, "Oh, sweetheart."

Mrs. Bulwark picked up a jalapeño popper from her snack plate. "I love Mexican, don't you?" she asked.

I didn't know what stating one's preference was supposed to mean in such a context. In such a house, in such a foyer, in such a space between people, everything I knew was losing its defining feature.

I ran out the door and slammed it hard behind me. I must have spent half my life slamming doors. I spent the other half looking for Mark. And there he was, on the front stoop, hunched over with a cigarette and a bag of iced animal crackers at his feet.

An hour later, all of the elephant crackers were decapitated and I was finishing my cigarette faster than Mark was his. It was the inevitability of winter that made me nervous, and suddenly, smoking felt like something you should always, always do to keep warm. I inhaled and inhaled and then inhaled again until all the trees became one, until I felt certain that the largeness of everything was mostly unfixable. I exhaled, soiling the sky with my breathy clouds of self-pity. Being an adult, it seemed, was horrible. But being a child was awful too, and moving from one state to the other only meant you were moving closer to death, with so much and so little to talk about all at the same time, and how was that even possible?

I wanted to smoke until I was so old, I would already be dead.

"Did he leave a note?" I finally asked.

"No," Mark said.

"I'm sorry," I said. "I'm not sure what to say."

"Say anything," he said. "I don't really care."

"Okay," I said. I paused. If I did not look left at Mark, the curb we sat on could have been any curb, in any neighborhood, anywhere. We could have been any two people. So I began.

"Once in the third grade, I wrote a story about a bee detective in search of stolen money from a restaurant," I said. "The story ended with the bee going home to find the money under his bed. He forgot he stole it. My teacher kept asking me, 'How did the bee forget that he stole the money? I just can't believe a bee would do that!'"

Mark laughed. For a moment, I believed I had fixed everything. Mark seemed interested. He didn't look at me but handed me another cigarette. I rolled it between my palms.

"The worst part was," I said, continuing, "it wasn't even my story. It was the plot to some stupid movie we watched in Spanish class. The whole thing happened in Spanish."

But when he didn't respond, it was clear I hadn't fixed anything. His father was dead. Buried. Bloodless. And Mark had not looked at me once during our conversation. This only felt like my fault. I was becoming too irrelevant to inspire awe, like Jesus Christ resurrecting in front of a bunch of Eskimos, less relevant every time my mother and father walked past me in the kitchen, my father with boxes in his arms, my mother with the phone, and me in the doorway looking down at myself, thinking, Are those even my feet?

I thought about reaching out to put my arm on his back, the way I had reached out to touch Mr. Basketball. But I couldn't. I spent the first half of my conscious life never being touched by anybody, except for pediatricians with toxic eyes who put stethoscopes under my shirts and against my chest, explaining that my heart beat too slowly for someone my age. "She has more in common with the dead than the living," one of them joked, to which my mother said, "We've always known this about her."

I put the cigarette in my mouth so Mark would come close to my face and feel my breath when he lit it up for me. I needed him to feel that I was still alive. But he didn't even glance over. He didn't even light my cigarette.

My mother suddenly interrupted. "What are you doing out here? Are you *smoking*?"

"I'm just being *outside*," I said coolly. She still had the blue cheese on her lip, which had dried into a crust, but the heat from the house had melted some of her eye shadow and made her appear to be crying purple blood.

The cigarette hung from my lips.

Mark stood up, paused like he was deciding something important. Then, he walked into his house. There, on his stoop, watching him walk away from me for a second time, I just couldn't take it. I was going to vomit. I opened my mouth wide and let the cigarette fall onto the stairs. It rolled down two steps, until it hit a tiny puddle left over from last night's rain.

My mother smiled a little, considered this a small victory. She had gotten me to stop smoking. She won. My life as a smoker was over. Every moment felt like a new kind of death.

"It's time to leave," she said.

"Why?" I asked. "Where's Dad?"

"He's staying. Come on, Emily."

"He's *staying*?"

We didn't speak on the way home. It was too difficult to know what to say. I hopped over cracks in the dirt like a five-year-old, using my youth as a form of communication with my mother, hoping it would remind her of another time when I was sure we were happier, when my father loved her and she loved my father, when everybody who was dead or pregnant was supposed to be, when I braided my pigtails without complaint and counted worms in the woods without ever getting bored, when my mother and I held hands and weren't embarrassed about how much we loved each other, neither of us compelled to scream how *okay* everything would be.

I thought about hugging my mother, but for some reason, the intimacy seemed rude, like a forced confession.

"You have blue cheese on your lip," I finally said to her as she opened our front door. "You've had it on your lip through the entire party."

She didn't respond. She didn't even say, "Emily, that wasn't a *party*." She didn't even wipe it off.

When we got inside the house, I said it again just to make sure she heard me. I was her daughter after all, and I couldn't let my mother walk around with blue cheese on her lip for the rest of her life.

"*Mom!*" I screamed. "You have blue cheese on your lip!"

"I know, Emily," my mother said. "I heard you."

My mother covered her face with her hands. Body language, Ms. Nailer told us, was a way of getting your point across without having to say anything. It was the easiest way to fight, without being accused of looking for a fight. Sometimes, I thought my mother exclusively communicated in body language. I remember walking through my front door after school with bloody knees from the playground, and my mother would just have gotten home. She wouldn't be surprised that I was bleeding. I was a child. That was what children did. They fell down and then bled. That was the only thing you could expect from a child. And yet, my mother's face would tighten, even though it was her job as the adult to wipe the blood off and tell me it would be okay, better than okay, but her lips would purse and her breath would shorten and she would be angry. That was what upset her the most. That was what upset me the most. How could she be mad at me for bleeding? How could you be mad at a tiny thing who only had questions? Why do I bleed and fish don't, Mom? Is that supposed to make me feel better about eating them?

"You had it on your lip throughout the whole party!" I shouted. I couldn't stop. "By the bookshelf, by the bar, even when you were talking to that ugly man."

*"I know I know I know I know!"* she shouted, louder with each recitation.

My mother took my father's antique Norwegian pewter bowl in her hands. She held it in the air like a trophy and threw it on the ground. So she had known about the affair. She kicked the broken pieces across the floor.

And the pregnancy.

She grabbed his dictionaries from the shelf and chucked them through the window, because who cared about a window? Who cared about my father's paintings, I thought, as my mother dumped his real Matisse print in the sink and ran water on it. Who cared whose baby it was, who cared if it lived, who cared about the blue cheese? What did it even matter if it was on your face? That was the saddest part about it.

My mother took his miniature ivory elephants and threw them against the wall. She smashed vases and ripped plants from the soil, tore curtains from the rods. She was destroying our house. And when my father walked in the door to see her dumping his Cocoa Puffs on the ground, he did the most surprising thing. He paused. He went to speak. He walked over to the Matisse print in the sink and said nothing. He dropped the mail and walked toward her. The cereal crunched under his feet. My mother didn't yell, she didn't move away. I wanted to scream, *Don't touch her!* but my voice was lodged in my throat like a gumball. He wrapped his arms around her. She laid her head against his shoulder, and for the first time in my life, I watched my mother cry. She sobbed hard into the pocket of his suit jacket, while my father repeated, "I'm so sorry." They held each other for what seemed like hours until my mother silently broke from the embrace.

I sat at the kitchen counter and drew my name backward with the juice of a stray tomato slice cut for the reception. Y-L-I-M-E. Nobody wiped my name for four days.

# 9

Mark returned to school in November and everybody wanted to either eat lunch with him or touch his hair. The suicide had given our daily routines an urgent and excited motion for which everyone was privately thankful. One of the Other Girls ran up to him in the cafeteria so fast she spilled her green beans on the floor when she halted, and told him that as soon as she heard the news she cried and changed her dog's name from Q-Tip to Mr. Resnick. In high school, everyone was always saying the wrong thing and then laughing too hard afterward.

"He's gotten super popular," Janice told me in the lunch line. There was always a crowd around him, offering Doritos and halves of their turkey sandwiches. "He's like a celebrity now. One of those celebrities that are, like, famous for no reason, or by accident, or for something horrible, like Selena who got famous from dying, or Magic Johnson for contracting HIV."

Things were changing for me too.

I had begun to feel haunted. My hair extended past my shoulders, my face sagged, and I didn't know if it was me that I felt like or someone I didn't even know or if those were the same exact thing. People I didn't know approached me in the hall, asking what it felt like to watch a man die, telling me that in some ancient religion a person who witnessed a man's death carried around the spirit of that man for the rest of her life, and could I draw an accurate picture of the corpse? They wanted to know: could I sleep at night? Why didn't I try to stop him? If I didn't even try to stop him, would that make me a murderer according to the United States criminal justice system—a debate topic Leroy Hannah posed to our social studies teacher.

The Other Girls followed me down the hall, asking, Why didn't you wake us up? What'd it look like? Did you scream? Did you touch it? And at first, these questions bothered me, but over time their curiosity proved harmless. At least they were interested. At least they wanted to talk about the suicide like it was something real that happened, unlike my father, who closed the discussion forever one night at dinner by saying, "It's their own private business."

"It was terrible," I said, closing my locker. "He was so still."

"Jesus," Brittany said.

"That's so sad."

Some of the girls mistook the suicide as their own tragedy, an excuse to no longer do homework for the month. "I just can't think," Martha said to Ms. Nailer, "knowing things like this happen."

"I just can't believe it," another one said.

"To think we were almost right there . . ."

"My mother's friend killed herself once after a boob job."

"That's dumb. Aren't big breasts supposed to be a reason to *live?*"

Janice explained how her brother Ed was never inspired by his big breasts. Janice and I used to make fun of Ed for being fat when we were younger, before he was paralyzed; it seemed like a good enough reason at the time. I cringed at Janice's mentioning of this, even though I had once offered him my bra and left a pamphlet on increasing breast cancer awareness in front of his door.

The Other Girls started waiting for Mark at his locker every day right before lunch. Mark and I never looked at each other. We stood at his locker while Mark looked at one of the Other Girls' perfect faces. Then we walked to Ms. Nailer's class.

"Nail-her," Mark finally said. "I'm going to nail-her, get it?"

We nodded our heads, even though I hated him when he acted like Richard, which was happening more and more frequently. But it felt wrong to hold his failings against him. So I nodded my head as though I knew why Mark wanted to fuck an older woman when I was standing right in front of him. I nodded my head because if we were forced to understand anything then it was that all men and women, young or old, were created equal under God, indivisible, with liberty and justice for all.

But, still.

"She's so old," I said.

"I heard Ms. Nailer slept with Socrates," one of the girls said, and everybody laughed except Martha, who said, "What's a Socrates?"

"Don't be stupid, Martha."

"They're an ancient people."

Mark took the lead. I was glad when Mark walked ahead of me, as my whole life became embarrassing around him now. I was embarrassed when he sat at lunch with us, watching me eat a sandwich. After all of this, I was still here, *just eating a sandwich*!

We passed a sign for the Ebony Club, which had sent the whole school into a recent uproar. Freddy Lawrence, the president, put up fliers around the school to advertise a meeting where black students could discuss being black in a predominantly white school. *Everybody is invited,* it said. *Even White and Jewish People.* Jewish students walked by the signs, offended, exclaiming, "What, are we not white? Are we not black?"

Martha walked by and said, "I don't get it: Is being Jewish opposite to being white? Is it?"

One of the girls said we should start a white people club.

"Our whole life is a white people club," one of them said.

"Sometimes, I wish we had a black friend."

"*Guys,*" one of them said. "I'm black."

"Shit."

"Sometimes we forget."

"It's not like you're, like, *black,* you know. I mean, you wear Skechers."

"And you want to be a pastry chef."

"And you take French."

One of the girls pointed to another group of girls by staircase B and said, "Look at those other girls. Just look at them. They're so freaking tarded." Martha flinched because she had a brother with Down syndrome and none of us knew how to appreciate imperfection. One of the girls asked, "Is Down syndrome when the cells divide too fast?"

The one who never made eye contact anymore said, "No, tard, that's what my mom has. Cancer." Another one asked, "Like, is she dying?" and none of us knew.

After lunch, a teacher always guided the special education students into the cafeteria. They were given napkins and 409 to wipe down the tables.

"It's so weird," I said as we watched them divide and pick tables. "It's like slave labor or something."

Janice approached a faculty member and said, "This is slave labor. I bet you aren't even paying them."

"Paying who?" the teacher asked.

"The retards!"

The teacher shook her head. "They like to have tasks."

"Yeah, that's what the plantation owners said too."

If I was pleased by anything during this portion of my life, it was my fantastic handwriting. I jotted down notes about the Great Depression before dinner while my father talked aimlessly about beef Stroganoff. I made neat lists about government-created labor, like it wasn't until all the suffering was over that you could appreciate something as an organized system of profit and loss. I got my best grades freshman year and nobody understood this—why now, they asked, why are you acting stable when your house is being disassembled, it's a sign of a contrary nature, of bad things to come. I heard my mother whisper this over the phone to a psychiatrist she had been trying to get me to visit.

Tragedy was making me a better and a worse person all at once. I said hello to the mailman for the first time. I had ignored him my whole life for reasons unknown to both of us. I suppose it was because the mailman was terrifying to me the way Santa Claus had been a bit terrifying, old hairy men who had private access to my life, both of them regarding my house as just another destination on the map, which, I guess, is exactly what it was, and we were just people who needed something, and every day they checked us off lists, like things, like *wine* and *gouda cheese* and *Emily Marie Vidal*. Because that was who I was. "I'm Emily Marie Vidal," I sometimes repeated in front of the mirror, developing a strange compulsion to remind myself. "Weird." Every day,

I was still myself, and yet constantly unrecognizable. And sometimes after school when I had nothing to do, I would draw pictures on the driveway in chalk of what I thought my brothers and sisters would look like. Then, one day when the mailman arrived, I picked up my hand and thought, I could be a different person, we could all be different people. "Hello!" I waved to the mailman. "Hello!"

But sometimes the mailman didn't wave back. Or he didn't hear me. Or he got so used to not seeing me, I started to look just like the lamppost. I started to feel just like the lamppost, flat and not like a real person at all, unlike Mark's new girlfriend Alice, who walked out of his house after school, ruffled and flushed and proud of her decisions. She was a happy girl who had been touched by a boy. She was never afraid. She was the last person in our class to change from shorts to jeans when winter came. I stared at her legs in algebra class and waited to see the slow rise of prickles on her skin that the cold weather brought, but her legs remained smooth like glass. Alice was smooth like glass and never regretful of her decisions, but on my lawn, she could not look me in the eye. "What's the math homework?" she asked.

"Page fifty-four, problems one through ten," I told her.

"Thanks," she said, and walked away.

And I began to understand the truth: I would always be alone like this. I had understood the idea in theory, and noticed the absence of siblings at family functions, but when the neighborhood quieted down after the suicide, and the rain fell hard and washed away my drawn family, I felt truly alone for the first time in my life. "Can you guys believe this? Dad is leaving. I can't believe this," I said aloud to the blurred stick figures.

# 10

We were cutting open fetal pigs in biology when the alarms went off. Two days before Christmas break and the school went into lockdown. Lockdown meant that wherever you were, you had to close the door, lock it, and not leave until Dr. Killigan came onto the loudspeaker saying you could. It was our first real lockdown and it was the most thrilling thing that had happened all semester, even though we had practice ones before and I had joked to Janice how absurd it was to practice being locked in a room. "How hard is it? You just sit there. Being locked in."

"Where's Ms. Nailer?" Martha asked.

Ms. Nailer was in the bathroom when the alarms went off. She told us she was taking this new medicine for her skin condition that made her pee all the time.

"I'm right here, class!" Leroy Hannah said in a high-pitched voice that resembled Mother Goose's more than Ms. Nailer's. He was in the front of the room, wearing Ms. Nailer's Dior glasses and her green cardigan.

We closed the door, turned the lock.

"Why is this happening?" Martha asked.

"Must be a homo in the building," Richard said.

"Don't be so gay, Richard."

"It's sooo hot in here."

"I know. Don't touch me."

"Rabbits are weird," Richard said, tapping on the wired cage. "How they poop little pellets."

"Yeah but, I mean, so do we," I said, standing next to him.

"No we don't," Richard said. "We poop out long logs."

"Yes, I understand that," I said, rolling my eyes. "But I'm sure to the rabbits, their little pellets look like long logs."

"I wish we could open a window," Brittany said.

"I wish I could take off my pants," Annie the Bird or Bear said.

"Should we be scared or something?"

"According to Satan."

Someone turned off the lights.

*"Not funny."*

"Anyone wanna bone?"

When the lights came back on, Leroy Hannah was in the front of the class, pretending to sip coffee out of a beaker. Richard was next to him, announcing to everybody that he was going to give his fetal pig a rhinoplasty. "A nose job," he clarified.

"Oh, good!" Leroy shouted. "Class, listen up! We are going to make the pig's nose proportional to the pig's face!"

Richard picked up a ruler. "Annie!" he shouted. "Come here!'

The class laughed. Annie the Bird or Bear glared at him. "Real fucking funny, dickhead," she said.

"Annie," Leroy said, still mimicking Ms. Nailer, "your nose is nearly four inches long. Have you ever considered reconstructive surgery?"

We waited for Annie the Bird or Bear to stand up and slug Leroy across the face. But she didn't.

"Yes," she said.

She lay down on one of the empty lab tables.

"So give me a fucking nose job already!" she shouted.

"Uhhh," Richard said, "technically, it's a rhinoplasty."

"Don't be a bitch, Richard," Annie the Bird or Bear said. "Just do it."

"You can't give ABOB a nose job!" Martha screamed.

"I hate my nose," Annie the Bird or Bear said. "But my parents are poor so I can't do anything about it. I can't live the rest of my life like this. So just *do it,* you pansy ass."

Richard didn't move. He looked at me for some reason. He stared. I shook my head. Annie the Bird or Bear sat up and took him by the throat. "Do it, fuck face. Is your father a world-class surgeon or is he not?"

He cleared his throat, straightened out his back, like he was remembering who he was. "Jesus, woman," he said. "All right, all right."

The class buzzed.

"Scalpel."

The fetal pigs lay still all around us.

"First," Richard said, "since you are alive, we'll need to sterilize the blade. Anyone remember how to use the Bunsen burners?"

Human Fart did. Human Fart had been Ernest Bingley's new nickname since he farted the previous week doing sit-ups in gym. When I heard it, I was saddened and relieved all at the same time. It had to happen to someone eventually, and I was glad it wasn't me, but poor Ernest, even though Ernest would eventually get laid on prom night, go to Columbia, and have a son who invented an electric bike that powered itself off its own energy, but still.

"You can't bring me into this when you get in trouble," Human Fart said. "I'm going to be a doctor. I don't need this shit on my résumé."

Richard told him to put this shit on his résumé. "This is the shit of résumés," Richard said.

But Human Fart made them sign a contract. Leroy drafted it, wrote down *Earnest did not light the flame* on the contract.

"It's E-R-N-E-S-T," Human Fart said, annoyed.

He lit the flame.

"Smells like gas."

"Like ass."

"What if Ms. Nailer comes back?"

"What if Annie dies?"

"Nobody is going to die," Richard said, holding the blade over the flame. "I've done this a million times."

"Now," Annie the Bird or Bear said. "I want you to shave off the bump. I want a Grecian nose. I want a one-hundred-degree angle."

Annie lay back again, her feet hanging off the end of the table. Richard put on the white lab coat Ms. Nailer never wore. Girls tee-heed from behind. Richard grabbed two rulers and took measurements of her face. We couldn't even speak. Someone yelled at Martha for breathing too loud. I stood in disbelief. This whole time, I had truly believed Annie the Bird or Bear was okay with who she was, as though she had somehow accepted her position in life and was, in that way, above everyone else. But here she was, lying on a table ready to be split. Of course she wanted a Grecian nose. We all did.

Richard began. He hummed while marking her with a purple marker, circling the bump on her nose. He pulled out a flask from his pocket, and everybody gasped, as though he had pulled out a rabbit holding a loaded gun.

"Drink this," he said to her.

*"You've had that this whole time?"* one of the Other Girls asked.

Annie the Bird or Bear opened the cap and sniffed like it was poison.

"The Bird's scared of a little whiskey?" Richard taunted.

"Hell no, I'm not scared," Annie the Bird or Bear said. "Just making sure it's real liquor."

She threw her head back and gulped. She smacked her lips. "Good stuff."

People passed the flask around. At some point, I took a sip.

"Okay," Richard said. "Leroy. I need you to hold ABOB's head against the table. She's going to move when we break her nose."

Leroy stood behind her.

"Break my nose?" she cried. Her long red hair was hanging off the sides like a tablecloth.

"Reset it," Richard clarified.

"No," she said. "Just shave the top off. That's all."

"That's not how it works," Richard said. "Trust me, I know what I'm doing. Maybe a book?"

One of his friends got his Spanish book with *¡Bienvenidos!* on the cover and Annie the Bird or Bear looked scared for the first time since I had met her. "Uhhhhh," she said, "nobody is breaking my nose."

"What'd you think was going to happen?" Richard asked. "That it wasn't going to hurt? I'm changing your entire face."

"You can't just throw a book in my face! This is supposed to be precise, do it *surgically!*"

Annie the Bird or Bear went to sit up, but Leroy had his hands on her head and held her to the table. "Don't move," Richard said, holding the book above his head, and a sudden panic striped my heart. "Don't you move!"

Human Fart's hand was on the door. "Guys, I hear Ms. Nailer coming down the hall. I'm going to open the door."

"You open that door I'll kill you myself!" Richard shouted, his face red, the book high in the air.

"Get away from me!" Annie shouted.

"I'm opening the door."

"You can't open the door!" Martha shouted. "We're in a lockdown! That could be a *school shooter* on the loose. We'll all get shot. And *die*."

"I'm opening the door!"

Richard slammed the *¡Bienvenidos!* book into Annie the Bird or Bear's face and she cried out exactly as we imagined she would, she squawked and squealed and howled. The moan was loud and never-ending, like a wolf watching the moon explode in the middle of the night, the blood we never knew she had instantly dripping off the sides of her face. "See, I told you she has rabies," one of the Other Girls whispered behind me.

Annie wildly kicked at Richard and Leroy and we were all searching for something to do, some way to help her without moving. Leroy held her down, and Richard approached her with the scalpel. "Now," he said. "We can shave the bump off." And still, nobody was doing anything, not even me, who was standing there, me, who was always just standing there watching with my mouth open wide.

Richard pressed the knife against her skin.

Afterward, in Dr. Killigan's office, everybody agreed:

Annie's blood was so red, it looked just like a girl's.

Annie's blood was so red, it was like she was alive.

She was just a girl with her wrists pinned; she was a girl with hair and eyes and a mouth and in the end, I couldn't bear it. I grabbed the Bunsen burner that was still lit on the table. I waved it in front of Richard and shouted, "Richard, stop it!" He ignored me. So I put the flame to his arm, and the flame caught on his shirt. He looked at me with wild surprise, and then, in the time it took for a single flame to turn into a fire on his chest, he shouted, "Fuck, *you stupid cunt!*" He grabbed his shirt by the collar and tried to rip it off. He couldn't. He ran to the emergency shower and someone pulled the cord. The smoke rose off his body toward the ceiling, and everybody was so distracted, Annie sprang free, her blood preceding her out the door, where Ms. Nailer was standing, suddenly, tucking her shirt into her white pants.

"What the hell has happened?" she asked.

Nobody spoke. Then, from the back, there was a voice.

"Human Fart lit the flame."

The Other Girls couldn't figure out why I lit Richard on fire. They kept saying, "But he's an honors student."

When my mother got the call from Dr. Killigan, she kept asking, "What?" and then, *"What?"* My father asked me if this was about what happened in October. "Do we need to be worried about you, Emily?" and I yelled at him from behind my bedroom door: "I don't know! Probably!"

My mother told me I had to see Ron the psychiatrist. When I refused, she looked at my father, who said, "We'll all go, as a family." It almost sounded pleasant. I agreed.

Mrs. Trenton threatened to put me in jail for the rest of my life. She tried to hold a town meeting about it, until Dr. Killigan threatened to sue the Trentons since Annie's parents were suing the school. Dr. Trenton was so afraid of what this negative attention would do for his reputation in the medical community, he urged his wife to calm down. Let it be. Kids will be kids.

I took a sigh of relief, a verbal slap on the wrist. Dr. Killigan expressed extreme disappointment in me, and then I was sent to lunch. Punishment enough, I thought.

At lunch, everything that happened during the lockdown came out slowly, like bedbugs crawling to a warm body at night:

Richard Trenton cut off ABOB's nose.

Emily Vidal lit Richard on fire.

A human fart lit the flame? Is that at all related to the group fingering in the girls' bathroom?

"I don't even know what that is supposed to mean," Janice said to me, biting down on her carrot.

She explained what really happened during the lockdown: Principal

Killigan got a call saying someone had a gun. "But it turns out," she said, "just one of the special ed kids. He saw a security officer with a gun in his belt, called the main office, and said he saw someone in the building with a gun."

I stared at her blankly.

"I know," Janice said. "I didn't know retards took everything so literally either."

**11**

All I remember about Ron the psychiatrist was that we went right before my father left us for good, and his house was decorated with silver New Year's streamers, and we sat down underneath them on the couch in his living room. A long peacock feather bursting out of a vase tickled my ear, African masks lined the fireplace, and there were books on everything from Christ to Andy Warhol to why men hate whores to Italian cooking. There was an entire wall made of glass, purple velvet couches flat as pancakes, a television emitting a virtual fire, lights that weren't supposed to look like lights but rather boxes, and a painting of an Asian woman handing a white woman a dildo over the fireplace, and on the way home, my father drove faster than the speed limit and got angry at stop signs. "What kind of lunatic hangs pictures of Asian women holding dildos?" he asked.

My mother swatted my father and mouthed "dildos" accusingly.

"And that book on his bookshelf," I said. *"Why Men Hate Whores.* Did you guys get a load of that?"

"He must not have any children," my father said.

"Three," my mother said. "I saw a photo."

"Well I'm not going back there," my father said. "I don't trust a man who decorates his house with genitalia."

"I thought he was nice," my mother said.


On New Year's Eve, we took down our tree together for the last time like it was a celebration. We spent the night recognizing the origins of ornaments—Nana, Jane's Boutique, Russia—and the ends of ourselves.

"You know," my father said, sprinkling nutmeg on his brandy Alexander, "if you sniff too much nutmeg, you could die."

"You can die from anything, really," my mother said. "You can die from eating too many apricots."

They were officially divorced. Relief jingled in the air.

"Too much vitamin A," my father said. "Makes sense."

"How *many* apricots?" I said, afraid that the World's Most Pathetic Death could happen to me.

"Some inhuman amount," my mother said.

"Blowfish," my father said. "Now, they have poison sacks. Tons of people die every year in Asia from eating blowfish."

"Or get paralyzed!" I added. "They're called fugu zombies. Sometimes, people think they're dead, and they get buried alive."

Nobody even flinched. We were taking comfort in the ways death could find us, beating it to the punch.

When the clock struck twelve, my father put down his brandy Alexander. We clanked my mother's new pans together, jumped up and down. My mother stared at the television, which was turning into virtual confetti, and put her hand over her mouth, as though she understood exactly what would be lost if she cried out, "Do you two know how much those pans cost?" She would have been accusing us of not understanding the value of things. So she was quiet, even though we all felt something drain out of us during the celebration. And then the phone rang.

"What?" my father shouted into the phone.

Mrs. Resnick was in labor. "This is two months too soon," my father said. He was worried, but I couldn't tell what exactly about. He had the same look on his face when the dishwasher leaked water all over the floor. My father kissed me on the forehead. "I'll see you in the morning," he said, grabbing his coat. I sipped on my apple cider and thought that if I didn't know my family at all, it would have been nice to see my father at the coat rack and my mother sad to see him go.


I woke at six in the morning to a cold frost covering our lawn and my father making a loud noise in the living room. He was sitting on the couch, with his hands on his knees. My father's face was always wrinkled, regardless of whether he was laughing or crying, and on a morning like this, it was hard to tell what he was doing.

I did not touch him or ask him any questions. I just stood at the window.

"Things will be different now," my father said, wiping his tears.

"Things have been different for a long time now," I said.

I put my nose to the window and everything outside looked so vacant, even the icicles, Ms. Nailer had told us once, were made primarily of nothing. The weather was the circulation of invisible forces, colliding over and over and over again, throwing dead leaves against the sides of our house like a stoning.

"I love you, Emily," my father said. "That's one thing that won't ever change."

My mother walked into the room with a bag of soaps, and my father suddenly clammed up and said, "Well I don't suppose anyone cares, but it's a girl."

My mother put the soaps down on the table.

"Her name is Laura," my father said. "We can all go see her if you like."

"No, thanks," my mother said.

"No, thanks," I said, and followed her out of the room.

My father moved out a week later. I hugged him at our front door and couldn't bear to watch him leave with so much luggage. I closed my eyes and rubbed the poinsettias between my thumbs as I listened to his heels click the cement, the hush of the cab tires taking him away. When I opened my eyes, the street was silent, only the exhaust still suspended in the air.

# 12

Mr. Basketball stood green-collared and tall next to the projector, wrote *Welcome to English* on the board, and asked us to please settle down. It was January, a new semester of freshman year, and already Mr. Basketball was employing pedagogical methods Ms. Nailer had not. Janice walked into the room with her breasts sticking out in the air as if she got points for hitting things. She snapped her gum as she walked by Mr. Basketball's pointy face and then quickly explained how she didn't mean to; popping her gum was an accident that happened because she felt so comfortable all the time. She blushed so deeply, Mr. Basketball was forced to forgive her. "All right," he said. "Please take a seat." He smiled a bit and then made eye contact with me, as though he needed my permission to start class. I nodded.

"I'm your English teacher," Mr. Basketball said. "Can you all speak English?"

Nobody spoke, nobody moved.

"Apparently not," he said.

We laughed. Everyone was already in love with him. We stood in small circles every chance we got, just to talk about him.

Mr. Basketball was so funny, he could split your spleen just by looking at it.

Mr. Basketball was so smart, you got smarter just by looking at him.

"No," Janice said at lunch, correcting us. "You have to get to third with him."

My father was in Prague, discovering the joys of smoking cigars in public rooms. My mother was at home, discovering the joys of Arbor Mist and White Russians at noon. Since my father had left, she had watched enough movies starring Sally Field to know that having a dead husband was the preferred option. It was perfect because nothing was ever your fault, not even loneliness, and nobody would ever come up to you at the funeral and say, "Now, at which point do you think he stopped breathing?"

My mother developed a heart murmur, or as I asked, "Maybe you always had one? Maybe the house is just quieter now?" Sometimes, when I walked by her in the kitchen, she put a finger to her lips and said, "Shh, Emily. Can you hear my heart? It's not working properly." Sometimes, I thought she looked too beautiful to be sitting at the counter all by herself, developing palpitations.

"I'm busy, Mom," I said.

She eyed me as I moved across the kitchen.

"You're not busy," she said. "I can see you. You're just drinking lemonade."

That made me want to cry so hard, I can't even explain it.

Sometimes, my father called our house from Prague to say, "Dobrý den!" Sometimes he called just to say, "Where's your mother?" My mother was always sitting at the kitchen counter, and she never wanted to talk to him, even though she always wanted to talk to him. "She's not here," I said, and when I hung up the phone, she stuck her hand in a box of Cocoa Puffs and said, "Did you know that your father hired the neighbor to assemble your tricycle when you were three?" My mother loved to revisit the fights she'd had with my father, as though this was a form of keeping him present. "And I said, 'What, are you going to hire someone to love her as well?' God. What a fool."

My father left us enough money in the divorce settlement so my mother would never have to attend another thing she didn't want to attend. "A gift," he said. But it felt like punishment. Some weeks, she didn't even leave the house. She quit her volunteer job at the hospital. She spent the day running her fingers across photographs of us at Hershey Park, Disney World, St. John's. She talked about memories she said she wasn't sure she even had. She made meatloaf and threw it to the ground. She tried to learn the piano. She played the first three chords of "Row Row Row Your Boat" and then quit. She blew off bikini wax appointments, PTA meetings.

She started taking antidepressants. Prozac at first. When I found the bottle and confronted her, she said, "It's just for three months, Emily. It's not permanent. It's like, well, sometimes when you get older you forget how to be happy. You probably don't understand this, but it happens. And these pills remind you how it feels to be happy. So then when you go off them, you know how to create the feeling on your own."

She spent her nights ordering cookbooks from other countries and cooking Mexican dinners with all the wrong proportions. She wanted a basil plant, a cilantro plant. She wanted to start growing things. This was a good sign. But she never grew any. She just squeezed lime juice into her wine and watched the meat burn. I began to choke on cayenne pepper and dry bread and roll up my jersey knit skirts so that three quarters of my legs were always exposed to the general public. I hung dice from my ears as jewelry, stopped washing my hair, and let the grease curl around my face like the Other Girls. I sat and stared at Mr. Basketball, let my eyes wander over his long torso that made him look like a fish, I thought, standing at the chalkboard writing *Haikus*.

"We're going to write some haikus," Mr. Basketball said. "But first, let's talk about images. Let's come up with some images."

"What do you mean, images?" Janice asked. "Like, colors?"

"There are such things as tired images," he said. "And fresh images. Let's examine what a fresh image is compared to a tired, hackneyed image."

He asked us to think of four basic emotions.

"Disillusionment!" someone shouted from the back.

"Simpler," he said. "That's more a state of being."

"Ennui!"

"Funny," he said. He wrote *mad* on the board. "What about mad? Can anyone think of an image that would illustrate anger? Raise your hands, please."

Janice raised her hand. "A gun pressed to an ear."

"Blood spots on a car."

"A man with his fingers bent backward."

"That's violence," he said. "You are confusing anger with violence."

He wrote *clenched teeth* on the board.

*Narrowed eyes.*

*Popping veins.*

"This is how we're going to start thinking this semester," Mr. Basketball said. "In images."

We were ready to write the haikus. But we didn't have enough construction paper. Mr. Basketball looked at me and asked if I would run down to the basement and get an extra stack. We were going to hang them on the wall as decoration. "Me?" I asked, pointing to myself, as if "me" wasn't specific enough. "Yes," he said. *"You."*

I hated going down to the basement. Teachers rarely sent students to the basement. It was frowned upon by most of the teachers since basements were dark, and terrible things happened to children in the dark, even if it was only in their imaginations. But people were lazy, and I was discovering that was exactly what high school teachers primarily were—people—so they would send us with an added, "Don't tell anyone I sent you there," which was the only reason I had ever considered telling someone. But I wouldn't tell anyone that Mr. Basketball had sent me there. He was handsome and from Greenwich, Connecticut, and he picked glass out of my foot.

I walked into the basement and breathed in the overgrowth of mold, stepped over stray wires, and ran my finger against splintered and unused furniture. I knew that when you walked into a basement you were agreeing to a whole new set of world rules. A bat could fly at your neck, your heart could stop for no reason, limbs could roll out from closets, rats could pop out from pipes, and you couldn't be surprised about any of this.

"Fuck."

Except another person—that was surprising.

"Oh, it's just you," Mark said.

Mark was sitting on a crate behind a bunch of turned-over desks, smoking a cigarette. The hot ash lit up his face like a tiny prayer candle. His hair was growing past his ears. I heard that he had taken a fifty-dollar bet from Richard that he would never cut it again.

"Hello," I said.

He didn't speak. I walked toward the shelf closest to him. I began sorting through different kinds of paper. "Hi," he said.

"Hi," I said.

He watched me for a few minutes and then finally spoke.

"You know what's weird?" he asked.

"What?"

He flicked his ash to the ground. "My father killed himself on Cheesecock Lane."

"I know," I said.

"That's like killing yourself on Jellotit Ave."

I was quiet. His stare was aggressive. "Hey, you don't have to be all strange about it. What, like I can't talk about it? It was something that *happened*. You saw the whole goddamned thing."

So I said, "Asscrack Circle."

"No," he said. "You don't get it. It couldn't be Asscrack Circle. The first word has to be a soft food and the second word has to be slang for a private part."

"Okay," I said. I was afraid to smile. "Puddingvagina Boulevard."

"That was just gross."

I blushed. I looked away, back at the shelf. I didn't know what to say. He pulled out another cigarette.

"My mom hates that I smoke," he said. "She said it's bad around the baby. Nothing's good for the baby. And do you know what I say to that? Good. I say, fuck the baby. Long live the smoke."

"Smoking is pretty disgusting," I said, not sure if I should ask questions about the baby.

"Yeah, well my mom is pretty gay," he said.

He pulled me down onto the crate with him. He was acting reckless. Mark had grown a lot since we had last spoken. *You're so tall,* I wanted to say, but I didn't want to sound like my mother in a moment like this, where mothers were strictly unwelcome, not to mention gay.

"You should get back to class," he said. "The bell is going to ring soon. I can tell by the amount of footsteps."

"Yep," I said. "Okay." I grabbed the paper and left.

This felt like progress.

When I returned, the class was rioting. I had missed a great injustice.

"When forty years shall besiege thy brow!" Mr. Basketball shouted.

He threw up his hands like he couldn't believe us, like he was mad. "Did you know that people used to memorize Homeric epics like the backs of their hands? Did you know that Thomas de Quincey had memorized Shakespearean sonnets by the time he was thirteen?"

"Who is Thomas de Quincey?" they shouted. "What is a Homeric epic?"

"All I am asking," Mr. Basketball said, "is for you guys to memorize six lines of 'The Waste Land.' Pick any image that strikes you. You will have to recite it to the class."

"What's an image?"

"Shut up, Peter, you *retarded* retard," someone shouted.

"*Hey,*" Mr. Basketball said warningly.

"Hello!" Janice said from the back, and laughed.


At Janice's house, her mother always stood by the oven waiting to take the pumpkin bread out. "Remember when you girls were little and you'd run home from school, fighting your way for the pumpkin bread?" her mother asked.

"Mom," Janice scolded. "Please do not harp on the things of yore." That was Janice's rule. The past was boring. That included funny things we said, things we used to feel, clothes we used to wear.

We cut ourselves a slice and went upstairs.

"Mr. Basketball and I haven't boned since last Wednesday," Janice said. "I think he's embarrassed that his dick fell out of me when he turned me on my stomach and he couldn't get it back in."

"Janice," I said. "God."

"What?"

"What if Mr. Basketball finds out you are saying this stuff about him?"

"He knows it's going to happen eventually. He knows what he is doing."

"Okay, Janice. You aren't actually sleeping with Mr. Basketball."

"How would you know what I was actually doing?"

We nibbled on our bread quietly until Janice became embarrassed by the silence. She continued telling me about the rest of her day. Mr.

Basketball said that T. S. Eliot once compared women to menstrual blood. Alex Trimble pulled his pants down in gym and cried, "Oh, God! The Martians!" Joseph Kimball shot half a carrot out his nose. On purpose. He proclaimed it his one profitable talent. Was going to major in it at college. Richard accidentally killed Mr. Kraft's classroom guinea pig Mickey by squeezing it too hard. Everyone called him Lenny. They shouted at him, "Stupid Lenny, you're so nice and sweet but so big." Since Mark and Richard had started snorting cocaine over Christmas break, Richard stopped going to English class and had no idea the joke was a reference to *Of Mice and Men*. He had no idea what was what anymore. He walked around the halls with Mark, kicking empty soda cans. He wore T-shirts with the faces of smashed cartoons and cracked skulls, and when people asked him about the burn running all the way up his arm and his chest, he told them to "eat vag." Then he laughed. Richard thought everything about him was funny, even if he didn't understand why anymore.

Janice smiled the whole time she told me what happened in class, and I laughed hard, harder than I had in weeks, because what we didn't know was that Richard would die four years later in a snowboarding accident, or that people would go to his funeral and nobody would cry, but instead laugh about the time he got so high he jumped off the roof of Stop and Shop, or that his virgin girlfriend in a fit of grief would scream out, "We never even had sex!" or that our new science teacher genuinely loved the guinea pig Mickey.

Richard loved Mickey as well. I saw him standing by the cage while I was walking past the classroom one day, petting Mickey's fur so softly, as though it was a body full of cotton, and he saw me too, held my gaze, and then said with unexpected honesty: "I've always kinda liked you."

"Oh," Janice said, continuing. "Also. The Other Girls decided we should start calling you Shiny Forehead."

## 13

My forehead was so shiny, my biology class had joked about using it as a light source all semester. Ms. Nailer was gone; she had not been fired, but rather "deselected" after the Annie incident. My half sister Laura had started eating solids, Richard had a crush on me, used to masturbate to my fifth-grade photo, and X was the substitute for the unknown number.

"But how does adding X make it any less unknown?" I asked Ms. O'Malley, my algebra teacher, during extra help. Ms. O'Malley crossed her long, smooth legs and sighed.

At home, my mother hadn't changed clothes in four days.

"The tiger lilies are dead," my mother said after school on our porch, while she sipped wine in the cold. My mother was not wearing earrings. She was never wearing earrings anymore. She was always on the porch, always in a robe.

"How many glasses is that?" I asked her.

"Just two," she said. My mother was the kind of woman who looked worse when she was relaxed.

"Just two," I repeated.

"Look at all the dead vegetation," she said.

Everything was covered in snow and my mother seemed to blame my father for this, even though it was February, even though I was sure I loved him more than ever now that he was gone. Because how could you blame a man for dead flowers when he was the one who planted them in the first place? He was obsessed with keeping the tiger lilies alive while he lived here, always trying out new systems. Once, I came home from school and caught him pissing on all the plants, laughing. "To keep the deer away," he said.

It was impossible to hate a man who had planned all of your vacations, who drove us through the corn farms and the honeysuckle beaches of Bridgehampton, Long Island, toward the ocean and asked, "Emily, what crop is that?"

"Beans! Potatoes! Ice cream!" I'd shout.

"No. Corn! What flower is that?"

"Honeydew!"

"Close."

"Mildew."

"Farther."

"Honeyflower?"

"Honeysuckle!"

"How do you always remember that, Dad?"

"I bet you there is nothing you know that I don't know!" he said, turning the wheel.

And there wasn't. Not until I started studying Canadian geography at school and I asked him, "What's the most northern province?" He shook his head and said, "Come on! That's not a fair question."

At night in Long Island, my father took us for ice cream in Sag Harbor. We walked the quiet strip to the end of the dock and looked at the yachts. "Can you imagine?" my father asked us, and I was always too impressed by the size of the boats to notice that this was him wishing for a different life. He bought us mocha ice cream cones. All I knew about Sag Harbor ice cream was that it was the most goddamn expensive ice cream in the whole country but what the hell, we were on vacation, weren't we? My father said that everything was too goddamned expensive if you thought about it long enough.

"How goddamned expensive is each lick?" I asked, cone in hand. My mother and father laughed until they had to sit down.

My father was always money conscious, and I thought it was because we didn't have any money. As I got older, I realized my father was only money conscious because my mother wasn't. Sometimes, my father would sit at the kitchen counter doing the bills and shout out, "We have zero dollars, people! Zero!" This was directed to my mother, who would roll her eyes and say to me, "Don't listen to him." Apparently, it was okay to have zero dollars. We seemed to get by. We had two fridges, a handful of white leather couches, four beds with memory foam, two electric eyelash curlers, and a blender that could puree a rake.

"You kids don't use any *color* in your poems," Mr. Basketball said. "Let's talk about how important color is. Let's take a good look at these walls around us."

We would have revolved our heads if we could.

"What color are they?"

"Is this a trick question?"

"Gray," Janice said.

"Right," Mr. Basketball said. Janice smiled, proud she had vision. "And does it matter that they're gray?"

"No."

"Of course it does," he said. "Because why would they be gray?"

"Why wouldn't they be gray?" Lillian Biggs asked.

"Good question," Mr. Basketball said. "There are plenty of reasons why they wouldn't be gray. They could be yellow. They could be red. They could be striped or wallpapered or glass! They could have holes. They could be made out of papier-mâché."

"That wouldn't make any sense," someone said.

"Why not?" Mr. Basketball said. "Why wouldn't it be reasonable to paint these walls red?"

"Because school is boring. And so is gray. It makes sense."

"But maybe school is only boring because the walls are gray. Maybe if the walls were red, things would be different."

"Okay!" I shouted after school, barging into the living room. "Let's redesign the house!"

"Huh?" she asked.

I turned on a brown, dull lamp. "Get up, get up! We're going to change this place!"

"What? Why?"

I looked around at the room. Nobody had ever really cleaned up properly after my mother tore down the curtains and threw the books to the floor.

"You can change your attitude just by changing the colors that surround you," I said.

Surprisingly, she agreed. She was ready for a change, too. Like she realized that we needed this, and this was one small thing we could do. We signed up for one of those community interior design classes offered by the town at night. "What do you want to feel like when you are home?" the instructor asked us during the first class. My mother shrugged. "Like I'm not home," she joked in my ear.

"Foreign," I translated. "Norwegian!"

"Your homework," the teacher said, "is to find out what that looks like."

There were so many ways to live just one life, I found out. I spent my nights researching and drawing models of what our house would look like if we lived in Italy and kept "slow hallways," or in France with checkerboard floors. And when I thought of Mr. Resnick's broken neck, I thought of the most neutral thing I could and said, "koi fish koi fish koi fish." When I fell asleep, I had nightmares about old men Tasering me in elevators for no reason at all. Richard lifting up my skirt, putting his middle finger inside me. Mr. Resnick on a canoe, looking for a pen. Bleeding out his toe. "That's where the blood goes, Emily," he said to me in my dream. I woke up in a cold sweat and for a moment, I thought his blood was all over me.

All day long, I sweated. I sweated so bad, I cut out washcloths and safety-pinned them under the armpits of my shirts. Every few days or so, my mother would approach and say, "Please, Emily, wash your hair."

"It's shinier this way," I said. When I looked in the mirror, it was. I was glad to see the grease coating my hair.

My mother and I stopped going to the design class two weeks in, but I continued my plans to redesign the house. I asked my mother for her credit card and went to local furniture stores after school. I bought bright red curtains, gold lamps with braided tassels. I stored my father's paintings of random rivers and empty docks in the basement, and hung pictures of koi fish over the television, gingersnap roses over the couch.

My mother looked around at the new decoration and made the soft face she always made when she said, "Darling, you are my angel. Did you know that?"

Her voice lifted at the end of the sentence in an attempt to make it sound like the responsibility was something to be happy about, but by the time my mother's words reached my ears across the new room, being her angel merely sounded like another chore around the house, a game we had to play where my mother got to be god and I got to be the celestial attendant. Like cleaning the toilet bowl. Like wiping down the shower after I used it.

My mother believed that everybody had their own personal angel who inspired them to do really undesirable things: taking out the garbage in the middle of a snowstorm when you could only find your open-toed heels. My father's angel was Mr. Lipson (an accountant who apparently spared him jail time). My mother said my angel was Ralph Lauren, who was the only designer she could think of who made sweaters with proper shoulder lines.

"And I'm your angel?" I asked. "That doesn't seem fair somehow."

"That's just how it works," she had said.

In reality, it wasn't all that difficult being my mother's angel. Her needs were tangible and immediate. I got the Belvedere, the heating pad. I buttered the bread, shelved the *Home and Garden*. I hung the curtains, dusted them once a week. I didn't mind. Movement felt productive. But when my mother lay on the new couch for too long and asked questions like, how could a husband get up from the kitchen counter and leave her sitting in the middle of her own conversation, the new couch began to look just like the old couch and I became selfish and fourteen again, more concerned about the state of my hair than the state of my mother, and I said, "Are you sure it happened exactly like that?"

When my mother wanted to know what a woman had to do to make a man fall in love with her again, what a woman did to be completely different without changing a thing, I tried to convince her of how unqualified I was to be an angel. I had lungs and blood cells and undeveloped opinions on floral patterns. My mother's eyes fluttered shut like she could barely believe the consistency of heartbreak.

When I was younger, my mother used to turn off my light and pull the covers to my chin. I put on my pajamas and wished for stupid things. She rubbed my head and sat at the edge of my bed, telling me to say my prayers. I told her I just said them in my head. She told me I had to say them out loud. "Why?" I asked. Why couldn't he just read my thoughts if he was so all-knowing? "Your prayers take on more urgency if God hears them directly," she said. She said there was a whole bunch of people out there just thinking, and did I just want to be one in a bunch?

"Can he hear me over my fan?" I asked.

"Oh no," she said, laughing. "I didn't mean it like that. Don't make it *that* complicated."

But that year, my mother slid into her bedroom each night without saying a word. The only sounds from her room were the pills rattling out of the bottle. Her lights never turned off. "I just can't sleep," she sometimes said, getting into my bed at night, cold like a fish. "Help me sleep. Why can't I sleep?"

I was expected to know. "I don't know," I said. Maybe she should try *not* sleeping. Maybe she needed a job. Maybe she needed a hobby. Maybe she needed to read a book.

"But I can't focus," she said. I called my father. He said maybe she needed to go outside. Maybe she needed to go get a coffee. Did she try yoga? Did she try not eating meat? Did she try only eating meat? Maybe she didn't need to eat so much meat. Maybe she didn't need to get out of bed as much. Maybe she should try sleeping. Try the hobby thing again. Try painting. Eat meat.

But I told him that she couldn't try painting because her hands weren't steady anymore and she couldn't get a job because she hadn't had a real job in years. She couldn't go outside because it was too cold and she got coffee yesterday and she does yoga but stretching her muscles didn't make the bad thoughts go away.

"What bad thoughts?" he asked.

"I think she wants to kill herself," I said.

"No," he said. "She won't kill herself. When she tells me that, I say, go ahead! Let's see you do it. And she won't."

## 14

My father sent me a birthday card from Prague. *Happy Bastille Day!* I thought my father's jokes about pretending not to care for me were a lot funnier when he was down the hall, shouting, "Just kidding! I care for you!"

At lunch, one of the Other Girls said, "Hey, Shiny Forehead, isn't it your birthday?"

I refused to answer.

"Guys!" cried the one who caked herself in so much foundation, bits sometimes fell off into her yogurt. "Shiny Forehead's parents fucked fifteen years and nine months ago!"

I opened my mouth to argue, to defend something, until I realized there was nothing to defend. It was true. My parents fucked fifteen years and nine months ago. Should I have been embarrassed about that?

In English, Mr. Basketball got everyone to sing "Happy Birthday" for me in unison. Janice sang the soprano harmony and pissed everyone off.

"In addition to memorizing lines from 'The Waste Land,'" Mr. Basketball said, "you all have to write a paper. On the origin of poetry."

"What do you mean, origin?"

"Like, the beginning of time?"

"When poetry began," Mr. Basketball said. "How poetry has shifted through time."

The students informed him that was, like, four billion years ago.

"Try to limit the scope of your paper to a particular topic," Mr. Basketball said. "For example, free verse and its beginnings. When did free verse become popular? When did it start? These are the questions you should be asking yourself while writing this paper."

Lillian Biggs said she thought we were supposed to be answering questions while writing our papers. She said she thought that was the whole point of writing a paper.

"School is stupid."

"So fucking stupid."

"This is all so stupid."

"The next person who swears, to the principal's office," Mr. Basketball said.

"Tampon!" someone cried from the back. "That's not a swear."

Mr. Basketball sighed. I looked out the window, watched the sun slip behind a tree, and convinced myself that the world was ending.

Dr. Killigan knocked on the door and walked in with a student I didn't recognize.

"We have a visiting student today," Dr. Killigan said. "Do you mind if she looks in on your class?"

Mr. Basketball looked around for an empty seat. The class was full, so full in fact that Lillian Biggs had to sit on top of a table in the back of the room.

"Emily," Mr. Basketball said, "will you run to the basement and grab another chair?"

I had become Mr. Basketball's errands girl. I didn't mind. Every time Mr. Basketball sent me to the basement, it felt like an affirmation of his love for me, an I-trust-you-with-big-things gesture. Like when my father would unload the car after our trips to Long Island and he'd call to my mother and ask her to hold something for him. My father needed the help of another person and my mother had agreed to be just that until death did them part, even if she failed and dropped the laundry basket on the ground.

I got to walk the halls when other students didn't. I went to the art studio and ran my finger over other people's dried paint. I peered into classrooms that weren't mine. I learned that everyone was equally bored at all times. This was comforting. I went to the courtyard and saw Marianne Stein and Nick Ross making out. Their tongues crossed. I went to the bathroom and picked at my hair, applied lipstick. "I can't believe I am you," I said to myself in the mirror. "I am you." Sometimes, I practiced my lines from "The Waste Land." "You cannot say, or guess, for you know only a heap of broken images."

I rubbed the lipstick off as soon as another girl came in. Sometimes there were girls already in the bathroom when I arrived, and I had to pretend to use the bathroom. I stood in the stall, flushed unnecessarily, and walked out without washing my hands because what was the point if you didn't even take your pants off, and I heard the girls in front of the mirror say, "Ew, she doesn't even wash her hands. Don't touch her or you'll probably die."


"I didn't actually mean my mom was gay," Mark said in the basement after a long period of silence. I was searching for a stack of chairs. There was an edge to his voice, something alien about him. "She's not *gay* gay. But you know what I mean."

"I didn't think you meant she was actually gay," I said.

"You gave me a funny look when I said it."

"Did I?"

"If my mom was gay, then that means your father is a transsexual."

"That's not necessarily true," I said, hoping to put an end to the conversation.

"I'm just joking. You don't know how to take a joke anymore?" I couldn't open my mouth without breathing in the entire basement, the dust, the dead moths stuck to the dirty windows, the mold painted on books.

"*Joke*," he said. But we couldn't laugh or look at each other, not even in the dim basement light that made everything look and feel and taste like a stale performance of someone's past.

Richard appeared out of a dark corner in the basement, licking the top of a vodka bottle.

"Did you know that Socrates could drink a shot of vodka every hour and still perform basic tasks?" he asked. Richard stepped fully into the light from the half window and revealed a wide and sloppy grin on his face. "It's twelve thirty." He took a shot. He counted to three with his fingers. "One. Two. Three. Basic task."

I just stared at him.

"Do you want some?" he asked.

"I came down here for a chair, actually," I said.

"That's too bad," Richard said. "These chairs are ours."

"They aren't yours."

"The thing is, Emily, we spend three-quarters of the school day down here. And possession is nine-tenths of the law. You do the math."

Mark broke into a crazed laughter. "That makes no fucking sense, dickhead."

I walked toward the chairs, which were stacked in neat piles behind Richard.

"Oh, no, no!" Richard said, stepping in the way and blocking Mark completely from my view.

"Move," I said.

"Shake my hand," Richard said. He stuck out his hand.

"Why?" I asked.

"Basic task."

I shook his hand.

"Say you're sorry now," Richard said, his grip tightening around my hand.

"For *what?*" I asked.

"For *what?*" he mimicked. He stuck my hand under his shirt. I felt the scar from his burn all over his chest. Mark was still laughing, not even paying attention. "For this," he said. "Feel it. It covers my entire chest, you bitch."

"*Richard,*" I said. "Let go of my hand!"

"Feel it."

"No," I said, kicking him away. "It was your own stupid fault!"

He pushed me against the wall. I pushed him back. He cupped his hand around my throat.

"Don't be *stupid,* Emily," he said. "Do you know what I could do to you?"

"I'm not scared," I said. "You're pathetic!"

He laughed. His hair fell in front of his eyes. The basement door swung open.

"Hey," Mr. Basketball shouted, the light flooding the room. Richard released his grip. "Emily, class is over! Where are you?"

Mr. Basketball walked closer until he could see us, and then Richard and Mark ran up the stairs and out the door.

"It smells like smoke down here," he said, walking closer to me. "You know, Emily, this is a smoke-free zone."

"I wasn't smoking," I said, my neck red around the throat.

"Sorry, sorry, I was just kind of joking," Mr. Basketball said. "You all right?"

"I wasn't smoking," I said.

"I believe you. What was going on down here?"

"Nothing," I said, looking at my feet.

"Oh," he said. "Well, what do you say we get you out of here, huh?"

Mr. Basketball held out his hand and stepped closer to me. If Mr. Basketball really was sleeping with Janice, this must have felt normal to him, his face close to mine, his gritty stubble compared to the youth of my cheek. I knew that if I reached out and touched him, the way I touched him on the stoop, he would step even closer, press himself against me. He would lift up my shirt and slide off my bra. He would put his mouth on my breast, and everything would feel soft again.

I was shaking. Inside my shoes, my toes were cramping.

Then he did the most unexpected thing. He laughed.

"It's all wildly confusing, I know," he said. Then I laughed too, like we had some kind of understanding. I took his hand and we walked out of the basement. We walked back to class so I could get my bag. On the way, Mr. Basketball explained how adolescent confusion was a prerequisite to knowing something absolutely when I was older.

# 15

When I got home, I was relieved to find a note from my mother saying she was shopping for my birthday dinner. I took off my shirt, bit into an apple, and put the radio on.

The phone rang. It was Mrs. Resnick.

"Hi, Emily," Mrs. Resnick said. "I'm really sorry to bother you, but I need to go to a doctor's appointment and I just don't know where Mark is. He was supposed to watch the baby. Will you come over and watch Laura for a bit?"

Laura was tiny. To be expected, I suppose. In her crib, she was wrapped in a pink blanket. She had eyes and a nose in reasonable distance of each other, but the most surprising thing about her was that she looked like nobody, some kind of generic baby you'd see on television.

When I first stood over her miniature body, I didn't know what to say to her. I picked her up, looked her in the eye, and said, "Your mother slept with my father." She didn't blink. So I tried playing peekaboo with her and that was when she started crying. "Peekaboo!" I said, and popped my head up over the crib. She kept crying until she tired herself into sleep.

I stood in front of Mrs. Resnick's bed. My feet were soft on the burgundy carpet as I walked around the mattress, staring at the plaid bedspread, trying to imagine if my father had ever slept here, if they rolled around and touched each other's thighs and laughed about their stupid, stupid families. I lay down, turned on the television. *The People's Court* was ending.

It turned out, I never cared who won. I got bored. I searched through the desk drawers. Stamps, pens, paper clips, cough drops, Post-its, Mr. Resnick's death certificate. In her closet, I tried on all of Mrs. Resnick's shoes and kept the red silk high heels on my feet as I walked toward a brown box on the floor of the closet. It was the kind of box that held secrets: love letters from Mr. Resnick in college, *kissing you in the elevator, still taste it on my tongue.* A pair of dirty baby shoes, and then bills, tons of unpaid bills. Bills from Stamford Hospital and the psychiatric clinic and checks for thousands of dollars from my father.

In her dresser drawers, Mrs. Resnick's underwear was mostly nude and cotton like my mother's, except for a few lace orange and red pairs with bows on the back that didn't have much ass coverage. I imagined she wore these only when she slept with my father. I picked up one of her bras and wrapped it around my body to see if it fit.

"I'm home, I'm home *I'm home*, Mom!" Mark shouted loudly, walking into his mother's room. "Oh," he said, horrified to see me holding his mother's bra.

"What the hell is Emily doing here?" Richard asked behind him, eating tuna right out of the can.

"Playing dress-up," Mark said.

I was so embarrassed I stood there and waited to perish. Richard sat on the bed.

"So if tuna is the chicken of the sea," Richard said, turning over the tuna can in his hand, "does that mean chicken is the tuna of the earth?"

"Richard, shut the fuck up," Mark said.

"Jesus," Richard said.

Mark walked over to Richard and took the vodka. He walked toward the closet. He ran his hands over his father's pants.

"Remember when my dad would call us up to his room and count his pants, Emily?" Mark asked.

"Yes," I said.

Mr. Resnick had an unreasonable amount of pants. That was one of the things I remembered most about him. "Look at my pants," Mr. Resnick would say to us. "That's an unreasonable amount of pants. I haven't changed pants size in twenty years. You know how many pants you collect in twenty years? This many pants." He pointed to all his pants. "That's an unreasonable amount of pants." Mark and I would run to his room and laugh until we were sore.

"The night before he killed himself, he called me upstairs to say it again," Mark said. He took a blue pair off the hanger. He put his feet in the holes and pulled them up to his waist. "He had so many pants!" Mark repeated. He hunched over like his father, shook his arms, one hand holding the vodka, and kicked out his legs as he walked in circles in the closet. "Mark. *Son.* Look how many pants I have!"

Richard broke out into hysterical laughter from the bed.

"Shit," Mark said, sitting down on the floor of the closet. "Dad. You were just a collection of fucking pants."

It sounded cruel, but I knew what he meant. When my mother was volunteering at Stamford Hospital two or three days a week, she put me in charge of handing out the lollipops in the oncology ward when she couldn't find a babysitter for me. There were always sick children walking by and they'd be bald with illness. It seemed to me, standing there with a strong immune system and a fistful of candy, that illness stripped the youth right out of their bones, and there I was trying to hand it back to them. I was too afraid to approach the sick children, so I waited for them to come to me, these tired little people with bloodless faces and tiny sneakers, Jean or Harriet or Betsy who already seemed dead to me. Jean or Harriet or Betsy would usually smile at me, and ask for one of the lollipops while her mother was talking to one of the doctors. "Blue, please." Jean or Harriet or Betsy was still alive enough to know what color she always wanted—children, it seemed, were creatures of favorites. I gave out a blue lollipop and she smiled as she tore the plastic off with one hard tug. A few months later, Jean or Harriet or Betsy usually died, and nobody ever announced it or told me, I would just have an abundance of blue lollipops left in my hand at the end of the day and that was how I knew they were dead.

Mark opened the vodka and looked around for a cup. He couldn't find one, so he just drank out of the bottle. "Want some?" he asked me. He handed the bottle to me.

I looked at them both, smiling at me. These were my childhood friends. Bark and Prickard, captains of the Space Rock, my sledding partners, the boys who buried me in leaves, and tugged on my pigtails, and lent me their water guns when mine had run out of water. I didn't smile back, but I took the vodka. It was my birthday after all. If everybody was planning on being drunk for it, so was I.

I swallowed a mouthful. It burned down my throat but it felt surprisingly good. I took another one. "Happy birthday, Shiny Forehead," Richard said.

Mark kicked off his sneakers, and they hit the wall. This woke Laura up in her crib under the window and she started crying. Richard licked the bottom of the tuna can with his tongue.

"That's fucking nasty, prickhead," Mark said. "Do you know how much bacteria is on that shit?"

I walked toward Laura.

"Hey!" Richard said, throwing the tuna can, jumping in my way.

"Don't be stupid, Richard," I said. "She's a baby."

Richard's eyes were red. His nose was runny. "Exactly. She's *just* a baby."

Mark laughed.

"To the fucking baby!" Mark shouted. "Cheers!"

Richard took a shot. And then Mark. And then me again.

"Cheers," Richard said.

"*Salud,*" I said, something I heard my father say once.

"To god in the highest!" Mark said.

"Hey, your parents have a computer too," Richard said. It was 1997, and some people in the neighborhood just got their first computers. For about thirty minutes, the novelty of the computer and vodka made us all friends again. Mark sat at his mother's desk. Richard and I were on the bed thinking of weird things for the computer to say, and Mark typed the phrases on the keyboard, pressing Speak Text.

"Make it say, 'I ate my fucking parrot.'"

"Make it say, 'I ate my fucking blasphemous parrot.'"

And we laughed, and typed in more things, and then laughed, and typed in more things, and I was rolling on the bed, getting dizzy from all of the vodka, which was new and corrosive to my stomach, and Mrs. Resnick's picture frames swirling in my head. My head hurt. I couldn't tell if the ceiling fan was on or not. Richard was against the headboard watching me, holding on to the heels of Mrs. Resnick's shoes.

"Make it say, 'I ate my Mom,'" Richard said.

I closed my eyes, dizzy. I listened to Richard laugh a little, his breath audible, wafting air out his mouth. Mark typed on the keys. The computer spoke and stopped our hearts:

"Muh dad is fuck-een dayed."

"Muh dad is fuck-een dayed."

"Muh dad is fuck-een dayed."

Richard tickled my feet. I was drunk for the first time in my life, and I felt like a semisolid, like I was melting, or just about to harden, and I worried that Richard's fingerprints would make permanent indents on my ankles, the way I had pressed my thumb into a rose petal at Mr. Resnick's burial so that my fingerprint would fall with the rose and accompany him underground forever. I kicked at Richard's face.

"Don't touch my feet!" I shouted at Richard, and ripped my legs away from him, accidentally kicking over the vodka bottle on the nightstand. It broke and the vodka spilled out the cracks. Mark, who was at the computer, looked at the broken glass and then at me.

"Pick that up!" Mark screamed.

"*Jesus,*" I exclaimed, reaching over the edge of the bed.

I remember Mark walking over to Laura angrily and me calling out for him and Richard shirtless above me. I remember thinking, why hadn't I seen this coming? This was always coming. Richard had always been coming for me. Following me. Pulling my hair and poking my armpit and hovering above me. Richard's skin was smooth and hairless in the abdomen, but his chest looked like it was covered in asiago cheese. "Just touch it," he kept saying, above me.

"Where's Mark?" I asked, looking around the room. Laura was

screaming behind me, louder with every second. It sounded like her throat was cracking down the middle. I worried Mark loved me less every second. I worried that Richard would never get off of me and that somehow I deserved all of this. Richard widely smiled and I was scared. "*Get off!*" I yelled at him, and he pushed me back down on the bed. I lifted up my knee into his crotch hard.

"You *torched* my skin," Richard said. "Feel it."

Richard lifted up my shirt and lowered himself until our chests pressed together. He moved up and down on me, and I could feel the smooth parts, and then the textured parts. The scar felt like a zipper against my breasts.

"Feel it," he said, and took my hand to his lower chest. "This part."

I spit on his face. "I'd rather die." It was somewhat true.

"Then maybe you will." Richard took out his lighter from his pocket. "Maybe I'm just going to light you on fire, *cunt,* see how you like it." Richard opened my mouth with his finger.

I bit his finger hard.

"Dang!" he said, pulling his finger out.

He started kissing me. Richard's mouth was heavy on mine, and it was hard to breathe. I put my hand at his throat, and he was ripping at my shirt, his hand cupped around my breast, his saliva acidic and thick.

"*What the hell?*" Mark said when he stood over us with Laura quiet in his arms. He stood there for a moment and watched Richard jump off me.

"What the hell were you doing?" Mark asked.

Standing there in the dark of Mrs. Resnick's room, I looked around at my childhood friends, and Laura sitting in Mark's arms, and that was my question exactly: what the hell were we doing? We weren't children anymore. Laura was the child. She was the one sitting in Mark's arms, asking something large and permanent of us. And I was fifteen, drunk and underneath a boy for the first time in my life, and nothing was as I wished it to be. I was drinking vodka while my half sister cried, and the thought never occurred to me that I would have to do more for this girl than just be her neighbor. Before she was born, I imagined Laura as this thing in the corner of our lives that we'd rather not mention, but no; she was alive and breathing. She needed bottles and shoelaces and pump-kins with her name cut out in bubble letters, she would wobble down the need-to-be-gated stairs, she would need moments upon moments of everybody's happiness, happiness that sometimes didn't wake up before she did. She was crying and the sodium chloride down her face was real.

Mark was waiting for an answer. "What were you doing?" he said to me. "You *like* Richard?"

"*No!*" I shouted. "He forced himself on me. Why didn't you try to help me?"

Mark looked angry.

"Why didn't I try to help you?" Mark shouted back. "Why didn't you try to help my father!"

"What?" I asked, confused.

"You just stood there! How could you just stand there while he was killing himself?"

"I couldn't do anything! He was too far away!"

"How long were you watching?"

"I don't know," I said. "I don't know!"

I started breathing heavier. My chest felt tight, my fingertips tin-gling.

"I dropped my glass," I finally said. "I'm sorry. I dropped my glass and it broke all around me."

At first Mark didn't answer; then he turned away from me and said, "Just leave."

He put Laura in front of the mirror in an attempt to get her to stop crying. Laura's face was red and loud and I felt a sudden gush of love for her. I remembered the night of her birth, I had felt her arrival like a bursting capillary in my heart, I could hear her breathing from across the street, and when I looked at Mark in the dark room, holding his, our, sister, I started to see him through her eyes, this sullen teen, this boy with long ratty hair who waited a couple seconds to watch before he yelled at his best friend to get off my body, this boy who would never love either of us the way he was supposed to. And there was Richard by the window, who had spent his life not knowing whether to rip my throat out or fuck me, Richard who ran his hands through his dark hair and sat down on the bed and sighed. Richard who took a long swig of vodka out of the bottle and said, "Your mother is next, you know. My mother says she looks like a ghost around town now. The White Lady. Like we're going to find her hanging from an electrical wire or something, any day now."

And there was me, not understanding why they let me leave like that, screaming, "Fuck you both!" and Laura gently making the soft coos of what could someday sound like my name.

We had crab legs for my birthday dinner. I loved my mother again, for opening the cookbook and putting on her THIS IS NO ORDINARY HOUSEWIFE apron and singing loud to the Frankie Valli CD that Janice put in the stereo. My mother had come home from the store just like this: "I got crab legs for your birthday!" She smiled, and then we dropped them into the boiling pot. They hit the water with a *plop-plip-plop-plop*.

Then while trying to crack them open at the table with our fingers, one of the crab legs slipped out of my mother's hand and sliced the tip of her thumb. With the blood dripping down her finger and onto the plate of crab, she looked at me and said, "I'm sorry." Before she even moved to stop the bleeding, I thought, She is not even trying to stop the bleeding. She was just sitting there, bleeding.

"Don't be sorry," I said. "I'll get a washcloth."

We continued the rest of the dinner in peace. There was a pleasant consistency to birthdays, the way we got reminded of our favorite things, as though it was an annual checkup to see what you grew out of that particular year. Favorite meal (Alaskan king crab), favorite cake (boxed), favorite dishware (ours). I got socks, underwear, a sweater, and a book called *The Best Book of Your Life,* "a collection of very interesting pictures for children."

"This book is for chill-dren," I said, emphasizing the space between syllables, which is what, at the time, I thought a French accent was. I was still a little too drunk to hide it.

My mother said nothing. Janice scraped icing off her fork and giggled.

"Chill-dren," Janice said, following my lead, "are ze worst. Don't zoo agwee?"

We laughed hard. My mother drank some wine. It started raining outside. Janice looked out the window and said, "It's raining like five bitches out there."

My mother didn't even scold her.

"Which is a lot of rain," Janice added.

"Are you *alive*?" I said accusingly to my mother. She ignored me.

Later, Janice whispered, "What's wrong with your mom?"

After dinner was over, my mother went to take a hot bath, the dishwasher stopped running, and the silence became disenchanting. Frankie Valli was just an asshole who got uncomfortable when little girls cried. Janice was a basket case who lied about sleeping with older men. My mother was a naked woman in the bathtub.

I knocked on the bathroom door. "Mom?" I asked through the wood.

No answer.

"Mom?" I asked again, opening the bathroom door. In the tub, my mother's eyes were closed. There were tears down her face. Broken glass bobbed in the water like ice cubes.

The bathwater was red.

"*Mom!*" I screamed. I tugged on her arm, checked for slit wrists.

"Oh, hell," my mother said, startled, opening her eyes. "What are you *doing*?"

"Did you slit your wrists or something?" I screamed.

"No, Emily Marie," she said. "I accidentally broke my wineglass in the tub and I'm a little drunk."

She laughed wildly to prove this was so. She took a drag of her cigarette hanging over the tub. She had been smoking on and off ever since my father left and she gave up volunteering at the hospital. My mother talked like this was a good thing: too many children walking into a hospital, saying hello with their sweet and sad faces and never coming back. After a while, she said, you start believing children were never meant to be anything but children.

"You aren't going to get up?" I asked. "You're going to sit here in the wine? Is that even sanitary?"

"Emily, please, you're being loud."

"And you're smoking! Inside the house. This house. I redesigned this place for you!"

"Honey, I've always been a smoker," she said, and splashed some water on her face.

"No, you weren't," I said. "Not always. Did you come out of the womb with a cigarette in your mouth?"

"Don't be like that, Emily."

"When you get sick and die, don't come crying to me," I told her.

"When I'm dead, I won't be crying to anyone. I'll be dead."

"Good!" I said. I stuck my hand in the tub to drain her filthy bath. "Good. Just smoke and hurry up and die already so we can get on with our lives!"

My mother didn't even drop her cigarette. She stood up, pale and nude and wet. My mother. The White Lady. I ripped the cigarette from her hand and threw it on the ground, hoping the shower curtain would catch fire and burn this whole neighborhood down. It wasn't like anybody would be surprised. Emily the Arsonist. Emily the Murderer. Emily the Cunt. Burned Richard and her whole house down. But who cared what people said? I was done with people. I was tired and angry and fed up with people. I couldn't even sleep anymore, not with the nightmares, not while imagining all the ways my mother might kill herself, at two in the morning, awake with the owls, wondering if she would do it by pills, if she would swallow all the Drano, where I would find her, who I would call first, what I might say.

"Did you even hear me?" I screamed in her face.

She pulled back her wet hand, and at first I couldn't believe it. My mother was going to hit me. No, she would never hit me. But then she did. She smacked me hard across the cheek, and the saddest part about it was that it felt good. It was my mother's touch, something I hadn't felt in so long.

"I am your mother," she said. "And don't you ever talk to me like that again."

I put my hand to my cheek. Janice was quiet behind me in the doorway. Wet and in the bathtub, my mother looked holy, like somebody else's mother, like a biblical figure. There was a sudden rush of heat to my head and my mother brushed the wet bangs off her forehead, and for one quick moment, she was my mother again, and I felt calm. Her nudity was familiar. I remembered when I was no more than three and forced to shower with her, I would be at her knees looking up, asking how her breasts were any different from clouds. "That's the nicest thing you've yet said to me," she had said.

# 16

"Would you be able to drive me home?" I asked Mr. Basketball after school the next day. "Richard has been calling me Emily the Cunt on the bus."

"Oh," he said, his feet still up on his desk, seemingly not affected by my mother's Planet Red lipstick on my mouth. "Of course, of course."

He picked up his briefcase, and we walked silently to the car. When we got inside, I couldn't help but search for signs of Janice on the seats. Long brown hairs, or strawberry ChapSticks, a striped sock, a portable comb, a bobby pin, a piece of chewed gum, a corner of her notebook paper, anything. But all I saw was . . .

"What?" Mr. Basketball asked.

A hamburger wrapper. A sweaty wristband.

"Your car is a mess," I said.

"Two sides to every stone," he said.

"I'm not saying it's surprising," I said, and he laughed, started the engine. The engine was too loud.

"Your poems are getting better," he said, driving out of the parking lot. "They've taken on a sort of dream logic that's really interesting."

"I have a wildly active prefrontal cortex," I said.

I had been waking up screaming. In the nightmare, I was never sure where we were driving, but it was somehow important to get there. Mr. Resnick was sitting next to me in the backseat of the car, dead. But his hair was alive, growing in fact, and I remember knowing for certain that all the hair was going to strangle me by the time I woke up. I kept forgetting he was dead, asking him, "How's work going?" My parents were in the car too, talking about an electrician with a pedophilia charge.

This made everybody laugh for some reason. Except for Mr. Resnick. He was swaying back and forth, and so I asked my father, "Why isn't he speaking? Don't you think he should be speaking?"

"Everybody is different," my father said, and the dream ended.

I told my mother this and she was concerned. She ordered tests. Thousands of my father's dollars later: "Her prefrontal cortex is wildly active during sleep. It's like she's drunk. No inhibitions, too much emotion."

"Me too," Mr. Basketball said. Mr. Basketball turned down my street. I did not tell him to turn. He remembered where I lived. "My parents made me go through a lot of sleep tests as a kid. That's what happens when you grow up in Greenwich."

He said he had CAT scans after falling on grass, allergy shots because he sneezed at his grandmother's house once. Later, Mr. Basketball would tell me that his parents paid ninety thousand dollars to store his umbilical cord in a hospital somewhere. It would protect him in case he ever got MS.

"I have dreams that make me feel like I'm awake," I said. "Or drunk. And awake."

"Horrible dreams," he said. "Cinematic all-night conquests that make no sense."

"Like last night, I was standing under the St. Louis arch. It was on fire, impossibly, and I was responsible for putting it out. But I couldn't because someone was holding my hand and I couldn't let go."

"You know what this means, right?" Mr. Basketball was looking straight ahead, serious about the road. "We're too smart. Smart people can't turn their brains off."

"If we were so smart, shouldn't we find a way?"

"Why would we want to?" he asked. "We're smart enough to know that, in the end, that's not really what we want. Self-awareness is a gift, really. You'll be happy for it one day."

"When I'm a better person, maybe."

"When you can control it, sweetheart," he said.

We laughed. I wasn't sure why. I looked out at the road and watched all the familiar areas pass by me. In Mr. Basketball's car, everything looked smaller and more manageable. I stuck my hand out the window, ready to press myself against the world.

*   *   *

The next day, I didn't even have to ask. "If you don't feel comfortable riding the bus, I don't mind giving you a ride again," Mr. Basketball said. "We live so close."

I agreed.

"Last night," I said, while we were halfway to my house, driving through the town, "an orange giant picked me up by my overalls and threw me over a stone wall."

"Last night," Mr. Basketball said, "I had to play soccer with books for feet. And then all my teeth fell out."

"The stone wall, turns out, was bordering the edge of the universe. I fell into the sky, which wasn't really the sky, since it was the space outside of whatever is the universe."

"They call that hyperspace," he said.

"Well," I said, "I was thrown into it."

"Your dreams are pathetically transparent."

"Should I be embarrassed? I'm so embarrassed."

He laughed. I stuck my hand out the window. The air was soft. Spring was coming.

"You should," he said. "You feel alone. Pushed out of the world, expelled by some godlike figure."

"And you. Chained to your academics, too stressed to function in real life. Aging."

I swallowed.

"The overalls," Mr. Basketball said, not skipping a beat. "That's what doesn't make sense to me. The overalls. Very unlike you."

Did he know me?

"Infantile state?" I asked. "Clothes worn by people who aren't usually me?"

"Oh, yes yes," he said. "I can see that now."

I smiled.

"See, you are smart," he said.

*   *   *

The next day after school, Mr. Basketball had a cupcake waiting for me on his desk. He was leaning back in his chair, reading the *Fairfield Times*: TORN FLAG TOO HIGH TO REMOVE. He had on khakis and his plaid shirt was unbuttoned to show off a T-shirt with a wagon and a warning: I HAVE DIED OF DYSENTERY.

"It's a little late," he said. "But happy birthday."

"Thank you," I said. Even though the cupcake was for me, I felt awkward touching it, as though it still shouldn't belong to me. Because why would he get me a cupcake? Did he buy the cupcake for me? Did he leave school at some point to get me a cupcake, think about what flavor I might like best, and then pay money for it?

"How old are you, Emily?" he asked.

"Fifteen."

Ms. O'Malley popped her head in the door. "Johannes," she said. Her clothes always looked so soft and muted and British. Her long curly hair was like a yellow mane around her face. "Faculty meeting."

"Your name is Johannes?" I asked when she left.

"It is."

"Why would your parents name you Johannes?"

"Why wouldn't they?"

"Did they not want you to have any sort of childhood?" I asked. "Who sees a baby and feels okay calling it Johannes?"

He laughed. "They wanted me to be a lawyer or something like that."

"Really?"

"Really. That and some hereditary shit. Long-lost grandfather I never met, who died in the war. I'm supposed to carry on his qualities. Be virtuous. Heroic. Johannes."

"I could never be a Johannes," I said.

He stood up from his desk, walked toward me.

"You can be anything you want to be," he said. "For example, I tell some of my friends to call me Jonathan and some to call me Jack."

We were quiet. He had friends. It was something I never considered before.

"You haven't eaten the cupcake," he said.

"It looks cancerous," I said, poking the cupcake. "It's very neon. You eat it and if you don't die, I'll try some."

He laughed. He buttoned his shirt back up to cover the wagon. "I have this faculty meeting. We're getting a new vending machine. Shouldn't take more than twenty minutes."

In his car, I threw an empty Sprite bottle in the backseat, pleased at my power to rearrange his life. His window was cracked where a rock had recently hit it. I picked up a twenty-dollar check from "Grandma."

"I thought you were rich," I said.

"My parents are," he said. "A lot of it doesn't trickle down. Like I said, they really really wanted me to be a lawyer. They're still waiting for me to go to law school. I told them not to hold their breath. The day I go to law school, Emily, that's the day I've surely sold my soul. But for now, they say they won't fund this life of Shakespearean gooblygok. A direct quote. And I look them in the eye and say, 'Gooblygok? I'm no lawyer, but I know that's not a word.' That's why they don't give me money, because I say annoying shit like that."

I didn't know if it was seeing his grandmother's curly handwriting or Natalie Merchant that came blasting on the radio, but something made me feel outside myself. I looked down at my legs and they barely looked like mine.

"Do you remember me?" I asked. We had never talked about what happened on my stoop and I was starting to fear I was the only one who remembered that moment.

"Remember you?" he asked. "From two seconds ago when you spoke?"

"No," I said, laughing. "From October. My porch."

He sighed. He turned left.

"Yes," he finally said. "Of course. You had glass in your foot."

"I did," I said.

He pulled into my driveway.

"And you didn't even flinch."

"Not once," I said.

"Right there," he said, pointing to my stoop. "You looked like the saddest, bravest, most alive girl I had ever seen. You were so alive. I can't explain it. Your face."

"What do you mean?" I asked.

He sighed. "When you get to be my age, Emily, that's the kind of stuff you start noticing. People have two deaths really, their physical death and their emotional death. People just start to emotionally die at some point. Some earlier than others. Take Mr. Heller, for instance, barely alive. But you, you are definitely alive, my dear."

Mr. Basketball leaned over and opened the passenger door for me. He hovered over my lap for a moment. He was so close, his face was suddenly terrifying. There was a tiny wrinkle in the corner of his eye, a coffee stain on his collar, a patch of dead skin on his temple where he must have forgotten to wash. He slid his hand down to my foot.

"Has it healed properly?" he asked.

"Yes," I said. "It has."

I got out of the car and walked slowly into my house so he would know I wasn't afraid.

"Who was that?" my mother asked when I threw my backpack on the tiles of our kitchen floor.

"Who was who?" I asked. I poured myself some lemonade.

"Who was that man dropping you off?"

"That man?"

"Emily, who was that man?" she said.

I took a long cool sip of my drink.

"That man was the man who dropped me off."

I put my glass down. The liquid settled in my stomach. I was alive. How exciting. My mother put her hands on her hips. "Fine. Fine. Be that way."

"Oh relax, Gloria. It was my friend's dad Maximus."

I pulled my homework out of my bag. My mother took an orange out of the refrigerator and began to peel it using her hands.

"Listen, Emily," my mother said, throwing the peel into the garbage. "I just have one thing to say. If a man tries to have sex with you and you don't want it, do you know what you say?"

I put my hands over my ears.

"Don't scream," she said, removing my hands. "That will only make him violent. Just confuse him. That's what your Nana always told me. She said you start singing something crazy, real crazy, like, 'Somewhere over the Rainbow.'"

My mother was so beautiful. She was biting into an orange and the juice ran down her chin.

"I know that sounds crazy," she said, wiping her mouth. "But that's the point. You have to scare him more than he scares you, get it?"

## 17

I was pleased with your haikus," Mr. Basketball said in class the next week, handing them back to us. When he stopped by my desk, he said, "See me after class." "You all seem to understand the beauty behind a haiku and that's a good thing."

When the bell rang, I nearly skipped up to his desk.

He explained to me that while the poems I wrote were interesting, they were not haikus.

**Emily Vidal's Haikus:**

*Mother is always the next morning,*
*A painted river of Maine*
*Framed and frozen body of water*
*Father said he had affiliations with.*

*Here are two brown lamps*
*And Mother dressed in scotch*
*For the season (whichever it may be)*
*The weather here never seems right.*

"But they are still poems," I said. I stood very still. I thought it would somehow help.

"I have to give you an F, Emily."

"But why?"

"You're so smart, sometimes I forget how young you really are."

"You're giving me an F because I'm young?"

He handed me the poems with the F on it. I felt like a dog that just pissed all over the carpet.

"I can't bring you home today," he said. "I have a dentist appointment."

I closed his door behind me. Janice was in the hall, leaning against the lockers.

"What did he want from you?" Janice asked.

"I'm not a bad person just because I don't understand what a haiku is," I said.

"I know that," Janice said.

"Well Mr. Basketball doesn't. He's mad at me."

"Maybe he's not mad at *you*."

"Huh?"

"He has a polyp. In his colon."

"I don't think that's it."

"It might be."

"Why don't you go and ask him then?" I asked. "He's your boyfriend, right?"

"What's your problem?"

"I don't have a problem, other than you've been lying to me about Mr. Basketball all year now."

"I'm not lying," she said.

"Why don't you go in and say, 'Mr. Basketball, since we are fucking I need to know if you have a polyp in your colon.'"

"That's too suspicious, Emily."

Janice was in a tight black shirt that said LOOK on the front. There was saliva bunching at the corners of her mouth. For some reason, I wanted to hurt her.

"Janice," I said, "Mr. Basketball touched me."

"Of course," Janice said, shrugging it off, refusing to look surprised. "He touches all of us."

"No," I said. "I mean, he touched me."

"Where?"

"On my leg."

"Here?" she asked, and put her hand around my thigh.

"Yes," I said. "He ran his hand all the way down my thigh and to my foot."

"So what's the big deal? That's baby stuff."

"No, you aren't listening."

"I hear you," she said. "And I'll tell you what happens next."

I felt the urge to put my hands over my ears but I didn't.

"First, Emily, you'll suck his dick. And then once he's hard enough, once it feels like a sausage in your mouth, you have sex until he comes."

"Janice," I said. "Stop it."

"Is this grossing you out, Emily? Because this is sex. This is what he'll want from you. You arch your back at a forty-five-degree angle and scream."

"No," I said.

"Yes," she said, walking away from me.

"Janice," I said, running after her. "Why do you have to be like this?"

"Like what?"

"I don't know," I said. "You're scaring me."

"I'm scaring you?" she asked. "You're the one who scares us."

"Huh?"

"You lit Richard Trenton on fire, Emily!" she said. "And I defended you. I've always defended you! I've always said, hey, guys, we all know Richard was the crazy one, Emily was just trying to help Annie. And what do you do in return? You stand there, and you say, 'Mr. Basketball touched me.' And you know I love him. I *love* him."

She walked out of school and into the parking lot where the Other Girls were sitting on red and white cars, nibbling on peanut butter and jelly matzoh sandwiches. When I first saw them eating matzoh sandwiches, I asked, "Are you guys Jewish?" Only two of them. Fewer calories.

I chased after Janice.

"My third cousin was a child actress," one of the Other Girls was in the middle of saying. "She was in hair commercials, she was so beautiful. And now she's in an insane asylum."

"Go figure."

Janice's eyelids were coated in tragic skid marks of one-dollar eyeliner and red eye shadow she stole from the mall. She licked her finger and used her saliva to smudge her eyeliner into one smooth line.

"I know a guy whose cousin went to an institution after he tried to commit suicide," Janice said. "Cost the guy's parents twenty thousand a year, which doesn't include the food in the dining hall. And after three years, he was still fucked-up, running around in Santa pajamas, talking about tits and dicks and the Apocalypse."

I told Janice I thought it was rude to use words like "tits" and "dicks" to describe the dead or almost-dead.

"Dead or almost-dead, they still have dicks, right?" she said. Then, Janice fluffed her hair and asked us about clits and whether I thought hers might be covered in scar tissue—was that why she couldn't orgasm anymore with Mr. Basketball? I didn't know.

"He's gained, like, ten pounds in the last week," she said. "Maybe that's why."

I told her maybe we were getting too old to make fun of people just for being fat.

"What I'm too old for is breaking habits," she said, and I worried that this was the only reason we were still friends.

One of the Other Girls announced she was going to ask Mark to the Halloween in Spring.

"You can't have a date to the Halloween in Spring," I protested. "It's an after-school dance where we'll play Spud and suck corn syrup through straws."

"So, you can still have a date," Janice said.

"Yeah," Brittany said. "Exactly."

Janice turned to the Other Girls. She started telling them about the new kind of sex she had been having with Mr. Basketball lately: desk sex. She said that by the end of the year, they were going to have had sex in all the classrooms. The Other Girls got excited, saying, "If you have sex on my desk, I'll kill you, Janice." Janice got excited too, and her stories took on the epic quality of a fairy tale, stock characters, predictable endings: of course it's the middle bowl of porridge, of course the duck is actually a swan, of course Mr. Basketball fucks you after school, Janice, of course his penis is the size of a baseball bat. Of course the baseball bat goes inside you, why else would love hurt so much?

"You're such a liar!" I screamed. "I want to see you dance with him at the Halloween in Spring."

"Fine," she said, but still wouldn't look at me. "I will."

# 18

At the Halloween in Spring, one of us went dressed as a super-hot kitten. One of us went as the country of France. One of us went as Saran Wrap. One of us went as a banana.

"I can't believe you came as a banana," one of us said.

"I'm a *slutty* banana," Martha said.

One of us was wearing jeans and a T-shirt. Janice was so disappointed.

"Brittany," she said, "jeans are so boring."

Janice thought anyone who didn't dress up for the Halloween in Spring was a loser who cared too much about being "ridiculous." "I don't care about being ridiculous!" Janice had cried in the bathroom, wrapping the colored Saran Wrap around her naked chest like a tube top.

As a defense for being costumeless, Brittany held out a bottle of liquor that she stole from her parents.

"Sweet vermouth?" one of us asked. "What is that?"

"Adults put it in martinis," Brittany said, holding the green bottle to her mouth. "It's really expensive."

One of us passed the bottle around, one of us exclaimed, "I can't believe they drink this," and one of us killed a fly against the wall with a hairpin. This felt like a cleansing.

In the cafeteria, the girls stood on one side of the room and boys on the other. I ate potato chips and sweated hard in my super-hot kitten mask and watched Mr. Basketball by the vending machine flirt with

Ms. O'Malley. Another teacher walked over to them, drunk off her flask of vodka that wasn't as secret as I overheard her telling them it was, and asked who the fuck the president of England was. "There's no president of England," Mr. Basketball said. Mr. Basketball and Ms. O'Malley laughed together and I saw myself in the reflection of a vending machine. I looked ridiculous. I wanted to claw my eyes out, rip off my costume.

I watched Mr. Basketball and Ms. O'Malley sip on their Hawaiian Punch martinis out of paper cups, and the other teacher spilled her drink over what a prankster Mr. Basketball was: *What do you mean there's no president of England?*

Ms. O'Malley left to bring Janice into the bathroom. "Plastic is not a costume!" she screamed, and tugged her arm.

I walked closer to Mr. Basketball. We stood, not speaking. It felt like a competition of who was going to forgive who first, and for what?

"You're a cat," Mr. Basketball said to me.

"And you're a clown's nose," I said.

"That's me," he said, and touched the red ball at the tip of his nose.

"That's you?" I asked. "That's all there is?"

He didn't answer. He took a sip out of his cup and I could feel the vermouth burn through me. So I said, "I can't believe you are all drunk."

"We're not drunk," he said.

"You're a teacher. Don't you *realize* that?"

"I don't think this is an appropriate conversation."

"I'm just saying. If you take back my F, I won't go tell Dr. Killigan that all the faculty is drunk."

Mr. Basketball sighed. "It is not a negotiation. I don't negotiate with my students."

Student? I was just a student? Mr. Basketball walked away from me, out of the cafeteria.

In my last dream of Mr. Basketball, he was standing at the chalkboard writing out lines of "The Waste Land," the ones I had been memorizing all semester. *There is shadow under this red rock.* My hair was matted to my desk in the front. (*Come in under the shadow of this red rock.*) Nobody in class laughed, and this surprised me, even though nobody had made a joke. All of a sudden, the other students were gone. Mr. Basketball was at my ear, saying, "Let's listen to dead men not rhyme!" He put on a sombrero and then flicked the end of my cigarette. The ash collected in a tiny pile on my desk. "I will show you fear in a handful of dust!" he said. Then, from the back of the class, my mother laughed. "My mother is dying," I said to him. He walked over to my mother, put my cigarette in her mouth. "Stop it!" I screamed at him. "She's dying!" They both looked at me as though I was guilty of something. "Stop killing us with those turtle shells," they both said in unison. He introduced himself to my mother. "Hi, I'm Jonathan," he said, and they shook hands.

I followed him down the hall. "Are you sleeping with Ms. O'Malley? Are you sleeping with Janice?"

He stopped. He walked back to me, took my arm. He pulled me into a classroom. He pointed his finger at me. He yelled. Something was wrong. Men, they pointed their fingers at me like they were scolding, and I just wanted to touch them.

"I don't want to yell, Emily," he said. "You're a sweet girl, who is perhaps a bit confused at the moment. But it is inappropriate to bribe your teachers or ask them questions like that!"

I took off my kitten mask and twirled around the room to prove how little he could affect me. "Well, if you are dating Ms. O'Malley," I said, "I just thought you should know that she slept with Socrates."

Mr. Basketball opened his mouth. He was going to let me have it. Then, he burst out laughing like a drunk. He laughed and he laughed and he laughed.

"That's just what I've heard," I said, and laughed with him.

It felt so good to laugh with him again that I started crying. That is when I whispered to Mr. Basketball, "My mother is dying."

I repeated this because even though it wasn't true, it felt true. It felt like she was gone, and wasn't that the same thing?

"Emily," he said. "I'm so sorry." He sat down next to me on the desk and looked at me like he knew exactly what I meant.

"My mother is dying," I said.

We looked at the chalkboard and then back at each other and then out the window.

"Do you know how I know you are drunk?" I asked. "If you weren't drunk, you would smell the liquor on my breath."

Mr. Basketball leaned in and put his mouth close to mine. "Smart girl," he said.

He hovered close to me for a moment, looking into my eyes. He seemed afraid of something and this was nice, because I was too, and it was mostly him. My psychology teacher had explained that this kind of terror was perfectly normal. In fact, you weren't healthy unless you feared something violently. "There is so much to be afraid of," she said.

Mr. Basketball was just a boy, I told myself. Only twenty-four. He wasn't like Mr. Heller or Mr. Foster, who both had hairs growing out of their ears. He was smooth, with a trimmed beard. Nothing to be scared about. He put his hand on my thigh and kissed me. I pulled away just to look, to make certain this was happening to me, to make sure it was his tongue in my mouth, and I said, "I can't believe you are doing this," as in, I can't believe this is finally happening to me.

"Would you like for me to stop?" he asked, to which I said, "No," and let him pull me closer to him. He grabbed the back of my neck like I was in a dream, at the opera, falling out of my seat toward something dramatic and incomprehensible. I wanted him closer. I wanted him to put his hands everywhere. How could I ever have tolerated being alone? There was nothing better than this warmth. He pushed my legs apart and pulled me toward him. He put his hand on my chest and pushed my body down so my back was against the table. He dragged his hand down my stomach. This is movement, I thought, this is two people against each other, this is the violence of attraction snapping a nerve in my heart. We didn't even hear the door open.

"Oh my fucking God!" one of the girls screamed.

"Oh my fucking God!" another one shouted. "This is amazing!"

"Mr. Basketball," Martha said, "this is a Hug-Free Zone!" and fell to the ground laughing.

Mr. Basketball jumped away from me. "Are you girls drunk?" he asked. "Come here," he said to all of them. They approached, giddy smiles spilling from their faces. "Now, look. You don't tell anyone what you saw here, and I don't tell anyone that you're drunk. We're both happy. Got it?"

"Yes, Mr. Basketball," said the country of France, her baguette limp at her side.

The slutty banana threw up vermouth and licorice. They scattered. Behind them was Janice, pale and faint as a haunting, in a sweatshirt.

"Janice!" I said.

"Emily," she said.

I wanted to cry out to her. I wanted to wipe the lipstick off my mouth and hold her to my chest and sob until she felt how sorry I was, but she was gone. She had run out the door.

I ran after her, next to her. She didn't look at me. Maybe she was running from me? I didn't know. I didn't try to speak. There was no point. Janice would never forgive me; even if she did forgive me and called me the next day, she would never look at me the same way she had since we both dressed up as bowling pins for Halloween in the third grade and she pointed at me across Mrs. Dagny's room and shouted, "Hey, that's me!"

We congregated in the Cunts R Us bathroom with the Other Girls. The one who hadn't eaten since Saturday sat on the ground and wanted to know how Mr. Basketball tasted: like sugar like honey like aren't those the same exact thing? Brittany, who had always secretly hated me, said she couldn't fucking believe any of it, not even the honey part. Another one looked at Janice and said, "You're such a liar! She was doing Mr. Basketball the whole time!"

The one who had six straight shots of vermouth slid down the wall and passed out on the floor. "Martha!" we shouted. "Are you okay?" We ran to tell Ms. O'Malley there was an emergency in the girls' bathroom. Because there really was. One giant emergency. One of us held Ms. O'Malley's hand as we pulled her through the crowd of students I hardly recognized, arctic animals in miniskirts, Cool and Not Cool, human thongs, science teachers with signs that read FAILED ASTRONAUT, Fuckables masquerading as Unfuckables and vice versa. Fringe members of the Jew Crew came as priests and the president of the Ebony Club came dressed as Tony Blair. We pulled Ms. O'Malley out of the cafeteria, to the bathroom where toilet paper was standing outside the door as a joke. "Need me?" he asked.

"Not at the moment," Ms. O'Malley said. Sometimes, I loved Ms. O'Malley. Sometimes, she reminded me of what our mothers should have been. Corny, lovely, her silk shirt extended all the way to her neck. She held our hands tight as if she didn't even care how little we knew then about being good people.

"What's the emergency?" she asked in her smooth British accent.

We pushed Ms. O'Malley hard through the bathroom door, as if she were stumbling upon a carnival, lit up and spinning and sick to the stomach with thrill.

An ambulance was sent for Martha, who would eventually be fine, who would never drink that much vermouth again. She would become president of the Spanish Club and get into the University of Rochester, where she would lose her virginity to a thirty-year-old from Cork, Ireland.

Ms. O'Malley took us to the principal's office. We sat down in front of Dr. Killigan. One of the girls told Dr. Killigan that she had a brother who was very retarded, even though she didn't. "*Martha's* brother is retarded!" one of us cried.

"But my mother is *dying*!" screamed Brittany. Breast cancer. "*My mother is dying!*" she screamed again, and cried so hard I was afraid she was going to throw up her liver. Dr. Killigan nodded his head. Jotted down a pardon for her on a piece of paper. She got up and left for the school psychiatrist's office. I bit my nail down to the skin and thought of all the dying people I knew. But I knew only dead people. George Washington. T. S. Eliot. Mr. Resnick.

"I don't know anyone who is dying," I said. "And. That. Just. Fucking. Figures."

"Emily, do not swear in this office," Dr. Killigan told me.

"Fine," I said. "Fine." I won't swear and I won't lie. I won't touch older men. I won't roll my skirts up to my thighs. I'll wear stockings made of sheep wool, stockings so thick even my nostrils will sweat. And when I wake up sad about my nightmares, I won't cry. I will put on my best dress and my highest of heels. I will get back into bed and try to wake up all over again, spread my arms wide and shout, "Good morning, everybody!" I will feel like I'm shouting, but nobody will hear. I will grab my backpack and see my mother on her bed in a silk nightgown. She won't be under the covers and this will convince me that she's dead. I will check her heartbeat with two fingers. "Alive," I will say to myself.

"Dr. Killigan," I said, and I wanted to stop but I was blanking out on other things to say. "You can't get mad if I tell you this."

"Tell me what?" he asked. He leaned closer. He scratched his mustache.

But I couldn't move my mouth to say what I thought he should know: Mr. Basketball touched me. He touched me and it hit me to the core and he is my favorite thing. He spread my legs with his thick arms and laid his body on top of mine and it scared me, but only in the really good way, when the pressure was too much and the terror was what kept you alive until the very end.

"Nothing," I said.

"And you?" Dr. Killigan asked Janice.

"Nothing," Janice said.

Dr. Killigan suspended us for a week.

To comfort my mother, I started watching a lot of reruns of *Family Matters, Full House,* and *The Cosby Show* to prove to my mother that a return to family sitcoms was a return to good habits, a return to myself. My mother looked at me during commercials, and instead of telling me I was her angel, she poured out all the liquor that was in our cabinet. She held my hand and asked me to promise that I wouldn't ever be like that again.

"I won't," I told her. "I won't ever be like that again."

"Good," she said. "Now, let's watch the movie." She cradled me in her arms. She rubbed my head. She cried and hummed the opening song to *Sabrina.* She held out a pack of cigarettes.

"I'm not going to smoke," I told her.

"Neither am I," she said. "Let's just pretend."

We put the cigarettes to our lips and watched a movie about a girl who cut her hair short and became happy. We dwelled on how severely the movie departed from logic. Normally, girls cut their hair short and then cried for two to three days. We pulled the unlit sticks from our mouths and laughed like there were haircuts we were too sensible for, and when I put my head on my pillow later that night, my mother didn't tell me to say my prayers, but rather, she said, "Thank you, Emily. Thank you for being my daughter." She turned off the light.

Dr. Killigan swore the drinking incident would go on our record, but it never showed up. The idea of a stained record was enough to make Janice cry right there in her chair, even though senior year, Janice and I applied to the same universities and she was the one who got into the Ivy League–reject schools. I was relieved by this forced separation. I applied to art programs in New York, Los Angeles, and got rejected from all of them except for the Rhode Island School of Design, which was two hours away in Providence.

When we graduated, Janice and I were on two different sides of the auditorium. We were under orders to wear white dresses, white flats, white robes. We were instructed not to throw our caps in celebration. Very dangerous. And under no circumstances was being naked allowed. Smiling, photographs, cheer: welcome.

"Can we hug?" a boy asked.

"Not until you've graduated," Dr. Killigan said.

At the graduation ceremony, the valedictorian preached about living on an island made entirely out of recyclables, while I sat next to girls I never talked to before. We walked. I kept my cap on my head. I watched my mother and father fan themselves with the programs. They were in a room together for the first time since he left and this felt sadder than anything. Mark was in upstate New York with his aunt, graduating from a different high school. Mark got caught with marijuana sophomore year and his mother thought it was best he got a fresh start away from Fairfield. Alex Trimble scratched his crotch. Brittany Stone painted her breasts red and then flashed everybody when she walked. Richard tripped on a wire and face-planted on the ground and everybody laughed, even though Richard cut his face and bled throughout the rest of the ceremony. Mr. Basketball sat with his legs crossed like a choirboy and clapped when I received my diploma.

On the way home, my mother and father chatted politely in the car like strangers, updating each other on their new lives. Prague was nice. So was Fairfield. "So few trees," my father said.

"A lovely daughter you have," my mother said about Laura, but my father thought she meant me. He talked about my accomplishments as a young being: taught herself to read and play the piano, rode a two-wheeler bike when she was three. "So creative," he said. At one point, my father looked at my mother and said, "You look beautiful, Gloria."

"Turn left, Victor," my mother said. "That's our house, right there." We pulled into the driveway. Laura was four, waddling around her driveway with a Welch's grape juice container in her hands. Mrs. Resnick watched her from her stoop. Laura ran to my father. Laura had become a chatty child, a product of Mrs. Resnick constantly placing her in the care of the adults in our neighborhood. Laura learned to read at the Bulwarks'. She grew up watching *Sesame Street* at my mother's. Took her first steps at the Trentons'. Alfred taught her how to check the oil in the car, how to know when the gutters were full. "Learn it while you're young," he said, "and the boys won't be able to stay away."

My father got out of the car, twirled Laura in the air as though he knew her. I smiled, and even though I tried my best to understand it all, my heart broke a little.

Nobody ever talked about what happened between Mr. Basketball and me, and this surprised me at first. Every day, I waited for the truth to come out. Every day, I waited for Mr. Basketball to be taken down the hallway in handcuffs. But every day, nothing. Every day, Mr. Basketball stood outside his classroom door, welcoming students inside. I supposed my criminal justice teacher was right; when one person witnessed a crime, there was an 80 percent chance he would report it, but if four people witnessed a crime, there was a 10 percent chance one of them would report it.

Junior year at one of Martha's elaborate birthday parties (Martha still on occasion wanted to be my friend and invited me to things even though nobody else did), Janice waved her beer in the air and asked me what happened with Mr. Basketball. She took a long sip and then demanded to know what it was about her that didn't work exactly. Why couldn't she just look like me, and if she did look like me, would that have been enough? Would Mr. Basketball have fucked her instead? Just tell me how many times, she said. Just tell her. Did he ask for her while he was with me, and if he did, what did it sound like when he said her name? Was it even possible to feel romantic with his dick so old and large, expanding like a drying sponge inside me?

"I don't know," I said. "Maybe."

Janice took out her ponytail. She tousled her hair and prepared to walk away. "You were my best friend," she said. "When I saw him on top of you, I said to myself, 'Who is that man raping my best friend?'"

# 19

My mother made me go see Ron the psychiatrist one more time. I hated Ron, the way he stared at my mother when she dropped me off at the door. I hated how my mother wore a black dress with a shiny red plastic belt, like dropping me off at someone's house was something to look sexy for, or how she let him take the check out of her hand so slowly that their index fingers touched and it became obvious she wasn't wearing her wedding ring anymore. I hated the way he talked so flatly, "Emilywhydon'tyoucomein," his words strung together like sterile white Christmas lights. When I sat in his chair and listened to him ask me about my life, it felt like sitting in my father's luxury car that rode so smooth I vomited all over the leather seats. I was so horrified to have ruined his seats, I kept quiet and put my sweater over the mess. My father was in the front seat driving, saying over and over again, "Tell me the truth, Emily. Did you vomit on the seats?" And I would never admit it, shouting, "No, it wasn't me!" and even when my father stopped the car to check the seats, even when he held me in his arms and said, "It's okay, it's not your fault you are sick," I refused to claim the vomit as my own, because the way I saw it, it wasn't the truth that solved our problems; the truth was always just the beginning of our problems.

"There's not much to talk about," I told Ron.

"Why do I feel like that's not the truth?" he asked.

The truth was a week after the Halloween in Spring, I sat in Mr. Basketball's car in some corduroy skirt thing and purple strappy sandals that laced up my ankles. We drove to the valley, the low swooping forest between Fairfield and Westport where Janice and I went as younger girls to watch the older kids smoke weed and make out against trees. On the way there, I listened to Mr. Basketball talk about how inappropriate it was for us to touch. He was sorry, *so* sorry. He was *twenty-four,* he kept saying. I was *fifteen*.

"When I was in *college,*" he said, "you were in *fifth grade*."

He looked straight ahead at the dirt road and said, "It's just not a good idea." He was regretful.

I put his hand between my legs.

"Stop it," he said, but didn't take his hand back.

I pressed his fingers harder against me until he moved his fingers around my underwear and inside me.

"I don't know what I'm doing," Mr. Basketball said. "But I can't stop thinking about this."

His hand was a tight fit. That was fine. Better that way. He took one finger inside me. I held tightly on to the door handle.

"Don't open it by accident," he said, and locked it, and for one never-ending second, I felt like a child again, my excitement something to be feared, something he couldn't control. *I am not a child,* I wanted to scream.

Mr. Basketball put another finger inside me as if he heard me and I remember it feeling like a tampon but a little bit better. He rubbed them back and forth against me, his other hand on the wheel. He even put his blinker on at some point, even though there were no other cars. I heard the clicking of the blinker, back and forth and back and forth and back and forth, a metronome. My eyes were wide open.

"Relax," Mr. Basketball said.

"*You* relax," I said.

He filled me, slowly, with every finger, every turn, and I felt my legs spread. I am free, I thought, free and pressed against the world and hoping that everything I learned from my past as an optimistic child was true: a gentleman never asks for anything in return.

The first few times Mr. Basketball and I had sex, we managed to do it without having to see each other naked. The first time we did it we were parked in his car in the valley. We climbed into the backseat. We didn't even speak, except once when he said, "This may feel strange for the first few seconds." He didn't even fully take my pants off. He slipped them down to my thighs. I remember the constriction feeling the best. Then he pulled out. His penis was scary to me at first. His penis looked like an alien in my hands, growing with my help, and I found ways not to touch it, until he guided my hands up and down. He groaned when I moved it fast, closed his eyes and rested his head against the window, and I got less scared each time, accepting the power such a simple act offered me.

And then once in the music storage room. It was cold. The room was small with thin gray carpet and I cried after in my bed thinking of how sad the violins looked alone in the corner. It was embarrassing to have sex in front of the wrong things, especially a violin, which was so dignified at every angle. I was sure Mr. Basketball felt this way too while I was bent over on the table. We were disgusting at that angle. He even went soft while he was inside me, and it felt like my fault, the violin's fault.

"It's my fault," Mr. Basketball said, pulling out of me. "Don't you ever think this is your fault."

"I don't," I said. My insides burned. We didn't speak for weeks. Freshman year ended. I stood up in front of the class and recited my verse of "The Waste Land."

" 'For you know only a heap of broken images,' " I said. " 'Where the sun beats, and the dead tree gives no shelter, the cricket no relief, and the dry stone no sound of water.' "

Mr. Basketball wrote things down on his clipboard.

" 'Only there is shadow under this red rock, (come in under the shadow of this red rock), and I will show you something different from either your shadow at morning striding behind you or your shadow at evening rising to meet you; I will show you fear in a handful of dust. *Frisch weht der Wind. Der Heimat zu. Mein Irisch Kind, wo weilest du?*' "

Mr. Basketball corrected my pronunciation. A knife sent straight to my spleen.

"How would you know?" I asked him, standing in front of the class. "You're not even *German.*"

Mr. Basketball clenched his jaw, like I was going to scream the truth to the entire classroom. Like I was that stupid.

We were over. He ignored me in the hallways, didn't return my glances. I saw him touch Ms. O'Malley's arm in the lunchroom and then open the door for her as they walked out.

But then we did it late one night at school on Lillian Biggs's table at the back of the room. I wasn't expecting it. I had returned to school to clean out my locker. My mother was in her car waiting for me in the parking lot. I walked by Mr. Basketball's classroom and saw him taking down our haikus from the wall. He asked if I wanted to help.

"Sure," I said. I took a tack out of the board and after a few minutes, he came up behind me. His hands were warm on my hips. I wasn't even ready for it. I was taking down the poems thinking of how little my mother knew about my life; how I was inside the school about to have sex with a man nearly twice my age and she was drumming her nails on the dashboard wondering if we should have asparagus for dinner. Mr. Basketball was pulling down my pants from the back. He was hard and I was dry and the sun was setting. I was reading the last line of Lillian's haiku when he came into me, which wasn't a haiku either: *the wind whistles in winter and for who?* It felt like newspapers being shoved inside me. I bled, even though it was our third time, and the blood collected in the balloon that Lillian had carved into the wood when she was bored. He looked at it, and then at me, apologizing for something, like for a second he thought he had killed me.

# 20

I was seventeen when my mother went on her first date: Ron the psychiatrist had asked her to go to an art gallery opening in Stamford. She danced around the kitchen all morning, hummed along with the gurgling coffeepot, told me how nice it would be to date a psychiatrist since a psychiatrist would already know what she needed. "He's my *psychiatrist*," I said. "Emily," she said. "Be serious. You only went three times." But when she came home from the date, she kissed me on the forehead and said, "Too weird."

After that, she went on dates nearly every night. The next guy was Seth. He worked for an advertising firm in Westport. He was balding. His feet were larger than my head. He said, "Nice to meet you," and then asked me about my schoolwork like I was a seventeen-year-old on the brink of discovering a cancer gene. "It's going very well, thank you," I said.

My mother hated him. I could tell by the way she was stiff at breakfast, polishing her nails, cucumbers for eyes all morning on the couch. And by the time he arrived, dressed head to toe in suede, she hunched her shoulders and threw on her fleece coat like she was already disappointed about the night she had.

Then there was Max, and then Nate, and then Gary, who she met off a dating website my aunt Lee convinced her to join. "Gary is seventy percent my match," my mother said to me, reading off the screen. "Sixteen percent my enemy."

I laughed.

"Whatever that means," my mother said. "We're going to the opera. His idea."

When Gary arrived at our front door, he was incredibly handsome with a full mouth. Gary was also 90 percent blind from a car accident ten years earlier, something he hadn't mentioned on his web profile.

"Blind? How did you get here?" my mother asked.

"Cab," Gary said.

"Come in," she said. My mother took me in the kitchen. "Don't pester him about being blind," my mother said, pouring out salsa in a bowl. "He's probably a very normal person, just like you and me. No wonder he wanted to go to the opera. If you are going to speak, ask him about the opera."

I didn't know anything about the opera other than the fact that "opera" was the plural of "opus," so said my vocab teacher Mrs. Miller, who kept holding me after class saying, "I'm worried about your vocab, Emily, you didn't do all your vocab sheets."

We sat down for chips and salsa at our coffee table, and I said, "How do you feel about being blind, Gary?"

My mother crunched loud on a chip.

"Well, Emily, blindness isn't really the problem you might think it is," Gary said, picking up a chip. "It's all the confusion that exists around the blindness that's the shitter."

I licked some salt off my finger. What a perfect face.

"With enough help, I barely notice."

Gary finished his chip, and I asked him about the last thing he ever saw: a road sign that said CAUTION DUCKS.

"Gary, we're going to be late," my mother said, standing up and swinging her white spring jacket around her body.

When she went on dates, I went on dates. Junior year, I had my first real boyfriend, Daniel Blank, who had been coming over to my house every other night for the past two weeks. Even though my mother wasn't home, for some reason I didn't want Daniel to know this; I didn't want him to think that there was nothing we couldn't do in the freedom of my unsupervised house. So when he asked if he could come over, I said, "Only if we take a vow of silence. My mom is sleeping upstairs."

Daniel arrived in a hoodie and corduroys, and we sat on two separate ends of the couch, and he wrote me a note on a piece of paper that said, *Do we break our vows when we sneeze?* These were the questions seventeen-year-olds asked, these were the questions we easily answered: yes, of course. Daniel was afraid to kiss me, so every night he left holding out his arms, saying, "Hug?" I hated Daniel against my breasts and I hated him a little more every time he came over. I guess the thing about regularly having sex with an older man was that when you tried to touch someone your own age, it felt like touching a child, Daniel's smooth jaw like a baby's bottom.

After Daniel left, I slipped on the green dress with bulky pockets that I wore almost all throughout my junior year in high school and ran through the dark to Mr. Basketball's. I passed Mark's house and thought of Laura inside, two years old now, learning how to form "oh's" and "ah's" with her mouth.

Mr. Basketball was having me over two, sometimes three, nights a week. I used the fire escape to get in.

When I got inside, the bathwater was running.

"What took you so long?" Mr. Basketball asked.

"I have homework, you know," I said.

Mr. Basketball liked to watch me bathe. I rubbed the soap over my breasts and he watched from the doorway. "You are so beautiful," he said. "I can't stand it." He stood by the toilet and dropped his pants. His penis hung large and twenty-six years old against his thigh. He lit a vanilla candle on his sink. He climbed in the warm soapy water, and I measured our waists with my eye. Mine was half the size of his. I laid my head against the back of the white tub. I put my hands around his waist and on his butt.

"You have hair on your ass," I said.

"I know that," he said. We laughed. I felt the coarse hairs with my fingertips.

He put his mouth on me under the water. I liked him better this way. Clean. Sterile. There was nothing dangerous about a naked man in water. Even though he weighed one hundred and seventy pounds he felt as weightless as a bedsheet. There was nothing he could do to me in water that wouldn't wash away. I held on to the sides of the bath with my hands, and his touch was different. He was an unpredictable fusion of body and water, and even with all the pressure on us, I could hardly feel him.

The water rose as he moved up my torso with his head, some of it filling my ears so when he came up for air and spoke, his voice was muffled. "Bub bum boat on bib," he said, pointing to his dick, which was now lying on top of my chest like a hot dog. I sat up out of the water.

"*What?*" I asked.

The candle flame throbbed behind us.

"Rub some soap on it," he said.

I climbed out of the tub.

"That's barbaric," I said.

"What? The soap makes it more sensitive."

I rubbed my legs with the towel. "I'm dating someone," I told him.

"What?" he said. "Who?"

I stood there naked. The oil from the tub made the water bead down my chest.

"Daniel Blank, right?" Mr. Basketball asked. "With the lip ring? I've seen you two together a lot lately."

"We're almost in love."

"We call him Lip Ring Boy in the lunchroom," Mr. Basketball said. "He's nice. Apparently, not very good at chemistry."

He climbed out of the tub.

"You're a terrible teacher," I said, and this made him pull me close and kiss me hard until my back hurt and his beard scraped my lips and my cheeks were wet from his hands. I was on his sink now, my legs separated by his hips.

"Don't do this to me," Mr. Basketball said, holding the ends of my long wet brown hair. "Don't date boys. Don't date Daniel Blank."

"I like boys," I said. "Boys don't have hair on their asses."

"Don't be cruel like this, Emily."

But I didn't like boys. Boys never made sense to me. Their bones were too long for their skin, their acne-faces so red and wilting, they were too embarrassed to look you in the eye, too embarrassed not to look you in the eye, their mouse voices you could barely hear over the music, which was always blasting in my ear. Their breath was irregular and scentless, these boys were always overbrushing their teeth and overminting their mouths in cars, always playing music with no detectable melody, and no matter how long you listened, they never successfully communicated anything. I hated sitting in cars, and on couches, and hugging with closed fists. I liked beards and full calves and throaty, fire-crackling voices that crashed right into my throat, I liked men who tasted like something, who were a part of the world, who felt heavy on my chest, Mr. Basketball warm inside me.

He put his hand on the back of my neck, and I held on to the towel rack. The screenless window was wide open at my head, and I waited for the air to fill my ears, the tiny mosquitoes to come sink their teeth into my cheeks, to suck out all the evil that was in my blood, and before I felt any of this kind of healing, Mr. Basketball whispered in my ear, "You are so good." He kissed me on the mouth.

"There is nothing better than this," he said, and I worried he was right. I worried that once something had entered you, it would never leave—he would plant himself inside me and grow and grow until I was nothing but him. I held on to the sides of his body, and as he came, I heard a tiny push of breath in my ear and we nearly cried.

Mr. Basketball dropped me off at the end of my street and while I sprinted through the dark to my house, the yard felt predatory, but I was full inside. I didn't even care that I was going to be in trouble. I knew my mother was already home because I knew she didn't really have it in her to date a blind man; as much as she would have liked to believe her heart was as golden as that of our new neighbor Mrs. Wallaby, who was married to a quadriplegic, we both knew my mother wouldn't go home with Gary. She didn't want to be the one who had to drive, or open the door, or boil the tea.

"Your hair is wet, Emily," my mother shouted as I ran up the stairs. "Why is your hair wet?"

"I liked Gary," I shouted back, and shut my bedroom door.

After Gary, my mother didn't go on any more dates. She was back to her bed again. She was almost forty, she complained. She was back to the therapist, a new therapist. Seeing this one two times a week now.

The more my mother saw the therapist, the more sex I had with Mr. Basketball, about three times a week at this point, and during my health class I worried that perhaps it was too much sex, that perhaps tampons would someday be too small for me. I wished somebody would have asked our health teacher Mrs. Blumenthal if something like this was even possible, so I could know if I was being ridiculous or not, but nobody did. Only Leroy Hannah spoke in health, raised his hand to ask Mrs. Blumenthal if vaginitis was the condition of constantly having a vagina, if there was any documented case of a cheerleader getting pregnant while doing a leg kick, and she just shook her head, reminded us that it only took one little sperm to make life bloom inside you; too many girls my age gave birth without even knowing they were pregnant, fetuses drop from our hips like underwear, "and it's an awful thing," Mrs. Blumenthal said. "A kind of murder." Then she passed out a test issued by the government with questions nobody could understand:

Most genital infections are transient, producing no sequelae (True?)

Where do condoms come from? (Trees?)

The female condom can be inserted into the vagina for how long before vaginal intercourse? (Condoms can be *female*?)

Mr. Basketball and I never had sex with condoms, male or female. We tried, but there was always an excuse; the condom was too far under the bed, or he bought the wrong kinds, or etc., etc., etc. I pressed down on my stomach and it felt harder than usual. How could I have been so stupid? Nobody was this stupid. I sat at my desk and convinced myself I was pregnant. I went to the bathroom, sure that you immediately detected anything foreign inside you, rubbed my hand over my stomach until I felt a giant, hard bulge swell between my hips.

I rubbed my breasts. The flab was tender. But my breasts had been tender since I had gotten breasts. I put my finger to my underwear. It was wet. Janice would have known what this meant, but Janice wouldn't even look at me anymore. She walked down the hallway with Brittany now and ignored my gaze, the two of them in matching brown boots, the two of them growing out their hair and nibbling on ecstasy pills between class, spreading rumors: Emily Vidal has regular sex with Satan.

I waited at Mr. Basketball's car after school.

"You can't wait at my car like this, Emily," Mr. Basketball said.

"I'm pregnant," I said.

"Jesus," he said. "In the car."

We got in the car.

"You're not pregnant," he said.

"How would you know?"

"I've only come inside you once," he said.

"So," I said, furious. "If you shot me in the head once, I'd still be dead."

We were silent until Lake Avenue.

"I'm seventeen," I said. "That's when my body wants me to have a baby."

"If you are so concerned take a pregnancy test," he said. "But you're not pregnant. Do you know how many times I've ejaculated inside a woman and not gotten her pregnant?"

"You're disgusting," I said. "That's a disgusting thing to say."

"I'm trying to reason with you here," he said.

At Stop and Shop, he said, "I'd go in with you, but . . ."

"I can walk from here, thanks," I said, and gave him the finger.

"Emily," he said. "Please calm down."

I walked away, determined to hate him forever. In the grocery line, I put a pregnancy test and a stalk of broccoli on the conveyor belt.

"Twelve fifty," the cashier said.

"I only have ten dollars," I said.

She removed the stalk of broccoli. "Ten dollars and five cents. I'll cover the five."

"Yes," I said. "Thank you."

I couldn't wait until I got all the way home to find out if I was pregnant, so I ran through the woods between the two main streets of my town, Lake and Bolt, and squatted behind an oak tree. I urinated on the stick and some splashed on my pants around my ankles and I closed my eyes. "It will be okay," I repeated to myself, as I waited for the two pink lines to appear. "It will be okay." Mary or Martha or Katherine or Geneva will be a lovely girl, I thought, nothing at all like myself, she will have long blond hair, and she won't cry at night, and she will eat tuna sandwiches without complaint, she will read the entire newspaper every morning and she will never date boys who don't have a GPA of 3.5 or higher, she will wear wool socks and polish her toes and she will emerge from my womb acutely aware of the fact that a female condom is an internal device used to prevent pregnancy and can be inserted in the vagina at least eight hours before vaginal intercourse.

Negative.

I threw the stick to the ground and ran all the way to Mr. Basketball's apartment.

I arrived breathless. He was behind his screen door, biting on a carrot.

"I'm not pregnant," I said.

"Come in," he said, opening the door for me.

His apartment was a tiny condo in a complex next to the commuter parking lot. It was carpeted, brand-new, and bare of anything essential, but at first, this was what I liked about it. I was impressed by the mere idea of having your own home and never feeling compelled to fill up the space. This was a good sign. He was a man who kept only what he needed and that included me. I walked around the apartment thinking, Wow, this is where your microwave could be. Wow, this is where you could have a fruit basket. This is where the light could hit the mirror on your blue walls and make everything feel like the outside.

Mr. Basketball had a slab of beef on the counter. He cut the meat into squares. He was going to make a stew, he said. He was upset. He was throwing chunks of butter into a pot. He sliced carrots on a board. He wanted to know why I behaved the way I did earlier.

"Don't say 'behave,'" I said.

He said he understood I was young, he knew that and was ready to deal with that, and I said, "Deal with my youth? Like that's the problem?" I asked.

"I know this is scary for you," he said.

He said it was scary for him too. "Don't you understand that?" he asked. "I'm a part of this. I'm a person."

I dragged my hand across his chest and unzipped his fly.

"No," I said.

I put his penis in my mouth, and I could still hear him above saying, "This is scary." I heard him slide the carrots into the pot. They sizzled. His life hung by a thread when he was around me, and we both knew this. I could be anyone I wanted around him, my good self, my hateful self, my needy and terrible self, and he would love me because at the core, I was a young girl with long brown hair and as I continued to hold him in my mouth, the quieter he became, the better we both felt.

He slid down the kitchen cabinets and took my face in his hands. "Jesus," he said. "You are so young."

He had red wine teeth. I wiped his mouth with my fingers.

"Oh for Christ's sake," I said. "I'm seventeen. In a different century, I would already know how to skin a chicken with my teeth and feed four children off my breasts and have five years left to live."

"Fair enough," he said. "Are you staying for dinner?"

"Yes," I said. "Yes I am."

We ate at his kitchen table and over the silence of the meal, it occurred to me that even though I'd just held his semen in my mouth—"babies," I had joked while I inspected the fluid like a scientist—we had never eaten together before. I had never seen him take his knife and fork and cut into his steak, just as he had never seen me drag a carrot across my plate. He was sipping on wine and I was drinking water. I reached out for his wineglass and drank some. This made us both nervous.

"Thanks for dinner," I said. "You're a real Batali."

He smiled.

"You don't even know who that is, do you?" I asked, imitating the tone he used to ask questions of Lillian Biggs, who never ever knew the answer in English class.

"Fat man," he said. "White shirt."

It was official: it didn't matter what I knew. It didn't matter if I read the dictionary from front to back or if I could conduct a twenty-minute conversation in Spanish or solve a math problem with three variables. It didn't matter if I learned how to get my mother to stop crying at night (hand on back, goofy grin on face) or if my legs grew thin, my breasts sturdy and reliable things, my face strong and lean now, my skin tightening at each cheekbone (eat a cheeseburger, my mother kept saying). It didn't matter if Mr. Basketball and I had sex backward or forward or with my knees at my ears or if I swallowed or spat or *put soap on it,* it didn't matter how careful both of us had been never to mention the word "rape"—there would never be one thing I knew that Mr. Basketball didn't already know. This was why all of our teachers and parents warned us about getting involved with adults; this was why they passed out sexual abuse pamphlets during school assemblies and grown-up women perched on stools and talked about the time that Benny (the uncle) showed his penis to Karen (the ten-year-old) and that when Benny put his privates to Karen's privates (privates being anything that was normally covered by a bathing suit) it felt good, Karen told all five hundred of us in the auditorium, even though it also felt bad.

"It felt good to my nerve endings," Karen said, and I couldn't even open my eyes because I knew that Mr. Basketball was bright red in the front of the auditorium, and that the whole school was staring at me in my seat. "But bad for my heart."

"Thank you, Karen," Dr. Killigan said, taking the microphone from her.

Mr. Basketball and I cleaned the dishes, and he put his hand up my shirt. It was soapy. When he kissed me, his tongue was gritty down the side of my neck. When his mouth reached the tips of my fingers, I practiced distancing myself from him, pretended it was just a cat, licking butter off my finger with its tongue.


My father called home to say, "Your mother tells me you need to eat a cheeseburger."

"Very funny, Dad," I said.

"Your mother tells me you have a boyfriend," he said.

"Oh, cut it out, Dad."

"Is he nice?"

"He's all right."

"What's his name?"

"Daniel."

"Is he smart?"

"He wants to be the president of the United States."

"That doesn't sound very smart."

"He can be kind of mean."

"Mean how?"

"He makes fun of fat people," I said. This was true.

He laughed.

"A lot," I said.

"Then why is he your boyfriend?" he asked. "You can do better than that."

\* \* \*

Daniel confessed to me late one night on my couch that he wanted to get to third with me, that he's been afraid to unbutton my pants out of fear of how I might react. He was sweaty and red and breathless, like this was a confession he had been holding in all summer long. "You make me feel like I can't or something," he said. "Well you can't," I said.

I discovered jean shorts that summer. "Daisy Dukes," my mother called them.

Mr. Basketball and I were better during the summers. The sun made us feel like better people. Before I entered my senior year, Mr. Basketball and I slept together on a real bed nearly every day. Mr. Basketball started to ask me if I would call him Jonathan. I was almost eighteen. "No," I said. We were in his apartment. We lay on his bed and spent too long next to each other, amazed at how normal touching each other felt out of school. We were just like any two people: we laughed and we slept and we loved each other and when we got hungry, our stomachs growled.

"That's our stomachs saying hello to each other," Mr. Basketball said.

"I can't understand what they are saying," I said.

"They speak Spanish."

"I didn't know my stomach was fluent."

"Oh, they're just saying hello. No need to be fluent for that."

But then high school started again and in the hallways, Mr. Basketball would look at me like I was any of the other students, like I was Janice or Martha or Lillian Biggs, and I would go into the bathroom and cry until it hurt.

People graduated, dyed the underside of their hair pink, cut the legs off their jeans, screamed out windows of cars, drank and drank and drank until Marcy Livingstone got pregnant and made everyone feel guilty for it. I sat on my driveway at home, sober and anxious, waiting for Mr. Basketball to bring me to his apartment.

My mother kept a watchful eye. She found me in a skirt on the stoop and bent down to look at me. "Why are you dressed like that?"

"Dressed like what?" I asked.

"Like *that*," she said.

"This doesn't even go above my knees," I told her.

"It's not how short it is. It's how tight it is. Do you want everyone to see the outline of your crotch?"

"Maybe."

"Since when do you wear skirts?" she asked, and this did not make me angry as much as it saddened me. I was wearing skirts and this made my mother sad because where could she wear her skirt to? That was what she was asking me, and we both knew that she would never ask it like that and I would never answer her the right way.

My mother sat down next to me and lit a cigarette. "A woman wears skirts when she needs to look pretty. I know this, Emily," she said.

I could not look at her face. I heard the sound of her cigarette leaving her mouth and felt the trail of smoke reach my nose.

"You're sleeping with that man, aren't you, Emily? That man who drops you off at the house sometimes?"

I pretended to be offended. "What man?" I asked, standing up. "I don't know what man you are talking about."

"I'll call the police right now," my mother said, and so I protested as I walked away from her: Mom, please stop it, you are overreacting, you are being embarrassing, who is feeding you this bullshit? I can't help it if there are men who want to drive me home, and well, who can blame them; she said, Emily, you are beautiful and you need to be aware of that, you need to start being real aware of that.


"Were you not going to pick me up?" I asked when I arrived at Mr. Basketball's apartment, sweaty and red, my legs chafed between the thighs.

"I was on my way," he said, sipping on some wine. There was the beagle, Penelope, quietly sleeping in the corner of the room.

"Mr. Basketball," I said, walking through the door, "your place is a mess."

"Please, Emily, I told you to call me by my name."

"Why?"

"Why? It's my name."

But I couldn't. I was afraid to. So I just stopped addressing him. And he was still secretly afraid to see me naked during the day even though I was eighteen now and my breasts hung circular from my chest, full at the bottom. He took off my shirt like he was removing a Band-Aid. Then my bra. He turned me around. His stomach was against my back, and he kissed my neck with his mouth. Then my ear, my spine. He watched me drop my skirt, then put me on the bed slowly like I was sick.

I was in awe of Mr. Basketball when we were in school and embarrassed of him out of school, especially in the morning, when his hair was greasy and clumped, early bald spots exposed. His bed was really just an elaborate futon, and he didn't even have a sheet on it. Just a black comforter and a worn-out pillow, and crumbs sometimes stuck to my legs. He had a poster on the wall celebrating the achievements of Quentin Tarantino and napkins that hung out of the pantry. He had so many TV dinners stocked in his freezer he joked about nuclear fallout to avoid feeling embarrassed. Frozen broccoli, turkey medallions, chicken breast with a mysterious sauce. Orange juice from concentrate. A sock in the utensil drawer. A key chain that said IRELAND and when I asked him why Ireland, he didn't even know.

"This is where you could put a fruit basket," I said, pointing to the bare table. "And this is where you could hang curtains. You can choose to block out all this light if you wish."

"I like my place the way it is, thanks," he said.

"I'm just saying. You have more choices than you think you do."


Two weeks before I left for college, he kissed me on the mouth and got out of bed. "I can't believe you're leaving me in this shit hole." He turned on the gas stove and cracked an egg into a bowl. With my eyes closed, the world sounded angry. "What am I supposed to do without you?"

"You're not making eggs, are you?" I asked sleepily in my white bulky underwear that I only wore at the end of my laundry cycle ("Harriet," he sometimes called it).

"Sure am."

"I hate the way you cook."

"And what way is that?"

"Like nobody ever taught you how."

He said nobody ever did teach him how.

"You scratch the pan with a fork. You're not supposed to do that."

"Says who?"

"I'm leaving."

"Don't leave like that," he said, and walked over to me. "Don't leave complaining about my pans."

"You don't live right."

I picked my jeans off the floor and stuck a leg in each hole. He walked over, pressed his stomach into my back, put his hands around my waist. "Don't leave," he said.

"You don't have extra things like cheese," I said. "You don't have amenities. You don't have soap that smells any good. You're twenty-seven and you hate your job and you have nothing besides a sock in the utensil drawer."

"You're eighteen," he said. "What do you have?"

"My whole life," I said.

He moved his hands down my thighs, until I turned around and met him with my face. "Just eat the eggs," he said.

He said that sometimes when he was alone in his bed, he worried he was becoming obsessed with me. Consumed in a way he felt too old for, too tired for. He said he'd draw the lines of my body with his finger at night. He used the white ceiling as a canvas. He slept next to someone else to feel independent of me, someone his age, someone who wore too many gold rings and went to the gym every day just to feel good, someone who understood exactly what he meant when he said, "I'm bored of Nietzsche, just so bored of him," someone who posed questions in his head about the strangeness of feeling.

"Whose beagle is that?" I asked.

"A friend's," he said.

"You *cannot* sleep with other women," I said. "That's not fair to me."

"I'll stop sleeping with her when you can say my name properly," he said.

"How can you sleep with someone else?"

"How can you keep calling me Mr. Basketball, like I'm some kind of a joke or something?"

"You are a joke!" I said, angry. "You've always been a joke. You were just supposed to be a joke."

Janice and I had always dreamed of touching him since the moment we saw him walking down the hall freshman year. We laughed on the bus thinking about touching him, how crazy to have Mr. Basketball's balls in our hands and his hands on our tiny bodies. "His butt is sooo amazing," Janice said sometimes, but this was always supposed to be a joke because we didn't even know what separated a good butt from a bad butt ("It's all just butt," I told Janice).

And when it was real, it wasn't funny, when you touched someone, they were always with you. When his mouth was on mine, we held the same breath in the same moment, and when he was naked, his body was covered in tiny black hairs that stuck to my clothes even after I washed them. He had slowly become a part of me and when he was cruel, or cold, or acted like we couldn't go on like this anymore, it felt like he was ripping my limbs off, one at a time. Janice had always understood this kind of pain, but I didn't, not until now, listening to Mr. Basketball explain how easy it was to be with me one day and someone else the next. He would feel the woman's curly hair against his chest, and he'd think about me. Her hair would itch like a wool carpet against his skin, and mine was smooth like silk, and that was when he knew: it was only in difference that we realized whom we loved.

"What does that *mean*?" I asked.

"I love you," he said. "I love you I love you I love you."

I loved him so much I let him take off my shirt right there while the eggs were burning. I loved his sand hair, his accidental handsomeness. It was all too human and overwhelming. He touched me the same way every time, the neck down to the chest to the pubic bone. He made my shape seem so contrived, planned just the way he would want me, as though he charted and mapped me, a body so simple he had already memorized it. He held my hips with his two hands, centering me under him. This man could kill me, I thought, snap me in two if he so pleased. Hang me from the back porch to dry. And then his grasp would soften. His fingers would dance on my skin. He was so surprising in his features, a different person at every angle. He was sleeping with other women.

"Sometimes, randomly and unexpectedly, I don't even know you," I said, pushing him off me, backing away.

"Maybe you don't," he said, moving toward the stove, scraping the eggs with a fork. "Maybe I'm not myself. Maybe I'm reincarnated, an ancient Egyptian goat herder."

"Impossible," I said. "You're too lazy."

"Not impossible. There are so many reasons to believe in reincarnation. So many accounts, Emily, so many children who know other languages, never having been exposed to them before. Or people who can describe their old bodies down to the tiniest fatal wound that matches with the corpse they claim to have been in."

"Okay, teacher," I said. "Cut it out."

"What would you want to come back as," he said, scraping the burnt parts onto a dish as though that was suitable breakfast, "if you could come back?"

"A chair," I said. "That couch. A crumb. You?"

"Be serious," he said.

"Well, to be serious, I don't think we come back."

He took this personally. "You have to come back," he said. "You are coming back."

"I'm not," I said, shrugging him off me. "I'm not coming back."

He threw the dish in the sink, and I closed the door to his apartment quietly.


We didn't speak for a week, and a few nights before I left Connecticut, my mother asked me to put on a nice dress because a man named Bill was coming over for dinner.

"Gross," I said.

"Emily, please be nice," she said. "Go take a shower, clean yourself up."

"Sorry," I said. "I have plans tonight."

I woke up that morning panicking at the thought of never seeing Mr. Basketball again. I put on a nice dress and left my mother, who had begun to drip olive oil over a pan. Mr. Basketball was reading when I showed up, and he welcomed me with open arms. I lay down on his bed, and he kissed my bare shoulder. I rested my head on his chest and listened to his heart beat. We were both sorry.

The beagle was in the corner of the room, chewing on a string.

"Let's go for a drive," I said.

We started driving to Westport, the town over. He suggested maybe getting some frozen custard; there was this place he said, far outside of Fairfield, that was real good.

Everything was fine until Mr. Basketball ran a stoplight on Bullfrog Lane. The stoplight was so well placed in the middle of a four-way intersection it took you to any part of Fairfield you'd ever dream of going to. You could go north or south or east or west and either way, you could drive for ten minutes and you'd be in some other town in Connecticut that looked entirely the same, and there, you'd have to make another decision about whether to go north or south or east or west.

"Jonathan!" I shouted, gripping the door handle.

"That's the first time you've ever called me Jonathan," he said, ignoring the fact that he ran a stoplight. As soon as I said his name aloud, it felt good to call him Jonathan. Why hadn't I before? "I thought I would like it," he said.

"Jonathan, do you realize you ran a stoplight? You could have killed us."

"Stop calling me that. It sounds so strange. Too strange."

"You can't just run stoplights and ignore me. That's not what a relationship is."

He looked over at me. Then he pulled over on the side of the road. The car was so silent, I could hear the brown tuft of hair slip out from behind his ear.

"A relationship?" he finally asked.

"Yes," I said.

"Tell me, Emily. How come your mother is still alive?"

"Huh?"

"Your mother. You told me when we first kissed that your mother was dying, three years ago."

I looked out the window. "My mother wasn't dying," I said. "I lied.

She was perfectly healthy. I'm sorry, I don't know why I said that. In fact, I forgot I even said that."

"So she wasn't even dying?" he asked, and hit the steering wheel.

"Would you prefer it if she had been?"

He put his head against the wheel. "What the fuck have I done?"

"You ran a stoplight," I said.

"What are we going to do?"

"I don't know," I said. "I don't know."

I cried as though crying were a reasonable substitute for making a decision.

"You're a little girl," he said. "Look at you, you're crying."

"Don't diminish me," I said, rubbing my eyes.

"You are a tiny girl who is in pain."

"Shut up!" I yelled.

"Who are you, anyway? What are you doing in my life?"

Trees hung above the roof of the car and blocked the last of the day's sun. Every moment, there was something new to want.

"Please don't," I said.

"I'm sorry, Emily," he said. "This isn't right."

"What isn't?"

"You are too young."

"No," I said, crying. "I love you."

He dropped me off at a gas station. He drove away, and poof, just like that, he was gone. Mr. Basketball was here, and then he wasn't. He was someone to me, and then he wasn't. I looked at the aisles of Oreos and Clorox cleaner, pretending to shop, but window-shopping at a gas station minimart, I found out, was nearly impossible. I turned over packages of Pringles, waiting for my mother to pick me up, and I didn't even cry as I saw his car turn left for the last time. That was the difference between children and adults.

"Children have a problem with that kind of stuff," my mother said after I babysat for Laura and I told my mother that she cried when I tried to play peekaboo with her. "That's what Ron said. Someone goes out of their sight and they believe that person to be gone forever. You cover your face, and Laura can't imagine ever seeing you again. You were like that."

At home, Bill was standing in the kitchen. My mother picked up the wine and loaf of anisette dough she had left in order to come get me.

"Hi, Emily," Bill said. Bill wore pleated khakis and parted his almond hair down the middle.

"Oh, Jesus," I said, rolling my eyes. "Bill's here."

"Emily," my mother scolded. The phone rang. I picked it up. It was Mrs. Resnick.

"Mrs. Resnick needs someone to watch Laura," I said, grabbing my purse.

My mother held up her hands covered in dough. "We have a guest."

"You have a guest," I said. "I have to go see my sister."

"You aren't going to help me with the cookies?" she asked. "I can't make these all on my own."

"I don't think Bill would like this victim psychology you are harboring," I said, walking out the door. "Would you, Bill?"


"We're going to eat like queens!" I said to Laura.

Laura clapped her hands. Laura was almost four. Old enough to talk, old enough to walk, and old enough to understand that queens did not eat gummy bears for dinner. I opened the food pantry. I was legally an adult now, eighteen and able to smoke and go to war and no longer able to be statutorily raped by men who were nineteen. I could have sex with anyone I pleased. I was proud of my body and I was wearing a thirty-dollar bra, so I lit the stove and pulled out everything from the cabinet that looked expensive. I fried Salisbury steak medallions in walnut oil, which I covered in quail eggs and tahini. Laura was mumbling parts of an Elvis song on the radio, braiding a chunk of her hair at the counter. I was surprised how I felt so much affection for Laura; she was the consequence of the terrible affair that ruined our lives, and yet, she was so small at the counter, so unaware of this fact, that all you wanted to do was possess her and be a part of her world. All she had to do was wrap her tiny fingers around my pinky and laugh when I picked her up and told her I was going to throw her in the trash. "Throw me in the trash again!" she shouted as I tickled her into the fold of the couch ("the trash") and how glorious it was to Laura, this idea of being thrown away.

"Meat's burning," I said.

I turned down the temperature and looked around at how neat and clean the house was, how much of a home it still was, the chairs in nearly the same exact position they were during the funeral reception, their family photos still hanging above the fireplace. Everything was so familiar and unfamiliar at the same time, even their smiles behind the frames, and I couldn't stand any of it.

I took out a bag of frozen shrimp and placed it on the counter. "Are those things animals?" Laura asked.

"Once upon a time," I said.

"They don't have any eyes," Laura said.

I defrosted shrimp in the sink, steamed broccoli, microwaved a Trader Joe's cheesecake and forgot about it, made a pesto sauce for the pasta that was burning in a pot, and when Laura went to bed, I unbraided her hair and kissed her on the forehead. "Are you my sister?" she asked.

"Yes," I said. "I am always your sister."

"Good," she said, and my heart was confused.

When a child goes to bed, a dark house begins to feel like a playground. I went downstairs and I opened up a bottle of Brane-Cantenac Red Bordeaux from France to celebrate my independence and poured some on the remaining steak and most of it in my mouth. There. We were even, I thought.

But, no, we still didn't feel even. I went upstairs and rolled on Mrs. Resnick's red and green plaid bedspread. Still plaid, how titillating, I said aloud, putting on her broken gold watch, how boring and unsexy and old.

In her bathroom, I smeared on her Red Salamander lipstick and pulled her lace knee socks to my thighs. I wrenched her lime green dress out of her closet, the one she wore to my father's birthday party. The linen felt used and vintage on my body, old and sad and retired. I put on her black pumps. We had the same size feet by then, which both depressed and comforted me. I called Daniel, who came over and smoked pot with me on her bed, *doobies,* he still depressingly called them as he told me to breathe in deep and not open my mouth until I fully swallowed. After, I jumped up and down with the ceiling fan spinning a little too close to my head. Daniel pulled at my arm, and I crumbled on top of his body like that whole time I had been a sand statue. "What are you wearing?" he finally asked, tugging at the green linen, and then my underwear, discovering that I had been wet for hours. He licked my vagina a few times and then gestured toward his own crotch. Laura woke up in time to see us leaving the master bedroom and cried out, "Mom?"

"Not yet, honey," I said, not quite ashamed.

Mrs. Resnick came home and walked through the door with a bunch of evening gowns draped over her arm and saw the empty bottle of wine on the table, the dirty burnt dishes in the sink, the melted cheesecake in her microwave, and me, costumed as an exaggerated, tired, whorish version of her. Without missing a beat, she stuck her hand in her wallet and pulled out forty bucks. "Here," she said, and gave me the money, but wouldn't look at me. "Thanks," I grumbled, and left into the night, my insides wet with a boy's saliva, my stomach spoiled with half-cooked meat and wine, my skin suffocated in another woman's clothes, and Mrs. Resnick didn't try to stop me, like she was glad to see herself go. I walked proudly across the lawn in a woman's heels, trying to feel pleased with all of my recent decisions, but when I got to the rock between our lawns, I stood on top of it and felt ashamed.

I stood and I twirled. I jumped off the rock, and my heels sank into the ground, making me fall to the grass.

By the time I got to my front stoop, I wiped my mouth clean with my arm. As I walked into my house, I couldn't help but notice how loud the heels cracked against the tile and wonder how much she had paid for them, if Mrs. Resnick cried when she found my clothes sprinkled on her unmade bed.

"Do you *love* Bill?" I asked my mother, flinging open the door, throwing myself into the kitchen. She was rolling the last batch of anisette cookies.

"Emily!" my mother said, shocked at my appearance. She never finished her sentence.

"After I graduate college," I said, calmly, picking up some dough like I just came home from a war and the only thing I needed to do was not talk about it, roll the dough in my hands, and perform simple and comforting tasks and remember *the everyday,* "I'm going to live with Dad in Prague."

"What are you wearing, Emily?" my mother shrieked.

Bill walked into the kitchen with his sweater and glass of red wine. He laughed at my outfit. "You're a hoot," he said. It sounded like he spent the week thinking of how to address me.

My mother gestured for him not to mention the outfit any further.

"I'm moving to Prague," I repeated. "As soon as I'm done with college."

"Prague?" Bill asked. "Why would you want to go hang out with a bunch of Commies? Aren't all the kids going to Latin America these days?"

"She's not going to Prague," my mother said. "She hasn't even started college."

I informed Bill that the architecture in Prague was amazing.

"Well," Bill said, holding up his wineglass. "Here's hoping they let you back in."

We clinked glasses, and it sounded like a contract. Bill left the room and my mother and I continued to roll the last of the anisette cookies. We held the cold dough between our palms and my mother asked me to please please take off that outfit, and I got flour all over Mrs. Resnick's dress and my mother demanded I tell her the truth about that man, and I asked my mother to tell me the truth about Bill. What was Bill *really* like? I asked. Oh, tall, she said. Brownish hair. Strong chin. Smooth skin. Loves all modes of transportation. And dogs. He really just loves dogs.

In Plain English

# 21

My father's apartment in Prague was covered in filth. This was something his fiancée Ester noticed every night while we waited for my father to return from work. Ester usually made the announcement while we were in the common room, and the television was loud. On the news, they were broadcasting live footage of the clear sky, evidence that the thunderstorm had passed.

"This apartment is covered in *špínu* and smells like dog," Ester said, looking at the dog hair on the windowsill. But Ester believed perfumes disturbed the natural scents that brought people together, so she didn't ever try to fight the smell, just held her nose and looked accusingly at Laura, who rolled a ball to her dog on the floor.

My father bought a dog for Laura, a cocker spaniel she named Raisinet. "That's French, right?" Laura asked.

Laura spent the summers in Prague with my father, but this time she was staying for the year, one solid year for her to learn how to speak Czech and go back to third grade bilingual. She was happy here in Prague. "It looks just like Disney World," she had said once. But my father told me before I came, she was a little lonely. He caught her singing a song to the bedposts. He thought a pet would be good for her. "It helps you more than you know to cultivate a life," he told me as he took the puppy out of the cage for the first time. I wanted him to elaborate, but neither of us knew what to say after he said things like that, and the dog began barking loud.

"Ruffski!" Laura shouted at the dog, which barked back at her, and she clapped her hands. Laura stood up, did a successful pirouette, and fell on the floor. Laura was eight. I was twenty-two. She was dancing in the living room, twirling her blue skirt, explaining how sad it was that "fish didn't know about elephants."

"You mean to tell me that's a fact?" I asked Laura.

"Laura," Ester said, holding a large painting in her hands, "what is that even supposed to mean?"

Two birds with sharp beaks sat on the edge of the screenless windows, worms jammed in their mouths, like really patient vampires waiting for an invitation to use the formal china.

"They don't know about each other!" Laura said. "One is in the sea forever, and the other has to be on land forever."

"That's why there are zoos," I told Laura. "The fish and elephants see each other there."

Laura stood up. "The zoo is dead!" she shouted.

"Dead" was the word Laura sometimes substituted for "closed."

Last year, the Prague Zoo had drowned in the one-hundred-year flood, along with a rhinoceros and an elephant. The flood had touched nearly everything in the city.

"Emily," Ester said, struggling with the painting. She placed it on the floor. "I need your help."

Ester was in front of the French doors guarding the balcony. She was red haired and beautiful with large threatening blue eyes, and stood still only with purpose. She was always and suddenly in a rush to notice everything—Laura wasn't wearing underwear today, my father had been coughing up a sick green storm all morning, I was getting home too late at night (what was I doing? What could I possibly have been doing?) and so was my father. "Where does he go?" she asked. I shrugged, as if I already understood the larger truth. "This is what it's like with him," I said. And that whole time, Ester's feather earrings hung as still as the red hair around them, like peacocks stashed in a maple tree.

"Shouldn't you have art handlers helping you with that?" I asked her.

"It's ony an imitation," she said.

"Well, shouldn't you wait for my father to come before you hang it?" I asked. We both looked at the front door.

"French doors," I had told my mother over the phone after I first arrived.

"And a balcony?" my mother asked.

"Of course," I said. "And a bay window in the bedroom."

"Well, that's just fine," my mother said, and changed the topic.

My mother was doing better now with her new fiancé Bill. Bill was richer than we had previously thought. It turned out that his dead wife had invented MazelTof! when she was pregnant during Passover. MazelTof! was matzoh dipped in chocolate and toffee. Her factory was in Brooklyn and she made four million dollars a year off the product until she died of cancer ten years ago. Bill inherited the company, sold it, invested all the profits, and bought a plane.

"I'm barely home anymore," my mother said like there was a direct ratio between time spent at home and unhappiness. "Bill flies me everywhere. It's marvelous, Emily, you wouldn't believe. So nice to just get out of Connecticut. I thought this place was going to kill me."

Ester measured out a decent space for the painting on my father's wall, which I could now see was a da Vinci painting, *The Virgin and Child with St. Anne*. "No need to wait for your father," Ester said. "You're the expert. Where should I hang this? Where would be the most feng shui?"

I stood up. For every one of my movements, Laura made four.

"Directly above the fireplace," I said. "It will make the living room a conversation space. If that's what you want it to be, of course."

I was studying for my master's in interior design, and somebody always assumed this meant I knew something about feng shui. But I had never learned a thing about feng shui, not in graduate school, and not in college. In college, it was always and simply, you have to meet this poet-art-installation guy who felt my breasts last week, and you have to meet this singer-songwriter-actress person with amazing legs, not to mention the best homegrown weed, and come see my dining hall, come to Waterfire, yes literally floating fires sent down the river that cuts through the city and makes your eyes glassy with their passing, and my flip-flops they are disgusting, yes, but that is the fate of a flip-flop, some woman in Indonesia made them from the rubber of recycled automobile tires, yes, my flip-flops were once the wheels of a sedan stuck on 95, and now they are growing mold, and yes, my roommate is disgusting too, she lets cheese sit out on her desk for days but guess what? She has white, sterile nipples.

My father called me in the middle of my senior year and said,

"Honey, I miss you. Nobody here understands my jokes. Why don't you come out and live with me in Prague? You can meet Ester."

"Who is Ester?" I had asked. "And why would I want to meet her? And why is Ester not laughing at your jokes?"

My father's other girlfriends were brief things he only mentioned in passing, as if he got a new credit card or something. Jana with the forty tennis rackets, Radka, whom he met at a café, Petra who had a daughter named Hanka, which was short for Hana, despite having more letters. But Ester was not Czech, and mostly from Delaware. She loved Delaware. She said loving a place like Delaware was as complicated as fondly remembering one's unhappy childhood. She said it was as complicated as her faith, which was Roman Catholic. She inherited the religion from her crazy mother, she said, and she was always paralyzed by the limitations and the freedoms of it. When she was younger on a camping trip, she accidentally got a nail jammed in a girl's forehead. "Don't ask," she said. The nail gave the girl brain damage and Ester had been going to church ever since. "Church offers forgiveness," she said, "but only if you always feel guilty. So I'm just not sure." She moved far far away from Delaware and became a psychologist in Prague.

The closer Ester came toward me while holding *The Virgin and Child,* the less blue her eyes appeared. The front door swung open. My working father had returned from work.

"Hi. Bye," Laura said to him. "Guy!"

"Hi, girls," my father said. He put his bags down and went to the wine rack. "Sorry, I'm late." He opened up a bottle of wine. "The trams were so packed with all these Christian teenagers singing Jesus campfire songs that we literally could not fit."

"I've seen them," I said as I held up a nail to the wall. "Red and blue sweatshirts. The teenagers who look like they are afraid to be naked even when they are alone in the shower."

My father laughed.

"Did you guys know that this painting is unfinished?" Ester asked, not hearing us. "That Leonardo da Vinci's other hobbies distracted him, and he stopped painting it?"

My father poured the three of us glasses of wine, and I hammered the nail into the wall.

"No, I didn't know that," I said.

The air came through the half-opened balcony door like a leak, stiff and cruel in its persistence. Ester was waiting for me to say, well, what hobbies? But I tried to look bored, *just hammering a nail*.

"Geology," Ester finally said.

"Understandable," I said. "Layers of sediment."

"Are you being sarcastic?" Ester said.

The nail was in.

"Try not to be so sarcastic, Emily," my father said from the kitchen.

"We believe it to be a sorry defense!" Laura said, mimicking Ester.

"And do you see Mary's arms? She's trying to protect Christ from the cross. Do you see?" Ester asked.

"No," I said. I walked away from the painting that was now leaning against the wall. "I'm not being sarcastic. I really don't see any cross."

"Come on," Ester said, pointing to the painting. "Look! Mary's arms are freaking outstretched!"

I looked. I laughed. Ester smiled.

"The Virgin Mary shouldn't be '*freaking*' anything," my father said, approaching with the glasses of wine.

"Don't be so Victorian, dear," Ester said. She took her wine. "At the core, this painting is about a mother loving her child. It makes me miss my mother. Is that weird?"

As soon as she asked, it suddenly felt like it was weird. Ester was thirty-nine. She should have stopped missing her mother a long time ago. We couldn't go on missing our mothers forever, could we? It was even weirder that nobody asked, "Why would you miss your mother—where is she?"

"But it's not just about a mother loving her child," Ester told me. "Freud thought it was the result of some kind of suppressed homosexuality. See, here, the shape of a vulture?"

Standing in front of the painting, Ester turned all her statements into questions. This bothered me, but it felt shameful to be upset about something stupid in front of something masterful. It was shameful to be this upset in general. I was twenty-two, with a college degree and long brown hair and thighs that looked more like my mother's every day. And yet every day, it seemed, I was discovering new ways to feel fourteen again. Every day, there were new ways to be disappointed by the conversation, by the weather, which according to the television was partly sunny, temperatures steady in the midsixties, a light breeze, particulates good.

"Da Vinci once had a dream about sucking a vulture's tail," Ester said, continuing. "Or maybe it was a kite?"

The more she talked about the painting, the less I understood.

"No respectable psychologist references *Freud*," my father said with a smile.

"Freud's all pseudoscience," I said. College was all about calling everything a "pseudoscience."

Ester's eyes flickered away in disappointment. Nobody wanted to share in her discovery, not even Laura, who had lost interest and picked the dog up over her head.

"Be careful with the dog," my father said.

"The dog, the dog, the dog," Ester said. "Always the dog!"

Ester didn't want the dog, and even less so when it turned out the dog had epilepsy. But she was too refined to ever express disgust; she just looked at him distantly as his lips curled back and his limbs went stiff (the first phase), and then he started chewing the air (the second phase), and then urinating all over the floor (the third phase). She looked at him like the dog was an empty thing, a leaking coffeepot, while my father monitored him, like the vet told us, see it through until the end of the seizure and take notes. Ester couldn't stand the smell of his urine, so she walked out the door and went to the movies. "Take notes," she sometimes laughed. "The urine is *yellow*."

Sometimes, I went with her. On the way, Ester complained about our faucets, which were striped with red rings of rust. And the water. It was a dingy brown for the first thirty seconds in the morning, and my father kept forgetting this, Ester said, kept forgetting he was in Prague, cupping his hand to bring the cool drink to his mouth before opening his eyes.

"At least he wears an undershirt," she said. "That's one thing I can say for the man."

The men on the street rarely wore undershirts so their thick chest hair lurked like shadows behind their shirts. On the tram, a pack of

American boys argued over who had been wearing the same pair of underwear the longest. The man who gave us the movie tickets had what I thought was a leper lesion on the back of his hand.

At the movies, the popcorn sat flat in glass cases. The Czech children were in various groups listening to each other speak, and American men were stooped over water fountains. There were bigger hands in littler hands, flashing golden tickets. I sat in my seat and the movie was usually not good, not bad. It was usually about a (black) woman and a (white) mother and another woman with a (shitty) mother who knew another (taller shittier) woman and when the (black white shitty) women visited some kind of waterfall and looked at the water rolling over the edge of the cliff, they compared the dropping movement to liberation and I could feel the dog falling down the stairs back in the apartment. I could feel the dog falling off the couch. I could feel the dog falling all the time, and I could feel Laura's stomach drop every time she saw the thing she loved most shake on the ground. Everybody thought I was always on the brink of despising Laura, scared that at any moment my hatred for her would fly forth and break all of our hearts. But the truth was, I felt incredibly sad for Laura. There was a sadness to her that she seemed to be born with. When the dog shook for the first time, my father, Ester, and I closed in around the animal asking, "What's it doing? Why's it doing that?" and Laura walked over to Raisinet and said, "Figures." She held him tight around his torso and I loved her for this. Laura was always on the noble mission to just love the dog. She was just a little girl who believed she could control the world with her own strength; she was my sister, something I never thought I would have. She combed her hair about fifty times a day, and I felt purposeful when she looked at me across the room and stared at my breasts until I felt compelled to hide them or explain them. She acted out imaginary scenes from imaginary plays and passed out imaginary playbills after dinner, asking the dog for imaginary feedback, while we stood in a circle, trying to decide what was wrong with it.

## 22

Your father is the only man I know in all of Prague who goes to an Italian restaurant most nights of the week," Ester said when we were settled into the cab. My father smiled. He was proud, like he was moving us toward something better.

"I will show you the best Italian food in all of Prague!" he shouted. Sometimes, my father was always shouting.

"Sometimes," Ester said, "your father will go to a Spanish restaurant in Prague and order the only Italian dish on the menu."

While we ordered, my father told jokes in Czech that nobody understood, except the waitress, who laughed, and to whom my father said, "Hey, here's a woman who likes my jokes!" as if this kind of woman wasn't always sitting across the table from him, mouth open. Ester laughed too, as if to say, *No, here's a woman who likes your jokes, Victor.* Ester squeezed my father's arm. My father didn't notice. My father told me later he was placing a bet with the waitress that 50 percent of the women in the room would order a limoncello for dessert.

"*Ano!*" the waitress said, and slapped his arm playfully. "Grappa!"

I looked around the room. Everybody was either talking in a different language, or bored, or drunk, or pissed off, or all things combined. Conversations in Czech naturally sounded angrier. The words barely had any vowels, just hard consonants and exclamations. Laura tried to strike up a conversation with Ester about something benign like the mating habits of clams and Ester waved her off with a quick, "Yes, mhmm, I heard that too."

Ester was threatened by Laura. Even though Laura was four feet tall, she was the tangible product of my father's infidelity, sitting across the table from her smiling. She was complication, a sign of my father's weakness that needed to eat, and drink, and be tucked into bed.

"*Strč prst skrz krk!*" Laura shouted at her.

"What's with that, honey?" my father asked. "Why do you keep saying words that make no sense, pumpkin?"

"It's Czech! It means, 'Stick finger through neck!'" Laura said. She giggled. Ester looked appalled. "My teacher told me it's the only sentence in Czech with zero vowels."

"Honey," he said. "Don't go around saying that, please."

My father was sickeningly sweet toward Laura. Laura was Honey and Pumpkin Face, and when my father was drunk off three glasses of wine, a Sweet Pea. I suspected his syrupy behavior was a product of guilt, his way of compensating for offering her a broken life from the very start. I excused myself to go to the bathroom. It was hot in the bathroom, and my skin felt coated. I splashed water on my face, looked in the mirror, and whispered, "Relax." When I walked back to the table, Ester leaned into the crevice of my father's shoulder, and he pulled her into him. Her long red hair covered parts of his arm. Laura kept asking the waitress for a crayon.

"Cray-*on*," Laura said. "Like a marker. But not."

"I do not understand," the waitress said.

"She doesn't need one," Ester said.

For the rest of the night, I couldn't think of anything to say to anyone except the Russian cabdriver, who smiled and said, "You Americans so quiet because you Americans don't know anything for real. You know your gas prices, you know your baseball numbers, but do you know that no piece of paper can be folded in half more than seven times?"

Even though we all had our own bedrooms, Laura ran into mine at night.

"I'm scared," Laura said. She got under my covers. Her bangs were stuck to her forehead with sweat.

"Don't you want the breeze?" I asked her, lifting up the comforter. Her eyes shone in the cave.

"No," she said. "The moths are coming inside the house. And they sit on my nose."

"That's right," I said. "To come and kiss you good night."

She started crying.

"No," she said. "They are coming in to touch everything. They are going to crawl in my nose."

"They won't," I said. "I'll swat the moths before they reach you. Just fall asleep."

I put the comforter back down. "Wait!" she cried, poking her head out.

"What?"

She looked around the room. "Ummm, *strč prst skrz krk*."

Laura fell asleep quickly after that in my bed and snored like a kitten when it had a cold. I pushed her bangs off her forehead and traced her hairline with my finger, and she shifted toward the wall. I closed my eyes, but couldn't sleep with Laura next to me. I couldn't sleep on the couch either. The leather was too sticky, like Saran Wrap on my skin. So I left the apartment. I went to the nearest bar, called Alcohol Bar. It was a bar for tourists, with a New York sensibility, where businessmen, or me, or anybody in an outfit, really, strolled in with a headache from being awake so long. They took off their jackets arm by arm as if to say, *I hate the day*. They wore thick lipstick and messy hair. They all sat on steel stools drinking malt whiskeys or Krušovice.

"Becherovka," I said to the bartender. "With tonic." A man named Patrick was loud and Irish in my ear, wearing a hooded sweatshirt backward so the hood was directly under his chin.

"Why are you wearing your sweatshirt like that?" I asked him.

"I'm just trying to make a statement," Patrick said.

"I don't get your point," I said.

He told me he was just kidding; he didn't know why he was wearing his sweatshirt backward, honestly, it just felt like the right thing to do at the time. I laughed. I took a sip of the Becherovka. I was embarrassed at how rude I was to a man just as accidental as I was, who was very attractive, with proportional features and brown hair that reminded me of Charlie Brown and suddenly turned me soft.

"Do you know how American you sound?" he asked.

"Do you realize you are not pronouncing your th's?" I asked.

I asked him to say other things. "Ask me how I am," I said.

"How you getting on?" he asked.

"The bus? How'm I getting on the bus?"

"Yes, the fucking bus!" he said.

"Ask me if I want a cup of tea," I said, leaning over the bar.

"Do you want a cuppa?" he asks.

"A cuppa what?"

He punched me on the arm. "Get the fuck outta here," he said, and laughed.

I stood up and pretended to leave. "Get the fuck back in here!" he said.

By three in the morning, we were drunk and had talked about everything from astrophysics (we both had cousins who swore they were involved with it) to Mexican restaurants in Prague (optimism reaching new heights every day) to Eskimos.

"Now, there's a fucking laugh," he said on the way back to my father's apartment. "What the fuck are they doing up there, like?"

"It's like they don't know we have electricity down here!" I said.

"Someone should let them know."

"Though, there's a chance they could be happy as they are."

"I'd fucking doubt that, like. Who's ever been like, gee, I'm so fucking happy because I'm so fucking cold!"

"You're right," I said. "You're right right right. The women have to gnaw on the men's shoes after they come back from hunting to melt the ice. By the time they are old their teeth have usually worn away."

"How the hell do you know that, like?"

"My teacher used to talk about them a lot."

"What else do you know?"

"Well we watched a video on how miserable their lives were. How the men have to sit in front of the ice and wait for a whisker to move slightly because that may mean there's a seal underneath them, so they go to stab it but if there's nothing then they likely go home hungry to die. But also, they have fun too. They showed a naked baby and his mother dangling a stick in front of his face and the baby was laughing."

"You fucking Americans."

We made out on my father's couch for an hour. His teeth turned out to be too large for his mouth, my first instincts about him were right, and when my lips got sore I pulled away and asked questions.

"What do you do?" I asked. "Do you work?"

"I work with fucking computers," he said.

Fucking computers sounded complicated. I asked no more questions. Ester came into the room, sleepily, to get a glass of water. She saw us on the couch and rolled her eyes. Ester was a Catholic and thought I was a slut, but since she was also a psychologist, she was careful never to phrase it like that.

# 23

I n the afternoons, I worked on the hotel. The Crowne Plaza. I was
on seating duty. My job was to find a different assortment of chairs,
love seats, benches for the entrance, the rooms, the pool, the restaurant, the patio, which meant I was never actually at the hotel. I was
always somewhere else, at another hotel, taking notes about the furniture. Krištof Marens, my Belgian thesis adviser, said our goal was
to make the hotel look Modern with a capital M, not modern for efficiency's sake. A kind of Modern that was more about extravagance,
that took time and planning and careful cutting and amazed the world
with its impossibility.

The Crowne Plaza was famous for preserving its social realistic
design. But after the Crowne Plaza was damaged in the flood, it was
temporarily closed, and the new owner decided to use the opportunity
to modernize the hotel. It was 2003 and no longer a time for statues of
Russian war heroes guarding the entrance. "Russia has no hold on this
country," Krištof said. "Or this country's buildings."

The owner said that most of the statues of Russian soldiers had
already been destroyed all over the city, "So, why must my hotel be
imprisoned in the past? Like it is some *museum*?" Especially since the
guests at the Crowne Plaza were mostly rich businessmen, foreign yup-
pies in Italian business suits who wanted to walk into a building that
promised them the most contemporary of living accommodations, col-
orful and glossy banisters, futuristic green hues lining the entranceway,
countertops that were also mirrors, and a fitness center with bright yellow walls so everybody could exercise in peace without the legacy of
Communism literally hanging over their heads.

Krištof Marens was hired as part of the redesign team, and during the first few weeks of graduate school I had become an assistant to the cause. "You American, no?" Krištof asked when I met with him in his tiny office about registration. I was the only American in the program. "You know how to destroy history. You know modern. You don't even *understand* Communism. A perfect fit."

Krištof wasn't very nice so I took this as a compliment.

Krištof wanted me to find seating that called into question the nature of sitting down. Chairs layered in blown glass that were actually comfortable to have sex in. I couldn't find any. I told him such a thing didn't exist. After weeks researching, I found the Nelson Marshmallow Sofa. The Marshmallow Sofa looked like it was made out of a bunch of very elegant black marshmallows joined together at the corners. Krištof was disgusted. "The Marshmallow Sofa?" he said, as though I had offended him. "You fat Americans."

But when I sent him the picture, he wrote back saying, "Not terrible."

The French owner loved them. He eventually purchased forty for some of the suites. "I knew you would do it, Američanka," Krištof said to me after, filling my tall glass with pilsner. "Leave it to the Američanka to deliver the Marshmallow Sofa."

Ester was a woman who believed in favorites. Favorite dinner: breakfast. Favorite street: the main ones. Favorite people: the sad old men on benches who have nothing to do with their hands. Favorite nighttime activity: visiting the old chapels.

"We should go to the bone church," I said.

"Bone church?" Laura asked. "What is that?"

"It's a church built out of more than thirty thousand skeletons," I said.

It was in Kutnà hora, an hour outside the city. After the plague took out more than half of Europe, thirty thousand bodies were left without a burial. A monk collected all the bones, and a wood-carver was hired to assemble them in the church. "The chandelier contains every bone in the human body," Krištof said. "Now, that's interior design."

"Ew," Ester said. "Why would we want to see that?"

"Because it's remarkable," I said.

"Is remarkable the same thing as portable?" Laura asked.

"No," I told her.

"Not while Laura is here, Emily," Ester said, suddenly like a mother. As though she had to protect Laura from me. "We can't bring a seven-year-old girl to a house made out of bones."

"I'm eight!" she said. "I *have* bones."

Instead, we went to the St. Vitus Cathedral, the largest church in Prague, where we bought prayers for twenty crowns each.

"A bargain!" I said.

"You mean prayers aren't free?" Laura asked.

"Think of it as a donation," I told her.

After, we went to the Vltava and when we fed the ducks leftover bits of bread, it didn't bother me to watch Ester the way I had imagined it would bother me to watch my father's lover stroll around Prague all night in Gucci shoes, buying spinach paninis that she couldn't bring herself to fully consume, asking us questions about our "schoolwork." Sometimes Ester hummed the tunes to songs I didn't know and I barely even got annoyed. I was too tired from walking around all day to do anything but admire her stamina.

"How can you look out at such a thing and not believe in God?" Ester asked us, looking down at the water below.

"I never said I didn't believe in God," I said.

"It's just too amazing," she said. "Impossible to think that no one planned this. That's what I keep telling your father. Your father the atheist."

It was a long way to the water below. I tried to imagine what it would feel like floating to the bottom of the river. There didn't seem to be anything lonelier than a flood, a city of no sound. There were watermarks on the sides of the yellow and pink buildings and Ester, our tour guide, would point to the watermarks on the buildings and exclaim, "See that mark? See this? Last year, this whole thing was underwater," like drowning was some kind of an achievement. The river had gotten into every crack, and most of the life that was carried through the city was either dead or debris, broken storefront signs and wooden kitchen spoons floating at the top of the river, people at the bottom. Even after the water had drained and evaporated, homes and stores and parks had been dampened from the carpets to the ceiling, the streets to the clouds, leaving a thick film all over the city, and for a long while nothing could be understood or seen without using the watermarks and the damp scent of must as a benchmark. Life had been a certain way "before the flood." Nothing's been the same "since the flood," not the color of the walls or the feel of our hands against the brick.

When we returned to the apartment my father was still not home. Ester and I drank wine and waited on my father's balcony. Ester got drunk. She took large gulps of her wine and it occurred to me for the first time that she was nervous around me. She was drinking fast, playing with a strand of red hair, telling me about her clients.

"I'm starting to get so bored by my job," she said. "That's really the worst thing that can happen to you, I think."

I could think of worse things, but I let her continue uninterrupted. She seemed to feel strongly about this. She said she was bored by everybody's displacement. She wanted to be challenged by something other than what was so obviously different. Something other than herself, something wild.

"I used to be wild, Emily," she said. "When I first met my ex-husband. I was in the doctoral program at Charles University, and I'd spend my evenings cruising around with my friend Sylvia from Italy in her twenty-year-old car with no vinyl siding on the inside of the doors."

They'd park the car, smoke some weed, and she'd call her husband from the nearest pay phone. He would sit up late at night, waiting for these phone calls because he loved her so much, and listen to her talk about her patients.

"What kind of clients do you have?" I asked.

"Not very crazy ones," she said. "Like this girl, two weeks ago, who told me about how she was driving her car, and she was like, 'Ugh, I'm driving again.'"

"I can sympathize with that," I said. "Sometimes, when I'm brushing my hair, I think, Here we go again . . ."

"Clients who say they need an affair," Ester said. "People who feel no rush with their husbands. People who feel like nothing ever happens to them anymore."

But nothing does happen, I thought. Not really. Nothing had happened to me in years, not in the way that Mr. Basketball had happened to me, and on the balcony listening to Ester talk, the wind felt empty against my cheek. It felt like the air could hold nothing here. The wind carried nothing around all day. I can't explain how terrifying that felt.

"Like, what is supposed to happen?" I asked.

"That's what I always ask. So I tell them to go paddleboating."

"What's the weirdest thing you've heard?"

"This woman can't stop going to the town square. She's addicted to the chaos that she feels when she's there, watching the clock. Surrounded by all that *stuff*," she said.

"That's strange," I said.

"It's not strange," Ester said. "It's just how it is. Her son died seven years ago in a car accident. She's very upset that she can't remember what it sounded like in the car. If it was a *bam!* Or a *smack!* Or a *crash!* The chaos makes sense to these people."

Ester got too drunk. Ester told me that she thought her first husband was a closet homosexual because he didn't fondle her breasts with the determination to really get to know them, and he cried once after they watched *Sleepless in Seattle*. She figured that since she didn't, she might be a lesbian. Ester said she was sick with the idea that her husband even watched the movie with her in the first place.

"But then I met your father," she said.

"My father cried once while watching *The Wizard of Oz*," I said. "When Judy Garland sings 'Somewhere Over the Rainbow.' It was the same song that they played at my grandmother's funeral."

"I see."

"So do you think my father's gay?" I asked. "Because he cried over his dead mother?"

"Emily," Ester said, "of course I don't think your father is gay. That song has a beautiful range. It would be nearly impossible not to cry while one's emotions are enhanced by the death of a loved one."

"Then why did you think your first husband was gay?"

"Because I caught him fucking another man in our bed."

"Oh," I said.

"Very intuitive of me," she said. "I stood over the two of them and said, 'Robert, I am starting to get the feeling that you are gay.'"

"You did not say that," I said.

I was right. She said she threw a pot, then cried for ten hours.

We were quiet for a moment. Then we burst out into laughter. Ester ran into the other room, holding her stomach, trying not to pee in her pants, saying, "I threw a fucking pot!"

Laura ran out on the balcony, her hair flipped upward from the pillow, saying, "Raisinet! Raisinet!"

Laura hurried us to the bottom of the stairs, where Raisinet was having another seizure. Laura was crying and knelt down next to the dog.

"I don't think I love him anymore," Laura said, like that was the tragedy of the situation, and not Raisinet, drooling from the corners of his mouth, or Ester, who was still trying to smother her giggles behind me.

To be honest, sometimes I did hate Laura a little bit. I hated her when it was late at night and she cried while we were finally having a good time, or when her voice cracked with emotion over her applesauce that she refused to eat if there were lumps. I hated her when she left a ring of milk on the kitchen counter and when she got her brown hairs stuck in the toothpaste on the sink. I hated her when my father was on the phone, and also throwing out the garbage, and also putting on his shoes, and she would look at him as though he was the maid and say, "Dad, hand me that marker," and I would look at her and say, "Can't you see he is busy?" but really what I wanted to say was, *Can't you see that he is my father? Can't you see that we have the same exact nose, that we share a vocabulary? Can't you see that we have a history you will never understand?* She tugged on Raisinet's fur like he was a doll and not a living thing that was suffering and she left my bobby pins in the shapes of crosses all along the coffee table. She spit on her palms when her hands were dry, and she blew out candles before the night was over and got scared in the dark. She'd look over at me from across the room like I wasn't enough protection and say, "Where is my dad?" and I would have to correct her and say, "Where is *our* dad, Laura." I hated her when she looked at Raisinet and then at me, and said, "I don't love him anymore," and I wanted to scream at her, even though she was just a child. Even though I did love her, and sometimes at night, she would draw a little mouth on her hand and sing me the Cheeseburger Song, or sit on my lap and ask me if I had ever heard of sex before, and I would laugh and tell her that of course I had. Even through all of this, sometimes I wanted to lift up her chin and say, "Don't you see that is your dog?" Don't you see how we didn't want to have to love you, Laura? Don't you see how you have to love things forever anyway, no matter if it shakes, or drools, or barks in the middle of the night, or throws up food, or dies, because even in death, he is still your dog? You picked him out of a group and said, that is my dog, and the dog you picked shakes and drools and barks in the middle of the night, but you named him. And for that reason you should never want to give him up, you should always be grateful since your dog is one of the few things in life that you actually can choose as your own.

"He's a *boy,*" she said. "I didn't know it was a *boy* when I chose him. I should have asked."

I took her teary little face in my hands.

"You should always always ask for what you want, Laura," I said.

I wasted too much of my life not asking for what I wanted. I didn't even know how to pray properly. When we were at St. Vitus Cathedral, after we had purchased our prayers, we each got a candle to light. I had never been much for prayer because most of the time I wasn't sure what I was supposed to expect for myself. What did we have the right to expect? I took a match to my candle. I lit the wick, and we stood in a circle around the candle display and watched our prayers burn into tiny stubs, drowning in the white wax, and I thought of what I wanted, what I had always wanted those four years in college I spent undressing to the entire soundtrack of *Moulin Rouge* after theater parties, kissing various boys with spotty beards and dirty fingernails, half-naked architects who wouldn't shut up about Frank Lloyd Wright or the weird thing they just found on their penis, boys who ate pizza with joints hanging out their mouths, boys who held me and licked me like I was covered in wounds as they played Portishead and asked me questions late into the night, like would I rather have to kill my whole family or the whole state of Ohio, and I said, "Does the state of Ohio know I murdered them?" and they looked at me and said, "That's four million people, Emily, that's genocide," and I hated them, these boys with uncombed hair and too-short ties who didn't understand that it was all just a game.

Mr. Basketball. Jonathan.

This was why all those women sat on those stools in our high school auditorium and shook their fingers and said, girls, don't let them touch you, girls, don't let them hold you, because even if you hated them, even if their proximity made your heart pound in fear, when they were gone and you were alone, you could hardly feel your pulse.

I lit my candle and I prayed.

A man walked by and my candle was blown out by the wind. I took a picture of it, with Laura's face behind the candle. On the way home, I took pictures of things I didn't think anybody would ever want to remember, like the underside of a black bench in the middle of the city where the word "rain" was written in Wite-Out. A half-eaten sandwich thrown on the street. A sign that read FOOD STORE. An old man who got his foot stuck in a revolving door and didn't even notice until someone pointed it out to him. Until I put down my camera and said, "Mister, your foot," but he flinched like I was about to mug him since he didn't know any English, and I was coming closer to him, and I wanted to say, *Why are we always so scared of everything, why am I so scared of the watermarks on the buildings, or the silence on the night trams, or to sit down with my father and have a proper conversation?* but the man was gone, grumbled something in French and walked in the door.

Why could we never speak? Why could I never ask for what I wanted?

I got my photo album from my bedroom. It was full of all the images I never wanted to remember but carried around with me so I'd never forget. "A poem is a record of change," Mr. Basketball said once, and this felt true to me; I was a record of change, and this photo album was a record of change. My father and Mrs. Resnick in the woods at his birthday party, Mr. Basketball's red gym shorts, my mother on the couch holding a martini. I put the picture of the bench with the word "rain" in an envelope and sent it to Mr. Basketball. I didn't know why exactly, or if he even had the same address, or if I was just sending something out there to the universe, but it seemed to me that he was the only person who would understand exactly what I saw in all of this. *Image,* was all I wrote. Then I signed my full name: Emily Marie Vidal.

My father and I didn't get to spend that much time alone together, except when he took me out to dinner on Wednesdays, and when he ordered Shiraz, he always said, 'Let's celebrate,' like Happy Wednesday, Daughter, hope it was better than Tuesday, though I hope your Tuesday was great too, and I never asked what people clapped about during the middle of the week and he never held out his glass to toast anything. We just liked to say things: "Hi, Father," I said with a grin. "I'm your daughter Emily and we just like to say things."

He laughed. Sometimes I loved my father more than anything.

"What can you do with linguini?" my father asked me when our meals arrived. This was a game we used to play to pass the time when I was little. What can you do with a *blank*? What can you do with a stone? Step on it, put it on your desk, stick it in your pants and try to drown. What can I do with your mother? he'd sometimes asked. Put her in the closet, I'd say, take her to the moon, make her a ham sandwich, draw her a picture of the Grand Canyon.

"Spell your name with it," I said.

"Make a statue out of it."

"Feed it to the dog."

"Tie it all together and use it like a string."

"Wear it like a wig."

My father touched the top of his head. He was severely balding. He was balding in the front, the hair left around his head fitting like a horseshoe. "I'm getting old," he said. He sighed.

"You're not old," I said. "At least not old in the way that Betty Ford is old."

"I'm old," he said. "I'm old in the way that my back hurts as soon as I open my eyes in the morning. I'm old."

# 24

Winter approached. Jonathan was in the living room of his suite at the Crowne Plaza about to drop his pants in front of the zebra statue. It had been four years since I had seen him and he was so comfortable unbuttoning his jeans in front of me that I was forced to look past him and think about the way the zebra's mane covered its face entirely, except for the right eye, which was peeking through the hair and emphasized like red lipstick on a child. I was reduced to obvious body language.

"I've got to shower," Jonathan said. "It was a long flight."

I told him there was soap and shampoo in the bathroom. He walked to the door in his boxers and exclaimed, "Ah yes, soap and shampoo in the bathroom." I sat on the couch and listened to him sing soft melodies through the shower door and felt a bit calmer. This is my hotel, I told myself, and that voice is only Jonathan's. Jonathan was staying at my hotel. I got him a slight discount, but he said he would have stayed there anyway since the law firm was paying for his trip. *I'm looking forward to being surrounded by you,* he had written before he came.

It wasn't until Jonathan showed up in Prague that I realized I hadn't really known anyone in Prague. I knew my father and Laura and Ester and Krištof and a few of my European classmates who had all left over winter break to go to the Swiss Alps, where someone always had an available cabin, or to Milan, where somebody's grandmother was always dying.

I felt lonely in Prague, but not quite sad. In October, the snow started falling and I welcomed it on the tip of my nose. There was something about being in a foreign country that validated and glorified your own sense of isolation. My loneliness felt epic, and the Romanesque buildings all around me only affirmed this.

And then Mr. Basketball wrote to me. Jonathan, as Mr. Basketball described himself in his letters, was a lawyer in Manhattan now but still lived in his Fairfield condo. He had sent me a picture of a courtroom, a man in a suit wildly flailing his arms in front of the judge, who was yawning without covering his mouth. *Ennui,* he had written on the back.

I wrote him explaining that I was a not-yet-certified interior designer. That I was living in Prague, indefinitely. That living in Prague sometimes felt like a way to remind myself it was impossible to be happy anywhere. There was too much pressure to be spontaneous and in the moment and eating and touching and enjoying everything every second.

He didn't write back.

So I had Krušovices all month long with men in jungle-green blazers, thin ties, and ankle pants, men who mostly spoke Czech so our conversations sounded a little bit like, "Well-hello-how-are-you-do-you-cook-yes-but-only-with-easy-to-pronounce-vegetable-names."

I ate dumplings and cabbage and felt constricted. In the morning, I drank Algerian coffee for the first time and I liked how drinking it required all of your attention in order to keep the coffee grinds settled on the bottom of the cup. I liked how walking around in Prague required your attention; you put your head down, and then before you knew it, you were completely lost. You were at the crest of the river, the end of a road, and above you, the sky was overwhelmingly fresh looking.

*You felt the same way in Connecticut,* Jonathan finally wrote back. *Don't you remember?*

*Who are these people who go to Europe to find themselves?* I wrote. *I've never felt more like my unself. People should really say, I'm going to Europe to find out who I'm not.*

I read *The Trial* and felt ashamed about my lack of appreciation for everything that came before me, so I followed Kafka's footsteps around the city and tried to memorize inscriptions under different statues and smile at old people. I fed the ducks that congregated at the bottom of the Vltava and sometimes I liked to pretend that we were all at a business meeting discussing fourth-quarter revenue. "Quack," one of the ducks inevitably said. "I disagree entirely," I said, and shook my head. I thought of my mother walking through Fairfield, trying on wedding gowns that were no longer too expensive for her. I imagined her feeling lonely in a pleated bodice. I went to talks given at my father's university by Arnošt Lustig. I cried over other people's pain. About boys who died in the Holocaust as virgins, and boys who didn't. I bought scarves for two hundred crowns because they were pretty and soft around my neck.

*People should say, I'm going to Europe to act outside the confines of my character,* he wrote.

*I'm going to Europe to participate in nonevents,* I wrote.

*I'm going to Europe to expel negative energy.*

I sat in parks and watched the dogs. In Letenské there was an old man with two long-haired schnauzers that came every day, and he called them both Ferdinand. "Ferdinand, come here," he said. "Ferdinand, stop licking Ferdinand." I stood in front of glass food booths and made decisions between cheese, blue cheese, and ham-and-cheese paninis. I could never decide how much cheese I was ready for but always chose a ham-and-cheese panini that Vladímira with the black hair served to me begrudgingly every day. I never had the correct change and this bothered her. We didn't joke, and she never smiled because the fact that I never had the correct change really really bothered her.

*I'm going to Prague on business,* he wrote. *I'm going for three weeks over Christmas. I'm representing an American company that is being sued for making combs so thin they have become choking hazards. Correction, I'm going to Prague to see you. Let me know if that's not all right.*

Was it all right? I wasn't sure.

It was December now and the sun hung low in the sky like a pendant lamp and everything about my life these past four years suddenly seemed so fake; I was sure of it. Here was Jonathan walking out of the shower and into the common room and he was real. He left wet footprints on the rug and ruffled his hair with a towel. I was slowly remembering this man, his hair wet and playful like a seal.

"Well?" he said.

It was Tuesday so I took him to my Czech language course. On the way, we walked by buildings with stones from the seventeenth century and I started to feel confident in the fact that four years ago was not as far away as I had previously thought.

Outside, it was winter in the most serious sense. There was snow, and sleet, and hail, and then snow again. Every day that week had been a thorough snowstorm. There was ice on the tram tracks. There was an implied curfew by the sun that set so early the town might as well have been a movie set, a white wonderland that existed only from nine to five. We walked through it anyway, all the way to Charles University on the other side of the bridge. We tried not to touch each other on the way. But there was ice and sidewalks were slippery, and then we brushed arms while trying to open the door of the school, his hand catching the ends of my hair when he moved past me into the elevator.

Jonathan sat next to me in the classroom with impeccable posture, like a man who was used to being called upon. He was the first person to make this language course feel like a very casual meeting between friends.

"I'm a fucking lawyer," Jonathan said. Then he sighed. "I need to learn some basic Czech so I can function while I'm here."

On the other side of me was a thin brunette from Ireland.

"My name is Natalie Mullan," the girl said. "I've never really taken Czech before, but I'm in a singing group and we want to write a song in Czech. You can buy our other songs on iTunes. And, well, I guess the thing to know about me is that sometimes people call me boisterous."

"Your *kapela*," the teacher said. "Your band. What's your *kapela*'s name?"

"Hot Pocket," the girl said.

Jonathan and I exchanged smiles. When he smiled he looked about thirty. When he frowned he looked about forty. He was thirty-one now. He was a lawyer now. He wore white oxford shirts and genuine leather shoes now. He parted his hair with a comb now. He had more wrinkles around the eyes now, which were still powder blue. When I first saw him walk down to greet me in the lobby of the hotel, I remember thinking, We still have the same eyes. I had never met anyone whom I felt this way with, and honestly, I didn't even know for sure what my eyes looked like or if having the same eyes as someone else even mattered. It was just an intuitive feeling. He had my eyes.

"I am your *učitelka*," the teacher said, and wrote it on the board. "Your teacher."

We learned greetings. Hello. Good-bye. *Dobrý den. Nashledanou. Jak se máte?*

"Like, don't actually tell me how you are; just tell me that you're good," my teacher said.

*Kolik je hodin?*

"Like, *What time is it?*" she said.

*Je jedna hodina.* Like, *It is one o'clock.* We learned basic travel items. Deodorant. *Dětský pudr.* Baby powder. That's a basic travel item? Class dismissed.

*Nashledanou.* Or *ciao.*

"Depending on how well you know the person," I explained to him softly in his ear.


"See that space over there?" I said to Jonathan at the tram stop after class. "That's where Stalin's body used to be."

"His body?" he asked.

"Not his real body. There was a giant monument built in honor of Stalin. They blew it up after he turned out to be a mass murderer."

The 23 arrived. We stepped on the tram and held on to the red poles as we headed to the city center. He was looking at me the way my mother often looked at her favorite foods in the grocery store if they suddenly had a different packaging, turning it over and then asking me, "Is this the same one I have always liked, Emily?"

"You are different," Jonathan said.

"Well, of course I'm different," I said. "I'm four years older," I added, but this advertisement of maturity only made me feel younger. "How am I different?"

"In the beginning," Jonathan said, "you were the good but flawed one who fought to stay alive. The mild-mannered quiet girl who's always around but isn't noticed right away when the other characters are engaging in activities."

The trams in Prague were mostly quiet, except for the soft murmurings of another language and the American who was always speaking. When an American talked on the trams, it felt so noticeable and understandable to me, as though Jonathan was a violin playing the melody of a song, while the rest of the orchestra was on the verse.

"But then you're actually," Jonathan continued, "without anyone taking notice, the boisterous, please note my word choice, feisty, won't-take-no-for-an-answer heroine who always ends up doing the right thing, unless it takes too much effort, in which case you just sit around and make fun of other people."

"That classic, timeless character," I said.

"Like Ophelia," he said.

"The mild-mannered quiet girl?"

"Yes."

"Who turns boisterous?"

"But not crazy."

"But she was crazy."

"I contend Ophelia was actually the hero of Hamlet," he said. "She was the only one with a pure heart. And I only called you Ophelia because that's the only female character from Shakespeare that I still feel comfortable referencing. Besides Lady Macbeth."

"I see."

"But you're not her," he added.

"And who are you?" I asked.

"Well, I suppose I'm like Othello. Though I've never read *Othello* so I don't actually know. Do you have any idea what Othello was like?"

"He was black," I said.

"Let's get some *oběd*," he said. "I want to buy you some food."


At Apropos Restaurant, a woman's tiny dog was gnawing on her foot. She was trying to kick it away.

"How do you say 'bark' in Czech?" Jonathan asked.

*Hafhaf.* That was how you said "bark" in Czech.

"'Ruffski,'" I said. That was how Laura addressed Raisinet now. "Ruffski!"

"Of course. Ruffski," Jonathan said. As soon as I said it, I regretted it. "Why didn't I think of that?"

The waiter gave us menus.

"What are you going to get?" Jonathan asked with a mocking smile on his face. "The three cheeses on the hard board?"

It was the cheapest thing on the menu at Apropos Restaurant and the translation made us laugh.

"I'd like the four fruits on a plate, next to the spinach, inside the restaurant, thanks," I said.

When we were done eating he said, "Let's do something Prague-ian. Let's find some Gypsies or something."

"The Gypsies are all gone," I said. "Or at least, leaving."

The Gypsies were fleeing to Canada. The rumor was that Czech officials were even trying to help them buy plane tickets, so they could tear down their "housing units" as soon as possible.

We wandered around town. I told Jonathan I had always wanted to get my tarot read by a Gypsy with a haunted deck, and I wanted her to sit across the table from me and say in an accent that represented a life lived in more than one place, "There is a draining force in your life. Do you know anybody who wants to drain you?"

"Let's do it," Jonathan said.

But we couldn't find any Gypsies, only Asian tourists traveling in packs looking for cosmetics, old men sitting over lumpy plates of stew like they were about to eat the last piece of meat that would finally destroy them, and thin-legged Czech men with jewel-encrusted numbers on their jeans. We walked around the street vendors in the Jewish district and Jonathan joked about buying me absurd things: a three-dimensional head of a fox that also served as a brooch.

"I wonder what kind of music Hot Pocket makes," I said.

"Irish pop from the looks of it," he said. "Irish Pop Pocket."

We didn't find any Gypsies but we found a tourist shop with a girl named Marva who read tarot, who said she was an ex–graduate student from the University of Ohio who had fled to Prague halfway through her dissertation. Jonathan liked her immediately. "Some people flee," he said. "Some people become lawyers."

"Well, I'm not very qualified to read tarot," Marva said.

"Well," Jonathan said, "give us our fortunes anyway."

"Okay. Though I must warn you," Marva said. "I'm going to tell you things that you normally would not have thought to do before I told you. I'm putting ideas in your head that would never have been there. So just watch for that."

Marva put out three front cards. Those, apparently, meant everything.

"Ah, the Magician," she said to Jonathan. "A very interesting card. You see, the Magician is of this world. The Magician is young in his craft, he's, like, a magician that doesn't understand his own tricks."

"I don't know what the fuck that means," Jonathan said. We laughed.

"You will," Marva said. "You've got to figure out what you're doing. Because you don't want to stay the Magician forever."

"Oh, thanks," Jonathan said.

Then it was my turn. "The Devil," she said, and of course. I knew it. Why even play the game? I sat and listened to Marva explain how people misunderstand the Devil card. It was really not a bad card. It was just a sign of extreme attachment to earthly pleasures. Right, I said, and I nodded like I understood, as I glared back at the Devil, with his blue flesh arms spread wide, and the two child figures underneath him, attached at the skin.

"See how they are attached at the skin?" Marva said. "It's like they choose to be there, it's an earthly attachment, not an eternal attachment. So don't despair really. It doesn't mean you're going to *hell*."

I nodded again. Right, I said, as I looked at the Devil blowing fire into only one of the children's backs. The boy's face was sort of sad, but almost vacant, as if he felt the pain but couldn't understand the reason his skin seemed to be on fire.


"I'm scared," Laura said, coming into my room later, tugging on my arm.

Laura had strange, thick wrists, and sometimes at night, she barely looked human to me.

"Not tonight, Laura," I said. I was frustrated in bed, thinking of how Jonathan walked me to my father's apartment at the end of the night and didn't even lean in to kiss me on the cheek or hold my hand. How I put my arms around him, and felt he was heavier now, with flab around his waist like a thick belt. "You have to sleep in your own room."

"I don't want to!" she screamed.

I picked Laura up and took her out of my bedroom into the living room. My father was still up, reading the paper. "Dad," I said. "Here is your child."

I draped Laura over my father's lap, and we both laughed a little.

"Hello, child," he said to Laura.

"Hello, old person," said Laura, who had stopped crying.

"Now, that's just mean," my father said.

The fireplace was lit, and the da Vinci painting looked nice in the firelight. It was midnight. Sometimes, I felt calm and happy with my new family. I sat down next to my father and Laura and closed my eyes.

"What are you reading?" Laura asked.

"A story," my father said, turning the page.

"What kind of story?"

"A very long story about many different kinds of people."

"What's it called?"

"The newspaper."

Laura laughed. "Read it to me," she said.

My father dramatically opened *The New York Times* to the business section. "Once upon a time, in a faraway land, lawmakers promised that their opposing viewpoints would not harm safety-net programs—"

"Dad!" Laura giggled. "No more."

"I'm not finished yet . . . ," he said.

"Tell me a real story," she said. "Tell me how you and mom met again."

"I've already told you," my father said.

"But Emily doesn't know," she said. "Emily, do you know?"

I looked at my father, but I wouldn't open my eyes. I couldn't look at them.

"No," I said. "I don't know."

I didn't really. When did they meet? Was it twenty years ago, across the lawns at a block party? When did they fall in love? It could have been anytime, anywhere, in front of my face.

I heard Laura bang her fist on his knee. "Dad, tell us."

"Well," he said, "frankly, it's late, and I've got to get up early tomorrow."

"Daaaaaaad," Laura said. Laura banged her fist on my knee now. "They met at the movies."

"Oh yeah?" I asked, trying to keep my voice steady and calm.

"My mom started crying halfway through the movie because the movie was sad. She still does that. Dad took her hand and said, 'Don't worry.'" Laura picked up my hand and laced our fingers together. "Like this."

"That was nice of him," I said. I heard my father's knees crack when he stood up, folding the newspaper into quarters. "What movie were they seeing?"

"*Mrs. Doubtfire,*" my father said, his voice coming from the kitchen. "The Robin Williams one."

"Oh," I said. "I saw that movie when I was eleven."

"You couldn't have been that young," he said.

"I was," I said. "I know for sure. I was at the theater with you."

I remembered that day specifically because on the way out of the theater Mark didn't hold the door for me, and it slammed in my face, and I thought this was a sure sign he didn't want to be my husband, and afterward in the car, I was glad when my father lectured Mark on what it meant to be a gentleman. "You open the doors, you pay for the meal, and you drive," he said. "It doesn't matter if it's your goddamn grandmother or your wife, you got that?"

I heard my father place his teacup in the sink and leave the room.


"*Kde je hrob Franze Kafky?*" the teacher said. It was our second class together. "Like, *Where is grave of Franz Kafka?*"

"*Kde je,*" she repeated. "Where is . . ."

The class was silent.

"*Židovský hřbitov na Olšanech,*" the teacher said. "In case any of you are interested in visiting it. The Jewish Cemetery at O."

The class was even more silent, if that was possible.

"Oh, don't be afraid," she said. "Czech is not as terrifying as it looks. And we do have grammar, despite what any Germans might be telling you on the street. All you need to know, really, is that once you learn the alphabet, you're all set because every letter in Czech is always pronounced the same. And you pronounce, most of the time, every single letter in the word."

"For example," she said. "It is Thursday. It is *Čtvrtek*."

She led us through the word phonetically: Ch-trv-tek.

"Oh," Jonathan said loudly, as though he were still the teacher in the front of the classroom. "That explains it."

Everybody laughed. When somebody finally pronounced it correctly, she dismissed us.

Jonathan and I set off for the miniature museum. The miniature museum showcased microscopic exhibits like Kafka's head carved into a poppy seed, or a golden train sculpted on a strand of hair. Jonathan and I looked up the address of the museum and set off to find it. We walked for an hour until the snow started to accumulate on top of our hats.

"Maybe it's microscopic," I said. I stopped walking. "Maybe you can't actually find the museum without a microscope."

Jonathan put his mouth close to my ear in front of the St. John of Nepomuk statue. He whispered something I couldn't hear. It was something important, I know that, because it made him lift up my face with his finger. He kissed me, and it was new and welcome and familiar. I was electrified. Finally. The snow had started to melt; rain was running over our feet like rivers. Jonathan's skin was smooth and his dimples deep. The details of the city were emerging. Below St. John of Nepomuk, an angel appeared, her stone finger over her lips.

"That statue is supposed to grant you a wish," I said. "You're supposed to touch it and it grants you a wish."

Jonathan reached out his hand and touched St. John of Nepomuk. He closed his eyes. "I wish I wasn't such a dumbass."

I laughed. We began walking.

"Let's go get some absinthe," Jonathan said. "Have you had it here yet?"

"No," I said.

We went to the Café Louvre. Café Louvre was a giant restaurant with so much space it was like eating in a really beautiful department store.

"Hello," the waiter said when we sat down at our table. The waiters in Prague always spoke in perfect English, but I liked to respond in Czech for practice.

"*Dobrý den*," I said.

"We would like to have some absinthe," Jonathan said. "Not the cheap stuff. And a *pivo*."

The waiter took our menus and left.

"So how long have you been a lawyer?" I said.

"Too long," Jonathan said.

"You don't like it?"

"I like it the way I like stable things," he said. "It's boring. I do product liability. It pays well. Sometimes it's exciting. Sometimes it's not. Sometimes all I talk about all day is a fence."

The waiter came back with our absinthe. He put two cups of green liquid in front of us. It looked like antifreeze. He ripped open two packets of sugar and poured them into two spoons. He dipped the sugar into the absinthe, and then lit the sugar on fire. A flame grew over the spoon like electric mold, and the sugar caramelized. I laughed while Jonathan stared into my eyes. The waiter poured the flaming sugar into the absinthe and stirred. Jonathan and I picked up our glasses, toasted to nothing except transformation, which felt like enough. I swallowed the absinthe, and it was huge and hot down my throat. It felt like swallowing the sun whole, like a giant mistake.

"Am I different?" he said. "Sometimes you look at me like I'm different."

"You are different."

"I am," he said. "You'll be disappointed, I'm sure."

"I don't have very high expectations," I said.

"I like it here," he said. "I like who I am here. With you."

"Sometimes it's nice to get away," I said. "You take a step back from your real life. You find out things you didn't, couldn't, possibly know before."

I felt like I was lying, even though I was barely saying anything at all.

"What's wrong with what you know?" Jonathan asked.

"Don't you want to know what you don't know?"

"What *don't* you know?"

"Why the universe started as a singularity," I said to him. "For instance."

He laughed. My whole body was tender. If Jonathan reached out to touch me in that moment, he would have left hand imprints all over my body.

"What the fuck is a singularity?" he asked. "Can you explain to me, right now, what a singularity is?"

"It's infinitesimal."

"I still don't get it."

"Yeah, neither do I," I said.

"Well if you find out, do let me know. I'll be hanging off the edge of my fucking seat," he said.

He smiled to let me know his swears were always compliments.

The walls of the hotel served as lit storage cabinets designed to look like a giant, illuminated checkerboard. In the white spaces, thin statues of gaunt men and women were stretched at their heads and feet. There were stacks of round dinner plates and bunches of steel firewood. Maybe it was the absinthe in my blood, maybe it was the Marshmallow Sofa, but something about the room just didn't feel right.

"That's my sofa," I said, pointing to the black Marshmallow Sofa in front of the coffee table. "I picked out that sofa."

Jonathan sat down on it.

"Does it make you question everything you thought you knew about sitting down?" I asked.

He ran his hand over the leather. "I don't know anything about sitting down," he finally said. I laughed.

He took my hand and pulled me into his lap. My whole body felt limp. His touch had always been too powerful a thing. His touch was something I assumed I'd find in other men, but never did. He smoothed my hair away from my face. It was all happening again. Just like it used to. Except when we used to sleep together, Mr. Basketball always wanted me on my back, on a bed. He touched my breasts while he moved inside me, held my forehead down with his other hand. Jonathan sat upright and slid my underwear down my legs. "Is this all right?" he asked.

"Yes," I said. I nodded. "Please."

He unzipped his pants, and they dropped to the floor. I could see through his boxers that he wasn't hard. Mr. Basketball was always hard. Mr. Basketball was hard even when he was on the other side of the room reading the dictionary. Jonathan didn't get hard until we were both naked, until he was against me, and even then he wasn't fully extended, and as if to change the subject he said, "You don't shave anymore."

We were both embarrassed. I was embarrassed not for being unshaven, but for the way I had shaved when I was younger. I had been too scared to cut myself, so I only shaved the upper part and he had once said it looked like Bert from *Sesame Street*.

"Can we have this discussion after, please?" I asked. He laughed, took my face in his hands, kissed me, relaxed now that he was inside me, we were together again, and I thought, I can't believe Mr. Basketball is inside me again.

By the end, he was shaking.

"I'm sorry," he said. "I haven't had sex in eleven months."

"That's okay," I said. Eleven months?

Eventually he stopped shaking. Eventually, we were lying next to each other and ran our hands over unexpected body parts. The spine. The ear. The nostril. The underside of a wrist. His penis was smaller than I had remembered, but I was bigger than I had used to be. Part of growing up was watching the world get smaller, and I convinced myself the sex felt better this way, smaller, softer, on a nice padded leather seat. It never hurt. So he took me to the floor of the bathroom and we made love on the white marble tile. He said he wanted me to feel him all over my body. He said he missed me so much he couldn't understand it. Neither could I. I ached in my tailbone, but I pressed him closer anyway. He kissed me each time he pulled back inside me, and his mouth was different now. His lips were harder and stronger and more potent in taste. He was more restrained and careless all at the same time, louder with his noises, as though he felt better when he announced who he was touching, who he was headed toward: Emily Marie, Emily Marie, he moaned.

The bathroom was so pearlescent, it was possible to consider the idea that we both had died.

Naked, on the bathroom floor, I stared at the large raised Roman-style tub, while Jonathan told me about his childhood in Greenwich and how he was always jealous of people who lived in the desert and had nothing to wear. "Why?" I asked. But sometimes he didn't answer questions, which made me wonder if I was using the right intonation. Instead, he told me he used to be a drug dealer in high school. "But it's okay, because I only sold it to rich fucks who would have found it elsewhere."

He told me about all of the girlfriends he had between me because he could tell just by looking at me that I needed to know everything about the gap.

"I dated this girl once who was really into rap music," he said. "It was weird. We'd be sitting around and she'd be like, 'Who was your favorite rap artist of 2000?'"

"And you'd say, 'The one with the woodwinds,' of course?"

We laughed and when we stopped laughing I said, "Tell me the truth. Did you ever sleep with Janice?"

"Janice?" he asked. "Who is Janice?"

"That girl," I said. "That girl with the gum. She was always chewing gum in our class."

How tragically we are reduced in time. My childhood best friend. That girl with the gum.

"Emily," he said. "I didn't sleep with anybody in *your* class. Who do you think I am?"

The last time I saw Janice was at the grocery store right before I left for Prague. She looked shocked to see me, like she had expected me to be dead by now or something. She told me she was finishing her fifth year at Boston College, where she studied biology. "Yeah, I don't know why I study biology," Janice said, rocking her cart back and forth. She was wearing her hair short. "It's the worst place in the world to go if you want to study biology. Even my professors know that. Sometimes, they look at us like, *seriously*? Like, this is a Catholic liberal arts school. We have one rat, and we've done all of our experiments on him. He's got about seven tumors by now. Like, *do you ever see us smiling*?" I laughed hard, and then her expression changed. "Well, see you around," she said quickly, and walked away. "Wait!" I almost shouted out, but instead turned the cart and went to get yogurt.

"I'm hungry," Jonathan said. "Let's go get a sandwich. You eat sandwiches?"

"That's like asking, 'Do you eat things in conglomeration?'"

"No, it's like asking, 'Do you eat meat slices in between bread?'"

We picked up two packaged sandwiches from the grocery store that were called Stripsy. We paid for them. *"Nashledanou."*

"This sandwich," I said, biting into the stale bread and the fried chicken, "all at once, is intimidating."

"Suddenly, spicy," he said. "And then an unexpected white sauce that confuses as much as it cools."

"Is it good? It's okay. Was I expecting better? Maybe."

"Is there lettuce falling everywhere, including but not limited to the ground, my shirt, that guy over there? Yes."

"But where can we apply blame?"

"Maybe to Prague as a whole, for settling," I said.

"Prague," Jonathan repeated, but in a movie-announcer voice. "Where the meat is never fully pressed into the crevice of the bread. Where there is no satisfactory meat-to-cheese-to–white sauce–to-lettuce-to-bread ratio."

We held hands and I remembered feeling something in the pit of my stomach, something like love or terror or the need to possess him, like a woman who is never and always alone, the terror of a woman who is in love all the time.

## 25

At home, Raisinet was having a seizure, and my father was on the couch holding him. Laura stood by the microwave crying. "Jesus," Ester said, and grabbed my hand. "We're going to the movies, Victor."

Along the way, Ester and I picked up feathered hats and stroked pashminas as we walked by the street vendors and one of us always said, "Soft," while one of us always agreed. A crazy man approached me and asked if I would eat his Pringle. "No, thanks," I said. Ester laughed. We were getting closer. Most days, we drank a different flavored coffee, and we made up hypothetical relationships between the vendors. Merchant Love, Ester liked to call it.

The only nondubbed American film playing was *Lilo & Stitch,* and Ester cried at the part when Lilo sends Stitch away. "I just can't take it when cartoons are cruel to each other," Ester said. "It's harder to take than when real people are cruel. I think that means something is wrong with me."

On the subway, she told me what it had felt like to be married.

"You know," she said, "the only way I can describe it is that I could walk through our kitchen at home and, when it was clean and organized, feel nothing but depressed. Everything was so clean, and the Tupperware was back in the cabinets and the sauce had been picked off the stove and here I thought that was what the problem was, but standing in the middle of the kitchen, everything felt clean and wrong. I had all the answers to all the questions I ever had and everything still felt wrong. I knew everything about my husband and he knew everything about me. I knew that when he woke up in the morning it took him ten minutes to brush his teeth, five minutes to yell at me for leaving a scarf on the stairs, even if he didn't fall or trip on it or anything, it was always the *principle* of the matter that mattered."

"That's what my father used to say when I left a sock on the floor," I said. "I'd say, 'Dad, it's just one sock, it barely takes up any room.' And he'd say, 'Emily, it's the principle of the matter.'"

Ester said that when you were married, there was no sense of urgency anymore. "Like when one of us was leaving on a trip, we wouldn't even have sex. I would say, 'You didn't even try,' and he would say, 'You're on your period.' And I would say, 'You wouldn't even know that because you didn't even try,' and he would say, 'Ester, I can see the garbage can.'"

"Sheesh," was my only response.

"Anyways," she said, "that's what it's like to be married."

"It's like having tampons in a can and somebody you love noticing?"

"It's like putting up a giant scoreboard in your living room."

"Then why would you want to get married again?" I asked.

"Because," she said. "Sometimes, you win."


*ODKUD JSTE?* This was what the teacher wrote on the board in big white letters during our fourth class. "Like, *Where are you from?*"

"*Jsem z Ameriky,*" I said to the class.

"*Jaké je vaše povolani?*" she asked. "Like, *What do you do?*"

"*Jsem obchodník,*" I said.

Like, *I am a businessperson.*

"That's just so not true," Jonathan whispered in my ear. "*Jste. Lhář.*"

Like, *You are a liar.*

"*Jste jen člověk,*" he said.

*You are only a person.*

"*Jste jen* the Little Mole."

*The Little Mole* was a Czech book of cartoons that Jonathan and I stumbled upon in Shakespeare and Sons one day, two weeks into his trip, about a mole who never spoke but traveled around town solving crimes in the spirit of socialism.

"He's so cute," Jonathan had said. "He reminds me of you."

Then we overheard some Frenchwoman yelling at her son, who was peering under books, making them fall to the ground. "You are just like *le* Little Mole!" she screamed. The boy cried.

Afterward, on the street, Jonathan pretended he was yelling at me, a little child, "that was mute and inquisitive and politically active!" Jonathan said. This made us laugh so hard, Jonathan started calling me *le* Little Mole.

And when I opened the door to my father's apartment to let Jonathan inside, Jonathan said, "*Le* Little Mole!" I had thought the nickname was just a joke that bonded me and Jonathan until my father approached, stuck out his hand, and said, "Please don't refer to my daughter as a mole."

This should have made me feel better but it felt the same way when my father and I used to sit around making fun of our noses, and my mother would say, "Victor, her nose is fine." It only confirmed everything that was wrong with my nose: long, lumpy at the top, overall much too eager. And when my father had said, "Don't call my daughter a mole," it confirmed it: there was something inherently mole-like about me that needed defending.

I had convinced Jonathan to come over and babysit Laura with me while Ester and my father went to the opera. "I don't want to meet your father," he had protested at the hotel. "It's too weird. I'm nine years older than you."

"He won't care," I had said. "His fiancée is almost twenty years younger than him." But as soon as I said this aloud, I knew it didn't matter. I knew I was wrong, the same way I had been wrong when I brought my Barbies to Mark's house as a child, and Mark asked, "Won't my dad think it's strange that I'm playing with Barbies?" to which I said, "No, he won't care. I promise."

"I'm Jonathan," he said, and stuck out his hand to greet my father.

"I'm Emily's father," my father said as he shook his hand slowly. It occurred to me then that my father had never met a man I dated before. It occurred to me that neither of us knew what to do. My father looked strangely at Jonathan and did not let go of his hand.

"We've done this before," my father said.

"Pardon?" Jonathan said.

"We've shaken hands before. I know you. I've done this with you before."

"I apologize, sir, I don't quite recall."

My father let go of his hand.

"You are a teacher at Webb High," my father said. "I remember you from the graduation. You were talking to Emily. We shook hands."

And the most surprising thing about this was that I was pleased; my father remembered my life.

"Oh," Jonathan said. "I was, yes. But I'm a lawyer now."

"But you were Emily's teacher, no?"

I chimed in. "No. We didn't know each other until I was in college."

We were silent. It was an obvious lie. Ester walked into the room with Laura.

"All right, Victor," Ester said. "The opera waits for no one except Pavarotti, and even then . . ."

She stood in front of the door and eyed Jonathan, who I realized was about her age, and this was humiliating for some reason, perhaps mostly for Jonathan, the two people in their thirties, one off to the opera and the other the babysitter.

"Wait," my father said, grabbing his coat and hat.

"Don't go, Dad!" Laura shouted all of a sudden. She fell at his feet with a rubber cheeseburger and banana in her hand. "Let's play Eat!"

Laura was obsessed with pretend. My father had gotten her a pretend kitchen, and she tugged on his arm and asked if we would all play Eat with her.

"I already ate, sweetheart," my father said, trying to peel her off of him.

"That's why we won't eat too much," Laura said.

My father looked at me for help.

But I stood there with my arms crossed, angry that my father called us out. *Laura is your responsibility,* I thought. *You had her.*

"What are we going to eat?" I asked as I scooped up Laura from the floor.

"You can eat the banana," she said, and stuck out her hand that held the rubber banana. "I'll have the cheeseburger."

"How come I get the banana?"

"Because I'm the princess and you are just the Bunny Friend."

The logic of eight-year-olds. I put her down on the couch.

"Bunny Friend?" I asked. "What do you mean?"

She put on a tiara. She handed me a headband with rabbit ears. I put it on my head.

"Bye, girls," my father said.

"Wait! Want to see my skeleton?" Laura asked, and lifted up her shirt, sucking in so hard her ribs hung carelessly over her hipbones. "Look at my skeleton!"

My father walked over, swooped her up, and hung her upside down by her feet until the vein in the middle of her forehead popped out from laughing so hard. "I'm going to shake your bones out," he said. My father was a different father around Laura. He was like a loving big brother, whereas sometimes, I felt like my father's business associate. I remember when I was younger, and my father and I were at one end of the dinner table, a bamboo plant between us, and we were making up lists of words that rhymed with our last name. Midol, I had said. He laughed. That's not a real word, he said. Then what is it? I asked. If it's not a word, what is it?

You got me there, he said, and we both took sips of his bitter coffee.

My father put Laura down. "Good night, girls." He looked at me and then at Jonathan. "You all be safe now," he said, closing the door.

To play Eat, you sit on a floor and you hold your head over plastic dishes with plastic carrot slices on them, then after, you throw the plastic carrot sticks behind your head and shout out, "All done!" only so you can ask for more plastic food to throw behind you, so you can ask for more plastic food to throw behind you, etc.

"This is getting silly," I said to Laura, chucking a stalk of plastic broccoli behind my head.

"You're right," she said. She sat down next to Jonathan. "I'll feed you pudding."

Jonathan opened his mouth. He was her prince, and princes, Laura said, should always be spoon-fed.

Jonathan seemed to like this idea. He smiled and said, "The best damn pudding I ever had."

Raisinet trotted happily into the room. Laura glared at him. "Go away!" she shouted. "Ruffski!"

"Laura," I scolded. "Be nice to the dog."

"Don't tell me what to do!" Laura snapped.

"And why not?" I asked.

"Because you are the Bunny Friend," she said. "Which is basically the same thing as the maid. Get us some tea, please, Bunny Friend!"

There were moments when Laura looked at me like she was trying to tell me how much she hated me. When she didn't understand quite who I was, when she admired and despised me all at the same time, and wrapped her arms around me and put her cheek to my chest just to feel the cold spots in my heart.

"Laura, go get washed up for bed," I said. "It's already nine."

"Oh, come on, Emily," Jonathan said. "I was just about to get more pudding."

"Come on, Emily," Laura mimicked. "It's time for more pudding. Don't be a bore."

Sometimes, she looked at me like she was already disappointed in what I could be. Children can make you feel like such a fraud in this way.

"All right," I said. "Eat the pudding." I looked at Jonathan. "But you'll have to put her to bed when she can't sleep."

Jonathan opened his mouth wide for pretend pudding, while I pretend smiled and, after, Laura rolled on the floor actually flipping up her skirt.

At ten, Jonathan put her to bed. He laid her body down on the mattress as though he had done such a thing before, his hand behind her head. "I love you," Laura said to him. "Not as much as Peter Pan, but I still do love you, very very much."

When Jonathan came out, he said, "Wow."

"What?" I asked.

"She is a spitting image of Mark," he said. "Her gestures, her smile."

"She's my sister too," I said, suddenly possessive of Laura.

"I know that, sweetheart," he said, and kissed me softly on the lips.

Later, when we heard Laura snoring, Jonathan and I climbed into the master bedroom, and Jonathan broke out a warm bottle of wine and I consented to the wall. Nothing ever really changed, I thought. Me in the master bedroom, Laura next door, and the wine was always warm. So I said, "No," to Jonathan. "Turn me around, I want to see the whole room. I want to see the room."

We were face-to-face. "I'm going to put my cock inside you," he said in my ear, and I pressed my nose into his shoulder. He put my arms against the wall, and as much as things might have looked the same, everything was different, like a discussion, upright as humans who had to carry their own weight.

"I am in loveski with you," he said after, under my father's silver sheets.

"How do you know that you loveski me?" I asked.

We tumbled over each other, thrilled to be in the master bedroom.

"I just know," he said. "I know like I know there are hairs growing out of my head."

"So when you're bald, I'll know it's over."

"Exactly."

## 26

Jonathan and I were going to meet at nine in Staré Město. He was leaving in a few days, and my skin already felt cold and dry as though he had gone. I was listening to one of Ester's CDs and thickening my lashes.

Laura was on the floor watching me apply makeup. Ever since Jonathan's comment about her face, I couldn't stop thinking of her as Mark. Like Mark was behind me, staring up from the ground, asking, "Why are you putting tar on your eyes?"

"Makes my eyes stand out more," I said.

"That makes *no* sense," she said.

Ester was behind me as well, watching from the table. I got the feeling that Ester wanted to come with me, as though watching me apply mascara was reminding her of a certain kind of happiness. Then she looked at my father, as if she were saying, Oh, I'd better not, I'm dating someone who is so responsible he'll probably wear his tie to bed. But then she went into her room and came back in a puffy blue dress.

"How do I look?" she asked. It occurred to me that she wanted to look attractive. That she could very well find Jonathan attractive. They were, after all, closer in age than any of us.

"Like you're about to blast off to the moon," Laura said, and I laughed. "Ester the astronaut, blasts off to Planet Snot!"

Ester grabbed her purse.

"Oh, you guys," Ester said. "*Please* don't hate me."

Ester and I went to Staré Město and sat on wicker chairs, waiting for Jonathan. Ester was crossing her legs and telling me her opinion on the most upsetting births of 2002. I wore black velvet stretch boots that I borrowed from my mother before I left, a black chiffon dress that bunched at the breastbone, and my mother's red paisley scarf, and I was so overdressed I felt like I was somebody's grandmother trying to get laid for the last time. I was so overdressed that when my father came into the apartment, he saw me standing at the fridge with my back toward him and accidentally said to me, "Hi, honey, I'm home."

"When is he coming?" Ester asked, looking at her watch. Sometimes, when I felt dry and worn-out, old and useless, I focused on the differences between me and Ester. Ester sprayed herself with too much perfume and wore a watch, while I just looked at the sun for guidance, and shrugged my shoulders and mumbled, "Soonish."

I drank two martinis before I could even feel them bubble down my throat and got drunk fairly quickly. I thought Ester was overdressed too, but she said this was impossible. She said that earlier we walked by a water fountain that was lined in golden horses, and being overdressed in front of golden horses in Prague was like being too prepared for the SAT.

"It's like wearing too much black to a funeral," I said.

"You can't wear too much black to a funeral," she said, like she was the authority on blackness and funerals.

"Yes you can," I said. "I've *seen* it."

Ester asked me if I was going to be protagonistic all night.

"You mean antagonistic," I said.

"See?" she said.

At the bar, I started talking to two Americans named Craig and Vince. Craig and Vince were in Prague on a business trip and they missed America. They worked with Nestlé. Craig handled the accounts and Vince handled negotiations. They hated cookies and they hated negotiations about cookies and they hated Prague, they said. Too many fucking cafés with too many cookies. Too many fucking places to sit down. Encourages nothing. What if they didn't want to sit down? And how the fuck do you say "cheese" here?

"*Sýr,*" I said.

"That's ridiculous," Craig said. Craig and Vince were hot all the time, like sweaty, they said, in the armpits especially, and everyone smelled like rotten cauliflower, and did we notice how the wine seemed watered down, like it was just another form of juice?

"You're drowning in specificity," I said. I had heard a tall blond woman make that comment about an exhibit at the Kafka Museum; she leaned into an older man's shoulder and said, "Frederick, this man was drowning in his own specificity."

Ester laughed. Ester was getting drunk as well.

We had been drinking for over an hour now and no sign of Jonathan. "Well," Ester said. "Who knows why men do what they do."

"He didn't change his mind," I said. "He's coming."

"Right," she said. "He is coming. Like my ex-husband is coming. Any second now, he's going to appear. White horse. Giddy up. Bullshit."

She told me that if her husband hadn't left her for being gay, he would have left her cleft chin.

"He didn't like my cleft chin," she said. "I said, 'I always *had* a cleft chin. I had a cleft chin when I married you, asshole.' "

I took a sip of my drink.

"He said, 'Doesn't that make it more upsetting or something?' "

Ester told me that he was concerned she would mother children with a million little cleft chins. That they would run around town and look like Harvey Birdman's offspring. "I don't even know what that means," she said. "Who is Harvey Birdman? Am I supposed to know who that is?"

"He's a cartoon," I said.

"You kids," Ester said. "You and Laura, always running around talking about shit I know nothing about. I'm sick of it."

"Well, we're sick of you," I said. "You and my father always running off to the opera. Always eating *gelato*. What's wrong with ice cream? Do you two ever listen to *music*?"

Ester laughed hysterically. "You're funny," she said. "You're just like your father."

I smiled.

"Not like Laura," she said. "Don't you think? She's so different."

"What do you mean?"

"Oh, I don't know," she said. "She's just different from you guys."

"Different how?"

"She says strange things," Ester said.

"Well, she's eight."

"And her widow's peak," Ester said. "It's pretty distinctive, don't you think?"

Laura had an incredibly severe widow's peak. That was why she looked so much more like Mark. My father didn't have a widow's peak, and neither did I. But Mr. Resnick did. He had a very severe widow's peak and I knew that because at a party when I was little he had come over to me and said, "Quick! A widow's peak, or a man's peak?"

"What's a widow's peak?" I asked.

He pointed to his. "*A man's peak.* Got it from my father. Not the only thing I got either. And I did my duty and gave it to Mark. It's the Resnick Peak, passed down through generations of us."

"She's not his daughter," I said aloud to Ester. "Laura is not my father's daughter."

Ester paused midmartini.

"You mean it's true?" I asked, not really believing my own theory.

She shifted her weight a few times in the chair before she began talking again.

"Please don't tell your father I told you," Ester begged. "He would kill me."

She told me that, at first, when Mrs. Resnick announced she was pregnant, my father had assumed it was his. But they had a DNA test done because my father wanted to be sure, and he was right for doing so—it wasn't my father's. But Mrs. Resnick was a wreck. Mr. Resnick had just killed himself, and she couldn't find the will to brush her teeth anymore, let alone raise a child with a dead father.

"She didn't have enough money," Ester said. "Not to raise Laura like she wanted to. So she guilt-tripped your father into fathering her."

"How?"

"She cried, banged her head against the bathtub, apparently."

Mrs. Resnick told my father he had to claim Laura as his, said he couldn't leave her alone like that, but my father said he couldn't lie to a child for the whole of her life. Then, Mrs. Resnick had looked my father in the eye and said, "We killed her father, Victor. We killed him. Now you need to be her new father." And he agreed, just like that.

"And my father told you all of this?" I asked.

"Yes," she said.

"That doesn't sound like him," I said. "Are you saying this just because you don't like Laura?"

"No," she said. "It's the truth. And I like Laura."

I felt sick.

"You can't say anything, Emily. This is a secret. This is serious stuff."

My tongue was damp and thick. "Are you okay?" Ester asked.

I went outside. I looked for Jonathan down the street. He's coming, I thought. Heads everywhere, but none of them Jonathan's. I went back inside and had the bartender call his hotel room. I listened to the phone ring. I went to the bathroom to splash water on my face, then looked in the mirror, and just like that, I was alone again.

## 27

E uropean interiors," Krištof said during our first class of European Interiors I, "advanced with the help of royalty."

"That is why Europeans trust their tastes," he explained, "while the Americans are always wasting everybody's time just trying to identify good taste." Europeans knew how to create their own private style, while Americans followed the latest trend. "Even if it meant lining your couch with baby's foreskin," Krištof said, and the class laughed.

My father the atheist, my father the capitalist, my father the man who was never trying to prove anything. I was often amazed at how little he tried to prove. He never hung paintings unless Ester made him. Ester said he didn't even have a mirror until she moved in. His curtains were dark brown, and he had curtains only because he couldn't sleep with the faintest hint of light. He never cleaned, and never defended the filthy apartment when we had guests (which was rare), not the way everyone else I knew always said, "Excuse the apartment, I'm in the middle of something." Once, I told him living there was like living inside a cardboard box with running faucets. "I left everything I loved about the inside of a home in America," he said in return.

"That's sad," I said.

In Prague, my father sat on chairs and read the paper in another language and never tried to defend anything. He never said, "Your mother, Emily, she was just too much." He never tried to prove that Laura wasn't his. Instead, he bought her pets and sent her to a horse camp last summer. He was very settled in his late fifties, comfortable in a chair he didn't care about. Resigned to a certain solitude. My mother had been wrong. He didn't need ivory elephants lining his desk or Italian vases on his dining room tables.

"What can you do with a pigeon?" my father asked. It was Wednesday. I hadn't heard from Jonathan in two days. We were at Findi, but I couldn't eat, couldn't think.

"Feed it," I said.

"Put it in the mailbox."

"Paint its wings."

"Follow it to the park."

"Say, 'Hello, sir, please don't shit on me,' to it."

"That one doesn't work," he said. "You can say, 'Hello, sir, please don't shit on me,' to anything."

"You can put anything in a mailbox."

"Certainly not. Not a tiger. Not a hot air balloon."

The couple next to us was loud, laughing. It felt like at any second, the wine could spill and we could start fighting. At any second, one of us could say something stupid, and anything could happen.

"I don't think it's going to work out," my father said. My father was light, airy, twirling his linguini on his fork.

"Huh?" I asked.

"Me and Ester."

"What do you mean?" I said, and I almost dropped my fork. I never saw anything that I was supposed to see, headed straight for me, and for some reason, my first tendency was to release my grip.

I had come to develop affection for Ester. Sometimes, she felt like a sister. A sister who was sleeping with my father, I suppose, but a woman who sat on balconies with me and laughed about the way my father shouted out "Groovy!" in his sleep.

"She's just," he said, and paused. "Not for me."

"Who is for you, Dad?"

"I don't know," he said.

"You can't run around by yourself forever," I said.

"As a matter of fact, you can."

"Dad."

"I don't need anyone, Emily. Why does anyone need anyone? I've always been on my own, and I'll die on my own."

"Don't talk like that."

"Talk like what?" he said. "It's the truth. You're not a little girl anymore. Time you face the facts. Your father is a loner. Your father just likes to be alone. Too much company creates too much fuss."

"You like the fuss," I said. "You like the wine and the chatter about fixing the coffeepot when it breaks. The fuss is annoying and who wants to argue about a painting or why the coffeepot is leaking water, but it's fuss and fuss is just what we do, right?"

"Truth is," my father said, "there's just too much. There's you, your mother, there's Laura, there's Mrs. Resnick. There's the dog. I just can't get involved in another commitment at this point."

"Drop Laura," I said, and as soon as I said it, I was horrified. But I couldn't stop. "We both know she's not yours."

"Emily," he said, "I don't like it when you're cruel like this."

"I'm sorry," I said.

I didn't necessarily want to prove that Laura wasn't his daughter, it was just that I couldn't stand not knowing.

"I wasn't around enough for you, Emily," my father said. "I wasn't. And I'm sorry for that. Sometimes I feel like I know exactly who you are, and sometimes, I confess, I have no idea. But I do feel we are close in our own way, and I feel that I have the right to ask you about that man in our apartment, your teacher from high school."

"Jonathan," I said.

"Okay then," my father said. "Jonathan. Tell me about *Jonathan*."

"He's my boyfriend," I said, and I felt foolish calling him my boyfriend for some reason. I'm not sure why other than the fact that Jonathan would not have described himself this way, if he were there to do so.

"What do you mean he is your *boyfriend*?" he asked. "He was your teacher for Christ's sake."

I chewed on my pasta. My father leaned forward over the candle and hushed his voice.

"Did he ever touch you while you were his student?" my father asked.

"Jesus, Dad," I said, wiping my mouth.

"Well I'm sorry if this is embarrassing for you, Emily, but it's an important question. The only question somebody in my position should ask."

"Somebody in your position?" I asked. "You mean, the position of being my father? It's not a job, Dad."

"I realize that, Emily."

He sighed. He took a sip of wine.

"I've spared you a lot of questions," I said. "I wish you would spare me this one. Just this one."

"You don't need to spare me anything, Emily," he said. "I am your father. If you have something to ask me, then ask it."

"Okay," I said. "How do you know Laura is your daughter?"

"We've been through this," he said, which meant, he had been through this—with my mother.

"You took a blood test?"

"I just *know*."

"But how?"

"You want to know the truth?" he asked.

What else would I want?

"Because Tom, Mr. Resnick, didn't sleep with her for years," he said. "That's how I know. He couldn't. He couldn't have sex."

I stared at him.

"He was a wobbler," my father said, and at first I was horrified because a wobbler sounded like the name for a man who couldn't have sex, a man whose penis was too unstable to be inserted. "He was a *wobbler*," Janice would have said, and rolled her eyes. But my father explained he had taken this antibiotic that ended up destroying the part of his ear that controlled his balance. It happened to a lot of people right after the drug came out. He had increased difficulty walking or standing up for long periods of time. A wobbler. Wobblers often did not attend social functions or perform regular everyday tasks.

"Joan started calling me during the worst of his condition, when he could hardly stand up. He would fall down the stairs sometimes, you know."

"Why did she call you?"

"I don't know," he said. "Proximity. I guess she trusted me. We were neighbors, friends."

"You wrote her checks for thousands of dollars," I said.

"Tom lost his job," he said. "They had no health insurance. They couldn't afford all of the bills."

"Did he know you were paying for all of this?" I asked.

"Yes, Emily," he said.

"He *knew*?"

"Yes."

"Is that why he killed himself?"

"I don't know," he said. "Who knows why anybody kills themselves?"

He was always so right, so dignified, so *the father,* and me, *always the daughter*. The waitress arrived with the check and this made us both feel grateful. My father thanked her, put his credit card in the book.

"Now it is my turn," he said. "How did you meet Jonathan?"

I stirred the ice in my glass with a knife.

"He was my teacher," I finally said. "So, go ahead. Put him in jail. He was my goddamn English teacher and he touched me. So *what*?"

My father sat there motionless. He did not look sad or upset or surprised or pleased; he looked out the window. When he faced me again, he had tears in his eyes. "We had no idea," he said. He picked up his napkin and put it over his face. I couldn't see his face, but I could see his shoulders shake.

"I mean, it's not your fault, Dad," I said. "It's nobody's fault."

He wouldn't remove the napkin from his face.

"I mean, there is no fault to be had. It's a good thing."

He put the napkin down and wiped his eyes.

"Right," he said. "It's a *good* thing."

Neither of us knew what to say. Talking about it felt wrong. Talking about it made me splice my words, stutter nervously, made me not want to talk about it. That had always been the problem and nothing was going to change that. Talking about it made us feel like people different from who we were, the kind of people who had failed, the kind of people whom other people rolled their eyes at, when we just wanted to be people who loved each other and sat around the fireplace and laughed about the way the shadow of the flames made the figures in the da Vinci painting look like cartoons. So we were silent until the waitress came back with my father's card, so silent I thought the people eating next to us were going to ask us to quit sitting there so damn quietly. We were quiet this way until the cab, when I looked over at my father and he was scratching the bottom of his throat, where his skin was loose and sagging, and he looked so foreign to me, an old man I might pass on the street and feel bad for. I felt panic rise from my stomach to my chest, the acute anxiety of not knowing my father anymore, of being coffined, in this black cab, this hearse, taking us past all the street signs: food store, bank, leftover generic storefronts from Communism, through the hilly dark in a country where nobody spoke our language. Talking was too hard—I of all people should have understood that. So I tried to. I tried to understand that my father had his reasons. Whatever they were, they were sure to be reasons. I made a peace offering. "What can you do with a dinner?" I asked quietly out the window.

"Make it unpleasant," he said back. He wouldn't look at me, and I worried that I disgusted him. That I wasn't who he thought I was, this whole time.

"Ruin it," I said.

We laughed so softly the cab driver probably couldn't even tell we had been speaking, and I wasn't even aware we were laughing until we were stopped at a light and it was silent again. The cane of a pedestrian hit methodically against the cobblestone, and walking sounded like a chore.

When we got back to the apartment, Ester was on the couch, painting her toenails. "*Dobrý den!*" she said, and laughed happily, as she leaned over to give my father a welcome-back kiss. "Honey, our new towel heater has arrived."

Then she turned to me.

"Who in the world needs a freaking towel heater? Your father does, of course. But we love him anyway I guess. Even if he is supremely flawed."

When my father did not laugh from the kitchen, I knew what he was thinking: I did not order that towel heater. If there was one thing my father *did* need to prove it was how much he didn't need a towel heater. He was looking at Ester from the kitchen holding up the towel heater, and I could see him thinking: How can I marry a woman who says "freaking"? That's teenage talk. That's little-girl talk.

My father only liked words that had been recognized by the *Oxford English Dictionary* for at least ten years, like "Internet," and "website," and he didn't believe in the immediate acceptance of slang. "It's irresponsible," he said once.

"How can you not be for progress?" I had asked him.

"It's a filtering process," he had said. "May the best functional slang win."

I sat down next to Ester and sank into the same spot on the couch. Our hips were touching. "Hey, scoot, Toot," I said, and she laughed like a little girl discovering rhyme for the first time, even though there were dark circles under her eyes that she didn't try to hide with makeup. Ester let me get close to her on the couch and share things with her like a sister, but there was still something that she kept shut down, moments when she would avoid eye contact or remind me which countries different perfumes came from even when I had never asked, as if to remind me, *I am older than you I am your father's lover and before you got here we used to drink wine on the balcony and analyze weather patterns.* It was a different kind of happiness, I could see her thinking, and so is sitting on the couch with you talking. But my father didn't notice any of that. What my father saw from the kitchen was his daughter and her red-haired friend on a couch, discussing episode 34 of *Merchant Love*, and his daughter asking her friend if she thought that the woman at the creperie was sleeping with the man who sold roses, because she saw them licking ice cream together in an alleyway all by themselves. They looked happy, the daughter said. "Anything is possible on *Merchant Love*," the redheaded friend said, and then leaned back in the couch as though she were at home.

## 28

I planned to tell Laura the truth when my father took Ester out to dinner to tell her it was over. It had started to snow. I boiled some tea and practiced telling her slowly, in pieces, but as soon as my father closed the door to leave, Laura was excited about something, running around in circles in the living room and then falling to the ground. She lay down with her arms spread.

"Let's play Dead," she said.

"Dead?"

"Yeah," she said. "You be fifteen years dead. I'll be recently dead."

She told me to lie down next to her. I wasn't sure what to do so I did.

"Okay, so you are wearing your dress with white socks. I'm wearing whatever I had on at the time of death."

She was breathing heavily.

"Then, when you see me for the first time across the bridge, you are going to say, 'Patricia, you're wearing *that*?'"

She put her finger in the air.

"By the way," she said, "I want my name to be Patricia once I'm dead."

She stood up.

"And then I say, 'It's what I was wearing at the time, Bunny Friend!'"

"I'm dead and I still have to be Bunny Friend?" I asked.

"Okay, you can be whoever you want. But, whoever you are, you have to get excited, jump up and down and stuff, and say, 'Why have you no underwear on, Patricia?'"

To be dead, according to Laura, you had to be on a bridge, and you had to have no underwear on. She would tell me that she didn't listen to her mother, that it was her mother's rule never to get in the car with-out any underwear on, in case you got in an accident, and then you'd be stuck around on the road all day, without any underwear on, and be really embarrassed.

"I was in a car accident," Laura said. "That's why I'm dead. See my scar?"

I told her I didn't think we should play anymore. I suggested dress-up, reading on the balcony. But Laura was too wrapped up in the imag-inary scene.

"Okay, so you see me on the bridge, and I say, 'Wait! Stop right there! I'm coming to you!' And as I walk to you we eat leaves that are really made out of sugar, and when you are dead, it's always a race against time . . ."

"But why? We're already dead."

"Oh, you can die a few times. I forgot to mention that. Once you die more than three, no, four times, you are officially dead forever. Any-way, so, the water is rising over the bridge, and it's getting in my ears, and I hate that, because it could lead to a forever infection, and at the last second, you pull me out of the river!"

I told her I was having difficulty imaging the landscape. She ignored me.

"And then," she said, "I say, 'Are you honestly going to tell me that nothing new has happened to you since you've been dead?' And that's when *you* say, 'It still feels really new to me, Patricia.'"

And that's when Laura started to get annoyed because she said I wasn't playing right. She asked me why I wasn't speaking, why I wasn't playing along. I told her I couldn't. I was dead.

"No, you're not *really* dead," she said. "You are only fake dead. Don't you get it? It's just a game."

Laura was getting flustered. Her cheeks were pink, and she looked like she was going to cry the way she cried when she couldn't sleep at night, a tired, overwhelming cry, exhausted by the length of one night.

"Okay," I said. "Okay, it's just a game. So what do I say next?"

"Never mind," she said, and started to walk away to the other room. "I'll play by myself. You are like the worst fake dead adult ever."

I tried to apologize for this, but she had already turned the corner. I followed her.

"Laura," I said, concerned, thinking of all the ways I could possibly tell her that my father was not her real father. That she was in Europe all alone with a bunch of strangers, that her only family was back in America, part of it buried in the ground. How weird, I thought. I could explain to this girl exactly what it looked like to watch her father die, his head crooked and his hands still. But what I said instead was, "Where did you learn this game?"

Laura was on the ground, petting Raisinet's underbelly. "Mark," she said.

The dog was silent. The snow fell harder outside.

"Raisinet," Laura said. "Shhh. Raisinet is dead. But he still has two more lives left."

I put my ear to Raisinet's stomach and when he didn't move, I decided I would never, ever tell Laura the truth because the truth was that this dog was dead. The truth was this girl was overwhelmingly alone, more alone than I ever considered myself as a child, and I didn't want to suddenly become the stranger who made her put her ear to the dead dog and listen to the silence.

"Take him away," Laura cried. "I don't want to sleep with that dead thing in the house."

"Okay," I said, brushing her bangs. "I'll take it away."

"Far far away," she asked.

"I promise," I said.

I sent Laura to bed. "Promise far far away?" she asked.

"Yes," I said. Laura closed her door and I looked for something to put Raisinet in. I found one of my father's small-sized suitcases and placed his body in. "Good-bye, Raisinet," I said, and when I closed the lid, I started crying. The room was dark, the way it gets dark after no one bothers to turn the lights on while the sun sets. I decided to give it one last try and called Jonathan at the hotel. He actually picked up.

"Hi," he said.

"Let's go to the bone church," I said to him.

I waited for my father to come home and sat on the couch with the dog in the suitcase. I practiced breaking the news to my father:

"The dog is dead," I said aloud, but it didn't sound right, so I added, "Dad, the dog is dead," and that didn't sound right either, so I said it in Czech, *"Pes je mrtvý,"* and that didn't sound right either, because in Czech, nouns could be masculine or feminine, but they could also be separated into living and nonliving, and so maybe it was not grammatically correct to still call the dog the *pes* because part of being a dog *is being a dog,* and it was now more dead, more *mrtvý,* than it was a dog.

By the time my father arrived, the truth didn't sound right in any language, so I just said it.

"Dad," I said. "The dog is dead."

"Where is it?"

"In the suitcase," I said.

"Why the hell is it in the suitcase?" he asked.

"I promised Laura I would go bury it."

"Now?"

"It doesn't feel right to fall asleep knowing the dog is in the living room, dead."

"I suppose not," he said, sitting down. "I suppose not."

He had questions: did Laura know (she was the one who found him), was she sad (about as sad as she got before she was forced to shower), how did it happen (like everything), well what does that mean (at some point, his heart stopped beating).

# 29

At the hotel, everything was different. Snow was piled high outside, and Jonathan was awake at the kitchen table. My legs were goose-bumped and cold.

"Heat's not working," he said.

The heat had been off since the middle of the day when the pipes froze and the temperature inside the room had dropped to fifty degrees. He called the front desk and they said they were working on it, a repairman was coming. We looked out at the tiny world covered in snow and as far as we could tell, there were no streets or people or things to say. The repairman was surely out there, somewhere else, never coming. Jonathan was across the room. The doornails were dead at the hinges. The dog was heavy in the suitcase.

"Where have you been?" I asked him.

"Here," he said. "Reading the paper."

Something about him was off. He looked broken. Like a wire in his brain had snapped. Like he had been staring at a plant for too long.

"A whale randomly exploded in Australia," Jonathan finally said, picking up the American newspaper on the table. "Scientists are still speculating."

I opened the window.

I put the suitcase on the table. "What's that?" he asked.

"It's the dog," I said. "The dog is dead."

"*Emily Marie,*" he said.

When he was sorry about me, sorry for coming to Prague, sorry for ever sleeping with me in the first place, he liked to use my full name as an imperceptible method of scolding.

"We have to bury it at the bone church," I said, holding up the suitcase.

"Now?" he asked.

"Yes," I said.

He looked at me like I was crazy, but we covered ourselves in our winter coats and hats and got on the tram. Jonathan was acting weird, like he thought I was weird, so I tried to lighten the mood. I told Jonathan that at Apropos Restaurant that morning, there was a sign above the vent that would have made him laugh. It said something in Czech, with the English translation underneath, DO NOT COVER SPIRACLES OF HEATING.

"Is 'spiracle' even a word?" Jonathan wanted to know. Before I could say, yes, dumbass, it's an external tracheal aperture of a terrestrial arthropod, before Jonathan could laugh and pull me into him, the undercover tram officer heard my English and wanted to know why Americans never thought they needed permission to be so dumb.

"*Jízdenku,*" the tram officer demanded, like, *ticket*.

The tram police in Prague were like a secret police left over from an expired Communist tradition, dressed casually in jeans and fleeces, riding the trains silently like they were just another tourist, and then flashing a gold badge.

"*Jak se máte?*" I said back, and I was learning from class that only an American would say this since when the Czechs heard, "How are you?" it was like, well, my mother's getting married and she needs to find a dress, and she will, I'm certain.

But not the tram officer. He did not even hear me.

"*Jízdenku,*" he said. "Or off tram. Or seven hundred koruny."

Jonathan and I looked at our empty hands. I couldn't find my tram pass. We stepped off the tram.

The first thing I noticed was the depravity of the situation. This was a trick my mother had once taught me. The snow was thick on the ground. My shoes were wet. A beggar was in a blue hooded sweatshirt kneeling in front of a yellow Lab that had a rat on its back. The rat was wet, rubbing his nose with his paws. The beggar had his cupped hands outstretched and was so still, his shape looked like a pipe that a careless passerby might decide to smoke. This was the traditional way of begging for money that I had seen all over Prague.

"Do you think the beggar trained the rat to do that?" Jonathan asked. He was so shamelessly American, the way he said beg-*ger*, the way he assumed this man was homeless only to be amusing. And the poor yellow Lab, I thought, no weapons, no money, no coat in this snowstorm—merely the instinct to kill. "Ruffski," Jonathan said, staring down at the yellow Lab. "Ruffski!"

The dog sniffed at my suitcase.

"Isn't it weird that to be homeless in the Czech Republic there are still all these rules to follow?" I asked Jonathan, and I thought that if I was going to answer a stupid question with a stupid question I could have made it a more efficient one, like, Jonathan, why don't we just go back to the hotel? How are we going to get to the bone church at this hour? Or, Where were you? Why can't you just love me in a regular way?

Instead, I said, "Like, you can't just be homeless and poor and beg, you have to sit in this uncomfortable position all day long and you are still poor and begging, but really uncomfortable."

Jonathan shrugged.

"Let's go get highski," he said.

We wandered through the city until we located Café Red, an underground bar where we could buy weed and smoke it right there. On the way, we walked through the streets. We were tourists who laughed at street signs. All the men in the street signs wore top hats and all of the little girls wore bows in their hair, bows that made them look less like pretty little girls and more like hybrids of children and bunnies.

"Hey, there's the underground bar," I said, pointing to Café Red.

"Why do you keep saying 'underground bar'?" Jonathan said. "What's so fucking great about an underground bar? It doesn't become cooler the farther underground it is. Like, nobody says, 'Hey, check out my fourth-floor restaurant, it's so cool because it's on the fourth floor.'"

We walked down the stairs. A black man with long dreadlocks was behind the bar, asking us what we wanted. "What you want?" the man said, and I noticed the Jamaican flag pin on his shoulder. "*What* you want?"

"Weed," Jonathan said. He turned to stare at the tall woman in the corner of the bar, her long blond hair like a sheet of ice melting down her back. She was beautiful, dancing, slowly moving her hips to the sound of nothing. She had her eyes closed as if she could not bear to watch her own body communicate, as if her subtle movement only validated the inarticulate murmurings of the drunk foreigners, who, she understood, were nobody. Watching her made me feel like nothing. Watching Jonathan watch her made me feel worse than nothing.

"Fucking Americans," the Jamaican said. But we got what we wanted.

We sat down on the seats. Jonathan put his hand on my leg so fast, I felt like part of the scenery, like the leather upholstery of the chair underneath him. He began to roll the joints.

"Jesus fucking Christ, this is worthless shit," Jonathan said after his first drag. "We'd be better off with oregano."

"Like that guy is even *from* Jamaica," I said. "It's fucking Disney World here."

"Like, hey, what part of Cleveland are you from?" Jonathan said. We both knew it was a joke, so we didn't even have to laugh. Jonathan was the only person who ever understood me like this, and he used this as leverage to get what he wanted.

I put the joint to my lips and apologized to Raisinet in my head. I felt the burn in my lungs and the panic rise to my diaphragm and I couldn't be sure that I wasn't choking. We sat in the booth for what felt like an hour, then Jonathan said, "Let's get the fuck out of here. Let's go find that bone church."

"We just got here," I said.

"Emily, there are chandeliers made out of peasant bones and that's something to see."

"I know that," I said. "I was the one who told you about it. And I said it exactly like that."

"All right, then, why are you fighting?" he said. "Let's go to the bone church."

But I was tired. I inhaled and thought: We are never going to find the bone church. How exhausting. The poor dog.

I didn't move. And Jonathan didn't stop staring at the blond woman while muttering, "Ruffski." Jonathan didn't think I could hear him. The burning oregano was regulating my breath, and I thought it was possible that I had never properly breathed until this moment. My stomach extended, and the smoke burned my lungs, like an old newspaper on fire, quick to light, quick to burn out, then: ash and I felt gone. The Jamaican from Cleveland had returned to our table, his face hovering in the smog around us. I couldn't tell if he was on fire or if the place was on fire or if nobody was on fire at all but me. "What you want?" he asked. Jonathan waved his hand for the man to go away.

"Nothingski," Jonathan said.

There was a man I presumed to be French staring at me from the other side of the bar, sitting under the long red fluorescent light that read: DOBRY DEN, like, *good day*, like, this is what it looks like when the Devil says hello in the morning. The presumably French man winked. I could barely move my mouth to explain the urgency of this to Jonathan.

"Why do you make Shakespeare references when you haven't actually read much Shakespeare?" I asked him instead.

"I don't knowski," he said.

"It scares me that you make references to books you haven't read," I said.

"Hey," he said. "Let's never mind that. Let's just go to the bone church."

The presumably French man winked at me.

"*Le* Little Mole, can you hear me?" Jonathan said. Stop staring at her, I thought. I wanted to scream in his face. The blond woman was only the most beautiful woman I had ever seen. "*Le* Little Mole!"

"Stop calling me *le* Little Mole!" I shouted at his face.

The French man was staring. The blond woman was touching her thighs. Jonathan sighed. "*Le* Little Mole, I need to tell you something."

"What?"

"You're not going to like it."

"Then don't tell me, please."

Which is what I should have said to my mother when she told me that she and my father were getting divorced: I don't want to know how a man can get up and leave his three-thousand-dollar desk behind him. I don't want to know if he buys a new one. It should have been what I said to Mark when he leaned over my shoulder and said, "Who's over there behind that tree?" It should have been what I said to Ester right before she admitted Laura wasn't my sister. It should have been what I said to Janice when I sat passenger in her old car: don't tell me. I don't want to know how many fingers Mr. Basketball can fit inside you, Janice; I already know. Two, sometimes three, depending on how relaxed you are. It was like I already knew: to be happy I am going to have to stop listening to everybody I love.

"Okay," Jonathan said.

"Okay," I said.

This was an example of a warning sign: as a child when Jonathan had walked into his kitchen and said, "I'm bored," his mother would make him do things like wash all the walls with a toothbrush or count out five hundred toothpicks just to put them back in the box; then she'd lean over his shoulder and say, "Are you bored yet?" He would shake his head, no no. "Good," she'd say. "Jesus was *never* bored."

"Just say it," I said. "You're bored with me. Is that what you have to tell me? I'm nothing like what you thought I would be."

He leaned over and covered my mouth with his. He pulled away, and we looked each other in the face.

"I'm not bored," he said. "I'm married, Emily."

The French man was calling me over with one finger. The blond woman was still touching her thighs.

"All right," Jonathan said. "I just had to say it. There, I said it. I'll say it again. I'm married. I'm married, I'm married, I'm married."

I felt the tiny fire start at the tip of my throat.

I thought maybe this was just another joke, so we turned to each other and laughed. We laughed until we were in tears. I did not look at the French man, though I knew he was staring. If I made eye contact, he became part of the joke too, which, I slowly realized, was not a joke at all. Nothing was even funny. The dog was dead. But Jonathan couldn't stop laughing, his face almost a dangerous shade of blue, so he pointed to the door and walked out of the café, like, *Excuse me, I have to remember why this isn't all that funny so my lungs don't explode inside me*.

And, to think, *still*. I was still definitely not an adult. No adult looked at another adult and laughed about nothing until their face turned blue. I was never going to grow up if I continued to sit here; I knew this for sure. We needed to leave. We needed to go to the bone church, bury the dead dog like responsible people, go back to the hotel, and walk through the doors and stare up at all the vaulted ceilings and trace our fingers on the French windowsills. We needed to sneak into the warm pool and swim lazily next to the glass swans, wash the chlorine off in the shower, scrub our bodies with free soap and love each other because the sterile scent of our skin reminded us of luxurious things we used to love.

But I was still there with a half-smoked joint and a dead dog and a table with *stůl* written on it in red marker. *Stůl*. Table. And Jonathan was *married*? In this underground bar with no windows, everything was dangerously without context, especially the English language: tay-bull. Mare-ead. What did that even mean?

I sat back with my head against the seat and my hands on the *stůl* and my feet itched. It felt like there were cockroaches at my ankles, live scorpions in my mouth, fire rushing up my leg until the whole of me was devoured, my body not quick to burn, but slow to catch. Pathetic flesh crumbling to ash.

The French man slid up next to me. Jonathan was nowhere to be seen.

The French man wanted to know all about me, like my habits and hobbies and preferences regarding all things, but he didn't know much English.

"*Salut,*" the French man said, like, *informal hello,* like, *Nice pants, babe.* "*Ça va? D'où viens tu?*" like, *Where are you from, but only in a really casual way.*

We discovered that our common language was functional Spanglish.

"*Quiero saber* you," he said. Like, *I really want to know you in a scholastic way.*

"*Le* Little Mole," I said. "Like the cartoon. I fight crime."

And then, even as I felt sure I hated Jonathan, I knew I loved him more than anything I had yet loved in my life. Soft food against my tongue, Mark and I lying on the stone wall as kids, the memory of my parents' laughter in the kitchen, bobbing in the backwaters of my brain: all slowly drowning evidence that I was worth more than this.

"*Le* Little Mole," the French man said, and shook my hand. I peered around the French man's head. Where was Jonathan? He could have been anywhere. Jonathan never said, "Be right back." Though why would he? Wasn't it always implied?

"*Le* Little Mole," he said. "*États-Unis?*"

"America, *sí*."

"*Te gusta Praha?*" *Are you happy here?*

"*Pan muy malo*," I said. *Have you noticed there is a bread problem here?*

"What *es tu* address *en Praha?*" he asked. *You're funny, I will find you,* like, *You're already the arrow in my heart and where have you been shot from?*

"No address," I said. *I would never tell you where I live, WEIRDO.*

"*Por qué no?*"

"*No libro.*" *No book.* I meant, *No pen.*

"*Maquillaje*. Or, how do you say, lipstick?"

"No."

"Write in *mi sangre*," he said, and pointed to his arm. *Mi sangre*, my blood. He smiled, and I sensed his instant dedication, like I was already the skin over his muscles and he had no choice in picking a covering. He put his hands in his pockets to find a pen, a pin, a tiny knife to release the *sangre*, and I understood I must leave before this was no longer a really weird experience. But the man had moved closer. I was lead against the leather of my seat, his hand was on my thigh, and I measured how fucked-up I was becoming by how normal this felt.

"Here," he said. "*Listo*. Tell me how it is I can . . . *ver* . . . you . . . again?" Like, *I am ready to see you again.*

I thought about saying, *Dumbass, I'm still here*—but Jonathan was the only person in the world who would have laughed at this, so I just shrugged my shoulders and felt my grasp on Jonathan slip. Even though I wasn't releasing my grip. Perhaps that was the problem; I was holding on to something that was dead. Walking around the city with a corpse in my hand. I couldn't see Jonathan anywhere through the smoke. I nearly choked understanding that this whole time, I had felt his hands against me, but this whole time, he had been married.

"Aha!" said the French man. The man found a bottle opener on his key chain.

"*Escribir* on *mi* arm," he said. "Scratch *suave*. Leave *solo blanco* marks on *mi* skin."

I wanted to tell this man to go away, but I couldn't say the words. I was too disconnected from my lips.

"Don't you know where you live?" the French man asked, the only thing he said in perfect English.

Café Red's architecture was designed to make you feel like you were dying; how apocalyptic to place a window in an underground bar.

"No," I told the French man. "No, I don't know where I live."

I could feel ghosts climbing these walls, I could feel the dog attempting escape before the snow buried us in this concrete room forever. But I couldn't even get off my chair. I couldn't even feel my own hands. It was possible that a person could live their life and not really live anywhere at all. It was possible that Jonathan was never coming back. It was possible that I didn't know Jonathan at all. It was possible that once you left, you weren't allowed back in. It was possible that the woman with long blond hair dancing by the fake ivy in the corner followed him out and that this was entirely Jonathan's motivation in faking his own suffocation. It was possible that she was a better partner than me, that Jonathan could have better partners than me, even though he was always my best. I couldn't blame him. I would stop breathing if it gave me cheekbones as high as hers. Just like that, I had stopped breathing. I was suddenly so sad, I felt I could will everything out of existence, even my own breath. But how appropriate. I was dirty and alone and in love with a married man. I should have been out of breath. I looked down at my shoes. They were filthy. But the filth always counts for something. "The filth is what proves we drive the car!" my mother used to shout at my father when he complained about the car being too dirty. "The filth is what proves your father isn't paying any attention," Ester had said to me.

I was always acting as though I never had any choices, but in the end, that was the only thing I ever really had. So I made a choice. I took the bottle opener in my hand. I pressed it against the French man's forearm.

"*Suave,*" the French man said. "No breaky skin."

And my mother was right: the filth was what proved we were moving against things.

The French man slid his fingers through mine.

And then, "I'm backski," Jonathan said, just like that. He sat down and leaned against the back of the chair. He sighed. Even though I wanted to tear his face off, I was grateful for his return. I was always grateful for his return. Even though I had a million questions, all I wanted to do was just let go of the French man and put my head on Jonathan's shoulder. I wasn't even mad. There were too many things I always assumed. Too many people I tried to claim as mine. And that was wrong. If there was anything I learned when I was fourteen, it was that people were not yours. Jonathan was never my happiness to be had. I put down the bottle opener and decided to at least be kind to the French man next to me—Listen, go away, I don't need this. The French man looked at me and Jonathan and rolled his eyes. "Putain," he said, and walked away.

I inhaled the last of the joint and it crumbled to ash in my fingers. With my lungs now wide open, I felt calm again. I spoke to Jonathan in puffs of smoke: Nice. To. See. You. Againski. Jonathan looked back at me. Forgiveski me, he mouthed. I could see that he was sad too, but maybe this was my imagination treating him as me. Jonathan grabbed my hand. Jonathan was still the only one who understood my impatience with the world.

"Let's get the fuck out of here, le Little Mole. Let's go to the bone church."

I nodded. I agreed. It was time to go to the bone church. I grabbed the suitcase. We got out of our seats and walked out of the café. The night air came at me like a wave and I closed my eyes, bracing for something.

But we lived. And we walked.

"If you could put your bones in the bone church, what would you want to be?" Jonathan asked me while we were waiting for the late-night tram. He leaned against me as he explained why he wanted to be the chandelier: even after he was dead, he still wanted all his bones to be together in one place.

"I'd be the bell that tolls at midnight," I said.

"Is there a bell that tolls at midnight?"

"Fine, then," I said, and I can't explain why this felt like the cruelest thing he ever said to me.

When the late-night tram never came, Jonathan walked me back to my apartment. He wouldn't kiss me on the mouth. Now that I knew about his wife, he said it felt like cheating. He was sorry for coming. "I shouldn't have come," he said. Jonathan said he was leaving the next morning for London, and then New York. Susan was in Africa. She was coming home to be with him. I nodded like I understood something. I closed the door. I put the suitcase down. No matter where we went, we always ended up back where we started. I laid my head down on the pillow and when I tried to dream of some other life, Jonathan was right—there was no bell that tolled at midnight. But there was a garland of arms lining the entrance of the church. There were elbows flanking the altar. There were strings of skulls draped over windows like curtains, like, *welcome,* like, *hey,* like, *Why don't you kneel down and make yourself at home? Why don't you prepare your bones to be something more elaborate than yourself?*

# This Is an Example of a Warning Sign

# 30

I had a new family. I always had a new family. "Isn't that wonderful?" my mother had asked, popping blue-cheese-stuffed red peppers into her mouth on Christmas Eve.

That was how my mother liked to frame it: my stepsister, Adora, my stepbrother, Nick, and my stepfather, Bill. Bill kept his hair trimmed short and insisted on a real Christmas tree even though I reminded him that real things were too much work and pointed to his three dogs, chewing the couch. Bill smiled, stood in front of the Christmas tree, and proclaimed that this year, it was Functional Christmas.

I was twenty-six. I lived in Brooklyn, above a deli. Being in my apartment meant feeling like I was always eating something. Every day, I was forced to think of things on top of things on top of other things, or me, in this box, alone. Or the box that sat in the front window of the deli that read 3,000 PEPPER PACKETS. Nobody ever moved it. Nobody ever needed that many pepper packets. So it just sat there, forgotten, for a year. The apartment was too expensive to have floorboards that sank in certain spots when I touched them lightly with my foot, but it still did anyway. There was a leak in the ceiling and I called my landlord and he told me the toilet was running in the apartment above me and that was why it was leaking. "But nobody lives there?" I asked. Then he cut a two-foot hole in my ceiling and my heating bill doubled. I wore a hat to bed for a week and when I went home for Christmas, Bill made jokes about me being the star of some one-woman film where there were never enough vegetables.

"Santa says that when there is a girl riding the poverty line, Christmas becomes about the things she needs," Bill said to me, holding out gifts.

"This is how my new family talks to me," I told my father over the phone. My father was living in Moscow and called me to celebrate the fact that Russia had officially become a superpower again.

My father talked in jokes and Bill talked in code. Bill was always Santa and I was always this girl. Though I never sat on his lap. And we never drank eggnog and we never kissed. Heavy-cream-based drinks sat in our stomachs and made us feel ungrateful—so no eggnog, my mother said. I opened the gifts. Socks. A cookbook. Luggage identifiers. A printer cartridge. "Thanks," I said.

I was the kind of woman who got printer cartridges for Christmas, and Adora was the kind of woman who got an all-expenses-paid honeymoon to Hawaii, saying, "Thank you, Father," and then looked at me and my printer cartridges like she wished she could help in some way. My mother thought Adora was a phony, and I said, "What's she pretending to be?"

"That's what I'm not sure of yet," my mother said.

We were all pretending. Anyone who thought differently was just pretending. I was pretending that I didn't hear my mother in the kitchen crying into a cereal bowl most nights that week, and Bill was pretending that this didn't bother him. He woke up, walked down the stairs, rubbed her back, and asked her questions like, "What's wrong?" or "Are you sick?" as though her pain had nothing to do with the fact that my father was dying.

Not like I was any better. I coexisted gracefully with all of them; my conversations tended to be mere call-and-responses, ahh-choo-bless-you-thank-you-Bill. But at some point, Bill and I would both need something out of the refrigerator and reach for the door handle at the same time. "I'm really sorry to hear about your father," Bill finally said, opening the door. "I wish there was something more I could do. I feel completely helpless."

"Thanks, Bill," I said, and pulled out the last leftover slice of pizza. "Your helplessness means a lot to me."

He didn't laugh. He just closed the fridge.

"I'm joking," I said, and then he laughed a little, then I laughed a little, and he looked at my slice of pizza, then laughed a little bit more to show me how cool he was with the fact that I just took the last slice of pizza, the one he had bought last night and planned on eating for lunch today, because my father was dying, and whoever's father was dying was automatically the one who got the last slice of pizza.

My boyfriend Kevin seemed to be the only one who understood how to behave. When I told him that my father would be dead in three months, Kevin held my face in his hands. When I screamed and shouted and told him I couldn't stand the feel of my clothes against my skin, he said okay, and took off my shirt, and then my pants, and ran a cool ice cube down my back until it melted and I was calm.

"He calls me A," Adora complained, sorting through a pile of clothes in her bedroom chair while her breasts darted back and forth like nervous eyes. My stepsister, Adora, was the kind of woman who was always naked from the previous something or other. She was expressing doubts about her fiancé, Orrin, as I plucked her bra from the top of her desk. "Then he slaps my ass, like we're on the same sports team or something. Is that *normal*?"

We were in Greenwich dressing for her engagement party at Orrin's father's house, which was to become Adora and Orrin's house after they married. I was the kind, patient listener clothed in a black dress and amber earrings, hooking her strapless from the back, and I was the only one in the room, so it was my responsibility to ask all of the important questions, such as, "Is this what you really want, Adora, do you really want to be called A for the rest of your life by a man who gets his haircut from a *stylist*?"

"Don't worry, Adora," I was supposed to say, "we'll just call the whole thing off because this time, things aren't right."

"What do you mean?" Adora would have asked, and I would have told her what I heard Orinn's father say that morning after he thought I left the room:

Do you love her more than the Mets?

Of course, Orrin said. I *hate* the Mets.

Thattaboy. Hate the Mets. Hate 'em hate 'em hate 'em.

I hate the Mets probably more than I *love* her.

I hate the Mets more than I hate your mother.

And Adora would have found this confusing, but also appalling, and then would have expressed her concerns about dying alone, and I would have reminded her that she was only thirty-two, and there was always a next time, and next time was always better, and the time after that even better, and soon nobody would remember *this time*. This time was fleeting and already forgotten, and next time would be forever: crepe black minidresses that revealed knees and ankles and shins and we'd toast to your new tall dark and handsome man and we wouldn't care about anything because caring was what invited the suffering in the first place, right? Next time, maybe we would even invite Jesus— did you hear he can turn water into wine? "Imagine how much money we'd save," Adora would have said.

But I was done hooking the bra, and she was beautiful now in her engagement-party dress, a tea green that draped off her shoulders, and I was sipping on coffee, half-listening to her describe the pain of loving too much and half-listening to Phil Collins instructing us to Please Come Out Tonight.

"My name is *Adora*," she said, walking out of the bedroom to greet the guests. "That's what I tell him."

Adora had a beautiful name to get married in. It was perfect for the invitations, perfect in purple and pink and gold cursive. Bill had named her Adora, Italian for second person singular present imperative of the verb "*adorare*," Bill joked once. Then he started singing Adora for-a you-a, Adora for-a me-a, Adora for-a everybody! This is the song he used to sing to her at night in a fake Italian accent when she was a little girl, and a song he still sometimes sang when we were all together. But Bill was not here yet. Bill was not even Italian. And neither was my mother really; she was 50 percent, and if she had been there, she would have been not singing, but telling people that I spent a lot of time as a child learning how to spell my name backward.

At the engagement party, Kevin and I sipped on vodka by the yucca canes with Adora's friend from high school Melinda. Melinda was also an interior designer in the greater New York area. She had worked on Coco Chanel's house in Paris, which she got lost in three times because there were so many mirrors. Melinda and Adora were six years older than me, Orrin nine years older than I was, so this meant that all of their friends were in their early thirties, sons and daughters of minor celebrities, inheritors of three-floored town houses in Manhattan and paid tickets to the Ivy Leagues.

"Aren't you just dying to get your hands on the Capote house?" Melinda said.

I swirled the vodka in my mouth with my failing native tongue. It felt thick, like a piece of wet bread I couldn't swallow, filling with holes as it expanded to fit my mouth.

"I've seen pictures of it in *Architectural Digest*," I said.

"It just has so much space, so much potential," Melissa said. "It's like a ripe tomato waiting to be cut. Oh God, I can hardly stand knowing that house is out there."

When Truman Capote was alive he had designed his Long Island home himself. He told *Architectural Digest* that his design principle was "unfinished" and designers were a "bore."

Melinda sipped her drink. "Though, I suppose it's all right. Right now, I'm doing Woody Allen's apartment. This is his third redo in ten years. It's the most exotic challenge. He says he wants this apartment to reflect his current self-image."

I figured that was a lie as well but was proved wrong when a few months later, Melinda got sick with meningitis and called me to take over the job, with the promise that I give her 15 percent of my earnings. I became even more convinced when I stood on the terrace of Woody Allen's New York City penthouse, surrounded by a garden of lilies next to a small pond. I asked him whether he wanted his apartment to feel lived in, and he said, "Yes, of course!"

"By whom?" I asked.

"By me!" he said.

"A good place to start," I said.

"Or, well, by Kierkegaard," he added.

"All right."

"Or maybe Kokoschka."

I wrote them all down in my notebook.

"I don't know," he said, sitting down. "I like that question. I'll have to think about it."

* * *

"Jack is late," Orrin said, looking at his watch. "I guess everyone in this town is just late, late, late."

"That's because the fucking houses in Greenwich are too far apart!" Adora cried. "That's why I never trick-or-treated here when I was a kid."

Barbara Walters's third cousin was by the water fountain explaining the difference between Sunni and Shiite over the mashing of shrimp in our mouths, the African parrot was down the hall shouting, "Hello, banana!" There was the faint cry of the maid in the kitchen yelling on the phone, and the chitter-chatterings about the advantages of winter weddings—silky hair, red cheeks, frosted windows.

"You might even consider sewing seal fur into the bodice of your dress," one of Adora's friends told her.

We were on a red couch that cost the same as a second mortgage for a house (not as big as this), but in a house (as big as this) there was too much space for everything. The distance between Mondrian paintings was too vast. The house was like a museum in transition. The lamps were chrome, but the wood was dark mahogany; the pool was half-indoors, half-outdoors. The mirrors were kept too high up on the walls so nobody could see their own reflection, though Orrin was so handsome and Adora was so beautiful with blond curls down her back, this seemed like a nice thing to do for the guests since the last thing anybody wanted to be in this house was their actual self.

The more Orrin's friends talked, the less I understood: Williams is the new Harvard and has always been the new Harvard; being Indian is very fashionable right now.

"Has my mother arrived?" I asked Adora.

"My father just called," Adora said. "They will be late as well. He said to start without them."

"Start what exactly?" Orrin asked.

"The general partying, I suppose," I said.

"But the partying has started," Orrin said. We looked around at the room, the guests barely moving, barely talking, the room looking more like a painting of a party.

"Begin!" I shouted so loud, a woman in purple cheetah print spilled her drink. "Everybody, please begin amicably socializing!"

To be honest, by that point, I was a little drunk.

The room laughed.

"I *love* you," Adora said, putting her arm around me. This meant she was drunk too.

What we could not see: in the kitchen, the maid put down the plastic ladle on the hot stove and called her boyfriend. She walked into the pantry. She cried on the granite tiles and stared at the endless variations of jarred Italian imports, roasted red peppers and a rare olive oil, while she tried to tell her boyfriend she didn't want to be with him anymore.

I was in the dining room and my mouth was hot and burning with horseradish when the front door opened. I could feel the pool on my skin, like a hotel pool warm and sweaty like a baby, the humidity emanating to all the rooms, clinging to the sweat on my skin. I told my clients never to build pools inside their homes, water seeks water, and you, I would say, are 70 percent water.

A brown-haired man stood tall in the frame, snow drifted inward, and he hung his black trench coat on the rack. He brushed the snow off his Florsheim shoes.

"Jack's here!" Adora screamed. She interlaced her arm with his and walked toward us.

"This is Jack," Adora said to me, like she was introducing me to the president of the United States.

He stuck out his hand. I put my hair behind my ear.

"Emily," Adora said to me, "our friend is introducing himself to you."

"Hello," I finally said.

Mr. Basketball or Jonathan or Jack shook my hand, our matching eyes still wild with surprise.

"Well, what was *that*?" Adora said, looking at the two of us, standing in the doorway.

\* \* \*

Jonathan watched me from the bar, as if to say, so this is *Emily*: Emily is by the bar. Emily obviously doesn't know anybody here. Not even the cousins, and you should always always know the cousins!

And I watched him. Jonathan's hair was shorter now, and his skin was wrinkled at the forehead. He was thirty-five, and different again, except for his eyes. "Eyes can never wrinkle and are eternal in this way," my eye doctor once told me too close to my face.

Jonathan filled my glass two times in an hour and when he opened the vodka bottle to pour a third, it occurred to me that he had always liked to pour my drinks. It occurred to me his wife was not there.

"Who is this guy?" Kevin whispered in my ear.

"An old friend," I said, shrugging Kevin's breath off me.

The third time Jonathan tried to pour me a drink, Kevin covered my glass with his hands. He took the vodka out of Jonathan's, and I took it out of Kevin's. "I'll just pour myself a glass."

At dinner, everything was formal. We were given assigned seats and I was between Kevin and a man named Harry. Adora thought Harry and I could make a great couple someday, if we only set aside our major differences, and Kevin. Adora was sitting down, her name written out in purple cursive at the head of the table, where she was proud and long-haired like a purebred, nibbling on coleslaw vinaigrette, with fresh lime juice, Harry told me as he squeezed some onto my plate. Harry was staring at me. Adora was running her hand on Orrin's leg underneath the table. Orrin was not even smiling. Jonathan was asking me if I would like to pass him the bread basket as though it were an option to deny someone the bread basket.

"Hey hey, a toast to Orrin and Adora!" Harry said. "May their marriage be a long and loving one!"

I was jealous that Adora was the kind of woman who could spread butter smoothly and mine ripped the bread. I was angry that Jonathan had come back as Jack without telling me, that he had started to part his hair down the middle of his head, and shaved his beard so close to the skin his chin shined like some dope on a magazine we would have made fun of once. Jonathan started telling a story about his old law professor and everybody laughed, and I was certain it had become impossible to breathe at the table, so I went to the bathroom.

When I returned, Harry informed me that he was an arborist by trade.

"My campaign lately has been shallow roots," he said.

Jonathan looked at me, as though he was waiting for me to laugh with him. He was nodding his wineglass toward me like we were in on some great joke together, like we were always in on some great joke together, and when he did this, he looked like Mr. Basketball again, reaching over my lap to open the car door. When he stopped smiling and sat back in his chair to look at me, he was Jonathan again, calm and at a distance in front of the statue in Prague, reaching out his hand to wipe the damp hair off his forehead. And when he leaned forward and stabbed the meat on his plate with his fork, he was Jack and I felt I hardly knew him.

Kevin squeezed my hand. Underneath the table, everybody's feet were still wet from the snow.

In the kitchen, the plastic ladle was starting to melt on the stove.

The kitchen was so far away from the dining room, there was no way for us to know this. The fire alarm was installed only in the upstairs, and when Orrin found this out after part of the house burned down, he blamed the whole thing on his fucking father, who, according to him, was so fucking stupid he exclusively hired stupid fucking people who never took care of anything in his fucking stupid house.

The maid was on the floor in the pantry with the phone in her hand, and the doors were so thick with mahogany, even the maid didn't know a fire was starting. The maid was a twenty-five-year-old girl from Austria and she was lying down as though she were playing dead but she was alive, with a broken heart; she was a heaving chest of grief, she would tell the police later in broken English.

"You were in the closet when the fire began and you were a heaving chest of *what*?" the police would ask.

The only other part of her that was moving was her fingers, digging holes into a plastic garbage bag. She was telling her American boyfriend that she no longer loved him. I am crying, she whispered into the phone, but that does not mean I love you or that I can stop crying, and all the boyfriend wanted to know in response was if it was because he was from central Florida.

\*     \*     \*

After dinner and before dessert, we began to smell the smoke. Adora accused Jonathan of smoking in the bathrooms. "Adora, sweetheart," Jack said, putting his arm around her, "we're not in high school anymore."

"Well we have a *patio*," she said, and she motioned for him to go outside.

It was all too much. Adora and Jonathan had smoked in bathrooms together when they were young. She might have actually known him better than I did. I lifted my head toward Kevin, who was caught up in conversation with a man who worked on the marketing team for 7Up, who didn't even realize I had stepped next to him, so when Jonathan motioned for me to follow him outside, I traced his wet footsteps. "I need some air," I whispered in Kevin's ear.

Outside, Jonathan and I leaned against the fence surrounding the pool, where he handed me his cigarette and we blamed everything on the vodka.

"I only smoke because of the vodka," I said.

"I'm only here because of the vodka," he said.

"I go to the bathroom in the middle of dinner because of the vodka."

"I make stupid jokes about contractual integrity and everybody laughs because of the vodka."

"My shoes are ugly and wet because of the vodka."

"I only got married because of the vodka."

The moon was not visible.

"Don't make it a joke," I said.

"Sometimes, it feels like a joke. It's true, but yet, still a joke. How can that be?"

The clouds hung heavy in the sky like sacks, distracting us. Everything covered the stars, which seemed like an incredible feat; the whole universe disappeared and, yet, we were still alive, even if it was just for now, everybody was alive for now, even my father.

Adora popped her head outside to accuse us of things. Smoking! Ash! Being cold! Uncivilized! Were we aware that nearly everything we were doing could kill us?

"Isn't that the fun part?" Jonathan asked.

Adora huffed and went back inside.

"Tell me everything," he said.

"Oh," I said. "I don't know."

I couldn't think of one thing except, You loved me. I know he did. Despite everything. And we laughed so hard in the mornings over Algerian coffee, I thought my spleen would erupt like a swollen and diseased organ. But I was too sad, or too drunk, or too defeated to be angry in this way.

"What's new with you?" I asked.

"Ohhh," Jonathan said, blowing out a puff of smoke. "So much has happened, since. I don't even think it's possible to begin."

By that point in the night, the fire had spread to the kitchen cabinets and the maid should have known this earlier, but she was crying so hard her nostrils filled with mucous, and she couldn't smell a thing, couldn't articulate a thing. She put her hand against the door to help her stand up. She felt the heat transferring through the door. "Hot!" she told her boyfriend, and her boyfriend didn't understand. "Kitchen on fire!" she shouted.

The cabinets dripped like paints and Adora would have known this earlier if she weren't obsessed with checking the upstairs bathrooms for leftover ash in the toilet.

I was having trouble organizing my thoughts. The pool looked cold, like it was alone. Or like it missed the half of the pool that was inside or like it *was* the pool inside, just split in half like land divided by a highway, like sisters who shared the same blood but never spoke on the phone. Like sisters who didn't share the same blood but talked every day. How did that happen? Everything felt so split in half. My mother. My father. Laura. Adora. Me. Jack. Jonathan. Were we all supposed to love each other? I slid my hand across the metal rung of the fence back and forth and I was wondering if I was the kind of woman that Mr. Basketball thought I'd turn out to be, if I was the kind of woman Jonathan really wanted to be with, if I was the kind of woman Jack still loved. We were silent. I tried to think of other things, about what it would be like to live inside this giant house where it was impossible, I'm sure, to feel anything but cold, even when it was on fire. He was not able to look at me and I was not able to look at him but we felt the presence of something there between us.

Or maybe we didn't. I really didn't know anymore.

The maid said she called 911 as soon as she smelled the smoke, before she even left the food pantry. Orrin said this made her a hero; Adora thought this made her dumb. I agreed with Adora. The kitchen was on fire and when the kitchen was on fire, you just got the hell out of the house, like Adora, who popped her head out onto the patio after she announced, "Kitchen is on fire!" as though she were telling us, "Belts are fifty percent off at Caché!" She saw Jonathan's hand that wasn't on top of mine, but was next to mine, and our hands were clasped to the rung of the fence. I could feel him sigh like he was disappointed, and shake his head, and grumble, "Kitchen is on fire," as though when you were with a woman, the kitchen was always always on fire.

Jonathan walked into the house, only to leave through the front door, and when he got in his car and drove away, I stood on the lawn and I felt I could breathe again.

I looked for Kevin.

When my mother and Bill showed up, we were outside with the fire trucks and the firemen were inside with their hoses. Bill and my mother were running to us; they were adults who had left their children alone for too long in a house that was too big and this was what they got for it. The fire was under control, the maid was upset in the back of an ambulance trying to explain: "Language barrier," she said to the police. "Much hard." Adora and Orrin were looking at their house and everyone held their breath beside them, and then exhaled as the smoke poured out through the broken windows.

"You're late," I said to my mother, who was by my side.

"Dear God," my mother said like she was about to embark on a prayer. Like a prayer is some kind of journey toward something. "What happened?"

Everything. Nothing.

"The Austrian maid broke up with her American boyfriend," I said.

# 31

The inside of Orrin's house was ruined. Everything was covered in smoke. Everything in ashes. They were just going to start over. Build new cabinets, rip out the flooring. The perfect time to start a new life, anyway, Adora said. And I, Adora told me, would be the perfect person to help them.

"I won't even begin to tell you how much Orrin would pay you," she said. "I'm sure you know."

"I don't actually," I said.

She wrote it down on a piece of paper, as though she couldn't bear to say it aloud.

Then, she mouthed to me, *two hundred thousand dollars*.

"For the whole house," she said. "Everything."

When good things happened to me, I called Kevin. He took me out on Saturday nights. We ate Spanish food, and then Brazilian food, and then plain old pizza, and then talked about his job at the 7Up plant. We had gentle sex, and he read long historical novels in the park while I flipped through pages and pages of photographs of homes in the greater New York area. On the weekends, we ate brunch on floral patios where I sipped black coffee and sorted fabric prints while he announced news headlines to me.

"Florida Authorizes Python Hunt."

"New Jersey Has School Districts Without Schools."

We had sex on couches and looked up at ceilings while he talked about the changing face of soda (all-natural now) and I contemplated the consequences of circular skylights (were they just holes?).

"Did you know there was a psychological study that has proved certain colors can affect a person's sense of time and space?" I asked him.

"I like how you tell me things," he said, but what he meant was, he liked it when I defended my profession in the name of science.

We started bringing each other to major life events that required dates. His cousin's wedding, his cousin's graduation, his cousin's birthday; he was so Irish, he had so many cousins.

"For weddings," I told him half-naked, getting dressed for his cousin's wedding, while he watched from the edge of my bed, "I wear short black dresses with varying degrees of elasticity. For graduation parties, I wear knee-length skirts with unpredictable floral patterns. For Bat Mitzvahs, I wear box dresses that I got on sale from Macy's."

Kevin laughed. Kevin was good like that. We made each other laugh before we brushed our teeth in the morning.

At Kevin's cousin's wedding, the bride and groom were twenty-one-year-old college students. The reception was held in the basement of Village Care of New York, a convalescent home. Standing in the room with blue tables, I felt like I was at my confirmation. The carrots were serrated. The fruit platters were sectioned in plastic containers so the cantaloupe wouldn't touch the strawberries. The meal had been turkey and ham sandwiches with banana peppers and Coca-Cola. The bride was blond, young, excited, and leading a group of her friends in a choreographed dance of the Macarena. She was very nice. "Feel free to eat the food," she had said.

I sat on my leather chair and wondered why a bride would want to eat a ham and turkey sandwich in a satin backless wedding dress. Or why she would cater her wedding as though it were a middle school lunch. Or why a bride would allow her love to be celebrated beneath a building of old people who were mistaking their spoons for grandchildren. Then, Kevin, tall thin man, cousin to the bride, walked up to me with a plate of broccoli and sour cream dip and said, "You have got to try this B6." He smiled. So I did.

Kevin was a flavor scientist. He worked in Trumbull, Connecticut, at the 7Up plant, and started making the daily reverse commute from Brooklyn after he moved in with me. We were so different that our only expectation was miscommunication. When we watched movies on Friday nights, I made the popcorn. When he ate it, he licked the butter off his fingers, I kissed him on the mouth. When I brought him to dinner so my new family could meet the man they presumed I was spending the rest of my life with, he sipped on his Jack and Coke and said, "This phosphoric acid is awesome, Mrs. Vidal."

Adora rolled her eyes. My stepbrother, Nick, stared at me. Nick was the tallest one in the stepfamily, and he considered his height a certification in forming good opinions. He tapped a quarter against the counter as if to say, this is what you bring to our stephome?

"It's Mrs. Trimble now," my mother said.

My mother was patient and kind as Mrs. Trimble. My father had been diagnosed last month with lung cancer and this had somehow softened her, like all my father had to do was reveal himself as a mortal with failing organs and my mother would stop feeling so defensive. My mother, with an apron wrapped neatly around her waist, actually responded to Kevin. "And how is the 7Up going, Kevin?"

"Still all-natural," Kevin said. Kevin said this every time someone asked him about the state of 7Up. I became embarrassed for him in his short-sleeved plaid T-shirt, gray pants, and white tennis sneakers, spouting catchphrases, next to my stepbrother, who was always sincere in his brown cashmere sweater with black boots, who was finishing his PhD at Yale in engineering. I smiled at Kevin from across the kitchen to let him know he was doing fine.

But at night, I had horrible dreams about children who wouldn't look at me, who could see only ghosts plucking out their teeth behind me. I woke up in a sweat. I was trying to teach myself not to be scared of things. I was learning: every time I woke up, Mr. Resnick's blood was never on me.

I got up to make popcorn, to relax, turn on the TV.

Death was just an image, I told myself, a coming together of events in a single frame, and pain was just a part of the painting and haven't we learned our lesson? Meaning is most poignant when never fully accessed. I sucked the butter off a cold popcorn kernel. I became intolerably sad when I made popcorn, standing by the microwave, listening to the *pop pop pop* as if it were a ticker tracking all the moments I spent alone. I bit into the kernel and thought of bodies on top of mine.

I thought of Jonathan's hands at the engagement party. I thought of Jonathan's stomach in Prague, full like a smooth, sustainable weight. Standing up, Jonathan had the disposition of a man who might crush me, but lying down, he never did. Mr. Basketball was the one who always crushed me. He crushed me in the backseats of cars, on futons, in hallways, on desks. He crushed Janice too, standing in front of our freshman English class. Mr. Basketball stared at me from his desk, while Janice couldn't concentrate on what she was saying, because she was watching Mr. Basketball stare at me, and said, "The river that bears no empty bottles! No sandwich papers, no cigarette ends, or, God, what was it? No other testimonies of a summer night!"

"You forgot silk handkerchiefs and cardboard boxes," Mr. Basketball had said, marking it down in a notepad. "And 'The Waste Land' is not supposed to be read with that much enthusiasm."

I thought of all the empty bottles and cigarette ends I had created and all the men I had created them with. There were so many things I had loved as my own, and these things never ended up being mine. All of the glass lights strung on other people's porches, houseplants that were someone else's, rugs and paintings and lighting fixtures and curtains and different men who looked different in every room, and I closed my eyes, overwhelmed by the infinite ways to live a finite life. I wanted to run out of my apartment until the street signs and passing cars ripped me of my belongings, until the wind had worn me down to sand.

# 32

Two months later, Jonathan didn't even call, he just showed up at my apartment when I was packing for Connecticut. My father was home from Moscow, and I had been going to my mother's house every weekend to visit him. It was five o'clock, and Kevin was likely starting his commute home. Jonathan walked around my apartment, saying, "Wow, this is great," and it all felt so patronizing, like he couldn't even believe in the idea that I had my own place, like my toaster was just for pretend and he was going to prove this by sticking his tongue in the slots. "Really great," he said, and looked around, trying not to stare at the stained windowsills or the slanted kitchen floor.

Jonathan and I sat on my couch and listened to noise from outside. In Brooklyn, I could always hear the pedestrians shouting through the windows, no matter how well I insulated them in the winter, and no matter how loud the fan was spinning in my ear during the summer. "You ready?" a man by the lamppost asked another man. No, he wasn't ready, he had to go back and get something. "What the *fuck*?" the other man said, and then they were gone. We listened to the men outside disappoint each other while Jonathan ran his fingers across Kevin's collection of chemical science dictionaries and the woman downstairs played C-major piano chords. That was all she ever played.

Jonathan looked outside and put his nose to the windowpane like a dog. I wanted to wrap my arms around him and ask him why he was behaving like the dog. We could have had a dog together by now, I wanted to say. The dog could be sitting right there by the television. The dog could love us. And we could love the dog. But I didn't speak.

I watched him sit in my chairs and drink tea out of my cups until I couldn't stand the silence of waiting.

"Let's go somewhere," I said. "Let's go get coffee."

"But we're drinking tea right now."

We went to a coffee shop.

"Did you know that there are people in this world who complain about their necks all the time?" Jonathan said when we sat down with our coffees. "Since I've been back from traveling, all I do is sit at my beige office chair, press the Line 1 button, and listen to a lady tell me about the worst thing in the world: she can't turn her head left. Well, she can, it just hurts. You know, the way it feels when something doesn't hurt all the time, it's just a nagging sort of pain that hurts more in its persistence rather than degree?"

"I know what you mean," I said.

"And the paralegals," he said. "They're the worst. It's like they are constantly surprised by the world. At lunch, they sit together, and their mouths hang halfway open and they look at each other's lunches and they say, there are *Cheetos* in there? You got *what* on your shirt? Camels *don't* mate for life?"

"It's true," I said. "They don't. I saw that on the Discovery Channel."

I told Jonathan about the new company I was launching with Melinda, and we both sat in our brand-new office while she sank her teeth into the same lunch every single day: microwavable chicken marsala.

"She tells me it was her father's favorite," I said. "And now that he is dead, she just can't stop eating it. She is always on a quest to discover if that means something is wrong with her."

"Sometimes my day is only about a fence," Jonathan said.

"You've told me this before," I said.

"Or a boy, or a boy and a fence and whose fault was it? Maybe the fence's. But the fence didn't know what it was doing. That's what it sounds like, and how can you punish a fence that was unaware of its influence on the boy?"

Jonathan said the point of the workday was that someone always needed to be held accountable for the fence's mistakes. The unaccounted-for objects needed someone to stand up and say, hey, that's mine, I made that, and when it doesn't do what you programmed it to do, we're real sorry, sir, let me just write you a check.

"God, what do you *want*?" I asked him. I was almost done with my coffee.

"I miss you," he said. "Please let me explain. My wife's name is Susan."

"My boyfriend's name is Kevin," I said.

"I met her at Columbia law. We got married sometime while you were away at college. And after she graduated, she decided she wanted to help represent people in other countries with unstable governments. So four years ago, she left for Somalia."

"Kevin's a flavor scientist. He makes soda. Are you trying to make me feel ashamed or something?"

"You're not listening," he said.

Jonathan said that after Susan left, he spent two years having late nights at his law office on Fifty-fifth Street breaking paper clips in half for no reason. He missed everything: Susan, literature, inherent meaning, laughing at midnight.

"Without Susan, there was no difference between home and not home, you know what I mean?"

So he stopped buying fresh vegetables, since he couldn't eat them all before they rotted anyway, and bought frozen broccoli florets in a thick soy sauce. He ordered shrimp fra diavolo from Tony's. He did this every night at six or seven or eight or whenever because without anybody watching, he said that everything he did was suddenly inconsequential.

For nearly six months, Jonathan said, he ate pepperoni out of a bag as dessert and watched late-night talk shows to renew the sense of humor he lost fighting with real estate agents and battling Susan about the severity of the faucet leak. He became friendlier to the lawyers in the office. He found that having nothing to take up one's time left a lot of time just to be nicer. He talked to women at the grocery store. He had morning coffees with paralegals and late-night whiskeys with Jon and Jay, the two other product liability lawyers in his firm. They sat out on the balcony and he listened to Jon mock the blond stenographer from the courtroom.

"Who everybody secretly wanted to sleep with," Jonathan said. "Who would sometimes stop the proceedings just to ask the witness, 'Wait, did you say "no" or "*nah*"?' "

Sometimes, Jonathan said, he attended formal dining gatherings hosted by his law firm and talked to a young woman with blond or brown or red hair.

"Well, was it blond or brown or red?" I said. "You couldn't even take the time to notice?"

"I guess it didn't matter what color her hair was, that's not the point."

The point was that he wasn't interested in any of the women, not until one of the lawyers' wives would come up to him, stick her nose in Jonathan's cocktail, and say, "Where is your wife?" This was always an accusation, Jonathan said, "Like my words were unbuttoning the woman's shirt right there." Jonathan said he wanted to shout back, "Where is your sense of decency?" but he just sighed and said, "Africa."

So Susan traveled for two years, up the coast of Africa, where she stayed in run-down buildings that were on occasion shot at. Where on occasion, she sat stiff as a board on her cot with her male coworker from Nebraska whom Jonathan said he assumed she fucked when it got tense, and even though the violence was routine and they were locked in and mostly safe (that was what she always said before she left), she called Jonathan to say, "Jack, the building is being shot at," so he would be equally impressed and concerned by her dedication and say, "Susan, come home, just come home," and she would say, "Okay, Jack, I'm coming home." But he said he never really understood the exact danger she was in, or the exact country for that matter, because it seemed no matter where she was, she got heat rash, she drank bad water and ate rotten meat, she came home for Christmas with tapeworm, and she sat on the toilet and cried and said, "Oh, God, Jack, don't look at me." But Jonathan said he combed her hair and kissed her on the forehead and the worms crawled out of her.

"Jonathan," I said, "I don't think your wife would appreciate me knowing this."

"It's important," he said. "Because I would tell her, 'Susan, you are my wife,' but when we climbed into bed, I didn't put my arms around her. And that was when I knew."

"Knew what?"

"That I didn't love her."

And he said Susan couldn't stop talking about the look on his face earlier when she reached for the knob of the stove, like it wasn't even her home to cook in. She ran to the bathroom, and they both agreed that they couldn't believe how inhumane the intimacy had become. Jonathan said he lay in bed imagining what it would feel like when she left again for Libya or Egypt or wherever, and how kissing her on the mouth at the airport would feel like nothing at all, like licking an envelope closed, and the sour taste on his tongue in the cab would taste exactly like falling out of love.

"I was going to divorce her," he said. "Then, I got your letter. And after she left again, I thought of you. I just thought of you. I saw you so clearly in my mind. I thought of you for days. So I went to Prague to see you. And it was perfect. And I was going to tell her that it was over."

And then Susan called while he was in Prague to tell him that she was coming home early from Ghana because she was two months pregnant, and Jonathan—who looked at me at Café Red and thought, Oh God, oh how sad, when did Susan and I even make love? But he said good-bye to me and hello to Susan. At dinner, he was so sad to be home, and Susan was so happy to be home. Jonathan said he thought of me at every meal, while Susan sipped on ice water and started the Name Game. "Ben," she said, "or Peter or Judas," and then laughed to confirm that she would never name her child after a traitor. Ben, Peter, Judas, Jonathan thought. He knew that if he asked, "Are you sure it's mine?" it would be over before the wine glasses dented the walls.

"I don't think names really mean anything," Jonathan said. "I think children make their names, not the other way around, but really, why take the chance?" Susan agreed. No chances. So they bought a state-of-the-art stroller and waited for Ben or Peter or Judas's day of birth. One morning, Susan cramped at the dishwasher, and they rushed to the hospital in his car while he held her hand. "I kept saying, 'Almost, Susan,' like a fucking jackass," Jonathan said.

He said he stood in the room and listened to Susan's screams. He wiped the sweat off her brow and thought, even if it was Peter's or Ben's or Judas's, he was okay with it, because the boy would wear his hand-me-downs and mimic his dialect. He would love Susan and he would love the boy.

"And then when he came out it was like looking at a broken windup toy," Jonathan said. "And Susan looked at the doctor as if to say, *Why isn't my child working?* The doctor looked at Susan, as if to say, *Almost, it-is-almost-a-baby, please just give us a second.*"

Jonathan said Susan laid her head back against the pillow as if it was her fault for never giving the child a name. Jonathan buckled at the knee. It was his fault, he knew this, for falling out of love with her.

"Everybody always knows the truth," he said. "Sometimes, it's like the whole world can see you, all the time."

The doctors rushed Peter, Ben, or Judas to the table, where they strapped wires to his tiny chest and shouted one-two-three come on.

"But he never came back to life," Jonathan said. "Or never had life. I'm not sure."

"I'm sorry," I said. I really was. It sounded terrible. "That sounds very sad."

"It was. It is."

He took a sip of his coffee.

"So that's the story," he said. "Well, not the whole story."

He reached for my hand. I recoiled.

"Kevin gets annoyed that I never heard of the word 'amylase,'" I said, running my finger over the rim of my empty cup. "It's a chemical. He thinks I'm stupid sometimes. I can see it on his face. But he gets my jokes and he loves me and when I have nightmares, he sits up and tries to psychoanalyze them. We try to work it out together and that is why I love him. Please do not contact me again."

I walked out of the coffee shop, got on the Metro North to Connecticut, and made circles of fog on the train window with my breath. The sign on the window that was supposed to read EMERGENCY BRAKE had two letters missing. A Spanish man sitting beside me pointed to the sign, chuckled, and said, "Emergency bra."

"That's funny, isn't it?" I said. He nodded.

\* \* \*

When my father came home from Russia, he stood at my mother's doorstep and said, "*Überraschung!* It means, *Surprise!*" Surprise! I'm a dead man! Surprise! Will you let me die in our old house? The one that I bought for my family? That means *you* of course. I want to die around my old things. My old Norwegian pewter bowl. The brown velvet curtains that keep out the sun. Where is Emily? And where is my pewter bowl and what's with the red curtains and what did you do with the sun? It's raining. I have one month to live and it's raining. Call Emily. Tell her that her father is dying and he could use a *masáž*. She'll know what that means.

"Why do you and your father always talk in this secret code?" my mother asked.

"It's not code, Gloria," my father yelled from the bedroom. "It's Czech!"

I stood in the kitchen and cried.

"Don't cry, Emily," my father said when he walked in. "Don't think of it as dying. Think of it as changing shape."

"Like you are becoming a rectangle?" I said.

"Yeah," my father said. "Like that."

My father's brothers, Uncle Vito and Vince, were staying in the house with us. My father started having trouble swallowing food two weeks ago, so we were feeding him only soft foods now.

"How 'bout I cook you up some Bob?" Uncle Vito said.

My father weakly smiled.

"Sick son of a bitch," Uncle Vince said.

The story goes that when they moved from the Bronx to Connecticut, they got so excited about living in a house with one acre of land, they got six chickens as pets, Neptune, Harry, Belvedere, Jungle, Puppy, and Bob. One day Uncle Vito took Bob out of the cage and broke his neck, skinned him, and cooked him into a stew. My grandmother came home and was pleased to find one of her sons cooking dinner so she asked no questions. During the meal, Uncle Vito said, "Well, doesn't anyone want to know where Bob is?"

"We eat goddamn chickens every day, and you still act as though I'm some sort of psychopath," Uncle Vito said.

"They were our *pets*," Uncle Vince said.

I took out three eggs and picked up a pan. "We'll make eggs," I said.

"What the hell do you think those are?" Uncle Vito asked, pointing to the eggs. "You're the sick ones."

"No, don't use that pan," my mother said.

"That pan sticks," Bill said.

I cracked the second egg on the side of the pan.

"Not three eggs," my mother said. "He won't eat three eggs."

Uncle Vince argued. "Yes he will. He hasn't eaten all day."

"Give him a roll," Bill said.

"Rolls are for pansies," Uncle Vito said.

"Did you drink your prune juice?" my mother asked my father. "We should get him some more prune juice."

"He's not thirsty," Uncle Vince said.

"Something smells like it's burning," said Uncle Vito. "Emily's frying the little fuckers."

"I'll make the eggs," my mother said to me, taking the pan.

"Didn't they teach you to make eggs in college?" said Uncle Vito.

"She went to art school," Uncle Vince said.

"Oh Jesus," Uncle Vito said.

"People," I said in protest, "I know how to make eggs."

"I don't suppose anyone cares if I go in the other room," my father said.

When the empty plate got sent back from my father's room, more debate followed.

"How many did he eat?" Uncle Vito wanted to know.

"Three," I said.

"He left a bit of egg in the corner," Uncle Vince said. "That was probably two and a quarter eggs."

All month long we had been waiting for him to die like this. We had been waiting for him to die in the same way that we waited for the mailman. The mailman was always coming. The mailman was always coming and the dogs were supposed to bark to let us know this and all of this felt as reliable a pattern as a weather pattern that might go on forever and ever and somewhere deep down we all started to believe that maybe my father really couldn't die. He just didn't seem like the type.

Until one morning my father grabbed at his chest, and opened his mouth like he was choking, and we called the ambulance, which arrived quickly, despite the rush-hour traffic, despite the twenty-five-mile-an-hour speed limit on our street. "Your father's lung collapsed," the doctor said.

At Stamford Hospital, my father was so thin in his bed his collarbone sat across his neck like a thick metal chain. My father was nearing the end of his rope, the doctor told us, as though he was saying, your father is on a rope. Life is just a rope, and we are people with hands.

Now we had to wait. They'd patch up his lung, but he had only weeks now. Weeks. We just had to hold his hand and bring him green tea that he wouldn't drink and shout good nutritional advice in his ears. "Antioxidants help your heart!" my mother said.

"My heart?" my father asked. "What's that got to do with anything?"

"Oh, Victor," my mother said.

My mother sent Bill to Trader Joe's, where he could buy a roasted chicken. To visit someone at the hospital, my mother explained in the car, you need food. You need brie and chicken and napkins and you need to act like it's just so normal that you are there, sucking down a meal like you would at your own kitchen table. "Otherwise," my mother said, "everybody gets uncomfortable."

Mrs. Resnick showed up with Laura. My mother saw her walking down the hall and turned to me and said, "Emily, where's Bill?"

"You sent him to get a chicken."

"That's right," my mother said.

My father's friends from work came, neighbors came, Adora and Nick came, and when my father asked them how in the hell their lives were going, they both nodded. "Good, good, our lives are good." My mother and I listened on the chairs outside the room waiting for Kevin to show up. Kevin had never met my father and it was strange that the first time he did would be one of the last times he ever saw him, so for a moment, I considered not even introducing them. What was the point?

Mrs. Resnick sat next to Laura, combing Laura's bangs over to one side.

"*Mom,*" Laura said. Laura was twelve and embarrassed of everything now. Her braces, her mother's floral perfume, even her father a little bit, who was spitting up fluid in a dish down the hall. "Stop it."

She was shy around me now. I asked about her schoolwork, how her classmates were, did she have a boyfriend, and was he nice, was he an upstanding citizen, did he vote? And all she did was giggle and say, "I don't know anyone who votes, I don't think."

A woman in a wheelchair rolled by us, made scary eye contact, spewed crazy talk, asked if I thought all the demons were in hell. At first I refused to answer, but as she persisted I told her what I really thought: yes, probably. Did I think they were sorry for being demons? I didn't know. I hoped so.

"Of course they aren't," my mother told the lady. "They're demons."

My father was given a serious amount of morphine. "He won't even realize he's dying," the doctor said.

"Oh, he won't like that," my mother said.

But the morphine was pumped into his veins anyway—procedure, the doctor said—and my father started having trouble seeing and organizing his thoughts. He told everybody in his hospital room that one thing was clear: his big regret was that he wanted to see his only daughter get married before he died—so sue him—no, really, why didn't we?

"That's sad," said Uncle Vince, looking at me. "It's sad when you put it like that."

"If Emily is your only daughter," Uncle Vito said, "then who the fuck is she?" He pointed to Laura by the plant. Laura opened her mouth as if to speak, but she didn't.

"Oh, why, that's my daughter, Emily," my father said.

Nobody spoke.

"Emily, pumpkin," my father said, looking at Laura. "Come here."

We both approached my father.

"I'll try to die tonight," he said, not making eye contact with either of us, "so I won't ruin your wedding day."

"All right!" The doctor interrupted in his white coat. "He really needs to sleep. He's going to get panicky soon."

"No," my father said. "Something feels wrong."

We stared at him.

"That's because you are panicking," the doctor said.

"Everybody is being too polite!" my father shouted. "Especially you." He looked at me. He said he didn't understand why I worried about his neck position in the bed or if his feet were too cold. "It's so sad. Don't be so polite. It feels rude. Rude to be so polite about my death."

# 33

Adora's wedding dress was a Priscilla of Boston with an envelope-draped bust. She stood tall in the corner of the room, her dress wide at the bottom with an embellished beaded train flowing out into the hallway. There was a silk corset tight around her torso while the red lace crawled up her neck and ate her bare skin like a wild disease. The dress was so complicated, I couldn't decide what would be more impressive: to get it on or off. Adora stood in front of the mirror that morning, my mother wildly tugging at the silk ropes wrapped around her torso—pulling and tugging and complaining. "I can't breathe," Adora said.

"Of *course* you can't breathe," my mother said. "You're getting married, for Christ's sake."

Adora's wedding was held at the MoMa. "I want it to be as secular as it can be," Adora had said. "If somebody is to sneeze, I don't even want to hear a 'God bless you.' I don't even care if it's an old person."

Adora didn't wear white, and the priest was their friend Luke, who was just this guy. He conducted the ceremony, in which they were to eat herbs. Different herbs represented different emotions they were supposed to feel together, forever.

The caterer didn't remember to bring the serving spoons, and the guests pretended not to mind that the service workers poured the Italian wedding soup directly into their bowls from the pot. We all cheered and clapped for Mr. and Mrs. Orrin Hallaby when they entered the sculpture garden and the lobby, which was full of two hundred and fifty guests, three-quarters of whom Adora didn't even pretend to know.

They insisted on no cake (too tacky) and no first dance (so predictable). Heat was pumped into the sculpture garden so nobody got cold while we danced. Humans were hired to stand in the middle of the appetizer and dessert tables, with large frames around their heads. Human paintings. The tables had wheels on them, so the human paintings could move around the room and offer bacon-wrapped scallops, beef Wellington bites when they needed to. Between every course, the humans would crawl out from the tables and perform their painting. I stood by the bar, waiting for Mona Lisa to put on her show, while Kevin was dancing with my mother. Kevin was not wearing a tie because earlier that morning, he couldn't find it in the mess of our apartment. "Just wear one of my father's," I said.

And he said, "No, that'd be too weird."

"He's not dead yet," I said.

"I didn't mean it like that." He looked under the table and the bed. "How can you be an interior designer when you live like this?" he asked, picking up my clothes from the floor.

"Hairdressers don't usually have good hair," I said back. "But they can still be good hairdressers."

"Well, that's because they physically can't cut their own hair. You can actually clean up the bedroom."

"Oh, stop being like this," I said. "You're going to make me throw up."

Jonathan stood by the pond while little children threw in pennies, which were picked out by older children later when they thought no one was looking. Behind him, a statue of a naked woman, dipping her head in the water, classical Greek beauty—"Nudity," my professor said in my college sculpture class, walking around the naked model in the center of the room, "is being exactly what you are and, in that way, unfamiliar to everbody who knows you."

My mouth went hot, metallic, sore from something. Jonathan didn't see me at first, and I took advantage of the luxury of being unseen. I stared at him for as long as I could without Kevin or Jonathan noticing. He was playing with a chocolate-covered pretzel in between his fingers, talking to no one. He took a sip out of his beer. There were women everywhere. Women in party dresses, women in gowns, women with bows, women with problems. Then he saw me. Another woman. He didn't wave.

We didn't speak, until—

"It's like a fucking Broadway show here," he said, walking over to me.

"I know," I said.

"It's sick," he said. He stared at me. He stayed at my ear for a moment. He was a little drunk. I could tell by the way he touched my shoulder when he spoke. Kevin eyed me from across the room, doing the box-step with my mother.

"I can still feel you on my body at night," Jonathan said in my ear. "When I close my eyes."

"Don't be a stupid creep," I said to him. And then I moved to his ear and said, "I can't believe you had sex with me when I was fifteen."

"Gandalf sayeth, 'Even the wise don't see all ends.'"

"There. You appealed to a higher authority. Good job."

He twirled his finger in the foam of his beer. "I was crazy over you," he said. "You have to understand."

"I was a *little girl*."

"You were fine. You were always strong."

Adora approached.

"Where's the laser show?" Adora asked us like we were supposed to know.

Adora slumped down on a yellow lotus sculpture that also served as a chair.

We couldn't help it. All three of us bent over in laughter.

When Adora and Orrin left early at ten, she hugged me good-bye and whispered, "Emily, be careful with him. Jack's wife, she died three years ago. He just doesn't like to talk about it. He's a mess. And I don't know, with your father dying and all, if this is the right time for you to get involved with a man who's already in so much pain."

# 34

I stayed at the apartment for two days and worked from my kitchen table. Jonathan called me late at night there. His voice was raspy over the phone and this was when I hated him the most. I hated most people at this hour of the night, when nobody was as selfish as me, or as confused as me, and when I looked at the ceiling and at Kevin asleep next to me, and sometimes they felt like the same exact thing.

Then, the phone rang.

"Hi," I said.

"Just talk to me for a bit," Jonathan asked. "I can't sleep."

Neither could I. So I talked to him for a bit. I left the room and Kevin turned on his side.

"Might be up for sarcasm and *pivo*," Jonathan whispered into the phone when I was in the kitchen.

"Sarcasm just put on her shoes."

"I wrote an imitation of Chekhov today. Why?"

"You're becoming incredibly obscure."

"Meet me at Washington Square Park."

"Where are you? In Fairfield?"

"In my Manhattan apartment."

"Okay," I said, without even thinking about it, without even bothering to give Kevin a reasonable excuse when he woke up and asked me where I was going. I said, "Melinda just broke up with her boyfriend," and he didn't bother to say, "But you aren't really friends with Melinda," as I put on my coat and walked through the door; he didn't grab me by the waist, put me down on the bed. He never demanded to know just exactly who I thought I was, and this was my excuse.

\* \* \*

"This is actually a burial ground," Jonathan said as he came up behind me. It was one in the morning. We were in Washington Square Park. The cold fountain glossed our faces. We were both overdressed for the park, but the formality was refreshing so late in the night.

"Don't tell me that you asked me here so you can kill me," I said. "Because that would be disappointing."

Jonathan reached out for my hand. He ran his fingertips against my knuckles. He sat down on the ground. A child's shoe was left wet on the stone wall, and neither of us mentioned it. We didn't speak and then we spoke.

"This is a potter's field," Jonathan said, patting the earth. "There are twenty thousand corpses underneath us right now."

We stared at each other like we were relearning how to see everything: You still have Jonathan's nose, I thought, you still have Mr. Basketball's eyes, but you have a completely new mouth. Whose mouth is that?

"Imagine," he said. "Imagine if they could still see us from so far below."

"Who?" I asked. His wife?

I walked around the field trying to decide what to do while Jonathan never answered me.

"Why don't you come over here, sweetheart," he finally said, and this was not a question. I walked over to him and stood over his body. He spread my legs and put his mouth in me, and I wondered if he could see any corner of the moon from inside my body.

# 35

Kevin and I went to Central Park and took a rowboat into the center of the pond. We each had our own books, and we stretched our legs out over each other to make room for leisure. He was reading something fantastically grounded in the legal politics of contemporary America. I was reading up on the birth of the organic chair. I told Kevin that no matter how we treated something, at its roots, everything grows and then dies the same way. The ducks circled around us, the ducks quacked around us, and the ducks factored us into the reflection of their tiny retinas but never considered us in any real way. Weird.

Kevin didn't say anything until we were in one of those fusion places he sometimes admired so much. Something was wrong. They were serving Western macaroni and cheese with Vietnamese rice noodles. Smooth ceramic tiles on the floor, and gold-framed pictures of smiling women from distant lands, picking unidentifiable crops and putting them in their woven baskets. These were the happy women who lined the walls of Noodles N You. Kevin twirled the last of his rice noodles neatly around his fork just to be polite. Like what we needed was *more* polite.

"I think we should walk back home through the park after we're done here," he said.

"Okay," I said. "But I have to get back to Connecticut before it gets dark. I want to see my father before he goes to sleep."

When we walked through the park, Kevin wanted to know what was wrong. Kevin wanted to know who was calling at night. Kevin wanted to know how he could be dating a woman who was so unsubtle. We watched the tiny dogs chase after a ball in the dog park.

"This isn't just about your father," Kevin said.

Kevin leaned over the fence and asked a woman which dog was hers.

"That one," she said. "The schnauzer."

"I used to have a schnauzer," Kevin said. "But it didn't have hair like that."

"Well, then," the woman said, "you obviously don't know the breed."

Kevin and I looked at each other and when we didn't laugh, when he picked a piece of white lint off my shoulder and said, "I *know* the breed, lady," I knew I would never love him. I would never wake up in the middle of the night screaming for his touch, and I was stupid enough, watching a tiny terrier piss against the fence, to still believe that terror was such a large part of love.

"Since when do you *know* breeds?" I asked him.

"Emily," he said, "what's going on?"

Jonathan and I had been having sex in restaurant bathrooms where the toilet paper roll sat on the floor. "Men's or women's?" he always asked. "Men's," I would say. "Women are too judgmental."

"What do you mean?" I asked Kevin.

"Are you becoming someone else, Emily?" Kevin asked. "Someone I don't know?"

"You're the one who suddenly *knows* breeds. You don't even have a dog."

"Emily, whoever he is, I'd wish you'd say it."

"Say what?"

"You're cheating on me."

"I'm not."

"Yes you are."

"I'm not."

"Just say it, claim responsibility for it."

"It's not free will," I told him.

Jonathan had put me against the tiled wall and we had tried not to breathe out our noses. Sometimes we dangerously spoke like we had become the same careless person and said, "Let's go somewhere else?" and we were off to the basement stacks of the public library, where sex was a dark art and we were just students. Where I had to keep on my wool dress for decorum's sake and he just unzipped his pleated khakis and out he tumbled like a waterfall. We didn't even have to look down to feel what was happening to us. *The History of Russia,* the tiled wall, the bathroom door handle cut hard lines against my clothed back and it had all begun to hurt again.

"You're addicted," he said.

"I don't know what it is. Honestly."

"If I tell you to go be with him all you want, will you be done with it and then come back to me?"

"I can't. I can't stop."

"That's pathetic."

"He's killing me."

"Do you think about me?"

"Yes."

"Do you think about us?"

"Of course I think about us."

"Are you thinking about us always *always* like I am?"

"Yes," but I did not tell him the truth. Always *always* just sounded so exhausting.

"You don't need to sleep with another man to prove to me that you aren't ready for marriage. I wasn't going to propose yet."

"That's not what this is about."

"Of course it is."

On the subway home, Kevin asked me to explain in detail the sex I had with Jonathan.

"How do you know it's Jonathan?" I asked.

"It's obvious."

He said he needed to know if it was the kind of sex he could get over or the kind of sex that would haunt him forever.

"When did you first sleep with him?" he asked.

"Four days ago," I said. "Wednesday."

"That's where you went that night you left?"

"Yes," I said. "And then Thursday night."

On Thursday, Jonathan had picked me up in Stamford after I spent the day at the hospital, and we drove to his father's empty house in Greenwich (France for the winter), and this was where we finally had sex with our clothes off, and I noticed that Jonathan sweated more than he used to, sweated more easily indoors, more easily in the winter, and he didn't understand why but that had always been the case. I didn't understand why anybody would hire a maid to work in an empty house, or why Jonathan didn't take me to his real house in Fairfield since he wasn't technically married anymore, or why he needed to pretend like he was, and if he didn't love me, then why did he stick his nose in my hair and say, "I wish I could describe what you smell like," my very particular scent, that he just couldn't put his finger on, "and your hair," he said, my hair, oh my hair, he loved to feel his fingers in my hair, he loved to grab my hair, and I wondered if this was similar to the joy I felt when I held on to his back, if this was all that this was, the joy of needing and wanting and holding on.

"I barely remember Thursday," Kevin said. "What was I doing on Thursday? I guess I barely remember so what does it matter that you were with someone else? Right? Is that what I should be telling myself?"

"Remember," I said, "when you were at the dinner with your family and you called me to say good night in case I was going to bed before you got home, and I said good night?"

"No," he said. "But that sounds like something that would happen."

I thanked him for being funny. He said at a moment like this he was trying to find ways to be funny. But he didn't think it was possible. He didn't think this was going to be the kind of thing we laughed about ever, not even in ten years when we probably wouldn't know each other anymore. I started to cry. Tell me more, he said.

"I was sleeping with Jonathan when you called."

"I couldn't even tell," he said. "I can't even remember the conversation we had."

"I can," I said. "You told me your mother was upset because a pearl popped off into her drink, and she was convinced she accidentally drank it. Since that moment, I've been thinking of how sad that is."

"I don't want to hear any more," he said. "Don't return to the apartment until I'm gone, please."


I spent the week at home. During the day, we visited with my father, and after, we went out to dinner, where Uncle Vito always asked Bill to pass the salt and pecker, and Uncle Vince winked at the cute waitresses, then announced that my father and he were conceived in the same hotel, one year apart (something that had always made them close), and then once we finally got back to the house, I turned around and took the train to Greenwich, where I spent the night at Jonathan's father's house.

"Your hair," he said when he opened the door to the house.

"Yes," I said. I had cut my hair the night before to hurry the arrival of spring.

"Susan's hair is three days unwashed," Jonathan said. I didn't know what to say but:

*Jsi lhař. You liar.*

So I said, "Kevin knows breeds."

"Susan speaks four languages, including functional Arabic, and she can't remember what street the grocery store is on. The psychiatrist says she has pseudodementia. Dementia brought on by depression. And we had to go to a group meeting today," he said. "Coping with Grief."

He said that they attended this group once a week, Sundays at seven thirty.

"The lecture tonight was 'Suicide and Grief,'" he said, running his fingers down my legs in the kitchen.

Jonathan pressed his back against the chair and held his breath. "Good, great, you're just going to give her ideas, I thought," he said, and looked over at me. I was fixing the hem of my short blue sweater dress.

"Did you ever fantasize about a way to kill yourself?" Jonathan asked me.

"Yeah," I said. "After Mark's father killed himself, I was afraid my mother might kill herself. For a while, I thought that maybe I'd kill myself first, that way, I couldn't be affected by her suicide."

"How would you do it?"

"I knew that I could never kill myself directly," I said. "I'd have to get someone else to do it. I'd set up a gun with a pulley system tied to my door. When someone would walk through my door, the gun would be in my mouth and it would go off."

"That's selfish."

"I know. But suicide is selfish in general."

"I used to dream that I could die in an airtight room," Jonathan said, "my body laid out on a glass table, and I'd be on heroin. And somehow, I'd be on fire."

Jonathan took a long sip of his beer.

"It's not that glamorous," I said.

Jonathan didn't turn to look at me. He didn't even put his hand on my thigh. He wasn't impressed.

"I don't think we can meet in Greenwich anymore," Jonathan said, staring at the maid, who'd just come into the room to dust the tops of the counters in the kitchen. "It's starting to make me feel uncomfortable. The maid knows my wife."

# 36

Your father is really dying this time," my mother said on the other end of my cell phone. "Come to the hospital."

I hung up the phone with my mother. I was naked. I couldn't find my keys or my coat or my shoes or my hair elastic. I cried over his soccer trophies and Jonathan took my hand and said, "I'll drive you."

When we arrived at the hospital, Jonathan hung back. "Just come on," I said.

He followed me to my father's room but stayed outside on the chairs. After a while he said he had to get going. "I'll come see you later," he said.

In some ways it wasn't all that different from home: my father was so distant and thin in his bed, it gave me the same feeling that I got when he came back from a long trip in Europe and something about his face looked painfully unaffiliated with me. My father said, "Mhmm?" every time he thought somebody spoke, to which my mother said, "Emily, say hello to your father," to which my father said, "Gloria, I'm talking to *Emily*."

"Emily?" my father asked.

"Hi, Dad," I said.

"Oh, there you are, Emily."

I took my father's hand.

"Your hands are so cold," he said. "Put some mittens on, will you?"

"I'll be okay."

"Put some mittens on. Stronzo, give Emily your mittens."

Everybody looked around.

"Where's Stronzo?" my father said. "Stronzo, give Emily your mittens."

"*Stronzo*" was Italian for "turd," or "piece of shit," or "cheating liar," and was a specific nickname for Uncle Vito after he drove his car into our garage by accident one night. It was a specific secret nickname that only the three of us knew. My mother smiled.

"Shh," my mother whispered to my father.

"Where's Stronzo? Oh, there he is!" he said, pointing to Uncle Vito in the corner.

Uncle Vito pointed to himself. "Me?" Uncle Vito said. "I'm *Stronzo*?"

The doctor came in. "Your father should get some sleep for an hour," he said. "You all can come back in soon though."

"I don't need rest," my father said dreamily. "For God's sakes, people, I'll be dead soon! Let me live."

"*Victor,*" my mother said, looking at me and Laura. "The children."

"Why am *I* Stronzo?" Uncle Vito asked. "I thought *Vince* was Stronzo."

My mother ran her fingers over the IV. My uncles stared at the heart monitor. Laura took her fingers through her brown hair. The nurses walked by the room in a rush. I cleared my throat. My father opened and closed and then opened and closed his eyes.

"Property tax has gone up in Monroe and that's a crying shame," Uncle Vince said.

Silence.

"Emily," my father said, pointing to Laura, "is that your daughter?"

"This is Laura," I said.

"Why didn't anybody tell me I was a grandfather?" my father asked. The needles in his arm were crowded by blue and red patches of skin.

"No, Dad," I said. "This is your daughter, Laura."

Laura stood still. "*Dad,*" she said. "No. It's me."

"Victor," my mother said. "This is Laura. You know Laura."

"Is it overwhelming?" my father asked me. His lips were thin and crusty. "She is beautiful. Is it overwhelming?"

"Dad," I said. "This is your daughter. *Your* daughter."

My uncles shifted uncomfortably. Stronzo thumbed the fan.

"Oh, I know my daughter when I see her," he said. "Emily, honey."

"Dad, this is your daughter," I said calmly. "This is your daughter Laura."

"Dad!" Laura screamed. She was about to cry.

My mother put her arms around Laura. "Let's go, Laura," she said. "Your father is on a lot of morphine right now. He's very confused at the moment. Of course he knows that you're his daughter."

"You look at me, Gloria, and tell me when I had the time to have another daughter!" my father said, pointing at us but not quite looking at us. "I'm a busy working man! I have a life, you know that, Gloria! Remember how busy I was? That was always the problem, wasn't it?"

I kissed my father's shaking hand.

"Oh, there was never any problem, Victor," my mother said.

"I was very busy and I'm sorry," my father said.

"We'll let you sleep now," my mother said.

His lips curled as though he was about to cry. And then he was crying, blubbering, wholly sad. "Oh, God," he said. "Don't go. This is it, isn't it? This is it."

"No, this isn't it," I said.

"Let me count on my hand how many children I had, Emily Marie," he said. "One. Look. One child. And we felt so bad, you know that, Emily. We wished we could have given you a brother or a sister. You were always so alone. So alone. Out on that driveway. I cried. Forgive us? Can you forgive me? I am so old, Emily, too old to have a child."


Mrs. Resnick arrived. We sat in the chairs outside the hallway in silence, and we continued to sit like this for an hour while my mother tried to make conversation (the chairs did not hug her back well), the doctors were so tall (don't you just hate that), the coffee so-so (the way Emily likes it). Laura was droopy, slouching, confused in her chair, and Mrs. Resnick asked me questions about my business, if it was what I always dreamed of doing, if I thought it was going to sustain me throughout my thirties—and if not, what would I do instead?

I picked at my nails, pushed back the cuticle until I drew blood.

"Emily, stop that," my mother said. "Oh, I'll get you a napkin."

My mother left and came back with a napkin, a tray of corn muffins, four coffees. She swung her hair over her right shoulder, and I couldn't figure out where she thought she was. When my mother got close enough, she leaned over and presented the muffins to us like a consolation prize.

"I'm sorry your father is dying," she said to both of us. "I'm sorry your father is dying."

She said this as though my father and Laura's father and her ex-husband were not the same person. She said it like we were losing three completely different people. I didn't know what she was losing and she didn't know what I was losing, but the doctors kept making it clear that what we were all losing was an *organism*. This was what happened after too much time in a hospital. When someone died in a hospital, you just said, okay, well, that's sort of why we brought the organism here. The organism wasn't looking so good. But when someone died outside of a hospital, you shouted, you screamed for help, you looked at their face and you wanted to scream, *This is a man! This is a man who can no longer breathe! This is a man who goes to Spanish restaurants in Prague and eats Italian!* You want to scream, *How dare you put that man in a bag!* You want to scream, even though nobody would hear you, even though screaming is the first clear indication that somebody, somewhere, is drowning.

"Take a muffin," my mother said. She was still leaning over my chair. I picked out the largest muffin of the group. I was always a child, even in front of a child; I was still the child plucking off the tops of the largest muffins and handing the bottoms to my mother.

My mother ate the bottom of the muffin, despite her complaints, because at the hospital, she was the one whom people talked to; here, she was the one who kept her hair responsibly out of her face and I was the one who twirled the strands that fell limply across mine and thought, *We are running out of time to communicate with each other!* She was the one who knew the answers. She was the one who said to me on the bench outside his hospital room, "Emily, if nobody ever died what would be the point of living?" and I was the one who said, "The point would be to always be alive." She was the one who stayed at our house and watched our silverware tarnish and I was the one who traveled the world and was constantly surprised that the houses I decorated were not my own, the vases I put inside them were not my own, the arched doorways were not my own, the people I loved were not my own, the feelings I felt were not my own, my feet were not my own, my mouth and hands and eyelashes and teeth and skin were not my own, because one day, it would all be taken from me.

"Laura, honey, take a coffee," my mother said, handing the last one to her. "It's good for you."

Laura sniffed her coffee suspiciously. "I'll hold on to it," Mrs. Resnick said, taking the coffee from Laura.

We sat this way for hours, all four of us, shifting our feet to the solemn songs of machines, to nurses and doctors guessing which part of my father was next in line for shutdown. His lung. His leg. His brain. When I began to cry, Laura began to cry, so I stood up straight and regained composure.

"Your father once told me that fencing was a winter sport," I said to Laura about Mr. Resnick. "Your father once told me the only word in the English language with no vowels is 'gym,'" I said to Laura about my father.

"That's not a word," my mother said. "Because the actual word is 'gymnasium.' And that has more than one vowel. I don't know why your father never understood that."

"He only understood what he wanted to understand," Mrs. Resnick said.

My mother dropped her mouth to speak and I tensed. "Will you be all right?" my mother asked Laura, and I relaxed. "I worry for you."

"I think so," Laura said, and tucked the hair behind her ears.

"How is Mark doing?" I asked Mrs. Resnick.

"He's well," she said. "He lives in Norwalk. He's an engineer now. Very happy."

I wondered what Mrs. Resnick and Mark and Laura talked about when they got together, if they could look each other in the face, if they ever even got together. I wondered if Mark's empty bedroom was making a good storage room, if nightfall was the most appropriate time to be erased, if the body shut down painlessly in the dark, limb by limb, finger by finger, toe by toe, nail by nail, your life more like a faraway dream with every passing moment, the people standing above you merely shadows blocking the light. I wondered at what point during your death you could look down at your own body in the noose and think, What is this thing? I wondered if dying hurt more at dawn, when everything was green and crisp and beginning and you were ending, you were tired, you were unsure of what was worse—the things you understood or the things you didn't. Would Mr. Resnick have felt worse or better knowing that I was watching him die? Would Mr. Basketball think of me on his deathbed? I wondered and all four of us sat in our blue chairs and wondered. We held hands and ate muffins like children who couldn't feel their stomachs and when my mother dropped her muffin, she bent over and sobbed into her lap for the first time in years and I knew she loved my father. I knew she could feel him leaving her, and that it hurt just as much, if not more, than the first time he left, even if this time he was still down the hall in his silk robe.

## 37

Whuen Jonathan picked me up later that night he had a hard time looking at me.

"You okay?" he asked, driving the car.

"Yeah," I said. My father was a cold slab. My father was a ghost.

Jonathan told me that it felt like a Kafka short story at the hospital.

"Everybody kept going into the dark room to see the person that I couldn't see," Jonathan said. "Then everybody came out of the dark room crying."

I wanted to smack him in the face. A large acidic pocket of air rose in my chest, but I kept my mouth shut. "Don't get on the highway," I said. "Let's go to your place. It's so much closer than your father's."

"We can't," Jonathan said. "I'm sorry."

We turned onto Seeley Road, the street of my old high school. Webb High. A taupe and asymmetrical castle built in the seventies.

"Jonathan! Stop," I said. "Let's stop here."

"For what?"

"I want to see the school. I haven't been inside since I graduated."

"It's late," he said. "School is locked."

"Not the theater door," I said. "They keep that side door open all the time. I used it whenever I needed to come back to school and get a book."

We parked on the side of the school and walked through the door to the theater. We walked past the auditorium, where Jonathan had kissed me behind the curtain once. We walked past the music room, and the cafeteria, and ended up in the front hallway of the school where there was a big red sign that said DRESS CODE.

*NO muscle shirts, NO wearing of pants below the waistline, NO shirts bearing midriff, shoulders must be covered at all times, NO tube tops, NO see-through shirts, NO bandannas or hoods unless they are worn for religious or medical reasons, NO T-shirts that promote racial slurs or gender slurs, NO student shall intentionally expose undergarments, at risk of suspension and/ or restructuring of garment. Shoes must be worn at all times.*

"Girls started wearing thongs on the outsides of their jeans after you graduated," Jonathan said.

"I suppose it was inevitable," I said.

The front hallway was still packed with the same old trophies and some new ones: Yale Physics Olympics, First Place; National Financial Literary Conference Leaders 08. In the cafeteria, there were no more vending machines. Only big Gatorade bottles that dispensed water underneath a sign that said HOW ACIDIC IS YOUR BODY?

I walked quickly to find my old locker. On the way, I passed a large white sign that said THIS IS AN EXAMPLE OF A WARNING SIGN, and underneath there was a picture of a genderless child smoking marijuana, a genderless child with his/her head on his/her book, a genderless child drinking from a beer bottle, a genderless child mouthing "F**K!"

I walked faster down the hallway and I could hear Jonathan losing pace behind me, shouting, slow down, Emily, but I couldn't; I was feeling like my wild, destructive self. Slow down, Emily, slow down, he kept saying, as the white walls blurred past me, and I wanted his voice to go away. I wanted him smaller and smaller. I wanted to feel what life would have been like without him, if he had never walked the dog and found me on the stoop that day. I passed wall graffiti on the right that said JENNY CLIMP CLAMPS HER CLIT underneath a banner that read: HEY, GREAT THINKERS: IS THERE A GOD? WHAT IS MOST REAL? THE MOLECULES THAT MAKE UP THE AIR, OR THE FEELINGS YOU HAVE INSIDE YOU?

"Jesus," I said. I stood still at my old locker and caught my breath.

My locker was covered in a giant sticker that said VOLDEMORT IS REPUBLICAN. I leaned against the metal. Jonathan caught up to me. "I'm starving," I suddenly realized. Grief made me feel ten years old, crying and panting and barely thinking, and then suddenly, out of nowhere, my stomach ached.

"Here's home ec," Jonathan said, pointing to the classroom.

We walked inside the classroom where I had spent two years sewing an oversized stuffed camel. The home-ec room still had four full kitchens, one in each corner of the room, two refrigerators.

"Aha!" Jonathan said, a little giddy, finding a ready-to-make package of cinnamon rolls in the fridge. "Sit."

He pulled out a tiny yellow plastic chair for me.

"I'll make you some rolls," he said. "But first, we need some music. What's your father's favorite CD?"

"Jimmy Buffett," I said. "His earlier work," my father always added, as if he was talking about Picasso's Blue Period.

"Shockingly, there's no Jimmy Buffett," he said at the boom box on the windowsill, picking up CDs. But I couldn't have had a life without him, I thought; he was so good, standing there in the pretend kitchen, trying to cheer me up. "But there's Beethoven or Wagner or Spanish II."

He put in Wagner and while he took the dough out of the cardboard he made up words to the music just to watch me laugh. I laughed and I laughed and I laughed. Sometimes it was easier to laugh when you were sad. Everything felt more extreme. More romantic.

"I love you," I said from my chair across the room. And when he didn't say anything, the room felt as big as the ocean. Like I was drowning, in his car again, when I was eighteen and he accused me of my mother *not* dying.

The oven buzzer went off, and I flinched. "I know your wife is dead," I said. "You've been lying to me."

He had expected this, he said. "Let's just eat."

We sat on the tiny little yellow chairs and ate at the flat round table. I sat there wondering why I catered to Jonathan's guilt. *Suck it up,* I wanted to scream, *we're all shitheads.* But my stomach ached, and the rolls were warm, and the icing was slipping off the sides.

When I was full, I said, "Why couldn't you just tell me? Why are you lying?"

"Let's get out of here," he said, dumping the tray in the trash.

His tone bothered me. His tone implied that we were not really sitting there, surrounded by a stove, a table, and a refrigerator, like this whole time we were only playing in a poorly furnished movie about ourselves, and in this movie Jonathan always stole the last line.

"Take me to your house," I said. "Show me how you lived with her."

"No," he said.

I walked out of the room and down the hall. I walked and walked and I wasn't quite sure where I was headed, but I passed more signs: JOIN THE DISTRIBUTIVE EDUCATION CLUB OF AMERICA (DECA) AND GO TO CALIFORNIA! CHOICES HAVE CONSEQUENCES. I could hear Jonathan's footsteps behind me.

"Here's your old classroom," I said, standing in front of the door. B27.

The room was almost exactly the same, and that was what I had been hoping for, that was why I had come—to remember something. The slate tiles and the gray walls and the chairs in rows. The windows with no blinds. Everything sterile, the air disinfected. This wasn't romance.

"This is where you sat, remember?" I said. I sat down at the teacher's desk. I opened the drawer and pulled out a piece of paper. "Mr. Browsdowski. American Perspectives College Prep."

"This is where you sat," he said. Third row, fourth seat from the window.

Or maybe his tone bothered me because of the way he always used our intimacy as a way to distance himself. Like, let's get the fuck out of here, like, let's always start over, every second, let's start over and then relive the same life, it's easy and painless, like everything we've been doing for the last ten years actually had nothing to do with us.

"It's weird to see you on that side of the classroom," I said.

"Vice versa," he said.

"What was your English teacher like?" I asked.

"No man is an island!" he said, standing up. "Any man's death diminishes me because I am involved in mankind!

"And like this," he said. He put his hand over his heart. "How did Nathanael West die, class? How?"

Silence.

"Wrong!" he said. "On the way to Fitzgerald's funeral!

"And Oscar Wilde. Gay! Did you know that! Imprisoned for homosexuality!"

I was quiet. Jonathan sat back down and put his head in his hands. "That's what he was like."

"And what were you like?" I asked.

He put his head down on the desk. "Like this," he said, his voice muffled.

"And what was she like?"

"Smart," he said, his head still down on the desk. "Too smart."

"And how did she die?"

"I don't know."

He nervously started tapping his feet.

"You don't know?" I asked. "What kind of answer is that?"

"I mean, I'm not sure really."

We sat there in silence until I said, "Well, was it sudden?"

"Yes," he said. "Very sudden. But it felt slow. It felt like it took years."

He stood up. He sat on the floor between my knees.

"Do you miss her?" I asked. He rubbed my knees with his hands. He had touched me so many times, and it never felt repetitive.

"Most of the time," he said.

He unbuttoned my shirt slowly like we were going to make love. The buttons were pearls. The shirt was nearly see-through. In the dark, I was a skin suit lined with pearls. In the dark Jonathan looked expansive. As though he should take care of everything. He looked like a person who would take care of everyone he loved when he was older. He would put thermometers in his wife's mouth and he would make jokes about not being able to climb the stairs.

I undressed him.

I sat on top of the desk and pressed against him. We stayed like this, with our faces close together, until he became as solid as a color. At night, up close, we were solid like colors, but at dawn, we were edges and corners and had an unpredictable way of interacting with the light, and as we sat there naked, the sun rose through the classroom window, and I thought, My father can't feel his fingers.

"How can you *not* know how your wife died?" I asked him. "It's such a definitive thing."

And silence was such an imperceptible failure so early in the morning. For the first half of my life, I had mistaken the silence in our house for comfort. After Mr. Resnick died, we barely talked for three days until my father took out a pan and said, "I'm making you ladies eggs!"

"Scrambled, please," I said.

"Don't you think 'quack' is the most appropriate sound a duck could make?" my father asked, cracking the eggs into a bowl. "There is no better sound a duck could make."

"Balooga," I said. "Hypotenuse."

My father poured olive oil into the pan.

"Butter, Victor, you use *butter* for eggs," my mother said, and I only saw my mother's eyes narrowed now, and I only noticed my father's silence throughout the rest of the meal now. I only realized that he was making eggs to apologize to us. He washed out the pan and used butter and silently apologized. And during breakfast, my mother pushed the eggs aside and ate only her toast.

"In the delivery room," Jonathan said. "Is that what you want to hear? She just bled and bled and bled until she wasn't alive anymore."

Jonathan leaned back to watch as I picked my bra off the floor. It didn't feel right to be naked while he talked about his dead wife. None of it felt right: Jonathan stood up and pulled at his hair, his eyes suddenly red rimmed. This is what a crazy person looks like, I thought. This was a crazy man, crying. This was a man doubling over, holding his stomach, asking for me.

"I didn't want the baby," he said. "And I didn't want to be married. And that's exactly what I got."

I was quiet.

"I just can't believe it," he shouted. "It's all so fucking weird!"

Despite his unreasonableness, I knew exactly what he meant.

"I love you," I said. "I love you I love you I love you."

I said it and I suddenly felt rid of something. Free in my chest. He looked at me.

"*Mám tě rád,*" he said.

I love you, in Czech.

"Say it in English," I said.

"Huh?"

"Why don't you ever say it in English?"

*Mám tě rád, loveski,* who cared?

"It makes me feel different to hear it in English," I said.

"Don't you get that this is all very complicated?"

He waited for me to agree.

"Don't you get that I was never supposed to touch you? Don't you know that?"

But if he was right, if he wasn't supposed to touch me, and I admitted that, then it meant my whole life was wrong. It meant he had changed who I was supposed to be, and whoever I was, sitting on his desk, was wrong.

"You are always leaving me," I said. "You're leaving me right now, I can feel it."

"I'm sorry," he said. "You were just so young."

"I was young," I said.

"In the basement," he said. "I remember. Only seeing your eyes. You have old eyes. And on your stoop, you were sitting there so sad in that stupid T-shirt, your hair was a mess and your foot was bleeding and you didn't even cry. That's what I remember most about you."

"You are talking like I am dead," I said.

"I feel as though I have killed you."

I laid my back on the desk. I closed my eyes. I heard his footsteps. I imagined throwing up and just by imagining it I could already feel the lesions lining my throat. I felt him leaving my body. My father always said that we see things not as they happen but one nanosecond after they happen, so by the time I saw Jonathan put on his shoes, he could have already been gone.

And what's even harder to understand, my father said, drawing me a map of the solar system on his napkin, is that if I were 186 trillion miles away from Earth, I'd see things a trillion seconds after they happened. "And what if you were even farther away than that?" I had asked. He had said that if he were peering at Earth through a telescope from even farther away than that, he might still see us, sitting around our kitchen table, making the sandwiches, your mother making the coffee, and me at the table, me not combing my hair, me at the mirror with my hands over my eyes.

I heard Jonathan say good-bye, good-bye, as in, I won't be seeing you anymore, and then, "Look at me, Emily," but I couldn't look.

"Good-bye," I said. I heard the classroom door close and I felt short of breath, but I stood up, and thought of my mother, taking me away from her mother's funeral, in my urine-soaked dress, with my hands over my eyes. Even when you can't see yourself, my mother said in my ear, you are still yourself, and even when you can't see your father, he is still your father, just because you can't see someone, it doesn't mean that they aren't someone, and what a relief! my mother had cried, taking the hands away from my eyes, what a relief.

# Everything Is Like My Mother Says

# 38

For your father to die properly, we need three hundred and fifty slices of cheddar cheese, it was his favorite—do you remember that, Emily? How he used to slice too many pieces of cheese and eat them with a steak knife in front of the television? I'd say, Victor! You're eating cheese with a steak knife! Why would a human being do that? And he'd look at me and be like, it feels better this way—I can't explain it, Gloria. We need to clean the toilets and dust the curtains and put out framed pictures of your father looking his best. We need platters of cavatelli and broccoli and if Alfred walks by his picture and says, what in God's name is on Victor's head, we need to explain: he just thought that hat was funny.

"Alfred is dead," I tell my mother. "Remember? Four years ago. He had a tumor in his pancreas."

"That's right," my mother says. "I forgot about that."

My mother looks at the picture of my father and smiles anyway.

"Your father had a real sense of humor, Emily," my mother says. "You know that, right?"

"I know," I say. "He was a funny man. Did Bill leave to get the beer?"

"He did."

It's like my mother says: Italians love and then Italians die and then Italians cry and then Italians drink half a bottle of sambuca and say stupid shit.

I am by the eggplant when I see Mrs. Resnick and Mark and Laura show up. I am pretty sure I am the only one who notices the way my mother's mouth quivers when she sticks out her hand to take the bottle of wine.

"I'm so sorry for your loss," Mrs. Resnick says to my mother, holding out a bottle of red wine.

I cannot decide if this is a vengeful, or sweet, or forgiving act. My father's funeral reception has just begun.

"Thank you," my mother says. "I'm sorry for your loss."

Mr. Bulwark is beside me, explaining how the eggplant isn't falling apart in his mouth like he wants it to. Ladies are on the patio arguing over whose lipstick is melting faster.

"Dorothy, your lipstick is melting right off your face," Mrs. Ewing says. "See, it's dripping right onto your teeth."

"Yours is dripping down the side of your *chin*," the other one points out, and they both laugh.

Children I don't know are tossing carrots back and forth under tables. Adora is passing out clear drinks. Mr. and Mrs. Trenton have come and left, quiet and always absent now that Richard has been dead for years. The wind is starting to pick up. It howls in my ear like it's mad nobody is listening. I watch the two women stand by the gate entrance to our yard. Mrs. Resnick is wearing a black suit with a beaded collar. Her hair is gray. She has on bright red lipstick and thick black glasses that hide her eyes. My mother is wearing a black dress with a scoop neck. Her blond hair is not in her normal French twist. Her hair is not even blond anymore. I noticed the gray two years ago, when she stopped dying it, and cried all night until my throat scabbed. Her hair is half-up and curling around her face.

"I used to curl my hair for your father," my mother said, standing in front of the mirror earlier this morning. "Oh my, Emily, when your father and I first started dating, I would curl my hair for him every night. I'd sit up the night before we were to go out and roll fifty tiny pink rollers in my head. Then I'd go lie down and feel the pricks of the rollers dig into my scalp and I thought, This is what Jesus meant by sacrifice."

"*Mom*," I said.

"I'm just joking, Emily. Come on. Lighten up."

Mark stands between my mother and Mrs. Resnick, a six-foot-four man who is wide at the shoulders. Mark has dark brown hair that is parted to the left. He is in a black suit with a red striped tie. He is holding the card that has white lilies on the front. He is very sorry for everything.

I watch my mother give Mark a hug. I walk over to them. I think of something better to say with every step I take.

"Hello," I say.

"This is my daughter, Emily," my mother says. "She's all grown up now."

My mother started saying this after I turned twenty-three, as though my person before and after twenty-three was so different, nobody could tell it was the same person.

I make eye contact with Mark and we shake hands.

"Hello, Emily," Mark says. His voice is deep. He is a different person now too. It is so obvious how we don't even know each other.

"Hi, Mark," I say.

"Emily is an interior designer," my mother says. "She designed Woody Allen's apartment."

"Oh really?" Mark says. "You decorated that?"

"We try not to say 'decorated,'" my mother says. "Emily thinks it's offensive."

I shrug my shoulders. I am fourteen again.

"What do you do?" I ask him.

"He's an engineer," Mrs. Resnick says.

"I'm an engineer," Mark repeats.

"That's great," my mother says. "Mr. Jackson was an engineer. Still is an engineer. Once an engineer, always an engineer? Is that what you engineers say?"

My mother gets stupid around Mrs. Resnick.

"We could," Mark says to be polite. "We could start saying that, I suppose. I don't see why not."

I smile.

When Janice arrives, she pulls up quickly in a silver Infiniti. She steps out of the car in checkered black and white heels and with a baby on her arm. She hands the baby to the man on her right, who turns out to be her husband, Max, a forty-year-old vice president of People's Bank. She runs up to me standing with Mark and Mrs. Resnick and my mother. She wraps her arms around me and when I do the same, she feels frail in my embrace, like a feather waiting for a strong wind to take her to the bar, which I assume is usually Max.

"Let's talk," Janice says, and we sit down at a table.

We are women who barely know each other, sitting at a beautiful table, and my father is fifteen miles away at the cemetery.

"I'll get you a drink," I say.

"Vodka and soda," she says. "No lime."

At the bar, Mr. Lipson stops me. When the adults at my father's reception stop me, they put one hand on my shoulder and then smile. "You know, I was just telling Stephen that you've got your father's nose," he says.

"I do," I say. "Long. Lumpy at the top."

Mr. Lipson laughs. "Careful," he says. "I don't think your father would like to hear anybody making fun of his nose. Even you, young lady." Mr. Lipson puffs on his cigar and I shiver.

"I can't believe all this," Janice says when I sit down. "I'm so sorry about your father, Emily."

"Thank you," I say. "I didn't know you got married."

"What else was I supposed to do?"

My mother, Mrs. Resnick, and another woman I don't recognize sit down with us.

"I just eloped," Janice said. "There was no huge wedding."

"You always wanted a huge wedding."

"I wanted Oprah at my wedding."

"I know. That's weird."

"But we went on vacation and then just eloped. Just like that."

"What's he like?"

"Handsome," she says. "Charming. Snores. Yellowed teeth. But he's old. So what can I expect really? He knows shit. Like during breakfast sometimes he's just like, 'Did you know that you have to grow rice on a completely flat piece of land?'"

"I didn't know that."

"Yeah. That's what it's like with him."

"How much older is he?"

"Fifteen years older."

"That's pretty old."

"I was afraid the baby would come out with Down syndrome. I mean, we'd love her anyway of course. But still. It's not what you prefer for a child."

"I didn't know you had a baby either," I say. "You couldn't just write these things in a postcard or something?"

"I was scared you wouldn't have come to see any of it," Janice says. "I didn't want to invite you and then not have you come. You know?"

"Of course I would have come."

"You probably wouldn't have come."

I might not have come.

After a while, Janice says, "I wish you could have come when I had Betsy."

"So do I," I say.

"I needed you there for some perspective," Janice says, and as soon as she says this, it suddenly makes sense as to why we had always been friends. "When Betsy came out, I remember thinking, Wow, everybody is crowded around my vagina right now. And then when she came out, everyone was like, wow, it's a miracle. But really. For God's sakes, was it really a surprise? We had been planning this for nine months. And I kept hearing your voice in the back of my head, like, who *knew* the child came out of the *vagina*?"

My mother and Mrs. Resnick, who are sitting quietly next to us, both flinch at the word "vagina." Janice continues, saying that, at first, having a child was like babysitting. Except she never got to go home, and eating the food in the cabinet wasn't exciting because it was hers and she paid for it.

"And when Betsy finally said something for the first time I started to think that maybe she *was* a real human being, you know?" Janice says, sipping her drink with a straw, demonstrating habits she must have picked up from her daughter. "But then she would do something like spill her milk all the over the table and I would think, No, she couldn't possibly be a real person. Sometimes she just seemed like this large object that came out of my uterus to spill things."

"It takes time," Mrs. Resnick says.

"It *does* take time," my mother says.

"Exactly," Janice says. She says she has a few baby friends—other ladies with babies who sit around in the same floral room and talk about other ladies and their babies. They cured her.

"My friend Beatrice would always say, it's a new type of fun," Janice says. "New fun is the kind of fun that happens when Betsy says she wants to be a zookeeper when she grows up because she wants to be with animals and we all laugh and have a big hoo-ha. Not to be confused with a nickname for a vagina. 'Hoo-ha' is how Betsy says 'laugh.'"

"I know exactly what you mean," my mother says. "It's sort of like when Emily couldn't pronounce her *k* sounds so whenever she would chase after the neighborhood stray Emily would scream, 'Titty!' instead of 'Kitty!' and make me and Victor laugh."

Me and Victor. I have not heard my mother say that in years. It was always "your father," "Emily's father," "my ex-husband." Today, he is her Victor.

"I love my girl," Janice says. "I really do. Now, where'd Max take her?"

# 39

At the height of the reception, Mark helps me replace the empty vats of ziti. He picks up the empty dishes before they are blown away by the wind. When he is next to me, I feel the pressure to speak. But I don't know what to say. My father is dead. Your father is dead. Alfred is dead. Mr. Finnegan moved to Naples, Florida. Mr. Bulwark has even larger ears now, and then someday, he will die, and he and his ears will be buried. Oh, I fucked Mr. Basketball. I live alone. I have houseplants. I forget to water them. My favorite candy is oh-trick-question I don't have a favorite candy.

Mark and I stand quietly by the bar until Mr. Bulwark approaches.

"My wife," Mr. Bulwark says. He puts three carrots on his plate. "She was a novelist, did you know that? She was such a smart woman, that one."

"She was," Mark says. "I remember. She taught me how to play chess."

Mrs. Bulwark is also dead.

We stand like this for the rest of the night, until our feet can't take it anymore, until we sit down in the chairs and I open my mouth to say something and then I stop because I am afraid of who we both have become. Will our new selves like each other? Mark puts his hand on my back.

"Once, you threatened to murder my father," I say.

"I did," he says. "I'm very sorry for that."

A week later, my mother holds a tag sale, selling my father's stuff from the attic. There is so much left over from his life I joke with my mother that our yard looks like the Waste Not, Want Not display at the MoMa. We try to sell his collections of Herman Melville, business dictionaries, and Tom Wolfe, but it turns out that the people in my neighborhood won't want to read them. Someone buys his old electric razor that is ten years out of date. Some people buy his old college T-shirts. Some of them buy parts of his old Matchbox car collection. Then, they drive away in their Volvos and their Infinitis and their Mercedes and parts of my father become scattered all across town. Mrs. Resnick shows up late, right before the sun is about to set and we are about to close, as though showing up in the nick of time to collect the remains of my father is the art of their romance.

"Is there anything left?" she asks, tears in her eyes. She moves the hair out of her mouth, yet she still does not look at me. I almost cover my mouth with my hand. I am screaming inside my head.

My mother looks around.

"Scarves," my mother says. "There are some of his scarves left."

Must you take everything from us? I want to shout.

"How much?" Mrs. Resnick says. She brings out a wad of singles, and her fingers are shaking. One of the dollars falls to the ground, and nobody ever bends over to pick it up.

"Just take them," my mother says. "They're free."

Mrs. Resnick takes my father's plaid scarves. Even though I thought I had forgiven everyone for everything, there is a child inside me that wants to rip them from her and scream, "Those are *ours*! Those are *ours*!"

My mother says, "Okay, I'm going in to take a hot bath." Mrs. Resnick leaves and as she says good-bye, I think, That woman has never properly looked me in the eye and I don't know who is to blame for any of this.

Then Mark arrives. He walks across his lawn, and I drop candlesticks carelessly in boxes, and my heart pauses, as though it is taking the time to fall in love all over again, even though it will feel impossible to love at this moment, even him. But it feels equally impossible not to believe that anybody walking toward me on the lawn is not on a mission to return something.

He helps me put away the tables. We work silently. Things have to be categorized. Leftover socks. Golf tees. Old calculators. Empty binders. We sit in the garage and mark the boxes—*Total Junk*.

*Useful Stuff.* Then Mark takes the marker and adds *(Not Really Though).*

Mark pulls a silver necklace with a ruby in the middle out of my father's brown safekeeping box. He starts to speak, then thinks better of himself. We are silent.

"Is this your mother's?" he asks.

"No," I say. "Is it your mother's?"

Mark never answers. He reaches out his hand and touches my hair. People are always touching my hair. Why are people always doing this?

"Emily," he says, "I am so sorry."

"No," I say. "I am so sorry."

And then he leans close to my face.

"No, you must understand, *I am sorry.*"

"No, but *I'm* sorry."

We go upstairs to my room. We lay there and we rest like this every night for a month. Sometimes when we can't sleep, we debate over which appliance in my house is making the most commotion. Or he makes me do conversions to the metric system until I fall asleep.

"How many meters are in a mile?"

"Oh, Jesus, I don't know."

"One thousand six hundred and nine."

"How many miles are in a knot?"

"I don't know. Blah."

Then he says something like, "Well, it's like you don't even want to talk acreage."

And when I fall asleep, I dream that I am riding a bike, and the bike's parts are falling off as I pedal. I don't even notice. "What a magnificent sight!" someone shouts from behind me. Sometimes, this makes me wake up and cry. This person feels like the only thing missing from my life. Sometimes it feels like my father. And when I wake up in a panic, Mark is there. The problem is not the nightmare at all.

"How could your mother have slept with my father?" I say.

"How could your father have slept with my mother?" he says.

"Your mother had such ugly hair," I say.

"Your father had a fat ass," he says.

And then we laugh like children and lay our heads back down on the pillow and forgive each other. Sometimes, it feels like we are always forgiving each other.

"I slept with Mr. Basketball," I say once during breakfast, when we are tired. "I dated Mr. Basketball on and off for nearly ten years."

"You *what*?" he asks, but never drops his fork. Most of the time he isn't even holding a fork. He is by the toaster, burning bread. It is exhausting in this way, but also honest. He slams the burnt bread down on my plate as though I lived my past only to hurt him, and burnt bread feels like an appropriate punishment for being someone he can't recognize at the moment.

I dream of Mr. Basketball some nights, on the side of I-90 that curves around the bend of a mountain. I dream of Jonathan, swimming in hotel pools. In my dream, he is waiting for something that never shows up, a car, a lizard, a book. I am always farther away.

On the anniversary of Mr. Resnick's suicide, Mark has too much to drink and confronts me. He asks me to recount his father's suicide, step by step.

I explain to Mark that my mouth was dry that night. I saw his father through the window, walking. That I hadn't seen him in so long, I wanted to say hello. That even after he was dead, I still felt compelled to say hello, but I knew the only people who spoke to the dead were either insane or my aunt Lee.

Mark politely asks me not to joke around.

"Let me tell you how it happened for me," he says.

He tells me how he watched his father walk out the door that morning, hoping he would just keep walking down the street until he got lost. He was so tired of counting his pants and taking care of him, so tired of feeling bad for him, scared of him. "Did you know that I didn't laugh for forty days after my father killed himself?" he asks me. "Did you know that I tried on every single one of his pants? There are seventy pairs.

"One night, two months before he died, my father had a breakthrough. He walked all the way from the basement, into the kitchen, out the door, got the mail, and came back in. We all cheered, my parents laughed, even though now that I think about it, it was such a minor victory that it was almost more of a setback, really. They laughed, and my father walked over to her and kissed her right on the lips. We all thought this was a new beginning. That the new treatment was working. That my father would become a man again, he would go back to work, my mother would return to him. They made love that night. I know because I heard them."

Mark says that the night before his father killed himself he had another breakthrough. He didn't shake for hours. He walked up and down the stairs. But nobody smiled. Nobody laughed. He was angry, Mark says. He knew it couldn't last.

"I watched him walk out the door that morning," Mark says. "He was walking so well. I thought it was a good thing."

He says that he spent a long time hating my father. "I hated him for everything," he says. "Even Laura. But now I think it was good. She got a father, you know? At least for a little while."

And everything is always exactly like my mother says: your father's funeral was a dreadful success. Everything went according to plan—he was born, he got lungs and he got cancer and he died and we put him in a box and we carried him to his grave, well, your uncles did, but I put out platters of carrots and cheese and his position in the company is being given to some guy named Greg, who will really benefit from it, I think. Can you believe Mr. Bulwark made that joke, saying, It's about time Victor gave the company a free meal! That was a bit insensitive, don't you think? Don't look at me like that, Emily, I only laughed because I was the host. A host must make her guests feel comfortable. And I only walked away from his grave because honestly, Emily, I couldn't bear watching them put dirt on him.

"The Resnicks are leaving," I say to my mother. "Do you want me to go say good-bye to them for you?"

"No," my mother says. "I'll do it. Just let me sit here for a moment."

"Okay," I say.

"That was nice of Mrs. Resnick and Mark to stop by," my mother says. "She really is a nice woman, that Mrs. Resnick. A bit dowdy, but we can't fault someone for their shape."

Exactly. Her shape is so standard. Regular. Rounded at the hip. Her shape makes her look exactly like a person. "We can't fault her for that," I say.

"We probably should," my mother says. "But, of course, we won't."

"There are things we can't help," I say.

"Of course," my mother says.

It's like watching a man suffocate. That's what it's like, Emily. That's what it *is*. And how does it help him any to watch? And just because someone puts your husband in the ground and you drive away it doesn't mean you're leaving him. What are you *supposed* to do? You have to leave him. And when people come up to you in the receiving line and say, "I'm sorry for your loss," I want you to show them exactly what you've lost. Look them in the eye and cry hard. Cry your guts out because nothing is sadder than an adult who forgets how to be a child. Did you know there is a word for that?

"Mom," I say, "there are so many things I don't know."

"Honey." My mother sighs. "Your late twenties is not the time for playing dumb."

Neoteny! That's the word. Your father taught it to me actually. He said, Gloria, what's a seven-letter word for retention of youth into adulthood? And I said, Hey, Victor, I'll give you youth! Remember, Victor, being in your twenties and sitting in cars and laughing about how our parents didn't understand us? I played my music too loud and I was too glum at dinner and I was not putting in the effort a child needs to put in to continue being a child. He was too skinny and he was never good at caring about sports and he was always yelling at his father when he picked on his mother. Being misunderstood is okay around someone else, Emily, when someone else understands your misunderstandings, it is funny then. Just remember that.

"I try to remember that," I tell my mother.

"I know you do," she says. "You've always understood."

My mother gets up to collect the empty paper cups that are blowing off the table from the wind. She is still a beautiful woman, even when she is bending over, picking up trash. I sit there, and I watch my mother say good-bye to my father's friends. Children's lives are always beginning and adults' lives are always ending. Or is it the opposite? Your childhood is always ending and your adult self is always beginning. You are always learning how to say good-bye to whoever you were at the dinner table the night before.

I hear my mother through the wind, laughing, as though she is not the kind of person who could ever die, and I am proud of her, because it takes strength to live like this, even though she will die, someday when my hair is thinner and her heart is slower, when distance allows us to feel and understand everything much better. I am proud of her; even though the jokes she is telling aren't hers, the pride is: "It's about time Victor bought you guys a free meal!" I watch my neighbors and my father's coworkers laugh, as they stick out their hands, and pull my mother close and give her a kiss on the cheek. I watch as my mother never looks away from their faces. Her hair gets caught in her mouth. She brushes it away before anybody notices. Bill puts his arm around her. She says, Good-bye, and thank you so much for bringing the coffee cake. We loved it. And the bruschetta. Everybody just really loved the bruschetta. They nod and my mother doesn't even cry, even though the bruschetta was soggy and the coffee cake fell on the floor halfway through the reception, and my father's body is just a memory now, leaning over the plate of kale on the stove, singing, "And thus the carnivores went extinct!" And thus the carnivores went extinct, along with Alfred, and Lehman Brothers, and Top Hat Cleaners down the street, and the Norwegian pewter bowl, and 50 percent of the adults. I watch my mother stand tall and say good-bye to our life that is spread out on white tables and chairs, sectioned on platters, dripping in cold marinara sauce, next to a house that never really felt like ours anyway, even though it has to be ours, because that is where we hung our pictures on the walls and picked pennies out of the carpet and left coats on the backs of chairs as though this life belonged to nobody else.

# Acknowledgments

Thank you to my agents Molly Friedrich and Lucy Carson, and my editor Alexis Gargagliano.

Thank you to Kathryn Davis, Marshall Klimasewiski, Kellie Wells, Kathleen Finneran, and Peter Johnson for your support and guidance.

Thank you to my colleagues at Washington University in St. Louis for your friendship and feedback.

Thank you to Jacob Labendz, Kyle Winkler, and Dustin Iler for your editorial help.

Thank you to Joe for being my human thesaurus.

And thank you to my family for all those backyard barbecues.

# About the Author

**Alison Espach** received her MFA from Washington University in St. Louis. Her fiction has appeared in *McSweeney's* and other journals. She grew up in Connecticut and now lives in New York City, where she is currently teaching creative writing.

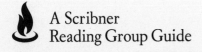
# The Adults

## Alison Espach

Emily Marie Vidal stands at the epicenter of a bizarre suburban universe where neighbors commit suicide, high school teachers have affairs with their students, and someone needs to be lit on fire to stop an even more heinous act from occurring. These situations send her on a physical and emotional journey that will take her from suburban Connecticut to Prague to New York City and back to Connecticut in an effort to find happiness, solace, and even love.

*The Adults* chronicles Emily's coming-of-age in a modern world where an adult and a child can so dangerously be mistaken for the same thing.

# DISCUSSION QUESTIONS

1. The opening scene of *The Adults* is a garden party celebrating Victor Vidal's fiftieth birthday. Discuss your first impressions of Emily's parents and friends. How does Emily struggle to identify with the people around her?

2. How do Emily's parents break the news of their divorce to her? How does she react? Why does Emily comment, "I was positive I had no family at all, certain it was not my mother but the solar wind that carried me into this universe" (p. 16). How does Emily's relationship with her parents change over the course of the book?

3. Emily is frustrated with her parents' and friends' lack of communication. Do you agree with fourteen-year-old Emily that "Nobody ever knew how to talk about anything" (p. 21)? Do you think her perception changes by the end of the book?

4. Emily's mother would "often use her youth as leverage to win arguments, something [Emily] didn't realize was even possible since it was youth that was always [her] handicap" (p. 22). Do you believe that Emily's youth is a handicap? Discuss this in the context of her ongoing relationship with Mr. Basketball. How did her youth affect the eventual outcome of the relationship?

5. Mark Resnick and Emily Vidal are both neighbors and good friends. They are together when they see Mrs. Resnick and Mr. Vidal kissing in the woods. What are their reactions? How does this discovery impact their relationship? Why do you think the author chose to bring Mark back at the very end of the book?

6. Discuss Emily's belief that "fathers were men who were just trying to understand, while mothers were women who were trying to change us" (p. 51).

7. Emily's father, Mr. Vidal, admits to his wife that Mrs. Resnick is pregnant with his child. What incident sets off the confession? How does her mother react? When does the "truth" about Laura finally come out?

8. Mr. Basketball suggests that Emily will one day appreciate being self-aware, as it is a gift. Is this true? Does Emily ever recognize the value of her "gift"?

9. Consider the relationship between Ester and Laura. Why does Emily believe Ester is threatened by Laura? What does Laura represent?

10. Emily remarks that Prague changed dramatically after the flood. She remarks: "Life had been a certain way 'before the flood.' Nothing's been the same 'since the flood'" (p. 182). Was there a "flood" in Emily's own life that changed her? Explain your answer.

11. Do you think Emily will ever truly be happy? Or is she stuck in the self-fulfilling prophecy of it being "impossible to be happy anywhere" (p. 190)? What do you think would make her happy?

12. What prevents Emily from telling Laura the truth about her parents? Should she ever tell her? Why did Emily's father decide to live a lie all those years?

13. How does the passing of Emily's father affect her and her mother? Do you think Emily's mother ever stopped loving her father? Does the experience of her father's death make Emily an "adult," or is she still the same child she always was?

## Enhance Your Book Club

1. Have some interesting high school experiences to share? Pick a night to swap favorite stories with your book club.

2. When Emily travels to Prague, she provides some background and history about the city. Pick a favorite city you have visited and research some interesting facts to share with your book club!

3. Emily begins working as an interior designer for wealthy socialites and celebrities, including Woody Allen. Which celebrity or socialite's house would you like to remodel? Discuss your decorating ideas at your next book club meeting.

# Author Q&A

**What's the most accurate thing someone else has said about your work?**

"There's too much sex in it." —My mother

**Do you think teenagers have changed much since you were one?**

I don't know if it's teenagers that have changed, or if it's just the technology that has made them seem different. I think teenagers can be fairly cruel to each other, and they will use every technological outlet available in order to spread that cruelty. I barely survived adolescence after three-way calling came into existence. I don't know how teenagers do it today with Facebook and Twitter.

**You are pretty brilliant at capturing teenage speak. How did you get to be so good at that?**

I guess I spent a lot of my adolescence listening. Which just means I was shy. This frustrated my parents a lot, to the point where they started buying books about it. *The Shy Child* and others like it fill our bookcase at home. I think I am one of very few kids who ever got in trouble for being "too shy."

**Did you start *The Adults* with a plot idea in mind, or did you come up with Emily and go from there?**

I started with the characters of Emily and Mark, as observers at Emily's father's party. I was interested in how their youth bonded them in that opening scene. I've always been interested in the position of "the witness," the person who is forced to see but doesn't quite understand. Emily's point of view as witness was what helped shape the rest of the novel for me.

**Do you think there is something distinctly Connecticut, or at least distinctly East Coast, about *The Adults*?**

I think growing up next to the Long Island Sound is something distinctly Connecticut (and Long Island). There's the excitement of being so close to a source of water, but on the other hand, the disappointment of it being the Long Island Sound. It's beautiful to look at, but hard to jump in without thinking about all the chemicals in it.

In my town specifically, there is a dense population of houses with nothing else for miles. I think this is why my characters spend a lot of time in hallways, kitchens, side yards, and basements. That's where most of my life took place.

**A reviewer (*The New York Times*) wrote that the central theme of your book can be expressed by this line: "You are always learning how to say good-bye to whoever you were at the dinner table the night before." Do you think that's true?**

I do think that's partially true, and I say "partially" just because I would have a hard time deciding on the "central theme" of my book. But the book is a lot about the many losses we feel day to day, the pain of knowing a person in a certain way, and then watching that person change into something else. It's not just death that forces us to say good-bye to each other. Life can be a constant shedding of the self, and while it's sometimes necessary, it can be sad or exciting, depending on the changes. Emily has to say good-bye to people who are still alive, her friends, her parents, her lovers, because they have either changed too much to remain in her life, or because they are too old for her, or because they have decided to leave. I think choosing to exclude someone from your life, or accepting that someone has excluded you from theirs, is one of the hardest, saddest things to do.

**Do you think going to Prague was good for Emily?**

In the way that some bad experiences can be good for you, yes. It's always good to travel, and to get far away from the town that has always defined you. In Prague she was forced to face certain truths about her life. I wanted her to be able to look back at the things she did, and distance makes that much easier.

**Have you ever been a starving artist, and did it make you brilliant, or just hungry?**

Mostly just delirious. In St. Louis, 2007, you could buy black beans, Prego, an onion, and white rice for four dollars and fifty cents, and the meal would last for two days.

**Any advice for writers who are currently trying to survive on such a diet?**

Most leftovers should be thrown out after seven days. Ninety-nine-cent shrimp is never as good as it sounds. The one-massive-meal-a-day diet will not sustain you. And at some point, start eating like a normal person. Start spending the extra dollar for the good tomato sauce. Or better yet, make your own. It feels good, and not just because it tastes better.

**Have you ever written anything that you'd like to take back?**

My eighth-grade diary, the one my mother read.

**What's the strangest or most interesting job you've ever had?**

I once had a job transcribing market-research interviews. Duties ranged from listening to married couples talk about their Honda CRV to watching a video recording of an "average American family" shop at Wal-Mart. As they shopped, I had to record their movements in detail (*Women in red shirt picks up Bic pens and hands to man, presumably her husband, in beige*), along with dialogue (*"The red pens? Why not the multipack?"*). Shopping at Wal-Mart is one of my least favorite things to do ever, but at least there's the satisfaction of buying things. Watching another family shop at Wal-Mart is boring in too many ways and really makes me wonder why I had to sign a confidentiality agreement that I would never tell anyone what I had witnessed.

**Have you ever made a literary pilgrimage?**

I drove to Iowa City once in order to look at the graduate theses of famous writers at the University of Iowa. I mainly went for Flannery O'Connor's but ended up reading Ann Patchett's, Chris Adrian's, and a few others'. It sounds creepy now but felt educational at the time.

**What makes your favorite pair of shoes better than the rest?**

It's hard to find shoes without heels that are not ballet flats and not ugly. So my favorite pair keeps me under six feet and is not that ugly. That's all I ask of shoes. I'm very boring and desperate when it comes to shoes. I wear large, obnoxious earrings to counterbalance.

**What is your astrological sign? How do you feel about it?**

I'm a Virgo, which mostly offends me. If you read about Virgos, they don't sound very affectionate, or normal, or pleasant to be around. Virgos are supposed to be obsessed with hospital corners and have hearts of stone, so I find comfort in the fact that I'm not organized or neat, and cried once while watching *Jack Frost*. But people tell me I can be militant in my refusal to be organized, that I'm a perfectionist about wasteful, unproductive things. Instead of cleaning my room, I'll randomly decide that my scarf is better served as a skirt and spend days trying to make it the best scarf-to-skirt ever. I've also been told that I'm a terrible hugger. So, who knows?

**What is your favorite indulgence, wicked or otherwise?**

Donuts. It's not wicked, and yet, not benign either. In fact, I've convinced myself donuts are a kind of poison. So I rarely eat them. Because I love them too much. But I'm confident I could eat an entire box, if ever challenged. Someone *please* challenge me.

**On a beautiful day, do you typically get outside into the sunshine or stay inside?**

I usually stay inside, but feel guilty about it the whole time.

**Do you have any writing rituals you like to stick to?**

I drink a lot of coffee, and listen to French music. It helps me to listen to music in foreign languages. Since I don't understand the lyrics, they don't distract me, and yet still somehow sound meaningful and pretty.

**What are you working on now?**

I'm working on my next novel, though I can't say what it's about. I'm still at that early stage where I might want to change my mind.